I0695257

THE KAEDIN SECRET

Book 1 of the Kaedin Series

A.K. Lee

Firewords

Published in Singapore by Firewords in 2017

Cover art by Anitta Menon

National Library Board, Singapore Cataloguing in Publication Data

Name(s): Lee, A. K., 1983-
Title: The Kaedin secret / A.K. Lee.
Other title(s): Kaedin series ; book 1.
Description: Singapore : Firewords, 2017.
Identifier(s): OCN 1001816200 | ISBN 978-981-11-4447-9 (paperback) | ISBN 978-981-11-4448-6 (ebook)
Subject(s): LCSH: Magic--Fiction. | Identity (Psychology)--Fiction.
Classification: DDC S823--dc23

978-981-11-4447-9

firewords.com.sg

To my husband, who wants me to be happy:

Because of you, I am.

Acknowledgments

I owe many people a great deal of thanks for helping me through this journey of learning and exploration. You have encouraged, supported, and guided me in my crafting of this brand new world and its characters, who are now far more real than they would have otherwise been.

My first thank you goes to Samantha, my wonderful editor. You believed this was a story worth sharing, and guided me through the many rounds of editing and re-writing so that it has depth and breadth. I have learned a lot about writing through your questions.

Thank you also to Firewords for taking care of a novice author through the gauntlet of self-publishing, from editorial to distribution, all the while making sure that I focus on what I'm supposed to do, which is to write my story.

To my colleagues and my friends who taught me about geography and military history, your advice has been invaluable. Thank you for not asking me why I needed to know any of it.

My gratitude also goes to my Twitter friends around the world who acted as my sounding boards and cheerleaders. To Mercedes, Lydia, Angel, Candice, Khrystyana, and Sarshi: thank you for reading my early drafts. Especially Sarshi: you were the first reader I trusted with this baby. Without your support of what it was, this story would not have become what it is. To JP Lab-Guru, Jay, and Bhavya, you are my cheerleaders and my confidants.

To Julie Cohen, thank you for freely giving me your advice and showing me so much hospitality and love. To Catherine Winther, my heart grew three sizes upon reading your review of my story, and the love you show my work. I consider you both my mentors in your professionalism and love of the craft.

My most important thank you goes to my loving husband, who cheered me on when I finished my first draft and re-directed questions about my book from curious colleagues.

Finally, I'd like to thank you, reader, for giving *The Kaedin Secret* a chance.

I hope you find courage, kindness, and authenticity within these pages.

PROLOGUE

Dear brother,

How are you doing in Kaedin Hall? I wish we were there together, you and me, and you didn't have to secretly teach me through these letters. But you was always the smarter one. Them thick books would have confuddled me no end. Still, I am making progress, thanks to you. Bet we'll surprise them stuck-up kaedine when two lowly peasants show them that the poor can be kaedine too. Mind no one sees you send these lessons to me, I don't want you getting into no trouble.

The last time you were home, you and I discussed if it were possible to tune and shape fire. There's a reason why Firas is named the Forbidden, aye? I been thinking about it ever since you returned to Kaedin Hall. We use fire every day. How much better life would be, if we had heat and light whenever we need it.

The past winter was hard on the village. Mam Gemba Mul and her toddling babe Reddis frozed after we was all snowed in. When Reddon came home after the snow and ice broke, I thought he would fair lose his mind, he was that stricken. Least Ma and Pa saw to the cremating of Gemba and Reddis. It would been too cruel to Reddon if he had to do it hisself. He spends his days sozzled in linnis brandy, but half-dead ain't no way for an honest man to live. Dara's a good lass and she makes sure he gets food in him two times a day. She says she wishes you was home, and that she's right keen on being the wife of a kaedin when you come back. Don't you disappoint her.

A journeying master kaedin came by for the season to help with the watering. Says he's Master Darram. He was right curious about you, little brother, and I told him how proud we was that we could pay to send you to Kaedin Hall. Them lords in town won't pay for you but the village did, aye, and right proud of you we are too. Little Pond's own kaedin!

He says he'd look out for you when he goes back. I asked him about kae resonance and whatnot, discreet-like, after I gave him enough beer to be well in his cups. He said more about your training and such. I might have some ideas about tuning into fire and the shaping and pushing. When you come home for summer break, little brother, maybe I can teach you some things. I bet I can be the first fire kaedin in the world. You'd be right proud of your older brother then!

Ma and Pa send their love, and Dara is pining for you like I said she would. She'll be happy when you returns with a kaedin badge and all. Get her something pretty, aye? She'd like that. Don't worry about the siller or gilt, the new linnis brandy will bring in a good sum. It's the best we ever made. Pa says we can even buy up our bit of land with it.

Your brother,
Velben

* * *

The young man crumpled the letter in his fist and let it fall onto the ruins of his home. Everything had burned to its bones. There was still a lit ember somewhere; a corner of the letter began curling up into ash.

Picking up the smoking letter, the young man stared unseeing at the words. He smoothed the paper out as best as he could and folded it up before slipping it into his pocket. With his hands in thin woven gloves, he fell to digging. He was not sure what he was looking for until he saw it after heaving aside one particularly heavy beam.

Two blackened skulls stared up at him. Which had been his mother and which his father? In death, all looked alike. Water—tears, perhaps, or sweat—dripped onto the burned skulls.

He pulled the gloves off. Reverently, he removed his parents' remains from the ruined cottage with his bare hands. One set on the left, one on the right. The pile of bones on the right was Ma. Her wedding cuff was on her elbow, and she still had part of her plain green dress left intact. Pa had protected her as best as he could, he noticed; the larger skeleton was wrapped about the smaller one, and it had been his motions that dislodged them.

He left the gloves off as he scavenged through the cottage, shifting what debris he could. When the adepts came by to offer help, he refused them. It took another hour of moving and sifting before he found Velben, coiled on his side, one hand open and the other clutched in a fist. His bones were charred black, still smoking lightly even though it must have been days since. Days. Velben was still burning.

Drops fell on the blackened bones and sizzled into steam. He sank slowly to his knees and took the closed fist, heedless of the searing pain on his skin as he pried his dead brother's hand open. He had been holding a flat metal disk, which was slightly warped. He rubbed away the soot covering it, revealing a simple design: a square set in a circle.

The young man covered his mouth and tried to rein in the scream perched under his throat.

All he had to keep of his family was this little bit of metal and a letter.

The entire village of Little Pond had been decimated; the fire had raged so wildly beyond control that the one new master kaedin had burned himself out trying to save what he could. Now Master Darram lay unconscious by the river, the heart of his palms shot through with charred skin and flesh. He would never be able to tune, shape, or push kae again. The silence of his resonance with his element would taunt him to the end of his days. It would surprise no one if Master Darram chose to end his life rather than live silenced.

You took away everyone I loved, the young man swore. *I will master you. And when I do, there will be a reckoning.*

AN END

The last wisps of smoke dissipated into a sky so pale as to be nearly white. One by one the mourners faded away too, returning to their work—some back to the fields, others taking single or double-horse cabs back to the city. Enthinas would not stop for a tutor's cremation, not even one as esteemed as Master Baelmin.

Rilt Arald stood where he was, face still reddened by the heat of the fire. His tears had dried on his cheeks. As heir to the Arald house and the main pupil of Master Baelmin, he'd had the duty of lighting the funeral pyre. His father could not deny him from carrying out that custom. It had been hard to watch the old man's body burn, and even harder to keep from dissolving into tears where everyone could see him. His half-brother Cedaran had stood very close, supporting him in his grief. While Cedaran had been fond of Master Baelmin, Rilt had loved the old tutor who had overseen his education since he was eight.

Ten years of warm conversations and now, just charred bones, ashes, and smoke.

"Forster, your home village is closest to the old man's. Walk him home once the bone collectors hand you the ashes." Duke Halden, head of the Arald house and duke of Enthin, had little sentiment for Master Baelmin to start with, and even less after the events of the past two weeks. In a way, Rilt was glad Master Baelmin had passed away. He doubted that the ailing tutor would have come away unscathed in a contest of wills against Halden. The duke gestured for his wife and children to precede him into the carriage that bore rough gray linen. When Rilt did not respond, Halden barked, "Come along now. There's the matter of the will."

The ride back to the estate took them through the straight paved roads of Enthinas. First south to north, then a turn at the main thoroughfare to the west. The geometric lines of blackwood timbers against stark white walls blurred into an indistinguishable tapestry of webs and nets, the repeated pattern broken only by colorful business signs. Rilt watched citizens go about their daily lives: haggling over prices, calling out to their friends, selling their wares… as if the day was just like any other and a great man had not left Creation bereft of his patient wisdom and gentle encouragement.

"We'll need to find new tutors for Cedaran and Rilt next week," Halden said to Selvina. "Can't have the boys neglecting their studies."

Before his stepmother could respond, Rilt said, "You only need a tutor for Ced. I'll have to leave for Izdahl soon if I wish to make the first day of term on time."

"You are not going to Kaedin Hall."

"I am." Rilt turned away from the window to look his imposing father in the eye. "Master Baelmin would have wanted me to."

Halden's face was as stone. "The old man is dead."

"Dear, not now. Not in the carriage," Selvina interjected. Her expression was hidden by her thin gray veil, but her hands were tightly clenched in her lap, wrinkling her ash-gray silk dress. "Cedaran, when we arrive at home, do tell Willa to send caffi up to your father's office and a washbasin also. There is a lot to be done today."

Cedaran nodded and nudged his glasses up his nose. "Yes, mother."

Rilt wanted to say more, but Cedaran squeezed his brother's fingers in a mute plea not to prod the angry bull in the pen.

* * *

"To Lord Rilt of the Arald house, Master Baelmin left this letter," said the clerk who was distributing the late tutor's belongings according to his will. "Along with the letter, Master Baelmin also provided for two years' education in Kaedin Hall, Lord Rilt, contingent on your clearing the entrance examina-"

Halden interrupted with a growl, "When did he write the will?"

"It was written in the presence of my colleague and myself, your grace, two months ago, ere he took ill." The clerk's voice quavered slightly. He did not wish to offend his employer, but custom was custom. "As you saw, we broke the seal only in your grace's presence."

"So you've been plotting this since two months ago?"

Rilt clutched the letter in his right hand. His late tutor had worried about his being able to attend Kaedin Hall even when he was gravely ill, the fact that he had anticipated the one way Duke Halden could have stopped him… His heart felt too full, as though it might burst. "I have kae resonance. The adept kaedin that visited a year ago tested me and confirmed it. So no, I've not been plotting this for two months. Master Baelmin and I have been planning for me to attend Kaedin Hall since I was seventeen."

"Two years-"

"Of education at one of the most prestigious halls of learning in this kingdom, Father, all paid for. All the Aleisan nobility know that I have passed the entrance exams. Are you going to forbid me to attend now?"

The duke rose to his feet, all six foot four inches of him. In his chair, Rilt squared his shoulders to face his father. For a moment Halden looked ready to strike his defiant son, but he strode out of the office, slamming the door behind him.

No one wanted to be the one to break the silence that followed. In the end, it was Rilt who stood and shook the clerk's hand. "Thank you, Pasmin. I will read it in private. Pellit, send a runner to Kaedin Hall. Have them know I will be arriving in ten days. Mother, Ced, excuse me."

Rilt swept out of the room and down the hallway in large strides while his valet, Pellit, hurried to catch up. Pellit knew better than to ask Rilt any questions now, but he did anyway when they came to the stairs where he would head down to the runner station. "Sir, would you like to have your meal in your room?"

"Pell, what could my father do to keep me in Enthin?"

"Lock you in your room, sir. Perhaps bar the windows."

"What would you do then?"

"Break you out of your room, sir, perhaps through the lavatory," said Pellit with a brief smile. "Though I would ask that you take my mother and me along on your madcap escape to Izdahl then, for I doubt we would keep our employment, should things become that dire."

Rilt smiled. His eyes felt sore and puffy. "Good man. Send up my meal, and if your mother would be so kind, some of her lemon and berry pastries as well. Enough for us to share."

Pellit bowed and scurried off. The valet was fiercely loyal to Rilt, and Rilt repaid that loyalty with affection and friendship. Outside of their private conversations, Pellit took care to address Rilt as "Lord Rilt" and "my lord", for Duke Halden and Duchess Selvina were sticky about protocol, but Pellit was the closest thing to a friend that Rilt had in the estate.

Once he was safely ensconced in the privacy of his bedroom, Rilt broke the wax seal and unfolded the letter. His vision blurred with more tears at the sight of the neat, curving penmanship, and the unique curl Master Baelmin used for his Rs and Bs. He crumpled the letter in his right hand and pressed the knuckles of his left into his mouth, trying to keep from sobbing outright.

There was a brief knock on the door. Thinking it was Pellit, Rilt swallowed and called out for him to enter.

It was Cedaran who came and sat beside him. Rilt sniffed and rubbed at the wetness under his eyes. The back of his throat felt tight and sour when his half-brother patted his knee awkwardly.

Once he could maintain his composure, Rilt managed a feeble smile. "I'll be alright."

"I know," said Cedaran. "I just wanted to tell you that—that he had had his favorite rosales bud tea before he … Before. At least he had that."

"A small comfort." Rilt squeezed his brother's thin shoulder. "Thank you."

"Yes." The younger boy inhaled sharply and stood up again. "I have to… He set me some assignments, before he fell ill. I should finish them before the next tutor arrives."

Rilt reached out and gently grasped his half-brother's wrist. "If you want me to look them over, you have the next four days."

"You're really going to Kaedin Hall?"

Rilt wished his brother did not sound quite so young and lost. "I am."

Cedaran bit his lower lip, as if he was trying to refrain from saying something. He breathed in deeply again, tugged his hand from his brother's hold, and left the room.

What could Rilt have said to Cedaran? His choice to attend Kaedin Hall in the face of their father's disapproval must feel like abandonment to the younger boy. Rilt sighed and unfolded the letter from his late tutor. It was wrinkled from where he had crumpled it earlier.

Dear Rilt,

Alas, my body has failed the test of time. I have told you this before, and now I will remind you again that I am exceedingly proud of you, Rilt: my protege, my student, my child. You have been the son I never had, and I hope that in my own way I filled your days with warmth and love you may not have had otherwise.

I have been your tutor for a mere ten years, and in ten years I have found you endlessly curious about life beyond Enthin. You are bright enough to understand that I should never have encouraged you to study towards a seat in the University, but you have never once asked about my motivations. I did not share them when I was alive for two reasons: the first was a promise I was loath to break; the second was an entirely selfish desire to remain wise and infallible in your eyes for as long as I could.

Yet, as I ponder the end of my days, I owe it to you to show you that there is much I have not grasped, in the hopes that you will surpass me in this. I told you that I left my post as Master of History at the University of Izdahl to pursue my quest for knowledge beyond its lofty walls, but I believe you will have a greater chance of success than I had once you know the truth.

Twenty years ago, when I was heading into my fifteenth year as Master of History, I unsealed a vault under the Hall of History without my dean's express permission. He and I were close friends from our boyhood, and so I trusted that he would not deny me my exploration. I found shelves upon shelves of moldering records from the days before Coleri Aleis established the kingdom. Imagine my joy at the discovery! I had all but guaranteed my name carved into the annals of great scholars. Here I made my first and greatest mistake. I immediately informed the dean, my friend, and it was decided that since the state of the records was so poor, I should be the only man allowed access.

I did not know the import of what I had found then. Even now, I wonder if my mind is playing tricks on me; perhaps all I remember of those yellowed, crumbling texts are but figments of an old man's mind. But the fragment of this one account remains clear as day to me:

'Bi eldr daues, wi croisen men drauen fier… deyre breith wer flaume yn fir, yn much men deid blacken to asshe. Creatirs bless us wir water yn extynguish deyr fir, yet in trothe deyre line havet inde.'

I will not spare you the headache of translation. By now you should find it as easy to read as our regular exchanges. That I had read an account of Coleri before he was king was indisputable, but what of this about fire-breathing men? And that their line had not ended? I brought my questions to the dean, who promised to search through the royal archives—to which only he and the royal house of Alcaronan had access.

The very next day, he invited me to his study. Poor man! He was paler than he had ever been, and the shadows beneath his eyes made him appear nothing more than a living skull. The curtains were drawn and that text, a simple yellowed parchment, was unrolled on his desk.

"My dear Bael, promise me one thing," he said ere he elaborated on why I was there, "One thing only: that you tell no one of what you've told me, that you share nothing of this even unto your last breath."

"I will promise, if you tell me what secret that is."

"Promise me!"

To him I gave my promise, and since I am dead, I am no longer bound to my word.

We have all been told that there are only four elements that resonate with those who would be kaedine, and that the Creator, Firas the Forbidden, locked away the secret to the fire's song. But that is the one element discussed in the parchment, suggesting that there were those who could wield flame as easily as breath. If that were true, how fascinating and how fearsome they must have been! Where are they now, and why is this not common knowledge?

Since I was summarily dismissed from the hall a month later by this same friend, I do not know if that text remains in whole or even in part. I could not seek the answers with my resources removed from me. I was firmly invited to take up tutoring in the noble houses. I had to leave the place I called home from my youth, bide farewell to my friends, and grieve the loss of my books. No longer was I free to wander the university as a master; the great libraries of the halls were closed to me. My successor never did reply to my queries; my old friend returned my letters to me, seal unbroken, and even until his death, he replied to not a single missive.

I do believe that this knowledge should not pass away with me while others who have the knowledge remain silent. Thus, I ask that you seek the truth behind this cover-up. I feel in my old bones that the fragment I read contains an essential truth. What this truth may be, I do not know. As I have told you before, we seek out the unknown so that we fear it no more. For them to have taken such pains of casting me far from my resources and for my old friend to turn his back on me tell me that what I stumbled on so many years ago was of great importance. All that they have done to ensure that even a small fragment remains secret is deeply worrying to me.

Forgive me, dear Rilt. I am leaving you with the burden of my doubts while my body is finally at rest. Grieve for me, brave and curious boy, and for the lessons we will no longer share, and then, look forward to your future. I see in you a good man, for your impulse is to protect and to trust.

Remember: be kind, be courageous, and be yourself, always.

With all my love,

Your tutor,
Baelmin

LEAVING HOME

It was bright, breezy, and beautiful—the perfect day to leave.

Rilt turned away from the window. It would be a five-day journey to Izdahl, and two years or more before he would return to sleep in his wide bed with its down pillows and silk sheets. In exchange, he would be living with a stranger in an unfamiliar room without any of the luxuries he was used to. This was a trade he was happy to make.

He could hardly wait.

If only Master Baelmin were alive to see me off.

"You know your father would prefer you to remain here," said Selvina by the door. The duchess brushed away a tendril of dark hair curling into her cheek. "Or you could marry a lovely girl. You have your pick from a dozen. That sweet girl from Eastdown, Niena Aredal; she's a good match. And her singing voice is just divine. "

Rilt restrained the urge to roll his eyes. That would be rude, and as an Arald he knew better than to resort to childish discourtesy. His stepmother had his best interests in mind, after all. "First, I've earned my place in Kaedin Hall, Mother. A place that's paid for by Master Baelmin. I'm not going to waste this chance. Second, I'm not getting married at eighteen! It's a ridiculous notion."

"I don't mean that you have to be married now, silly, but an engagement would reassure the people that you're serious about your duties. You know there's been talk, ever since … well." She sighed and added, "Besides, it's not as though you haven't been with quite a few young ladies. There must be one of them whom you like more than the rest, is there not?"

"Mother, you know they were just casual fancies," Rilt protested, mildly scandalized by her bringing up his numerous liaisons. "I will come home and learn to be a proper duke, as I have been doing for the past ten years. I just want to learn to be a proper kaedin, too.

That's all there is to it."

"An Alcaronan lackey," Selvina said, mild disapproval tinting every syllable. "You are of the Arald house, Rilt. We were the shield of the kingdom before they even came to power. And you're the firstborn-"

"And as firstborn, I have the rights to the title and to the lands, but it doesn't mean my education must be exactly the same as my forebears," Rilt interrupted. He ran a hand through his brown hair and tried not to sound too exasperated. Lackey. That was his father's favorite epithet for a kaedin. Halden had the grace not to use that term at Master Baelmin's funeral, but for the past four days, that word had been dropped whenever Rilt faced his father or his stepmother. "Two years at the university to refine my kae resonance, and then I have a whole lifetime of being Duke of Enthin."

"Just because you have resonance doesn't mean you have to become a kaedin. There are hundreds of men out there who aren't."

"That's because they can't afford the tuition or clear the examinations. Or both."

"The exams which you took in secret," Selvina scolded. "If you had told your father about your wishes-"

"He would have kept me locked in my wing until I'm too old to be trained," Rilt said. "Perhaps he'd be prouder if I became a member of the Kaedin Council?"

Noting Rilt's mutinous expression, the duchess sighed. "He wants only the best for you, Rilt."

"I want the best for me too," Rilt replied, "and the best thing for me to do right now is to attend the university. Mother, I've been accepted as a student in Kaedin Hall. Only forty students across the kingdom are accepted every year. Is there no one in the household that is proud of me?"

"I'd be much prouder if you didn't have to do the king's bidding for the rest of your life," she reminded him archly. "We are the counterweight to the houses of Alcaronan, Alwyth, and Awells. The kingdom relies on this delicate balance. You becoming a kaedin puts our house at a disadvantage."

Rilt bit his tongue to stop his retort from escaping his lips. He wanted to explore the kingdom and beyond its borders more than anything else in the world. However, he had a duty to his people and his lands, and he knew it. The lesson had been drummed into him since he was a toddling child. "The balance won't change, whether I am kaedin or not. As a duke, I am still a subject. Anyway, Father is still more than able to throw his weight around. I'm hardly necessary."

Selvina stared at him forbiddingly. "He is your father and you will respect him, Rilt."

"Sorry, mother." There was no contrition in his tone at all, but his stepmother did not comment on it. Selvina knew better than to force her headstrong stepson in any direction. She would have better luck herding cats.

Pellit had already taken his luggage downstairs, so all he had to do was make sure he had the necessary papers with him. He also checked that he had his blood mother's starsilver ring tucked safely in an inner pocket of his coat. Rilt was certain she would have supported his attending the university, unlike his father or stepmother. After all, his blood mother was once a member of the kingsriders, and a former student of Master Baelmin herself. Despite her sex, Lady Taniya had been one of the most respected kingsriders in the kingdom. Master Baelmin had been fond of her, and told Rilt stories of his blood mother as a headstrong and wilful young woman. Lately, Rilt found himself wondering what his mother had seen in his father for her to give up her honored place in the kingsriders.

The ring might have been one of the less valuable items of jewelry in the dowry his mother had brought with her into her marriage, but it was the one Rilt liked the most. Its design was simple: a starsilver band with a vividly blue star sapphire nestled in the band. As a child, Rilt had enjoyed looking at the rays of the 'star' and imagining white light bursting from the stone.

All the other jewelry she had left behind after her death had been gifts from his father, each more intricate and extravagant than the previous one. Selvina, with her dark skin and hair, wore them exceedingly well. Rilt was glad of that, and did not begrudge her the jewels. Beauty should not be hidden from view.

They strolled down the sunlit hallway. Rilt knew his stepmother was still trying to conjure up other arguments for him to stay, and decided to ask about the state of some of the tapestries on the walls before she could belabor her points about staying in the estate.

"We will have to commission new ones," said Selvina with an absent frown, taking in the shabby state of two particularly large ones. "The dyes they use now are barely lasting past two summers. I'll have to speak with the dye-makers and weavers. The ones in the Izdahli estate are centuries old, and still as vivid as though woven yesterday."

Rilt hummed agreeably in acquiescence. He could not care less about the elaborate tapestries. He would, however, miss the picturesque view from the tall windows lining the corridor. Right now, the estate's grounds were beginning to show the green of new grass, and the trees were dripping with blossoms. The sweet fragrance of whitesong and rosales perfumed the air, and every breath was a delight. Perhaps there would be whitesong trees at Kaedin Hall. He did not remember if there were any in the Aralds' Izdahli estate. He would have the staff plant some if there weren't.

That would be lovely, he thought, distracted while the duchess prattled on. *A slice of home away from home.*

"You used to be such a biddable child," said Selvina, her tone wistful, reminding Rilt that he was supposed to be listening.

"A biddable Arald? No such thing." Rilt's lips curved in a faint smile.

Selvina's answering smile was very telling. "You Arald men never know when to let up and retreat."

"There's a reason our house crest features two rams, Mother."

Selvina ceded this with a look of resigned exasperation and amusement. Their conversation petered to a halt when they came to the library. Rilt pushed the heavy door open and entered his and his half-brother's sanctuary.

* * *

Heavy drapes had been drawn apart to let sunlight spill over the library's hardwood floor and the portrait over the mantel. Rilt's mother gazed out from inside the frame: pastel, placid, and pale. Beneath, a small golden plaque discreetly stated, 'Lady Taniya Arald'.

Rilt hated it.

He much preferred the portrait his father Halden kept in his study—in that one, she was painted in profile, a confident smile on her lips, her chin raised in challenge at some unknown person outside the frame. Her white-and-blue dress was severe and brilliant, and in her right hand she held a sword, with the starsilver ring that now nestled in Rilt's pocket glittering on her index finger. Rilt had often wondered why that portrait had been painted at all, and why his father kept that one for himself.

As he expected, Rilt found Cedaran nose deep in a book, surrounded by stacks of records. Heedless of his brother's approach, Cedaran was jotting down notes on a separate piece of paper. "…seventy-eight acres… Yes, but how much of it is arable?"

He jerked upright when Rilt crept up from behind and slapped his shoulder.

"Rilt! Is it already time for you to leave?" Cedaran asked, barely managing to keep the books from toppling. He adjusted his glasses on his nose and frowned at his older brother for the exuberant greeting.

"Yes it is," said Rilt. His smile faltered. "Are you sure you'll be fine?" *If you need me to stay, I will.* The promise was not stated outright but it was evident in his tone. Words were not always necessary with the brothers.

Cedaran's answering smile was nearly as confident as he sounded. "I will be fine, Rilt. I've got something for you, in fact. Hold on a moment—where have I put it, now?"

"Thank you, Ced," Rilt said. The thanks was meant for more than the gift. He pulled his brother up from his chair and slung his arm over Cedaran's shoulders, still slightly resentful of the fact that the younger boy was the taller of the two. He would match their father in height soon. For a sixteen-year-old, Cedaran had yet to grow into his bones, and sometimes moved as awkwardly as a newborn foal. His features were reminiscent of Duchess Selvina's, especially his green eyes, though his complexion was just a shade lighter than his mother's. "You can keep your present to me for yourself, or send it along after. I'm sure the runners won't mind delivering it."

Instead of answering, Cedaran ducked away and started rummaging through the drawers of the antique table, putting Rilt in mind of a scholarly snowhop. Rilt felt a wave of fond pride when he noticed Cedaran's workbook, covered with figures and details. The younger boy was smart—smarter than Rilt, in Rilt's opinion— and hardworking. He liked learning how to manage the estate and its lands, whereas Rilt found it tiresome and dull. In the past few years, Master Baelmin had often used Cedaran's diligence to spur Rilt on. It had not always worked.

At least he knew he could count on Cedaran after he took the reins from Halden. For three months late last year, the situation in Halimgor had seemed too volatile for comfort. The fighting between Lady Liria and Lord Evvas of the Alwyth house had finally drawn to a close last midwinter, with Liria emerging the victor. Their father, so close to death that his opinion made no difference, had not been able to intervene. Selvina had been very distressed about the power struggle: the ailing duke was her distant cousin, and it had pained her to know that her niece and nephew had become thus estranged. Rilt could not imagine being so ruthless as to break all bonds of kinship just to secure his authority, but he was firstborn, and Cedaran was not power-hungry or avaricious in the least. Liria was to be confirmed this year at the Lords' Convene, and Halden had made it clear he found the girl too ambitious and smart by half.

"Got it," Cedaran said in triumph, after emptying a drawer's contents on the desk. He presented it with a flourish. "I bought it at the midwinter fair. The master tanner drove a hard bargain, too."

Rilt took the gift from Cedaran. It was a journal with a red leather cover, embossed with Rilt's name and the Arald crest. Inside were smooth unlined pages the colour of honeyed cream, waiting to be filled with notes.

"It's beautiful," said the older boy sincerely, and ruffled Cedaran's hair affectionately, knocking his glasses askew.

"Quit it, you big bully."

"Make me, Beanpole."

Cedaran then took the journal and flipped to its last two pages, thrusting it against his brother's chest. "I also copied out a list of the noble houses in Izdahl with daughters of marriageable age."

"Ced, you know how I feel about getting married early."

"So, Rilt, you just have to avoid these particular houses," said Cedaran blandly, and then added with a tiny smile, "You're welcome. Don't tell Mother."

The older boy laughed. "You've always been the smarter one. Thanks, Ced. All right, walk me to the door. You're not going to be seeing me as often as you'd like after today, so keep me company as long as you can."

"It'll be nice and quiet after you go too. No one to knock my glasses off. No one else to be the new tutor's prize pupil."

"Liar. You want to be just like me and you know it." Rilt tucked the journal into his pocket and said, more somberly, "Don't let Father bother you. He'll see how smart you are. How brilliant."

Cedaran's gaze fell to his shoes and he shifted his feet. "You think too highly of me. I can't ever … Not with Father."

"You'll have to learn to face him down, Ced. You're an Arald." Rilt squeezed his brother's shoulder. "And we Aralds always stand our ground."

* * *

The two brothers emerged from the library to find Selvina giving Pellit instructions. The valet was doing his best not to look harassed; Rilt knew how long-winded his stepmother could be.

"Zarin is to prepare all his meals," said Selvina. "And Rilt must have the best rooms. Pay as much as you must to ensure it."

The corners of Pellit's lips twitched almost imperceptibly when he saw Rilt roll his eyes, but the valet wisely stayed silent until the duchess had finished. He bowed to her and then to Rilt.

"Your coach is waiting, Lord Rilt," said Pellit.

"I will be there momentarily." Once Pellit was out of hearing range, Rilt said, "Mother, I have no qualms eating what everyone else does, and I can certainly sleep in any room available to us."

"Nonsense. Your father always has our people take over the kitchen when we travel, and as the heir to the title you should have the comfort due your station. You're not some common cattle-driver."

"I am also not Father," said Rilt, his patience dissipating rapidly. Cedaran cleared his throat and squeezed Rilt's elbow in warning. An argument now would only sour the mood, and Rilt wanted to leave on a good note. He took his sibling's caution and made himself smile. "Fine, Mother. Might as well enjoy my perks before I become a mere student."

The three walked together to the main door. With every step, his departure felt more real; Rilt could barely contain his excitement and apprehension. Two glorious years away from Duke Halden—

freedom from the endless lectures about politics, from the tedious checking of numbers, from the droning litanies about duty and honor and heritage … He could almost taste his freedom. He had been half-expecting the house guards to manhandle him to his bedroom and lock the door. He would not put it past his father.

It was only at the door that it truly dawned on Rilt: this was going to be the longest period of time he would ever be away from his family. The realization drew a lump in his throat. He would miss them—well, perhaps not his father, but he would certainly miss Selvina and Cedaran. As for Master Baelmin, Rilt had the old man's letter among his papers and kept his tutor's words in his heart.

"It's only twenty weeks before the break," said Rilt. He knew his smile was shaky. "I'll write often."

For a second, the duchess seemed uncertain. Then she smiled and embraced her stepson, kissing him once on the cheek.

"Take care of yourself," she told him. "We'll be seeing you. Pellit and Zarin will get the Izdahli estate ready, so if you need some proper food away from the hall, just go to the estate."

Rilt said, "I'll look forward to your visit. Get Ced out of his books for a bit too."

"You're going to have to show me everything in Izdahl," said Cedaran.

"Of course I will."

They hugged tightly, exchanging wordless encouragement. Rilt privately hoped Halden would at least notice Cedaran in his absence; his younger brother deserved better from their father.

As though summoned by Rilt's thought, the main doors swung open. Duke Halden strode in, dressed in his riding leathers. His valet Elais trotted faithfully behind him, carrying an armful of dead snowhops and a crossbow. Halden saw the trio and narrowed his dark brown eyes. "What is the coach doing out there?"

Rilt mentally braced himself before he spoke. He wished Duke Halden were less broad and imposing in build; each time they faced off, it was as though Rilt were facing down a mountain bear.

"Father. I do have to leave today if I wish to make the Hall on time," said Rilt evenly. "Mother and Cedaran are seeing me off."

"You're still determined to go through with this kaedin foolery?" The duke did not scoff. It would have been better if he did; he sounded as though this was a mere nuisance that could be swatted aside. He tossed his riding gloves to Elais without looking before removing his jacket. "Well, well. An Arald as an Alcaronan lackey. Imagine that. Creation is coming to ruin. Your Master Baelmin indulged you far too much, boy."

This was not the time to fight, so Rilt bit the inside of his cheek and said, "You were the one who chose him to be my tutor, Father. I look forward to seeing you at the Lords' Convene."

"You watch your tone, boy," said Halden. He scrutinized his son, slow and forbidding. Rilt did not avert his eyes, though he knew that his father was liable to strike him for the impudent remark. The duke's mouth curled with disdain. "You are attending Kaedin Hall only because I am permitting you to go. I can have you back here any time, locked and barred inside your rooms."

"I know." Rilt could feel a tic starting at his temple. "And I know the only reason you haven't is the gossip that'll flare if I don't attend, when all of Enthin knows I've cleared the examinations. Imagine the embarrassment when they start talking behind your back, Father."

Incensed, Halden grabbed his firstborn by his collar, as though to shake him. "You insolent whelp-"

"Your insolent whelp, Father," Rilt spat, forcibly tearing his collar free from the duke's grip.

Halden's raised hand would have landed heavily across Rilt's ear if Selvina had not interposed herself between father and son.

"Enough of this," said the duchess to her husband. She took the upraised fist in her hands and pressed a kiss to it. "Rilt is honoring Master Baelmin's last request. It is right to do so, and Creation knows that Rilt won't shame the house. If he does, we'll bring him home. Let him go."

The duke said nothing. He gazed at Selvina, his jaw clenched. Finally the tension in his shoulders eased. "So be it. We'll allow him go on this fool's run then. Let him be the most foolish Arald our house has ever seen."

Rilt was about to retort but a stern glare from Selvina silenced him. Instead, he raised his chin and stared his father in the eye before turning aside with deliberate discourtesy. "Mother, Cedaran, I'll miss you. Take care."

Rilt's pointed exclusion of his father in his farewells did not go unnoticed. Selvina shot Rilt another forbidding and exasperated look, but Halden only strode into the mansion, his heavy boots leaving mud prints over the dark stone floor. Elais trotted after him, laden with game and hunting gear.

The duchess shook her head. "You did not have to provoke your father."

"He did not have to make this unpleasant for us, either," Rilt said, his jaw taut with ire, and tried in vain to ignore the acid taste at the back of his throat. Without further hesitation, he boarded the coach and flung himself into the seat. Pellit raised his eyebrows at Rilt, then jerked his head imperceptibly in the direction of Selvina and Cedaran.

"Pell, shut the door." Rilt then took a few deep breaths the way Master Baelmin had taught him, before he peered out the window, forcing a smile on his face. "Mother, Ced, I'll write you when I arrive."

With a crack of the reins, the coach set off. Rilt desperately hoped it would be a good long while before he looked at the Arald grounds again.

* * *

They had been on the road for barely an hour when Zarin slowed the coach. Pellit peered in through the front window. "Sir, Elais is behind us."

"See what he wants."

Elais cantered up on a gray mare and stopped next to the cabin's open window, pink in the cheeks. "Lord Rilt, I was tasked with delivering an item to you."

Rilt plucked the small velvet pouch from Elais's hand. It was heavy for its size. Once he had tipped the item into his hand, Rilt gaped in shock.

It was an Arald seal ring. In fact—Rilt examined the inscription inside—it was Halden's own seal ring. It bore the familiar twin rams' heads of the Arald house crest, horns curved and heads lowered to clash. Rilt stared at it, as if he could command the ring to elucidate his father's reasoning through force of will.

"My father told you to pass this to me?"

"Yes, my lord."

"Did my father have a message for me?" Rilt asked, still holding the ring in disbelief.

"No, my lord."

That was uncharacteristic of Halden, both the gift and the lack of a message. Rilt dismissed Elais with a perfunctory wave. The vehicle set off again at a brisk pace, the clatter of hooves barely intruding into his thoughts.

He gripped the ring in his palm, the seal pressed into his flesh. It was too large to fit any of his fingers. It had been made for Halden, not Rilt. He wondered if his father had intended it as a reminder of Rilt's responsibility to the Arald line, to Enthin; a reminder of the threat that Halden could have Rilt brought home any time.

If so, Halden had succeeded.

FIRST IMPRESSIONS

It was the day he was to report to the university. Rilt was dressed in the uniform of Kaedin Hall: a plain gray tunic with blue cuffs and hem, black pants and laced calf boots, and a braided blue rope belt—Kaedin blue, recognized across the kingdom and reserved solely for the use of the kaedine. Only the dye-makers in the capital had the recipe for the vibrant color.

It felt odd seeing himself in the attire of a common student, despite the thrill of wearing Kaedin blue. Rilt tried to imagine himself as an adept kaedin, with the shoulder sash to match, then as a master kaedin with a staff. It seemed an unlikely image. Then again, a year ago he would not have pictured himself in this very uniform. A new way of life beckoned, as close to a new start as was possible for him. He took a deep breath, held it, and exhaled.

It's only for a little while, he reminded himself wistfully. The responsibilities and duties of the Arald house would be waiting when he emerged from this dream.

Rilt held no illusions about the limitations posed by his station. He knew the city of Enthinas well enough—the Arald estate lay about two miles outside its gates—although he was hardly allowed to visit it without an armed escort of the house guards. He could recognize all the merchant chiefs, calculate the values and weight of grain, fruit, beer and wine carted out of Enthinas on any given week, and even map the runners' routes against the patrol areas of the rangers and wardens. He could recite the various noble houses, from the royal Alcaronans to the least important houses of Enthin; he had memorized the boundaries of his lands and the sites of major battles. He could analyze any given move by one of the major noble houses and assess if it would benefit or endanger Enthin in the time it took to pour a flagon of linnis brandy.

Yet he did not know the kingdom the way he wanted to. All his knowledge was theoretical. He wanted to experience it all. Part of his reason for enrolling in the university was to gain understanding beyond what Master Baelmin could impart. The other reason was that small taste of freedom, away from his father's demands and expectations.

To be kaedin was to be free. Free to explore Aleis, to see the sights of the land, to know its people. To be unburdened, not constrained by the duties of being the firstborn of the Arald house. To be his own person, answerable to no one but himself.

"Sir?" There was a knock at the door. "We have to leave soon."

"Yes, I'll be down shortly," said Rilt, taking one last lingering look in the mirror. The firstborn of the noble House of Arald, the heir of the Duke of Enthin, and now, just another student in the University of Izdahl. He grinned and wondered what Master Baelmin would have said to him. Smoothing back his hair, Rilt Arald stepped out of the room with his head held high and a smile on his lips.

* * *

The shimmering blue ribbon of the river Dahl came into view not long after midday, and in the near distance a large, dull gray blob sprawled over its span. By the time the Dahl emptied into the bay, it was heavy with the weight of civilization.

Izdahl herself was essentially a squat spread of buildings, encased within five circles of thick stone walls and segmented with canals that webbed across the city, with the widest channel cutting straight through Izdahl. The city walls were old and strong, imbued with kae. Izdahl was the oldest of the four great cities of Aleis, and her history the bloodiest. She was the bedrock of the kingdom: a king who lost Izdahl did not deserve the throne.

The superstitious claimed that the Creators were the ones who raised the palace complex. Rilt had been told that the first Kaedine Council created it by tuning and shaping the foundations from bare rock. Even from this distance, Rilt could see the Eye of Izdahl—the watchtower of the palace—a black spike jutting out from the heart of the city into the sky. Master Baelmin had once jokingly referred to the tower as "the king's kae staff; with it, he changes our world".

Odd that Aleisans refused to accept any but a kaedin on the throne now. Rilt smiled wryly; one of his father's arguments against his enrollment as a student kaedin was that the other houses would suspect them of eyeing the throne. It was a silly argument, in Rilt's opinion. If he had been after the throne, the last place he would want to go was the capital. However, the truth would not deter those trying to twist the facts to their political advantage. Rilt was aware that there would be many eyes on him in Izdahl. Most of them would not be friendly.

He put the thoughts out of his mind. He was in Kaedin Hall as a student. He was going to learn, he was going to keep his head down, and he was not going to be one of those noble lordlings who flaunted their houses to get by with no effort. He might even meet a pretty girl or two to bed.

That reminded him to check the list Cedaran had given him; those were girls whose sights would more likely be set on the title than his good self, and he had to be sure to avoid them. A commoner girl, knowing her slim chance of climbing the social ladder, would likely settle for a few romps with no promises of more.

They had to get into the city first. Throngs of carriages, carts, and coaches were jostling to enter Izdahl, and some drivers were using the time-tested tactic of yelling colorful threats at each other to get ahead. Zarin skillfully maneuvered the coach to the leftmost path for passenger vehicles. The closer they got, the slower their passage became.

The congestion could not be attributed solely to the sheer volume of traffic. Rilt poked his head out the window and noticed, just a few vehicles ahead of them, another coach listing dangerously on its side. It was a marvel that it had not toppled. From what he could see, one of its wheels had popped off. Standing next to the stricken coach were two city wardens and two liveried men. The wardens were directing traffic as best as they could while the men tried to lead the horses to one side of the lane, but the animals were skittish and refused to budge.

A pretty young brunette in university's uniform stood a few paces away, keeping an eye on the men's efforts. She kept curtsying in apology to the drivers that had to navigate around the coach; her apologetic manner and sweet smile kept them from being rude about the delay.

Rilt liked what he saw. Her long black hair gleamed in the sunlight, and the bright yellow ribbons braided into it shone like gold. Judging by her green rope belt, she was a student from the Hall of Arts. Rilt told Zarin to halt when they drew closer.

"But my lord, we'll hold up the road," Zarin protested.

"It's only for a moment. We must offer assistance."

The valet leaned over and muttered to Zarin. The older man sniggered, but he did urge the horses closer to the damaged coach. Once they were level with the listing vehicle, Rilt opened his door and leaned out. "If you don't mind, miss, I can give you a lift to your destination."

"Oh, would you? That would be wonderful!" she exclaimed. Her voice was low and clear. "Belos, do send my love to Mother. I'll reach school in time with this gentleman's help."

Her footman, Belos, narrowed his eyes in suspicion before he noticed the crest on the open door. Then he beamed greasily. "Certainly, miss, and I'll pass along your regards to madam. Thank ye kindly, my lord."

The young lady boarded quickly, not wishing to remain out on the road any longer. Trail dust coated her boots, the sight of which made her grimace in dismay after she had sat down. Pellit and Belos loaded her luggage quickly and they were off. After they had passed the wardens at the gate— their entry papers had been scrutinized with disconcerting attention—Rilt asked for her name.

"I'm Galena Aedinal, from Rimir," she said. Rimir was a small but fairly prosperous town in Dunte, if Rilt's memory served correctly, known for really fine vinegar. He was rather rusty on places beyond Enthin.

"Rilt Arald, Enthin. Pleasure to meet you, Lady Galena."

"Just Galena, please, Lord Rilt. The house of Arald is recognized throughout Aleis," Galena said with a quick grin, nodding at the crest embroidered on the seat.

She'll do, Rilt thought, taking in the pale blue eyes framed by dark lashes and her plump lips. He could not recall the name Aedinal; it was probably one of the lesser Duntean houses. He put on his most charming manner. "Just Rilt as well, then. I see you're attending the Hall of Arts."

"The School of Music, to be precise. You know, when I heard that a lord of Enthin had cleared the entrance examinations for Kaedin Hall, I didn't know it would be the next duke himself attending. I thought it'd be one of the minor lords," said Galena, cocking her head to study the young man. "It should have been all over the grapevine, something big like that. However in Creation did you keep it secret?"

Rilt smiled blandly. "My family wanted my enrollment to be a low-key affair."

"Low-key? In this carriage?" asked Galena, who blushed and covered her mouth. "Sorry. Mother despairs of my ever finding a good match, the way I blurt out my thoughts."

"It's all right." He liked the way her cheeks flushed. She also had a point, and he wished he had seen it earlier. Changing the subject, he asked Galena, "Are you a first-year?"

"Oh, no! I'm in my second. I was given a place early on account of my voice. It'll be grand to sing at the King's Ball—if I can get the adept sash."

"You're a singer?"

"An alto and a harpist." Galena said with a self-conscious smile. "Mother is adamant that I give up all this silliness about becoming a master singer, but I love what I do. I simply must get my adept sash this year. She's keen on setting me up with a nice man by next summer." Galena sighed extravagantly and shrugged. "I can just imagine: Lady Galena, wife of such-and-such a merchant or minor lord or landowner."

"What is it with mothers and marriages?"

"Yours too?"

The young man nodded. "It's practically all she ever talks about when we attend or hold social events. Not that I mind the attention from the young ladies, but sometimes I wonder if they like me or they just like the idea of being the next duchess of Enthin."

"It must be difficult when you are the future duke of Enthin," said Galena, her tone almost sardonic. "Still, a girl could want to be a duchess and like you. These desires are not mutually exclusive."

"That's fair enough."

Leaning back in her seat, Galena put on an exaggeratedly dreamy-eyed expression. "Duchess Galena … It does have a lovely ring to it. I wouldn't mind, dear Lord Rilt. How much attention and favor should I shower upon your handsome self before I win the title?"

"It's not a competition." Rilt laughed and shook his head. "You've been here for two years. How would you recommend I spend my restdays?"

"Trying as much of the street food as possible. I usually avoid the spicier fare to protect my voice, but everything is so delicious," she said cheerfully, the pretense falling away. "Oh, and Riverbank Park is lovely. You take the path just behind the campus' back gate—it leads out from Kaedin Hall, you'll find it easily—is lovely. Very serene and tranquil. I go there often. And—once you find a lovely girl to go walking with—the arches are where the young couples go. It's private enough, with plenty of hiding places."

"Careful, or I'll think you're suggesting something," Rilt teased.

"When I want something, I don't bother to suggest it. I ask."

"That's something new for me, then."

Outside, vendors and peddlers called out an array of enticements and snacks. An assortment of unfamiliar scents filled the inside of the carriage, fighting for attention. Rilt called a few over and bought some, just in case he got hungry in the middle of the night. After all, he would not be able to send Pellit to get him suppers.

"Salted nuts! Only three coppers per pack! Salted nuts!"

"Chikskewers! Chikskewers! Hot and spicy chikskewers!"

"Newest textiles from Port Halim, from across the Aoril Sea! Look at the sheen! Feel its softness!"

"Sweet beans! Come getcher sweet beans roight herrrre!"

It seemed like all the colors ever dyed by the master weavers were on display in the streets. The canvas awnings of shops and vendors' stalls were riotously hued, battling for the eye of passers-by. Women in ethereal diaphanous dresses, their long hair bound up in jeweled combs and ribbons, squeezed past burly men in rough homespun cotton clothes. A few city wardens in black and silver stood atop raised plinths at road junctions like glinting rocks in a chaotic river of people and vehicles. Horses jostled for space alongside mules and hand-drawn carts, and the noise was terrific. Rilt was enthralled by the cacophony of it all. The coach eventually threaded its way through the crowded mercantile circle and crossed the bridge to the north bank. Soon, the air was no longer redolent with the scents of fried meats and dried herbs, and the sounds of trade faded.

Once they were across the canal, Rilt drew back the curtains fully. Tall evergreens lined the avenues while mansions lurked behind lofty stone walls; they could be seen only through ornate wrought iron gates. Trained canines behind the gates barked noisily when they passed and liveried house guards watched the coach with hooded eyes. Rilt knew the Arald's Izdahli estate was close to the water, and even had its own little dock. The coach rolled past the parade of mansions and through a set of tall iron gates that had the Alcaronan crest set into them.

"There it is, my favorite part of the journey," said Galena excitedly, pointing out the window. "Best view of the university."

Rilt saw what she meant. The seven halls of the university were spread out on the south side of the palace around a large, kaedine-made lake, and from here all seven halls were visible, their gleaming tiled roofs adorned in the seven colors of Creation with bright pennants flying from turrets and towers. Green for the arts, yellow for healers, red for history… Rilt wondered if he could visit every hall. If he could visit the Hall of History, perhaps he could see for himself the sights that Master Baelmin had gazed upon when the tutor had walked its hallways. The thought made him smile. The university halls of gleaming white stone stood proud in the sunlight. Huge arched stained glass windows spanned many of the walls, and Rilt could see students ambling around on the grounds, even at this time in the morning. The building with the blue roof would be Kaedin Hall, where Rilt was to live for two years.

A thrill fluttered just beneath his heart.

Galena chattered away about shortcuts to different halls and the general temperaments of students of the various schools. Rilt barely heard a word; he was rapt with the sheer delight of seeing his school for the very first time, outside of his imagination or faded illustrations in a book.

The two stared out the window until they turned down a different avenue and the view was lost. Flagstones gave way to the crunch of gravel. A large painted sign on the side of the road proclaimed that they were entering the grounds of Izdahl University, and that trespassers would be handed to the city wardens.

"Do the city wardens come into the university often?"

"Every hall has their own porters who patrol at night, but as long as you have a reason to be out of the dorm, they're fairly lenient. Just don't try to sneak out of campus after midnight—they've been known to lie in wait and then, once they catch you, take you to the dean." She paused and winked. "Or maybe that's just for my hall."

"I'm sure they follow the same protocol throughout." Rilt hesitated for a beat, and then asked, "Do you like staying here?"

"It's fun living away from home, once you get used to it," Galena told Rilt. "I'm not going to lie; it was tough in the beginning. I did get homesick a few times, but now I have friends from all over the kingdom, and we write each other over the holidays."

"We'll have roommates in the dormitories, I heard. What's it like living with other people?"

"Six girls rooming together creates the most incredible mess you can imagine." Galena laughed self-deprecatingly. "Usually I'm the culprit when it comes to the mess. As for what it feels like … Well, at first it was quite strange to have no privacy," she admitted, "but I got used to having them around at all hours of the day. You end up talking about everything and anything. No secrets. Of course, it also means that gossip and scandal travel at an accelerated rate. We always know who is sleeping with whom."

Rilt frowned. Even considering his dalliances, he had never shared a room with anyone overnight, except for a few times nearly ten years ago, when Ced was still afraid of thunderstorms. He felt uneasy at having to sacrifice his privacy.

"I'm just glad I made friends with them," said Galena. "By summer, I'm sure my mother will have found yet another gaggle of eligible bachelors 'for my consideration'." She uttered the last three words with a venom familiar to Rilt.

The beginnings of a plan started to sprout in Rilt's mind. He leaned forward and asked quietly, "I don't mean to be presumptuous, but would you be amenable to a date?"

"Excuse me?" Galena's astonishment was honest. "We've just met!"

"I'd like to get to know you better." Rilt put on his most charming smile, and then let his expression fall just a little. "I apologize, I didn't mean to put you on the spot."

"Oh, no, I was just—I'm surprised, that's all." She nibbled on her upper lip and studied him through her narrowed gaze, before her mouth curved in a small, shy smile. "It's rather flattering. I'll think about it."

It always works, Rilt thought, careful not to let his smugness show.

They were now trundling along the gravel path, following the lead of the stagecoach ahead of them. Dappled shade provided welcome relief from the bright morning sunlight. The steady crunch of hooves on the tiny stones filled the quiet of the cabin.

Rilt rubbed the tip of his nose in chagrin. "I didn't mean to make you uncomfortable. I'm sorry. I guess I just want to meet someone who isn't from the hall, so I won't end up talking about lessons."

"There is no need to apologize," said Galena. "I wonder what my parents would think if they hear I went out with a future duke. They might want me to push you for a wedding date."

"I have no qualms resisting your subtle pressuring. Or your parents', for that matter. I'm not keen on an early marriage."

"In that case, I might allow myself to enjoy your company." Galena relaxed against her seat. The assessing gleam in her eyes became more shrewd. "What do you want from me?"

"I merely wish to be friends. So, if I wanted to contact you, how would I go about it?"

"You can tell the university's runners to run your message to 4304, Hall of Music. That's my room number."

"I don't remember getting a room number," said Rilt, starting to feel worried.

"You're a first-year, so you'll be assigned one later when you report in. The Hall of Music is on the left, thank you," she called out the front to Zarin. To Rilt, she said, "Have fun at Kaedin Hall, Lord Rilt. I'm really pleased to meet you."

"Me too, Lady Galena. 4304, right?"

"Yes." Galena's pale blue eyes widened in mischief and she whispered, "Since I'm rolling up to the steps in your coach, I think it's safe to assume that gossip about us will reach our parents quite promptly."

When the vehicle rolled to a stop, it was Rilt who opened the door and helped her out. From the looks of surprise on some of the students' faces, both of them knew their arrival had caused a minor stir. It was all they could do not to maintain their expressions of bland politeness. Eagle-eyed students and adepts of the Hall of Music had identified the Arald crest instantly and were talking to each other, pretending they were not staring. Rilt did not linger. Leaving the unloading of Galena's luggage to Pellit, he gave Galena a quick kiss on the back of her hand, which made her blush.

"I look forward to seeing you again, Galena," he said with a smile and a wink. As they drove away, he wondered how he could make use of his new acquaintance. He and Galena could come to a mutually satisfying arrangement, he was sure; that should stave off the status-hungry houses. He might even get to have some fun along the way.

* * *

The university lake was a burning blue circled by a broad grassy bank, with trees bordering the water along certain parts of the lake. A pavilion stood in the heart of the lake, connected to the bank by a zig-zagging stone path that bisected the lake. Tall lampposts stood at regular intervals on the lake's circumference beside wooden benches. Shards of sunlight flickered over the surface of the water. It looked pleasant enough. There were already some students from the other halls strolling along the banks. Rilt wondered idly how cold the water was, and if they were allowed to swim in it.

His heart leaped in joy when he spotted the whitesong trees, their cascades of small white blossoms barely brushing the surface of the lake. It made Izdahl and Kaedin Hall seem a lot more welcoming, and home less distant.

The three main buildings of Kaedin Hall faced the lake, their many ornate windows reflecting the scenic view like facets of a jewel. The west building had windows spanning two whole floors—that had to be the library or the great hall. The middle building was the tallest, with ancient stained glass windows depicting the five Creators amid the seven colors of the rainbow. No one used stained glass these days. The east building looked the plainest, so Rilt assumed it held classrooms or dormitories.

They entered a broad semicircular yard in front of the building in the middle, where a handful of carriages and stagecoaches had halted for their passengers to disembark. Rilt bounced in his seat. Before Zarin had stopped the vehicle completely, he had flung open the door and hopped out. It was not proper for him to do so, but he could not contain himself.

Students stood in loose groups in the yard while the porters bustled about with luggage. A short, wide flight of steps led up to ornate doors carved out of solid blackwood with gleaming bronze fittings.

The young lord observed the people around him. This was the largest group of people around his age he had ever been in. Most Enthinian youths avoided the Arald sons, all too keenly aware of the difference in status. Here, he was very nearly another face in the crowd. Though a few older students glanced askance at the crest on his coach, they did not seem impressed. The younger ones muttered among themselves, but Rilt hoped they would not be put off by his rank.

He heard a heavy thump behind him, distracting him from his musings.

"Be careful with that," Pellit admonished sharply. "It's Lord Rilt's and worth more than your hide."

"Pellit, don't," said Rilt, casting a glance behind him. He gestured for the man to unload the luggage. "It's alright, man, go on."

The porter squinted at Pellit and then at Rilt, before bobbing his head at the latter. "G'morn, m'lord."

"Good morning," said Rilt. The porter seemed surprised that Rilt would reply. He nodded again, this time with a touch more respect, before carrying the trunk away. Something about his measured gait reminded Rilt of his house guards. He guessed that the porters here were trained in the use of arms. After all, most of the students here came from fairly well-off families. The university's fees were steep for commoners, if what Pellit told him was true.

The exchange between Rilt and the porter did not go unnoticed. Those who had been chatting nearby studied Rilt surreptitiously; he felt as though he was being weighed for sale. He pretended not to notice the scrutiny, however, and thanked Pellit and Zarin for making the long drive to Izdahl with him.

"Sir, Zarin and I have been told to stay and have the Izdahli estate made ready for the Duke and Duchess," Pellit said while Zarin sorted out the horses. "Her Grace has instructed us to leave the estate's address at the runner lodge here."

Rilt understood the underlying message. They had been ordered to watch him and report his actions to his father. He thanked the Creators that Pellit was more loyal to Rilt than to Halden. Rilt would even count Pellit a friend, but the latter was still a servant when all was weighed and measured.

"Then do as you've been told, Pell. I may drop by on a Sixthday or Seventhday when I'm more settled." Rilt paused and added, "Inform my parents of my safe arrival, and send my love to your mother. Remind her to make sure Ced eats well."

The young valet inclined his sandy head. "We'll be off then, sir. Take care."

"You too, Pellit, Zarin." He watched them get into the vehicle. Before the coach started moving, he was already running up the steps.

* * *

The foyer was crowded with young men, some looking as lost as Rilt felt, others—older students, judging by the casual familiarity with which they yelled at one another—strode about confidently. There was an ornate stairwell that swept up to a second floor, under an exquisite chandelier dripping with glass beads. Doors leading into the back of the building were shut, so the noise was contained to the foyer. Rilt peered around, looking for someone to guide him through whatever needed be done. Then he spotted four tables set up on the side of the room, marked with the numbers one to four.

I suppose that's where I need to report? Rilt exhaled and headed to the table that was presumably for first-years. He had his papers tucked under an arm. Two young men with adept sashes sat there, ticking off names. One was stoutly built and wore a friendly smile. The other one was lean and intense, with lank, dirty yellow hair that hung in his eyes, and he watched the room like a graywulf. Rilt strode right up to the front but before he could speak, the person near the front of the line took hold of his elbow.

"You should get in line, my lord."

It was a voice he knew and loathed. Rilt sucked in a deep breath and turned around, not bothering to hide the frown creasing his brow. "Naelen Barith. This is the last place I expected to see you."

"The feeling is mutual, Lord Rilt." Naelen smiled thinly. He nodded at the students behind him and said, "There is a line right here. You don't get to cut it just because of your name."

"I have a question, that is all."

"Nonetheless. The line, Lord Rilt."

One of the adepts at the table cleared his throat. "Do you both mind moving this to the side? Everyone else is held up." The friendly-looking adept looked vaguely worried and embarrassed about interjecting.

Rilt glared at Naelen. "I wasn't the one who-"

"Get in line," the other adept said, quiet and authoritative. His keen gaze flicked from Naelen to Rilt and back. "You, blond student, you're up. You, end of the line."

The adept's tone raised Rilt's hackles. "I am-"

"A first-year student," said the adept. He raised his chin, looking directly at Rilt with a small sardonic curl to his lips. "In this hall, I outrank you. End of the line, or go home."

Feeling a flush of humiliated anger creep up his neck and cheeks, Rilt was about to argue further when someone tugged lightly on his sleeve.

"Hey, how about we go to the end of the line together?" asked another student. He had bright blue eyes and a winning smile, and the lilt in his accent suggested that he was from the south near the sea. "Come on, it's our first day. Bet you're tired from all the traveling. Where are you from?" As he chattered away he led Rilt to the back of the queue; the other first-years watched them curiously and a few bore unfriendly smirks.

"My name is Kayle Radieri," the other student said, once they were lined up behind the rest. In front of them was a dark-haired student who bore a faint resemblance to Kayle, and he also bore a suspicious scowl now directed at Rilt. Kayle held out a hand. "I'm from Halimgor. Port Halim."

Rilt shook it, with some hesitation. "Rilt Arald. Enthinas."

"Really?" Kayle dropped the hand and covered his mouth. "I'm so sorry, my lord, I didn't mean any disrespect, I was just-"

"Don't grovel, Kayle, you're better than that," the other student drawled. He cast an eye over Rilt, barely concealing his distaste. "Why did you help him? He can fend for himself like the rest of us here."

Kayle elbowed the student. "Gareth, there's no call for being rude. Sorry, Lord Rilt, he can be uncouth."

"Actually, 'Rilt' will do, we're all students here." Rilt put aside his instinctive dislike of Gareth for the moment; he had no desire to be singled out again by the adept with the dirty blond hair. He remembered his resolve from that morning to just be a simple student of the hall and not the future duke of Enthin. "Are you two brothers?"

"No, we're just friends." Kayle grinned at Gareth who rolled his eyes and turned his back on Kayle and Rilt both. "He doesn't like meeting new people."

"I'd never have guessed that," said Rilt dryly.

Gareth flicked an assessing gaze over Rilt, then snorted. He looked away again, giving every impression of not caring.

"I'm surprised to see you here," said Kayle brightly. "I mean, I thought the son of a duke would be privately tutored, not be allowed to mingle with the commoners."

Rilt had to smile at Kayle's friendliness. The other young man was so eager to please that it was nearly impossible to feel anything less than flattered by his interest. Kayle had chin-length dark hair that curled fetchingly, and fair skin that contrasted with dark-lashed blue eyes. For someone who lived in the busiest port of the kingdom, he looked as though he had not seen the sun for some time. There was a feminine delicacy to his features that Rilt supposed could be considered attractive. Gareth was paler and thinner than Kayle, and his cheekbones stood out sharply; his straight dark hair had a rich sheen to it. It was his one handsome feature, Rilt considered. He had never met anyone quite as disagreeable-looking as Gareth.

"I had a private tutor, but I did have kae resonance when I tested for it, so I thought attending the hall would be beneficial," said Rilt, answering Kayle's query.

They were near the front now. Gareth handed his papers to the friendly-looking adept, who looked down the list of names. "Gareth Krell, you're paired with Naelen Barith, over there. He's got the keys and he's been briefed already, so you can go ahead."

Gareth looked over. "That one? I thought I'd be with-"

"You thought wrong. Barith's over there, the handsome blond lad with the stunning green eyes. Is that fine with you, Krell?" said the lean adept, voice heavy with sarcasm. "Do I need to hold your hand to introduce you?"

Gareth Krell scowled and strode off, leaving Kayle and Rilt to the adepts. Rilt hesitated. He was not sure how to address them.

The stout one with the friendly face helped him out. "I'm Terras and this is Wolvam. About just now? I'm sorry. Wolvam isn't the tactful sort."

"Don't apologize for me," said Wolvam. "I meant every word I said." He took Kayle's and Rilt's papers and looked them over. Lacing his thin fingers together, he stared at Rilt, not unkindly. "In the hall, I rank you. Everyone who isn't in your class ranks you. Best get used to that feeling."

Elbowing Wolvam lightly in mild rebuke, Terras shuffled the papers together and handed them to Kayle. "Rilt Arald and Kayle Radieri, you're been paired in Room Six. These are your keys. You'll have to pay for any losses or damages, and you're responsible for the cleanliness of your own room. That includes the bathroom you share with Room Five."

Rilt frowned. "Are there no servants?"

"There are servants. They clean the masters' studies, the library, the classrooms, and the laboratories. Not your rooms." Wolvam's mouth curved in a humorless smile. "Welcome to life without privilege, Lord Rilt. You're a student of Kaedin Hall now."

Before Rilt could respond to that jibe, Kayle jingled the keys and beamed. "I can't wait to see the room. Come on!"

* * *

As luck would have it, Rilt and Kayle were to share a bathroom with Gareth and Naelen. The latter two were in Room Five. Rilt was not glad about it at all, but he kept his displeasure to himself. It could have been worse: he could have been roommates with Naelen.

"I think it's wonderful," Kayle said to Gareth when they caught up to him and Naelen in a wide corridor leading to the dormitories. Gareth—Rilt was pleased to note—seemed as far less excited than his friend. "But it does mean we have to roster our timings. I don't want to fight over who gets to use the bathroom first."

"We have limited hot water, too," said Gareth, reading off a sheet of information. "That means the lordling will have to be the last to shower."

"What? Why?"

"I don't want you to use up all the hot water, taking long showers the way you probably used to back in your fancy mansion."

"Watch your tone, Krell. Keep that up and you will be in hot water."

Gareth narrowed his gray eyes. He tossed the sheet of paper aside. "Oh, you didn't just threaten me, lordling."

Rilt got in front of him. "What exactly is your problem? You hardly know me."

"What's going on here?" A master kaedin hurried over. He looked young, with a smooth brow and a beard that was dark brown and close-cropped. "Classes haven't even started! What is the argument about?" His accent placed him as a Halim, though it was milder than Kayle's.

Kayle cleared his throat and stepped forward. "Just a minor disagreement. I'm sorry, sir, it won't happen again." He levelled a glare at Gareth, who folded his arms. His mouth went thin and angry.

"Get to your rooms, young men. And comport yourselves with dignity proper to this institution. You are here to learn, not to brawl like street ruffians." The master kaedin huffed through his nose disapprovingly. Then he paused and stared at Kayle. "You look familiar… Have I met you before?"

"I don't know, sir, but I have a pretty common face," said Kayle politely.

"Hardly common," said the master kaedin thoughtfully before shrugging. "I will see you boys in class. Now get to your dormitories."

Kayle blew out his cheeks in an exaggerated sigh of relief. He mimed wiping his brow and said, "We could have gotten in trouble."

"Who was that man?" Gareth asked.

"That would be Master Jodius," Naelen said. Seeing the doubtful looks of the other three, he added, "He was on the same stagecoach as I was this morning. I asked."

Kayle swiveled on his heel to walk backwards so he could see the man wind his way into the corridor leading to the masters' studies. "He's very young for a master."

"Fairly new to his mastery, I imagine," said Gareth.

"Wonder what he'll be teaching." Kayle turned to face the front again. "We have the whole day to explore, correct?"

Gareth shrugged. "Other than dinner at the eighth bell, we don't have anything scheduled."

While Gareth and Kayle discussed their plans for later, Rilt stuffed his hands in his pockets and looked around the corridor they were strolling down, deliberately ignoring Naelen Barith. Kaedin Hall radiated a sense of age. Its stone floor was worn down not by skill but by the friction of thousands and thousands of people walking over it daily for hundreds of years. Tiles featuring the symbols of the elements were painted around the windows and engraved in the ceiling. To their left were arches that opened into a small courtyard, with stone benches and trees clustered near the corners, artfully cultivated to provide shade. The grass in the courtyard looked thick and springy, and the bushes were flowering with ebullient vibrancy. On their right were bright, airy classrooms. Rilt wondered which one he would be using the most.

"Well, if you're not interested, I'll just go alone," said Kayle. He bumped Rilt with his elbow. "Maybe you'd like to come with me?"

"Where to?" asked the young lord. He had not been paying attention.

"The greenhouses! I've heard that Kaedin Hall has the single largest collection of rare plants outside of the Healer Hall. I want to see them."

"Are the greenhouses open to us?" Rilt remembered the conservatory his stepmother kept on the grounds. It was huge, but probably not as spacious as the one here. It would be interesting to see what the Hall kept on hand. Selvina loved flowers from Halimgor, so the conservatory was usually filled to the brim with those.

"Even if we can't go in, we can see where they are, and look in from the outside," Kayle said. "Will you come with me? Gareth has no patience when I start talking plants."

Rilt agreed readily. He wasn't tired from his journey, and he wanted to see the full extent of the hall and its grounds. They soon reached the students' block.

"We're first-years, so our rooms are on the first and second floor. There we are!" Kayle jogged up to the door with the number 'six' painted on it in dark blue. Their luggage was set outside: the large trunk for Rilt, and a small, battered one of cheap board for Kayle. Room Five was to the right, and to their left the numbers went on to Room Ten.

When Rilt followed Kayle inside with his heavy trunk, he was not sure how to react. The entire room was smaller than his dressing room back in Enthin. It was painted a pale blue, and the stone floor was bare but for two undyed wool rugs. There was a sitting space for two squat armchairs set before a simple fireplace. Two beds were placed against the walls on either side, and at the foot of each bed was a wooden chest of drawers. Two writing desks with drawers were set side-by-side directly under the window, which ran nearly the width of the room. The view outside was uninspiring; just the tops of two skinny saplings and some shrubs, and beyond that, a brick wall. When he leaned carefully out the window, he saw that the other side was a six to eight-foot drop. It was probably to deter students from sneaking out of the room at night far more than burglars.

How was this going to be enough living space for two persons? He was about to say this aloud when he saw Kayle testing out one of the beds.

"This is amazing," said Kayle with a big smile. His gaze fell on the wall facing the other bed, next to the fireplace. "Oh, we get a wardrobe! Not that I have much to hang in it. But I guess you can always use the space."

Rilt peered into the shared bathroom that opened on the left of the main entryway. There was another door for Room Five. There were two shower stalls and a two sinks, but only one toilet.

"We are definitely going to fight over this," he muttered. He was also vaguely worried at the thought of having to clean the bathroom; he had never needed to tidy anything up in his life. That was what servants were for.

Kayle had lain down on the bed, his eyes closed. Rilt sat down gingerly on the other and was surprised that it was not as uncomfortable as he had been expecting.

"Not up to your standards?" asked Kayle, still lying on his back.

"I wasn't … I mean, this is not what I'm used to."

His roommate studied him. The sunny smile was still present, but there was a shrewd cast to his gaze now. "The more you show that you're uncomfortable with these changes, the less the others will accept you."

Rilt scrubbed the back of his head. "You sound like you've been through this."

"It's a survival skill." Kayle looked at the ceiling. When he next spoke, there was a faraway note in his voice. "I lived near a cliff for a short time. The trees that grow on the edge of the cliff are all clustered together, and they grow to the same height. I never understood why. Then one day, I realized out that the winds there are much stronger than elsewhere along the coast. Storms hit that part of Port with twice the fury."

"What's that got to do with-"

"If you stand out, you become a target," said Kayle. His brilliant blue eyes fixed on Rilt's face, reminding him of sapphires. "Be less outstanding, and others will overlook you. Of course, that means you don't get the full benefit of the sunshine or the rain. But if you stand taller than any of the others, you'll bear the worst of the winds and the storms. You break. You fall. You become nothing but feed for the bugs and the other trees. Blending in is a matter of survival."

The bleakness of the words was at odds with the cheery demeanor Kayle had displayed earlier. When Rilt finally found his tongue, he said, "You're satisfied with being just like all of them?"

Kayle sat up and cocked his head at Rilt, his disarming smile back on his face. "I said 'you' for a reason. Your birthright already forces you to stand out. To brave the storms for Enthin. However, right now, in Kaedin Hall, it's best for you to be a mere student. You think Gareth with his sharp tongue is the worst you'll face?"

"If you mean Wolvam-"

"Adept Wolvam was trying to help you. If anyone gives you preferential treatment..." Kayle trailed off and shrugged. "You know what? I think we should unpack and then get on with our exploring."

Rilt thought about his father's seal ring, safe in his luggage. "You think the others will be jealous if I received preferential treatment."

"Lord Rilt, I'm commonborn and I've lived with dock workers, sailors, fisherfolk. Generaly speaking, people who work with their hands don't like those who live large on the sweat of other people's brows." Kayle upended his suitcase and began putting his things away.

It was an unexpectedly stinging admonition. Rilt looked at his trunk, nearly half the height of the chest of drawers, and thought of the room full of clothes he kept on the Izdahli estate as well as the clothes left back home. Chastened, he quietly unlocked his trunk and wondered how much to keep here and what to send to the estate. He doubted he would need as much as he originally believed, though he'd keep all six sets of the uniform he'd had made.

"Hey, um, Lord Rilt?"

Rilt glanced over, a shirt in one hand and a belt in another.

"I apologize for speaking bluntly." Kayle nibbled on his top lip. "I was out of line and I should … I don't know, be more courteous."

"No, it was … it is helpful. I appreciate your candor. We are going to be living together and—well, Wolvam said it. In here, I'm just a student. Like you." He grinned shyly. "Just 'Rilt' will do. Truly."

Kayle's smile turned self-effacing. "You're nothing like me. You're the heir to Enthin."

"But that is all I've ever been allowed to be. Coming to Kaedin Hall is the first time I've ever done exactly what I wanted to become what I want to be," said Rilt quietly. After a heartbeat, he realized he might have shared too much, and then cleared his throat. When he met Kayle's gaze, he saw only gentle empathy, and that made an unfamiliar emotion flare up in his throat. He dropped the garments back in the trunk and gestured helplessly. "I think I may need help putting away my clothes."

The other student laughed and joined him to sort out his luggage. As the two young men put away the shirts, tunics, and pants, they talked about inconsequential trivialities, but there was now a rapport that Rilt found welcoming.

* * *

Once they were done unpacking—Kayle much sooner than Rilt—the dark-haired Halim declared he was famished, and dragged Rilt out with him to the cafeteria. Rilt was not sure what he thought of his roommate: bubbly and cheerful one moment, astute and perceptive the next. He could not help liking him, however. There was an innate warmth and genuineness that Kayle exuded which was refreshing. Most of Rilt's acquaintances put on a mask so perfect, it was difficult to ever truly know the person behind them.

The large cafeteria was bustling with activity, and there were multiple tables for four set up in neat rows. The kitchen was visible to those eating, with large pass-throughs for platters and trays laid out on long trestle tables at one end. Rilt watched in awe as the cooks stirred pots that could probably hold a small child and kneaded lumps of dough the size of Rilt's waist. All the students helped themselves. It was a novel experience to serve himself, and Rilt piled his plate with a lot more than he initially had planned. Thankfully, Kayle had a similar amount on his own plate.

"I wonder what this is." Kayle prodded contemplatively at a brown lump. "Already I'm missing fish. The Dahl has fish, right?"

"Dahl fish taste like mud, if you're lucky," said another student seated one table over. He touched his brow in greeting. "Oledan Puros, Izdahli, bred and born."

"Kayle Radieri, and this is Rilt."

"Pleasure," Rilt added with a small smile. He sliced up the meat and tasted it. Blander than he was used to, but there was a hint of caro spice that added a kick of heat. "It's just carochik, Kayle."

"That's the wrong color then," Kayle declared. "Caro gives a rich, deep red to the sauce, not this pathetic brown mess."

Oledan laughed, a rich, fruity sound. "You're from Halimgor? You have the best caro from the islands. What comes to Izdahl is second-rate, even if this is the capital. The cooks in the halls and schools skimp on the spices. But I know the best eateries and other pleasurable delights to be found around town, so let me know if you need anything."

There was a lewdness about the way he said 'pleasurable delights' that made Rilt uncomfortable, but he seemed harmless, so Rilt held his tongue.

"Will do," replied Kayle cheerfully. When he looked at his food again, he twisted his mouth to the side. Then he sighed. "Beggars can't be choosers. At least it's warm."

Oledan grinned again. "There are good restaurants out there with Halim cooking." He belched into his fist. "Excuse me. I'm going to get some seconds."

"You and Gareth seem friendly," said Rilt as they ate. "Have you two known each other long?"

"Two... no, three years, I think? Let me see..." Kayle calculated as he chewed. "Yes, three years by the end of the term. He's my best friend."

"He doesn't seem very nice."

Kayle flashed a mischievous grin. "He'll say the same thing about you to me. He can be sharp, especially to those he thinks are dumber than he, but he's good at heart."

Rilt grunted. "If he picks on those less intelligent than he, there shouldn't be that many candidates."

"Unfortunately," Kayle said, smiling, "Gareth is one of the three royal scholars. He's brilliant."

"Really?"

"Mmhmm." Kayle finished off the last of his plate. "That wasn't too bad. I might go back for seconds."

Rilt kept him from standing up. "If you don't mind, you can take what I have on my plate, please. I'm not that hungry."

"You certain?" Kayle picked up his fork and spoon.

"Yes." Making little motions for Kayle to eat, Rilt took the chance to absorb the new knowledge about Gareth. One of three royal scholars. Who were the other two?

He saw Naelen taking the table beside them. He was all alone, but he seemed absorbed in a book. Craning his head slightly, Rilt read the title: *A Comparative Study of Creation Myths*.

Kayle followed his gaze. "Naelen, would you like to sit with us?"

"That's alright," said the blond Enthinian. He flicked a glance at Rilt. "I'm good over here."

"We wouldn't want you to be distracted from that engrossing book," Rilt said smoothly.

Naelen smiled politely and resumed reading and eating.

Without waiting for an invitation, Oledan slid into an empty seat at their table, his refilled plate thunking noisily. He pointed a fork at Kayle. "You said you're a Halim. Port?"

"Port."

"So you've heard of the Night Pearl, Lady Liria."

"And seen her about on her walks a few times," said Kayle. "What of it?"

Oledan wrinkled his nose. "Is she really that beautiful?"

Kayle considered his reply. "Taken individually, her features are not appealing. But together, they form a most attractive face. She's also one of the most brilliant minds in Halimgor, the rumor goes."

"I've heard her body is more attractive than her face," Oledan said as he chewed noisily on more carochik. Rilt angled himself slightly away from the crude young man. "And that Port is her playground now."

Kayle raised an eyebrow as he polished off the rest of Rilt's food.

"She has the support of nearly all the sea-captains and guildmasters."

"Bet she sleeps with them," Oledan cackled. "Bet that's how she's getting that support for her confirmation."

Rilt was suddenly and violently put off by the other student's greasy hair and greasier leer. Before he could speak up, there was swift motion next to them. Naelen had got to his feet and was gazing steadily at Oledan. "Lady Liria is of the Alwyth house, Oledan. Do watch how you speak of her." He shut his book and took his food elsewhere.

Distinctly bemused by Naelen's defense of Liria, Rilt had to speak up for his peer's honor. She was going to be a duchess, after all, and it would not do to allow commonborn to denigrate her. "I'm sure Lady Liria is very capable, Oledan."

"That's right," Kayle added. "She's negotiated new treaties for more trade to the Deraq Islands just last summer. The sea-captains love her."

"She's a woman," Oledan said. He sniffed and gulped down the rest of his meal. "She's better off married."

Abruptly irritated by Oledan's comment, Rilt pushed away from the table with his now-empty plate in hand. "Come on, Kayle. We have quite a bit of the hall's grounds to cover."

His roommate nodded and stood up, excusing themselves from Oledan. As they returned their plates, Kayle muttered to Rilt, "He's very obnoxious, isn't he?"

"Rude, too."

"Unsavory."

"Objectionable."

"Offensive to women."

"Oily."

The two young men caught each other's eye and burst out laughing. That attracted a few curious glances but the two first-years hurried out of the cafeteria and ambled towards the west block.

* * *

"Your parents must be proud of your qualifying for Kaedin Hall," said Kayle. He squinted at the signs and led the way. Rilt trailed after, smiling at his roommate's obvious enthusiasm.

"It was difficult for them to believe at first." Unwilling to get into the details of his own family's reactions, Rilt asked, "What did your parents say when you told them you've cleared the examinations?"

"Nothing." Kayle shrugged and pressed his lips together. "I'm an orphan. Never knew my father, and Ma died a few years back."

"Oh. I'm sorry."

"It was a long time ago." Kayle stretched his arms overhead and winced. "I owe Gareth everything. If it wasn't for him, I'd be adrift at sea. He was the one who insisted on our trying for Kaedin Hall."

Rilt nodded. "That's why you're best friends."

"Among other reasons. Here's the library." Kayle pushed open the doors for them to enter. Rilt was crossing the main floor when he realized that Kayle had stopped in his tracks. He turned to call his roommate, but paused when he saw the other student's expression.

Kayle stood with his mouth slightly agape, his blue eyes wide with wonder and awe. It was as though he was lit up from within from pure joy. His entire being was still, even his breathing, as though even an exhalation would disturb the sanctity of the moment. He stared at the floor-to-ceiling windows, the soaring vaulted ceilings, the shelf upon shelf upon shelf of books.

It was humbling for Rilt to witness his new friend's rapt delight; books and libraries were part of his life. Yet to see someone so rapt for as simple a place as a library…

He swallowed. "Come on. We can spend the afternoon here, if you want."

"I want to spend my whole life here," whispered Kayle, his eyes fixed on the books.

"You can't shower and use the necessary in the library." Rilt chuckled and added, "Not without being tossed out by the librarians."

That made Kayle laugh quietly and shook him out of his wonderment. They browsed the shelves, moving from historical records to treatises about civilizations outside of Aleis to myths and legends about the Creators. There were also volumes about healing, law, the arts, and military strategies, as they applied to the kaedine. Rilt found himself looking for books about kaedine history before the Warring Years, but he could not spot any.

When he found his roommate again, Kayle was flipping through a volume on advanced kaedine-assisted healing. He shut the thick leatherbound book reverently and returned it to the shelf. "If only everyone out there could read these books."

"Then everyone would know more than they need to know," Rilt said. "What good will that do?"

"Better to know than not to know, you know? That there is more to learn beyond the little worlds we each inhabit." The student returned the book to its place. His fingers lingered on the spine, and then trailed down longingly. "The archives are downstairs. Shall we?"

Rilt was far more impressed with the archives than the library. Here, in an echoing, cavernous space, Kaedin Hall displayed its collection of extraordinary kaedin constructs and artifacts collated through the generations. Rilt could barely tear his eyes from an entire wall of kaedin-made weaponry, locked behind clear glass.

"Look, the battlestaff of Master Werino! It's probably a replica, but the workmanship is stunning." He jogged down the display, pausing every now and then to read the card attached to an exhibit. "I wonder if they have the sword, Dalmis. That would be quite a coup."

Kayle wrinkled his nose. "Weapons aren't my area of interest. They make it easier to kill people."

"These are works of art," said Rilt distractedly, staring now at an engraved saber crafted for a kingsrider for the first king of the Alcaronan line. He waved for the other student to come over, but Kayle had wandered off elsewhere. With a sigh, Rilt went in search of his roommate. He strolled past the racks, occasionally distracted by a finely-made weapon, and turned a corner. He was startled by a kaedin pointing the carved end of his kae staff at him. It took him a heartbeat to realize that he was looking at a mannequin.

"Very realistic," he murmured. He was in the armory section; the mannequin that had frightened him bore the garb, shoulder plates and bracers of a kaedin of the late Amago dynasty, explained a small placard on the side of the mannequin. Rilt took his time admiring various mannequins, momentarily forgetting Kayle. The kaedine of the first few years of the Amago dynasty wore simple robes, stark contrasts to the richly embroidered tunics worn by kaedine now.

The Alcaronan house had eradicated the Amago line of kings, and brought unprecedented wealth into the kingdom. The further he walked down the aisle, the older the artefacts were. At the end of the hall were a dozen helmets, used in the Warring Years prior to the kingdom's founding. All had mesh face plates. The mesh reminded Rilt of the lamps used by coal miners in northern Enthin, the sort that would burn blue in exploding gas. The mesh kept the flame from touching the gas directly and the miners would be able to flee and burn out the gas with controlled fires.

"Kaedine of the Warring Years clashed often against archers who used burning arrows against them. Mesh face plates kept the flames from scorching the kaedine's faces," Rilt recited quietly. He paused. Something did not make sense. Burning arrows were used to attack structures, not people. Furthermore, kaedine could easily deflect debris with their resonant element.

'Deyre breith wer flaume yn fir.' The words in Master Baelmin's letter came back to Rilt. His heart leapt to his throat. Their breaths were flame and fire. And what would protect men from being blinded by flames?

"Rilt? Are you still here?" Kayle called out, somewhere far behind Rilt. The young lord looked at the placard again and hurried away to locate his new roommate, even as his mind raced to put together what he had just found with what his old tutor had confided in his final letter.

He found Kayle in front of a replica of the king's coronation garb and staff. Wordlessly, Rilt stood beside him to study the elaborately-embroidered robe, the fur-trimmed cloak, the spray of white and kaedin-blue gems about the throat and cuffs. The thick cloak bore the crest of the greater ice hawk of the Alcaronan house. The staff was a plain black iron rod with a single moon-white gem set at its tip, its simplicity a stark contrast against the extravagance of the outfit. This was definitely a replica, for the original would be with King Eram; that kae staff had belonged to Coleri Aleis, founder of the kingdom. Only the rightful king could wield the staff, according to legend. For the past five centuries, the staff had changed hands from the house of Aleis to the Amagos and now the Alcaronans. It was tempting to think that the staff chose the monarch, but Rilt suspected that it was just a myth to justify the change in kings.

"We'll see the prince in this someday," said Kayle softly. He touched the glass and withdrew his hand immediately, leaving a smear. "There is so much history in this. The stories it could tell."

"If that outfit were able to speak, it would probably say that it came from a dresser's studio in Third Circle East." Gareth strolled over from the opposite side and came to stand with them. The light from the display fell on the planes on his face in odd angles, highlighting his sharp cheekbones and thin nose.

Kayle sounded annoyed. "I know it's a replica."

"How do you know that?" asked Rilt, inquisitive despite his displeasure that Gareth had interrupted their quiet meanderings.

"Because it belongs to the royal house and leaving it here is stupid," said Gareth, sounding bored, but his dark eyes were scrutinizing the display with hungry reverence. Apparently sensing Rilt's curios scrutiny, Gareth stepped away. "Another pretty wrapping that means absolutely nothing. Titles and nobles, bah! Useless things."

Before Rilt could react to the insult, Kayle caught Gareth's arm and murmured something to him, too low for Rilt to hear, but he could see the seriousness of his roommate's expression.

"So what?" Gareth yanked his arm away. "I don't care."

"Gareth, you're not-"

"No, I'm not. You are, playing up to the lordling. Guess you're still that same boy at the docks, deep down beneath."

To Rilt's surprise, a glimmer of hurt crossed Kayle's features before he stalked past Gareth and headed for the exit. Rilt took one look at Gareth's tight, pinched face and followed Kayle out of the archives. It appeared that the two friends were not that close after all.

WHISPERS

The greenhouses were in a secluded corner of Kaedin Hall's grounds behind a small fruit orchard, past the cafeteria and kitchens, and close to the tall wall separating the university from the path leading to Riverbank Park. Few students were headed that way—most seemed content to stay in the main buildings or to stroll along the lake path—so only Rilt and Kayle were picking their way across the lawns. It was still fairly cold outside, and a breeze had picked up to bite at their noses and ears.

Kayle shivered. "I was warned about the chill, but I figured since it's the spring and summer term, I wouldn't need autumn clothes. I was so wrong."

"We can go back for a scarf or coat."

"It should be better once we get to the trees."

It was not better. Though leaves were already sprouting, the foliage was not yet thick enough to provide shelter. Somewhere ahead, the massive domed roofs of the greenhouses loomed over the trees in metal and glass. Kayle hunched up his shoulders and jogged towards the first greenhouse. He brightened and waved Rilt to hurry up. "It's open. Come on."

It was much warmer and more humid inside. Kayle sighed in relief and shuddered dramatically. "That was a dumb decision. The next time I suggest going out of doors before full summer? Stop me."

"You'll get used to it," said Rilt heartlessly. He brushed a thumb over a leaf of the nearest potted herb. The name escaped him but he knew it was used for seasoning. "This is not bad."

"Not bad? This is amazing!" Kayle walked into the huge greenhouse, peering at different plants, touching some of them. Rilt trailed behind, hands behind his back; he could recognize a few from Enthin and some from his stepmother's conservatory, but most were exotic-looking flora with waxy leaves and strange, unsettling scents. Some had dangerous-looking spikes or a layer of fuzz that Rilt knew better than to handle. He had been stung a few times on hunting trips by the innocuous-looking leaves of gripebush.

The greenhouse they had entered was one of the three smaller ones set around the main greenhouse, which housed the larger flora. From what Rilt could see, it was made of bronze and glass. The floor was sandy, with flat stone slabs for walking on, and the air grew increasingly thick with moisture the further they ventured inwards. The first greenhouse led into a gallery directing them to the central dome, where stands of palms and slender saplings dominated. Shrubs and bushes of varying sizes were grouped according to their functions along the galleries and around the dome. There were so many that it felt as though they were in a jungle. Rilt read the names with interest. Other than the various crops Enthin cultivated and possible diseases that blighted them, Rilt had not received much education in botany.

Kayle was utterly absorbed as he studied the species of plants on display. He bore an abstracted look on his face, his mind far away while his body navigated the narrow aisles. Often, Rilt lost sight of Kayle, only to glimpse his roommate through thick fronds or variegated leaves. Rilt wondered what the other young man was thinking, but it felt intrusive to ask. The sound of their boot heels was absorbed by the soft sand and thick vegetation.

They were going into another gallery, next to the one they came in from, when Kayle waved him over. In a corner were a dozen chest-high saplings. Their leaves were pale green, thin and spongy, and when Kayle carefully bruised one, his skin turned purple. He waved off Rilt's alarm.

"These are charas trees. I've only ever seen them in illustrations," said Kayle. He sniffed the sap that stained his thumb and then thrust his finger under Rilt's nose. "Smell."

Rilt took a cautious sniff. The scent was sharp and refreshing, like a mouthful of ice on a hot summer day. "I've eaten charas berries, but I never knew the leaves smelled like this. Or looked like this, for that matter."

"Back in Port, one of my neighbors said that in Okunimaratsa, charas trees are worth twice their weight in gold." Kayle breathed in the scent again. "She said they make an edible paste out of charas leaf pulp, nuts, and honey, dry it into cakes, and eat it to keep alert through the long watches when they graze their herds."

Rilt bent to smell the leaves. Unbruised, their icy scent was contained. "You know a lot."

"I talked to many people back home," said Kayle. "In a port, you meet all sorts of people, and everyone likes talking about home, wherever home may be."

"Not everyone."

The silence lingered a little too long. Then Kayle asked, "Why are you really attending Kaedin Hall, Rilt? You don't need to become a kaedin to be powerful or respected."

"I want to learn something other than managing Enthin." Rilt looked at him sharply. "Why are you here?"

"You mean, given my choices of being a common dock laborer living in a stinking, one-cot room or being someone respected enough to live where and how I want?" Kayle turned away and wiped his hand on his pants. "Not everyone's as lucky in their birth as you, Lord Rilt of the Arald house, shield of the kingdom."

Stung, Rilt was about to retort when they heard other voices coming down the entrance gallery.

"The greenhouses are supposed to be locked," said the first voice, a faintly nasal complaint. "At least there aren't students barging around in here. Some of these plants are far too sensitive to be jostled about."

His companion replied in a rumbling baritone, the volume too soft for the two students to hear the exact words.

"Regardless, he's here. We just have to keep a close eye on him." The nasal person sighed. "Students of rank are the most troublesome, and his is about as high as it gets."

Rilt stiffened. The only student of notably high rank attending Kaedin Hall was him. He nearly jolted out of his skin when he felt Kayle take his wrist.

"We mustn't be seen," Kayle murmured. He tugged Rilt along with him towards some broad-leaved plants where they could hide.

The two unseen speakers continued their discussion, but Rilt could not catch a name. Rilt heard faint footsteps and wondered if he should risk taking a peek. He was just about to look when he heard the voices, now much more clearly.

They were all in the same gallery.

The baritone said, "I can guarantee that there will be an opportunity to kill him. I cannot guarantee that he'll be alone when it occurs. What then?"

"You'll just have to get to him before the others do. Five of the shera nuts, please. The largest ones you can find."

There was a quick sound of shears. "And what about Jodius?"

"He's staying."

"He's staying? After everything that happened…"

"Until and unless someone steps up and accuses Jodius directly, there is nothing we can do." The baritone speaker made a rude sound, and the nasal-voiced one added, "Everyone deserves the benefit of the doubt, child. Where would you be if you'd been condemned based on one man's word?"

There was a pause. "I understand, sir."

"It's alright, my boy. I need four pods from the red vellun and ten shoots from the po'a. Go get them."

Hiding made Rilt feel as though he had done something wrong. Nonetheless, he followed Kayle's lead and hunkered down as the baritone speaker strolled past and collected what he needed. Rilt held his breath and listened to his pounding heartbeat. Beside him, Kayle kept unnaturally still.

Mind whirling with trying to process what he had heard, Rilt did not notice that Kayle had not let go of his wrist until after they heard the door to the greenhouse shut and there was no more conversation for a few minutes.

"Are you alright?" asked Rilt. Kayle looked gray and tense.

"I should be asking you that. They were probably talking about you," said his roommate. "About killing you."

Rilt was privately alarmed, but he smiled at Kayle nonetheless. "I'll be careful. I am trained to defend myself."

"Trained against kaedine?"

Their eyes flicked to the passage leading to the entrance. For a fleeting moment, Rilt thought the two speakers would return and kill him; it took a few deep, slow breaths before he could calm his imagination and stay the lurch of terror in his gut. It was not lost on him that he was alone in Izdahl, far from aid. Halden had always insisted on having house guards with them when they left the estate, and now Rilt was beginning to understand the reason behind his father's precautions.

Kayle squeezed his friend's wrist before he let go. "Maybe it wasn't you. It could be someone else."

"The only one whose rank is higher than mine would be the prince, and he's not here," said Rilt. He chewed meditatively on his lower lip. "Unless he is, but there would've been more of a furor if he had enrolled."

"You've never met him?"

"Only once, when I was about four or five." Rilt stuffed his hands in his pockets to hide how cold they felt. "The king, the queen and the prince came to our estate, stayed for a night. I don't remember much, but we didn't play together or talk. I remember the queen, mainly. She was very sickly then."

"You didn't talk with the prince?"

"He stayed close to the queen. The king was there to discuss some matters with Father, I suppose, and I was more interested in playing with Ced."

Kayle glanced at him askance as they made their way out of the greenhouse. Rilt made sure to walk at a brisk pace. His eyes jumped from shadow to shadow, imagining that the two speakers were lying in wait for him. On unspoken accord, they returned to their dormitory, and it was only when the door shut behind them that Rilt felt he could breathe normally again. His pulse was still fast, but he put on a nonchalant air. There was no need to show weakness to his roommate.

As he gathered his composure and thoughts, a stubborn anger uncurled in his gut. If those would-be assassins thought Rilt would run just because they were going to try to kill him, they were sorely mistaken. He was an Arald. He would stand his ground.

"Do you think we should tell somebody about what we heard?" Kayle asked.

"And who did you have in mind?" He sat down on his bed, wishing he could ask Master Baelmin what to do. His tutor always gave him good advice. "One of them had to be a master. Whomever you tell might just be the plotter."

Kayle had started a fire in the fireplace and stared at it, as though hypnotized. "So we can't tell anyone? Can't we talk to the dean or, or maybe a warden? The City Ward has to take you seriously, right?"

Rilt did not even realize he was hugging his elbows until he stretched out his arms. The room had grown warm, but he still felt chilled to the bone. "We have no suspect. All we heard was a snippet of a conversation. There may be intent, but if the wardens go around arresting people with bad intentions, there wouldn't be enough space in the gaols." He exhaled slowly, feeling the last of his initial terror fade, to be replaced with resolve. "I have my resources, Kayle. In the meantime, I'll be vigilant."

His roommate stood by one of the chairs, drumming his fingers on its back, and then came to sit next to Rilt. He said quietly, "You're not alone in this. I'll keep an eye out, too. I won't let you be murdered if I can help it."

It should be funny, two first-year students on the first day of school talking about one of them potentially being killed, but all Rilt felt was a warm rush of gratitude.

* * *

Dear Pellit,

Keep the contents of this letter to yourself. Burn it once you've read it. I do not need Zarin running tales to my parents. Not yet, anyway.

I suspect that some of Father's enemies may be in Kaedin Hall. They know that I am enrolled, and I have overheard a worrying conversation suggesting that they may make an attempt on my life. Now that I'm aware of their existence, I will be triply vigilant. At least in Kaedin Hall, I am seldom alone, and I have reason to believe they will stay their hand until they can get me by myself. I will make it hard for them.

For now, I need you to seek out information. Find out who among the kaedin adepts or masters come from houses that Father has antagonized in any way, no matter how insignificant the slight. Be careful of how you go about retrieving the information. Outside of my concern for your safety, I do not wish to startle the plotters into hiding. Do not let slip that you are doing this for me. Instead, let your informants believe you are acting on Father's orders. The Duke of Enthin carries more weight than I do, and impress upon those you speak with that secrecy will benefit them.

I trust your lessons with Stationmaster Eilem and your experiences with your associates back home have not gone astray. It is time to exercise those skills. I am putting my safety in your capable hands, Pell. Find me names.

Be careful,
Rilt

FIRST WEEK

Their first lesson the next morning was in a classroom near the cafeteria. Rilt and Kayle were there early—courtesy of the latter—and sat in the second row near the front. When Terras walked in, he was taken aback to see the two students already in their places.

"Have you two had breakfast?" he asked as he set down a thick sheaf of papers. Pulling out two sets, he handed one to each of them. "I don't mind if you go and grab something to eat. Early morning classes can be very torturous."

"We've eaten," said Kayle cheerily. It was almost disgusting how alert he was, given that he had shaken Rilt awake before the first bell had sounded.

Rilt merely grunted. He had not slept well; the bed was unfamiliar, the room was too warm, and someone above their room snored like a cart-ox in heat. If Kayle had not dragged him out of bed, he would still be curled up under the sheets. Breakfast had been a rushed affair of two bread rolls and a lukewarm cup of caffi. He wondered if he would ever get a good night's sleep here.

Terras grinned crookedly. "You're a keen one. Radieri, right? One of our three royal scholars. I look forward to your performance."

"Thanks, sir."

"Terras will do. The only adept who's sticky about rank is Wolvam."

The words took some time to penetrate the fog wrapped around Rilt's sleepy mind. He straightened and stared at Kayle. "Royal scholar?"

Kayle shrugged, embarrassed. "That's why I can attend. I can't afford the university otherwise."

"Second-highest score too," said Terras, his round face beaming. "Gareth Krell is our top scholar, followed by you, and another with one mark less. We seldom have more than one royal scholar come into Kaedin Hall. The last couple of years, we had none. The dean is very pleased."

Rilt could not look away from his roommate. He had thought the other young man a pleasant, friendly sort, but not someone out of the ordinary. Yet he was one of the seven young people who won scholarships to the university. Seven, out of a pool of thousands.

Kayle bumped Rilt's elbow when he caught the latter staring. "Don't do that."

"I'm impressed," said Rilt honestly.

"It was a bit of luck," said Kayle, the tips of his ears turning pink. He leaned forward and asked Terras, "So will you take us for morning meditation? I see that it's the first thing every morning, even before breakfast."

Terras shook his head. "Wolvam will direct all first-years. He's the most disciplined anyway. Not to noise it about, but most of your seniors don't bother with the practice."

"Will you be teaching us in any classes?" Rilt knew Kayle initiated the change of topic and decided to play along. He could always find out more later.

Terras explained that, as an adept, he was not teaching the theoretical lessons, but he would be assisting in the tutorials and practicals. He was also training those resonant with stone and earth, the Terai-Dag class. "All first-year students have the same Kae Resonance theory classes under Master Whitsam. For tutorials, Wolvam and I will each take half the cohort."

Rilt suspected that he would be in the Aega class of water-resonant kaedine. Terras was handing out papers to the students now filing in, so Rilt missed the opportunity to inquire who was in charge of the first-year Aega class. The first-years settled down quickly, just before Wolvam, Master Jodius and two other master kaedine turned up and took seats in the front of the class.

Just as Terras was about to speak, Gareth strolled in and dropped into the empty seat beside Kayle.

"Apologies," Gareth drawled. "I got lost."

Dubious, Terras said, "This room is on the same floor as the cafeteria."

"I had an early breakfast and then went for a stroll," Gareth replied with a slow, insouciant blink. "I got lost. Would you happen to have a map?"

"Krell, watch your tone," warned Wolvam, straightening slightly from his slouch.

"Wolvam, it's alright, leave it," Terras interrupted. "Go to your seat, Krell. We are going to begin soon."

When Gareth opened his mouth, Wolvam snapped, "You will shut up or I will have you scrubbing the cafeteria floors, Krell. Learn to use your ears and develop a sense of courtesy."

"I-"

"Shut up. No one is interested." Wolvam gave a curt nod for Terras to continue.

Terras glanced nervously at the master kaedine behind him. Then he cleared his throat. "Um. Well, you've met Wolvam and me. In case you've forgotten, I'm Terras. If you have questions about your dorms, locations in the hall, where to get certain texts or supplies, look for me. But Wolvam is the one in charge of first-year students, so he will be the one you report to for disciplinary issues or other matters. Behind me, from left to right, are Masters Jodius, Whitsam, and Berras. They are your main instructors; Wolvam and I will assist as needed. You may be selected for extra classes at the instructors' discretion."

The stocky adept waved his copy of the papers he had distributed earlier. "Here is your full schedule, as well as the required readings for each subject and the assignments and projects you have to complete. Don't worry," he added hastily when the students groaned, "Obviously, you will have help from us. You can ask us questions any time. Oh, and the test dates are listed, on the final page."

Rilt felt his heart sink as he flipped through the pages. There was so much reading to be done! There was no way he could do it all. From the resentful murmurings among the students, he was not the only one who dreaded having to plow through so much text.

"We can form a study group," Kayle whispered. "Four of us. I mean, there's a reason why they set up the rooms or the tables in the cafeteria the way they did."

"Four of us?" asked Gareth, and then he rolled his eyes. "Including Barith the ornament? Please."

There was a soft cough from behind them. Naelen raised his eyebrows at Rilt when the latter turned around. Gareth looked over his shoulder and appeared to notice his roommate for the first time.

"Ah, Barith. Didn't realize you were there."

"I'll bet," said Naelen dryly.

The prospect of having to study with Gareth was already unappealing. Add Naelen Barith with his perfectly sculpted features, perfectly proportioned body, perfectly glossy blond hair, and their little altercation from before, and it was a nightmare. Rilt wrinkled his nose, determined to dissuade Kayle of the notion.

Wolvam unfolded from his chair and stood next to Terras. For all that he was leaner and a few fingerwidths shorter than Terras, Wolvam seemed to tower over the entire class. The chatter died down immediately. He swept the room with his assessing gaze.

"As I've said to one of you yesterday, in this hall there are only three ranks that we care about: student, adept, and master." Wolvam stared at Rilt, who did not avert his eyes. The adept's mouth twitched, almost as though he was amused. "You are all students. That means you listen, you learn, and you don't give lip. You could be the prince and I will still demand that you show respect. If you do break a rule, make sure you do it so well that I never find out, because if I do find out, I will discipline you. And then, I'll hand you to the mercies of the dean."

It was dead silent in the room. Some students looked unsure, as if they were measuring how serious Wolvam was. Rilt was certain that the adept meant every syllable.

"Now, about your practical classes," said Wolvam. "Master Jodius instructs the Trae class, in the greenhouses. Master Berras takes the Dagas class, in the workshop further down this corridor, unless you're told to go to the forge. Master Whitsam is in charge of the Terai-Dag class—that's usually the largest group—and Terras will help in your practical lessons. You'll report to the front courtyard for your lessons. I will take charge of the Aega class, until Master Orod returns from his journeying. He'll return next term. Aega class students will go to the lake."

Each master that Wolvam introduced nodded or smiled at the students. They all seemed more pleasant than Wolvam, and Rilt wished fervently that he would not be taught by him. Any of the others would be better than the adept who seemed intent on singling him out. The oldest master was Master Whitsam, who gestured for Wolvam to continue before he and the other masters stood and left the room. Only the two adepts remained.

Wolvam leaned his hip on the edge of the teaching table. "All of you are going to become kaedine. To be kaedine is to be extraordinary. Many men are born with resonance, but only a few become part of this select fraternity." Wolvam did not need to raise his voice; every student listened closely. "While we don't know why we can resonate, we do know that we feel a greater affinity to specific elements. Arald, what elements am I talking about?"

Why is he picking on me? Rilt mouthed at Kayle and then replied the surly adept, "Metal, wood, water, and earth or stone."

"Good. You will learn more about why kaedine are sorted into these- yes, Norwan? You have a question."

The red-haired Felas lowered his hand. "Th-there's also fire, sir. But there aren't any Firas class kaedine."

Terras cleared his throat. "There isn't a man alive who is resonant with fire-"

"We don't have fire resonance because the Creators knew it is dangerous," Wolvam interrupted coolly. "Unlike the other elements, fire has no weight, no volume; there is no means to control the scale of it. Firas is the Forbidden precisely because her element is without order and impossible to manipulate. Thus there is no Firas class, nor will there ever be a Firas class."

Felas mumbled a thanks. Rilt sat forward, leaning on his elbows. The adept sounded very sure of himself, but Rilt thought about Master Baelmin's letter. *Deyre breith wer flaume yn fir.* If those had not been the scrambled memories of a dying old man's mind, then long ago, there were men who breathed flame. They would have been Firas class kaedine had the University existed then.

Wolvam paused. He pressed his lips together as though thinking over his next words. "As kaedine, we do not rule the elements. Our resonance allows us to shape the elements by force of will, but only insofar as our bodies and our minds can withstand the strain. With resonance, we shape, we transport, and we enhance the elements. That is all we can do. Those who are not kaedine may think that we manipulate the elements for our own pleasure. This is the furthest thing from the truth. As kaedine, we are bound to better the lives of all around us. We serve and protect the people of Aleis. Never, never forget that."

Rilt reassessed his judgment of Wolvam; the man spoke with a passionate belief that made even his sallow face proud and handsome. He looked a little embarrassed by his speech, and rustled the papers in his hand.

"When I call your name, you will come forward and we'll see whether you've identified your resonance accurately." The corner of his lips twitched again. "We'll start with Arald."

Rilt was not expecting to be the first. He gulped and stood up, feeling vaguely sick.

Wolvam flashed a smile with far too much teeth. "It's not going to hurt."

The test turned out to be quite straightforward. Rilt had been initially assessed to be in the Aega class, so he was given a tiny glass of water and told to focus on it.

"Focus on it to do… what?"

"Whatever you want." The adept shook back the lanky hair in front of his eyes. "For instance…"

Wolvam gestured with two fingers and the water in the glass streamed upwards in a thin, silvery ribbon, and with another short motion, he returned the water into the glass without spilling a single drop.

Doubly anxious now, Rilt held his breath and stared at the water.

"No, don't hold your breath, you'll faint if you do." Wolvam stepped next to him and placed a hand on his back between his shoulder blades. "Straighten. Breathe into your diaphragm. Now focus."

Rilt gritted his jaw and did as he was told. He resented being used as an example, but he had to admit Wolvam knew what he was doing. Within a minute, Rilt heard a bright, high-pitched hum inside his head, and suddenly water sprayed out from the mouth of the glass. Since it was such a small volume, most of it just landed on Rilt's face. He almost dropped the glass in shock, but managed to keep his grip on it at the last minute.

Wolvam patted him on the shoulder. "Good work. Definitely Aega class."

"Thank you," said Rilt, and added after a slight pause, "Sir."

The only reaction he got for the courtesy was a faint twitch in the corner of Wolvam's mouth.

After Rilt's demonstration, the other students were more confident in their own turns. Oledan was also in Aega class, to Rilt's dismay. Naelen and Gareth were both assigned to the Dagas class after twisting a steel wire with nothing but their minds.

"That's Felas Norwan, the third royal scholar," Kayle murmured to Rilt. Felas nudged his glasses up the bridge of his nose and hunched his shoulders as he approached the front. When he was given a round river stone, he crushed the stone with one hand.

Everyone was impressed. Gareth let out a low whistle. "That'll be useful."

Terras grinned. "It's good to have someone this comfortable with their resonance, Felas. I look forward to your progress in the Te-rai-Dag class." Felas mumbled something and his cheeks turned deeply red. Terras gathered up the stone dust and, shaping with his hands, reassembled it.

Kayle was the next. The other students were busy talking about Felas, so only Rilt and Gareth saw Kayle gingerly place the proffered purple berry in his palm. With an encouraging nod from Terras, Kayle closed his eyes, inhaled slowly, and breathed out.

When the berry started sprouting in a rush, Naelen whispered, "By all Creation…"

Rilt was too busy gaping to comment. White root tendrils reached down to the tiled floor, vainly tapping about as they sought water; a light green shoot rocketed up and sprouted pale and spongy leaves.

The class was absolutely silent. Other than the rustle of the rapidly-growing plant, Rilt could hear absolutely nothing.

Terras knocked the sapling from Kayle's hold to the floor. The scholar gasped sharply and blinked, his blue eyes wide with surprise.

"That's quite a demonstration." Terras picked up the sapling and grinned at the student. "A fine young charas shrub for the greenhouses. Master Jodius will be pleased. Thank you, Kayle."

Kayle blushed and hurried back to his seat between Gareth and Rilt. Even the back of his neck was red.

Clearing his throat, Wolvam said, "That was remarkable, Radieri. Very good focus."

"Thank you," Kayle replied very softly, staring at his hands in his lap.

They got through the final few, but it was obvious that everyone's attention was on Kayle, whose gaze remained resolutely on his hands until the bell rang and Wolvam dismissed the class.

* * *

"That," said Gareth, "was possibly the dumbest thing I have ever seen you do."

Kayle rolled his eyes. "I know I shouldn't have, but it is rather difficult controlling something I haven't been taught how to control."

Gareth snorted. "You've just attracted the attention of every other student. Everything you do is going to be scrutinized."

"As royal scholars, you and I will be under scrutiny, whether you like it or not."

"All the more reason to be less than conspicuous."

The two scholars bickered as they stalked down the corridor side by side, with Rilt trailing behind them like an afterthought. Kayle abruptly halted in his tracks, causing Rilt to nearly collide with him.

Kayle ignored the near-miss. "Just because you're afraid to show your true abilities, Gareth Krell, doesn't mean all of us have to hide what we are capable of."

Gareth narrowed his eyes. "I'm not afraid. You're flaunting."

"I intend to prove my worth, Gareth, and that isn't going to happen unless I give it full sail. Come on, Rilt. Let's try to get a good seat in our next class." He marched off, chin held high.

Trying not to feel too smug, Rilt hurried to join his roommate. Kayle's lips were set in a thin, angry line, and his blue eyes sparked with ire. Rilt decided to change the subject.

"There aren't a lot sorted into the Trae class," he said. "Only five out of the forty of us. You're going to get a lot of personalized attention from Master Jodius."

"True. I wonder what he's like."

Frowning, Rilt recalled the conversation they overheard. Master Jodius had been accused of something that nearly resulted in his sacking. "You'll find out."

"I guess." Kayle glanced at Rilt. "What about you? Will you be alright in Wolvam's class?"

"I should be," he said. He knew what Kayle was referring to. Wolvam had a baritone voice, just like one of the men in the greenhouse. Unfortunately, Terras, Jodius, and a dozen other adepts and senior students sounded similar to that speaker as well. Rilt exhaled heavily through his nose. "There are twelve other students. I'm sure I'll be safe enough."

Kayle bumped their elbows together. "You'll let me know if you feel threatened, right?"

"Between the two of us," said Rilt, feigning annoyance, "who's taller and stronger? And trained in unarmed combat since he was ten?"

"Who's the one with the better focus and resonance?"

"Low blow, Radieri."

"Get used to it. I don't fight fair." They got to their second class well ahead of the other students and, again, took seats near the front. When Gareth came in, he shot Kayle and Rilt a dirty look before striding to the back row. Rilt peered over his shoulder. Gareth folded his arms and glared at Rilt before pointedly looking out of the window.

For the rest of the day, Rilt and Kayle were inseparable, and every time Gareth looked over, there was a sour glint in his eyes. Kayle ignored his best friend studiously. The two scholars did not talk to each other at all, not even at mealtimes. Rilt knew that their estrangement should not give him smug satisfaction, but it did.

* * *

Their first lesson in Kae Tuning was on the third day, immediately after breakfast. The students would be going to different places in the hall for training. Rilt and ten others headed to the lake, where they had been told to gather.

"What do you think Wolvam's going to do?" Oledan asked.

"I suppose we'll find out," Rilt replied.

Ladmos, a skinny, undergrown student who looked about fourteen said worriedly, "I hope he doesn't expect us to swim. It's still cold."

"I can't swim," Oledan said. "Still baffles the shit out of me why I'm in Aega class. I get seasick crossing the canals, for Creation's sakes."

Wolvam was there waiting for the first-years. Rilt hid a smile when he noticed a pile of towels on the grass next to the adept, as well as a stack of copper bowls.

"Seems like we are going into the lake after all," he said blandly.

Wolvam must have overheard him. "We aren't going into the lake.

Yet. Next month you will. Nothing like being surrounded by your element to test your resonance."

Rilt strolled up to the edge of the lake and peered in. The gravel bank sloped gently into clear waters. Tiny iridescent fish flickered and flashed amongst the pebbles, feeding on weeds. He bent and dipped his hand into the water. It was cold, but not chilly; it would be a delight to be able to swim in it when the weather grew warmer.

"Arald, get back here," Wolvam called out irritably. The other students were ranged around him. Reluctantly, Rilt left the lake, wiping his wet hand on his tunic.

Once Rilt had joined the group, Wolvam started the lesson. Apparently, the trick to effortless tuning was a clear mind, though the adept used far more words to explain the concept.

"You've already heard about the concept of kae resonance. In practical classes, I'll teach you how to use that resonance to tune, shape and push. We'll start from tuning. That means aligning your mind with your resonant element. The denser and purer the element, the easier it is to tune, so you have quite the challenge ahead of you in Aega. Water is the hardest to tune, but easiest to shape."

The students exchanged faintly worried glances.

Wolvam tossed a towel at each of them. "Of course, in the wise words of the Amago philosopher Dekai, 'Everything's easier said than done.' You'll have to quiet your mind and listen. If you can do that, you'll be able to hear a note played in your mind; a single note. Focus on that note, picturing it as a horizontal line. That's tuning. The more vividly you can hear the note and picture the line, the easier it is to tune water to your will. Every body of water is different, but with practice, you'll eventually find that it becomes second nature."

Rilt could just picture it: crashing towers of water onto faceless enemies; walking through a storm without fear of getting wet; making water fountain and spray in intricate dances to amuse himself; drenching the irritating Gareth and perfect Naelen in their beds.

"Fill the bowls with water to a finger joint's length from the brim. I will demonstrate when we are all seated. Let's hope at least one of you can do this without getting wet."

The adept took Ladmos's bowl and sat down, placing the bowl before him. He then put his hands on either side of the bowl, and closed his eyes. Within a blink of an eye, water rippled in the bowl and then droplets started dancing on its surface.

"It'll be more difficult than you had experienced yesterday." Wolvam removed his hands. "Remember: breathe steadily through your nose, close your eyes, and listen. Picture the line once you hear the note in your head. You will then see the effects for yourself."

What followed was possibly the most draining hour of Rilt's life. All he did was sit with his hands on the sides of the bowl and attempt to recreate the vibrations Wolvam demonstrated. What he got was splashed multiple times, another lecture on breathing properly, and a pounding headache at the end of the lesson. Sometimes he thought he heard a note in his mind, but when he reached for it, he lost control and water would spray over his shirt and face. He had to get up and refill the bowl repeatedly. At least everyone was damp, some more soaked than others. No one had succeeded by the end of the lesson, and the towels Wolvam provided were sopping wet.

"Keep the bowls." Wolvam smiled sardonically and, before strolling off, added, "You boys need the practice."

There was half an hour before the next class, so they returned to their dormitories to change. Braced against the slight chill, Rilt shucked off his damp clothes and was rummaging in wardrobe when Kayle came in. The scholar halted in his tracks when he saw Rilt emerge from behind the wardrobe door, dry tunic and pants in hand.

"Oh! I, uh, I wasn't. I wasn't expecting you," Kayle stammered. He hurried past the naked Rilt to place a potted plant on the windowsill. The tips of his ears were flushed pink.

Rilt tugged on his pants. "I'm bringing a towel to class next time. What's that?" He pointed at the pot. It was only a small twig with two tiny leaves. There were tiny blue thorns on the twig.

"That," said Kayle with clear satisfaction, "is a cutting from a deadly bluespine."

"Deadly bluespine. Judging from the name, I don't think that's a good thing to have in our room."

"Don't be a wriggler. The bluespine is completely harmless unless you ingest its roots, seeds, flowers, or bark raw."

Thinking it over carefully, Rilt frowned. "That means only the leaves are not poisonous."

"For the leaves, you'll have to boil them for fourteen to eighteen hours and then distil the resulting solution to get the poison. It's not even that toxic, really, it just burns your skin and irritates it till it blisters." Off Rilt's expression, Kayle said, "It's my term project. I'm supposed to grow this and when it matures, intensify the toxicity of the leaves. It's really challenging. I grew this cutting from a thorn for over an hour, and I'm exhausted. Turns out the deadly bluespine is the one plant most resistant to kae. If I can grow this well, then I can resonate with any woody-stemmed plants out there."

"All I had to do was make water vibrate in a bowl and it feels like I ran the perimeter of the university with rocks tied to my ankles." Rilt stretched and felt the joints in his spine crack. "We still have two lectures today?"

"History next and then Geography after lunch." Kayle groaned. "Safe to say, the hall's schedule is tough on us."

Rilt collapsed onto his bed, face buried in his pillow. He wanted to just doze off, but he knew he would not wake up in time for their lecture. In the end, he settled for lying on his side to watch his roommate fuss over the plant.

Kayle had delicate features suited for a girl, Rilt thought distractedly. Soft pink lips, smooth skin with a faint dusting of freckles if you got up close, dazzlingly clear blue eyes framed by dark lashes, and dark curls that—on a girl—would make Rilt want to tug and run his fingers through. He moved his slender frame with efficient grace. There was a slight sway to Kayle's hips as he walked from the window to his chest of drawers and then back again, as though he was shifting his balance all the time.

I'd be sorely tempted to bed him if he were a girl. Rilt shooed the thought from his head. He did not need such outlandish notions wandering around his mind.

Kayle, sensing the scrutiny, frowned at the noble. "Are you alright?"

"I'm just tired," said Rilt. He wrinkled his nose and sat up with a grunt. "Let's go. I'll fall asleep if I stay on this bed any longer, and I don't think Master Whitsam would approve of that."

* * *

Dear Mother,

This has been an eventful first week! I'm sorry, I should have written earlier but I was busy settling in. You'll be glad to know that the hall does not stint on food, so I am well-fed.

What should I share with you when there is so much that's gone on? I suppose I should start at the beginning. I've been sorted into the Aega class—that's the one for water-resonant kaedin—and my instructor is this infuriating, judgmental senior adept who doesn't possess a shred of humor. Still, Wolvam is competent and surprisingly patient when coaching us in class. He's in charge of the novices, and guides us through meditation every morning. I can't believe how difficult it is to sit without thinking and still remain alert. Unfortunately, Wolvam has an uncanny sense about who is dozing, and will douse the unfortunate boy with ice-cold water. I've been drenched once, but don't tell Ced—he'll never let me live it down!

Most of my classmates are alright. There are far too many lewd jokes and coarse remarks for my liking, but they are commoners after all, and have not been brought up with our sensibilities. I hope I don't pick up their crudeness. I can't believe I thought the grooms were uncouth; I've heard more swearing in this one week than my whole life in the estate. I'm surprised my ears haven't caught fire from embarrassment.

Can you believe Naelen Barith is also in Kaedin Hall? That boy who broke my nose actually cleared the entrance exams. He's not made any friends here yet. I'm not surprised. This whole week, he's always been in the library, or buried in some thick book. He's stuck in the dorm next to mine with a student named Gareth Krell, who is thoroughly unpleasant. He's sharp-tongued, abrasive, and contemptuous of almost everyone. I can't say I'm displeased that Barith has such a horrible roommate.

I, on the other hand, have the friendliest, nicest student of the lot for my roommate. When you're here in Izdahl, I'm going to introduce you to Kayle Radieri. You and Ced will love him. He's from Port Halim, so you can swap stories. He is in the Trae class, and he made this berry sprout into a sapling in no time! Everyone was stunned by what he did, but he didn't boast about it. I like that he's modest even though he is quite clearly the strongest. He loves the greenhouses here and I'm sure he can show you around them. Kayle also is a Royal Scholar, one of seven in the entire kingdom! He's brilliant, Mother, and he was so awed by the library in the hall, I'm tempted to invite him to the estate where he and Ced can spend days just reading and discussing books. It's strange though, how someone as lovely as Kayle can be best friends with Gareth, but I suppose Gareth lucked out in this aspect. While Kayle isn't from any notable house, he is definitely miles ahead of the minor lords that always congregate at the parties you throw. For one thing, he is lively company, appealing in his appearance, and lovelier to listen to; his Halim accent reminds me of the lullabies you used to sing. I can't wait for you to meet him.

Send my love to Cedaran and tell him to write me soon. I hope the horses are doing fine on the new spring feed, and that the ewes are prolific with lambs this season.

Lots of love,
Rilt

* * *

Now that he had written to Selvina, he ought to send a letter to his brother too. Yet how much should he include for Cedaran? He was certainly not going to worry his younger brother about the conversation he overheard in the greenhouse, and much of what he could share was already in the letter to his stepmother. He did his best to write about his impressions of the library and archives, knowing that Ced would like those places.

Dear Beanpole,

Mother has the bulk of the news, and I'm sure she'll share with you.

The one thing I am most unused to is the amount of assigned reading. We used to complain to Master Baelmin about the amount of work he gave us. I'm reading nearly twice as much now every week. Kayle is suggesting that we organize a study group with Gareth and Naelen. To be honest, I don't want to spend time with them at all if I can possibly help it, but Kayle is good friends with Gareth (Creation knows why) and it'd be rude to invite Gareth without extending an invitation to his stuck-up marble sculpture of a roommate too. I suppose I'll just have to take the bit. If only they weren't in Room Five. I'd rather have Felas and

Ladmos or some of the others. Such is the price of having the best of the lot for my roommate, I guess.

Rilt paused. Was it hurtful to tell Cedaran about life away from Enthin, away from the Arald estate? He knew that if Cedaran were here instead of Rilt, he would tell Rilt about his experiences too. The last time he'd left his brother out of his life was two summers ago, when Ledon Pol was around, and Ledon and Rilt had spent nearly every free moment together. Cedaran had not complained, but it had taken months after the junior healer moved on to the next city before the brothers were as close as before.

He chewed the inside of his cheek and went on, describing his classmates—Kayle alone took up a page—and how they got along, as well as some of the masters and adepts. Enthin had never felt so far away before. He knew the most about Kayle, of course. If Rilt hadn't been writing about him, he would not realize how much he'd learned about Kayle. Carefully, he sketched out the tattoo of the cliff rose Kayle bore behind his left shoulder.

I'm no artist, but it looks something like that, but with more detail and delicacy. He told me that his mother had that same tattoo, he wrote below that drawing. Kayle said that only the sea-captains bore tattoos on their arms. Apparently, some of the islanders who go to Port to trade even have tattooed faces. I can't imagine how painful that must be.

It was strange having to share living quarters with someone else, but Rilt knew it could have been so much worse if he had disliked his roommate. He shuddered as he imagined living with Naelen or Gareth—or greasy, crude Oledan. Kayle was the best possible option, and Rilt tried to be neat insofar as he remembered to pick up after himself. He also jotted down another note to Galena, making arrangements for their date. She had promised to show him about town.

Kayle was on his bed, reading one of the assigned texts. Every so often he would mutter in annoyance.

"I'm dropping letters off at the runners," said Rilt once the letters were written. "Do you have any messages that need running?" He tilted up Kayle's book and scanned the title. "*The Unity of Mind,*

Body, and Kae. Heavy reading. This is for Master Berras?"

"Not really, and yes," said Kayle. He jerked the book out of the noble's hands. "I'll summarize what we need to know. And you have the section on Ethics to do."

"I'm going on a date tomorrow. Would you like to come along?"

Kayle did not glance up from the dense text. "Sure. Why not?" Then his brain caught up with his ears. He set the book down and stared at Rilt. "Why?"

"Because I don't want my date to think that I want anything serious, so having you there with us will help make it more of a friendly outing."

His roommate snorted and picked up the book again. "I don't see how that's my role."

"Come on. Do me a favor."

"I'm poor, I've nothing decent to wear, and I don't want to play the second rudder. Besides, I'm not the sort to ask girls out."

"I'll pay for everything, and you can borrow my clothes." Rilt stood with his hands on his hips. "I'll even ask Galena to help invite someone else. We'll get to meet pretty girls! It'll be fun."

Kayle peered up at him and then sighed. "If you say so."

Though Kayle's reluctance puzzled him, Rilt said nothing more about it. He added a postscript to the message for Galena and paid the runners for the letters home. On the way back to the dormitories, he collided into someone around the corner and caused the latter to drop his letters.

"Sorry," said Rilt, helping the other young man pick up the envelopes. He was surprised to see that it was Naelen. "Oh, it's you."

"It's me, yes. Thank you." Naelen took the letters and headed in the direction of the runner station.

Suddenly, Rilt called out to the other Enthinian, "Would you want to join Kayle and me to form a study group?"

Naelen halted. He turned and studied Rilt carefully, as though analyzing him for a sign of a trick or an insult. Rilt stared back and waited.

"It's odd that you would want me to join you," Naelen said eventually. "If I remember correctly, the last time we met at my father's trade dinner, you swore to beat my face in after I had punched you in the nose."

Rilt stuck his hands in his pockets. "I did."

"Hence I do not see why you would want my company. Or why I should accept this invitation."

"You're always working on the readings. I figured you want to do well … and Kayle wants to ask you anyway."

Naelen regarded him coolly, his green eyes bright with suspicion. "Why did you attack me that day?"

"You were cornering that serving girl," said Rilt. "I don't like seeing them coerced. With your looks, you can bed practically anyone you want."

The blond student scoffed and shook his head. "That was what you thought was going on? That girl stole my mother's jewelry. I was trying to get it back. Thanks to your interference, she got away."

That was not something Rilt had considered. He had immediately assumed the worst of Naelen when he had come across the scene back then. Feeling awkward, he rubbed the back of his neck. "How do I know you're not lying?"

"Believe what you will," said Naelen. "My conscience is clear, and my mother still hasn't got her string of pearls back." He turned again to go to the runners, but stopped when Rilt called out to him again.

"Do you want to join in the study group or not?" Rilt asked bluntly.

The tall student waved a hand in the air. "I'll think about it."

Rilt fumed. It was rude of Naelen to be so dismissive of his peace offering. He decided to dash off a note to Pellit and ask him to investigate Naelen's account. Servants talked, and Rilt knew that the servants in the Arald estate ran messages around the city for the duke. It would not be difficult for Pellit to ask his contacts back in Enthin for the truth.

It made sense for him and Kayle to band together with Gareth and Naelen. They could pop in and out of each other's rooms easily. He supposed he and Naelen could tolerate each other's existence, even if he didn't want to befriend the other Enthinian.

Kayle is being kind, he realized. He's seen Naelen sitting by himself during lessons and at mealtimes, and he's always hiding in the library. That's why Kayle says he wants Naelen in our study group.

It was remarkable that Kayle noticed and, more importantly, cared that Naelen could be lonely. Rilt chewed on the inside of his cheek. Perhaps he ought to give Naelen a chance, if the latter did acquiesce to the suggestion.

* * *

Gareth was in Room Six when Rilt returned. He was sitting at Kayle's desk, bare feet propped up on its surface, and didn't even look up when Rilt opened the door. The other scholar was nowhere to be seen, though the textbook lay open on his bed.

"What in Creation are you doing in my room?" Rilt demanded. "Where's Kayle?"

"Kayle was told to meet Master Jodius. He asked me to come over. Something about a study group."

Rilt chewed on the inside of his cheek. "Fine. But get your feet off Kayle's desk."

Still with his feet up, Gareth leaned back in the chair and fixed his gaze on the noble. "We're going to clarify something right now."

Rilt folded his arms and raised his chin. "Yes?"

"Kayle is my best friend. There is no one else in Creation who knows him better than I do. We may have our disagreements, but if it ever comes to a storm, he will choose to board my ship." Gareth was smiling, but it was far from a friendly expression.

Anger began to coil red and ugly in the pit of Rilt's stomach. "And the purpose of you telling me all this is?"

"Don't put him in a position where he has to choose, lordling."

"Do you really believe you're in any position to threaten me?" sneered Rilt. "I am the firstborn of the house of Arald. You are no one. Besides, Kayle is his own man. He can decide what he wants himself."

The scholar levered himself out of the chair, his sallow face darkening. "Scorch it, Arald, I'm trying to protect him. He's not your friend, and you'd best stop pretending he gives a lubber's shit about you."

Rilt met him toe to toe. "Who is he that he needs your protection?" he snarled. "Who are you to say whether he is my friend or not?"

"You don't know what you're doing, lordling, so stay away."

"You don't seem to remember to whom you speak, Krell."

"And I," said Kayle at the door, "don't understand why you two cannot exist in the same space without fighting." He stared at both of them until they separated, Gareth retreating to Kayle's desk and

Rilt to one of the chairs before the fireplace.

Ignoring Gareth's presence, Kayle came in and dropped a large envelope on his desk. He stood there, just staring at his potted plant for a long moment, before he rounded on the two of them, blue eyes ablaze.

"I came to Kaedin Hall to study. If neither of you can work together with me, I will find others who can and I will join them." He motioned at the books on his bed. "We've a lot to learn, and I for one am struggling. I'm on a scholarship, a scholarship they can take away at any time. If I don't do well, what happens to me? Can I be a duke? Can I take over from my father? I have nothing to fall back on. If you two ballast-brains ruin this, I will stick bluespine cuttings up your respective arses, believe me."

He stalked forward and stabbed a finger into Gareth's chest. "I can befriend whomever I want, Gareth Krell. I don't scorching care if he's a commoner or a guildmaster or, horror of horrors, a noble. Don't you dare assume that just because you're my best friend, I'll let you do whatever you want."

Gareth did not back away from Kayle's berating. "Fine. Don't get your lines tangled."

"Don't try to steer my life again," said Kayle. "I don't belong to you."

The atmosphere in Room Six felt like burning fog. Rilt shifted minutely in his seat, wishing he was elsewhere and resenting Gareth for making him feel uncomfortable in his own dormitory. He drummed his fingers on his knees before he blurted, "I've asked Naelen to join us."

"The ornament?" Gareth sputtered.

"That's great!" Kayle exclaimed at the same time. He smiled at Rilt, and that lightened the mood somewhat. "Did he agree?"

"He said he'll think about it." Rilt did not talk about why Naelen wanted more time to consider. After all, here were two royal scholars. Rilt was, theoretically, the luckiest student in the first-year cohort to have such brilliant brains to study with.

Someone knocked on the door and Kayle went to open it. It was a runner, a lean young woman with her hair cut very short and her long, muscular legs bared to the world.

"Message for Lord Rilt," she chirped. She grinned at Rilt when he came to the door to collect the note and looked him from top to toe. The student felt very self-conscious as he signed for the message. "Haven't seen a lord around the hall before. Nice to meetcha. Name's Anya. Let me know when you want another message run to the singers."

Her effusive chatter was rather annoying but Rilt managed a polite nod. "Thank you, Anya."

"Welcome. Rem'ber, ask for Anya. I'm the fastest runner in the university. The most discreet too." She winked at Rilt before trotting off.

With a cheeky grin, Kayle peered at the retreating runner and then mimicked her wink at Rilt. "You are a real charmer, Lord Rilt."

"Don't be ridiculous." Unfolding the message, he brightened and nudged Kayle's shoulder with his fist. "You and I are going on a date tomorrow."

His roommate rolled his eyes. "You still have that reading, and we have Whitsam's assignment."

"One afternoon won't hurt," said Rilt. He put on his most appealing, forlorn expression. "Please?"

With a deep sigh, Kayle assented. He jabbed his elbow into Rilt's side. "You're paying for everything, lordling."

From Kayle, that word sounded more like a friendly tease than an insult. Rilt beamed. "No problem."

Gareth drawled, "Don't bed the girl on the first date. They should have a chance to see your true colors before you satisfy your itch."

"No one asked for your opinion, Gareth," Rilt snapped. Out of the corner of his eye, he saw Naelen striding down the hallway. When the blond young man stopped outside Room Six, the only one visibly pleased to see him was Kayle.

Naelen did not beat about the bush. "I'll join your study group. It's more logical than struggling through all the suggested readings alone." He jerked a nod in Rilt's direction. "I know you've probably sent someone to check on what I said. I expect an apology soon."

"Only if you deserve one," Rilt retorted.

Kayle looked at both the Enthinians. "Is this something I have to know about? Because I can go elsewhere."

Naelen shook his fair head. "There's not a lot to say about it. May I come in?"

"Of course," said Kayle, stepping aside for Naelen to enter.

Gareth and Naelen took the chairs at the fireplace, angling them to face Kayle's bed where the other two sat. Gareth propped his thin face in his right hand. "How are we going to do this?"

"We," said Kayle, prodding Rilt with his elbow to shift aside, "will split the work. Rilt and I have a system of summarizing key points of every chapter we're assigned to read. I can show you later. Rilt's good at History, I'm comfortable with Kae Resonance. Naelen, what subject would you like?"

The blond student seemed startled that Kayle would voluntarily speak to him. "I enjoy Ethics and Governance. I can take those."

"Why didn't you ask me first?" Gareth complained.

Kayle leveled him with a deadpan look. "You're good at everything. You can take what's left."

"Oh, come on. Geography is dull."

"You find everything dull."

"Not really. I like Basic Survival Skills."

"Then you can be in charge of organizing our term challenge," said Kayle heartlessly. He smiled warmly at Naelen. "When he gets too overbearing, please feel free to drown his ego. He can take it."

The term challenge was a four-night stay in the middle of the woods; the adepts would drop them there with only rudimentary tools, and they would have to take care of themselves for the duration until the adepts picked them up again.

Rilt settled at his desk and tapped a staccato beat with his fingers. "So that's it, then?"

"I'm tired. Kayle, it's the same system as when we were studying?" Gareth asked, sounding bored.

"Some minor tweaks-"

"That you can show me tomorrow." Gareth yawned and went back to his dormitory through the shared bathroom.

"I would like to see the summaries you and Rilt have written, please," said Naelen. He ignored Rilt entirely and spoke only with Kayle, asking about their symbols and debating how detailed their summaries should be.

After Naelen had returned to Room Five and they got ready for bed, Kayle went to sit beside Rilt on the bed. With his knees tucked to his chest, the young lord rested his head on his forearms and studied his roommate.

"What is it?" he asked.

Kayle cocked his head. "What happened between you and Naelen?"

"Possibly a misunderstanding." Rilt outlined the altercation briefly and pointed to the slight crook in the bridge of his nose. "That's the reason for this. Father didn't let the healers see to me, saying that I deserved it. Master Baelmin did his best, but he was not a healer."

Kayle peered at Rilt's nose and gingerly prodded it. Rilt smacked Kayle's finger away.

Apparently, the scholar's inquisitiveness had not been sated. "What was Naelen like, back in Enthin? Did you and he cross paths often?"

"Hardly. He has two older brothers, so I saw them more often, trailing after their father. Swaggering braggarts, both of them, and they've yoked their carts to their father's oxen."

"What?"

Rilt belatedly remembered that Kayle came from a port, not the countryside. "They relied on their father's reputation to get them benefits."

"Naelen isn't like that."

"He could be worse. Dunefruit, tree, you know the saying."

Kayle slid off Rilt's bed to settle in his own. There was a thoughtful silence before he spoke. "I've seen lots of people in Port. Naelen doesn't strike me as a liar."

Rilt rolled over and shut his eyes. "I hope you're right." Before he could nod off, he asked, "What's in the envelope?"

"Master Jodius laid out a special curriculum for me. He said I have 'potential'."

"That's great!"

"Insofar as extra lessons can be great, yes." Since Kayle seemed somewhat reticent, Rilt didn't prod him further.

DATES

By the time Rilt had dragged a reluctant Kayle to the meeting spot, Galena was already waiting at the back gate with a friend. They were laughing at some shared joke while other students strolled past them. A line of single-horse open cabs waited for passengers about fifty yards away on the bridge between First and Second Circles.

"Bad form, Rilt," Galena called out with a warm smile when she saw him. Her hair fell freely over her shoulders, with a delicate braid of colorful yellow ribbons circling her crown. Her summery blue dress had small, shiny buttons in neat lines down the bodice. "Late for the first date? I'm taking points off for that."

Jogging up to the two young women, Rilt took Galena's hand and kissed her knuckles lightly. "I apologize."

"It was my fault," Kayle apologized as he joined them. "Rilt had to drag me out of bed today."

The other girl scanned Rilt and Kayle from head to toe. Rilt felt as though he was being weighed for sale. His first impression was that she was very brown: light brown hair, brown eyes the color of tea steeped overlong, tanned skin. Her dress was the green of new leaves, her heeled boots a darker green. She spoke in a wispy voice that Rilt thought better suited to an invalid.

"Galena, you have to make the introductions," she said. She paid scant attention to Kayle, who held his hands behind him and was bouncing lightly on his heels. Her gaze lingered on Rilt.

"Oh, yes. This is Miryana Mendos. She's also a harpist. We're performing together at the King's Ball at the end of term. This is Lord Rilt Arald, whom you and the rest of the school have been gossiping about," said Galena. "This is his friend and roommate, Kayle Radieri. That's all I know about you, Kayle, sorry."

Kayle smiled. "That's all I am."

Rilt frowned at his friend. "You sell yourself short. He's a royal scholar, one of the three enrolled in Kaedin Hall."

That made Miryana's gaze shift to Kayle. A corner of her lips lifted. "A royal scholar? How wonderful."

Kayle shot Rilt a look of alarm when Miryana slipped her arm through Kayle's. Rilt bit back the laugh that nearly escaped him and offered his arm to Galena. "Shall we?"

They took a cab to the restday market. Rilt was looking forward to this. Back home, vendors sold everything from dry goods to crockery, weapons to fabrics. He had never been allowed to explore one freely; Pellit or a house guard would stay close on his heels. This would be his first foray into a market without constant surveillance. He wondered what Izdahl's restday market would be like, and how much it differed from the one in Enthinas, which specialized in dairy products.

The closer they got to the market, the thicker the press of the crowd. The stalls' canvas tops in myriad colors stretched across the entirety of the open square, and fanned out into some of the wider avenues. Rilt wondered if he would be dazzled if he looked upon the square from a tall building.

"It's huge!" Kayle exclaimed. "How many streets does this market cover?"

"It goes north-south from Kingsway to Hangs, and east-west from Red Bridge to Tower." Seeing the two young men's blank looks, Galena said, "We may be able to go down the main avenue today. You'll see."

The cab navigated to a street where other cabs and their drivers waited for passengers while their horses munched placidly on the contents of their feedbags. Galena had them alight on the west side, where the food and snack stalls were arrayed. Rilt's mouth watered when he smelled the tantalizing aromas of chikskewers and fried groundnuts.

"You simply have to try the komma here," Galena gushed, tugging Rilt by the hand to one stall with a long line. Rilt gazed longingly at the chikskewers stall further down but followed Galena obligingly.

Miryana and Kayle trailed behind them. She had stopped trying to cozy up to Kayle when he politely disengaged his arm in the cab on the pretext of pointing to various buildings they passed on the way to the market. At least she could not criticize his clothes or his looks.

Rilt's pale orange tunic was just a little loose for his roommate, but on the slender Kayle, the loose folds looked stylish, and the black buttons on the cuffs matched his pants.

"What's komma?" asked Kayle as they got into line. He craned his neck but there were too many people in the way.

"You don't know what komma is?" said Miryana in disbelief. "What backwoods did you come from?"

Kayle's cheeks colored.

"It's a fried pastry roll stuffed with meat, chopped greens and kom sauce," said Rilt. He pointedly turned his back on Miryana and asked Kayle, "What are the popular street snacks in Port Halim, Kayle? I know kom sauce isn't popular in the south."

"We have something similar," said the young man quickly, tossing Rilt a grateful glance for his intervention. "We have freshas—deep fried seafood rolls—and there's a spicy kelp sauce that you can dip the rolls in. And of course, the best caro in the kingdom."

Miryana made a face. "Ew. Kelp. That's a slimy seaweed, isn't it?"

"You can't exactly grow lettis and borads on the beach, and there's plenty of kelp to harvest every season. They keep really well too, except the airing rooms tend to smell of unwashed feet," Kayle said with an amused grin. "When I was a kid, we used to punish anyone losing a game with an hour in an airing room."

Galena laughed. "That's quite a punishment. Kom sauce is mild, but the komma here has a good balance of lean and fatty meat. Try the lamb komma, it's amazing."

As she had said, the komma was delicious, and Rilt paid for all four of them. Rilt munched on the crispy komma, delighting in the sweet and tart burst of flavor from the kom sauce contrasting with the meaty richness of the lamb, all topped with crunchy, freshly chopped greens. Galena called the wine vendor over and they each ordered a small glass of white wine. Miryana passed a handkerchief to Kayle when kom sauce dripped on his fingers.

"Thank you," he said.

"You're welcome. I'd like to look for some ribbons after this. Galena? What do you need to get?"

The brunette shrugged. "I was thinking of getting a new purse and a comb. Mine broke when Rekia sat on it."

"I can't believe that fat cow did it again. She should be buying a new one for you," Miryana said. To Rilt and Kayle, she added, "Combs are on the south side. Ribbons and fabrics are on the north, with other accessories and materials. We're here nearly every week, so we know where all the good things are."

"We can purchase the ribbons first, then the purse and comb?" Rilt suggested.

Miryana wrinkled her button nose. "That will take more than two hours, given the crowd, and we have to be back before then. We've to report for extra practice."

"Oh yes, Master Tilfa. She's bent on torturing us with the piece she assigned, I swear to Creation." Galena went on to describe the piece she and Miryana were performing, even humming a couple of bars for them. Apparently, it was so technically challenging that the master had already changed two harpists. So far, only Miryana and Galena had been able to keep up.

Miryana let out a long-suffering sigh. "It's the tempo changes and the sudden shifts from key to key. I know she wants to convey the character's confusion as she struggles between duty and desire, but does she have to put us through confusion to get there?"

"Well," said Galena, "in any case, we have to split up. Rilt and I can head to the south, and you two can explore the north. We'll meet back here once we have our things."

Rilt swiped at his lower lip, brushing away flecks of fried pastry. "Sure. Kayle and I will grab some chikskewers before we head off. Just wait here for us. Come on, Kayle."

Bemused, Kayle followed Rilt to the chikskewer stall, out of sight of their dates. Once he was sure the girls were not watching them, Rilt discreetly stuffed five silvers and a gold piece into his roommate's hand.

"What's this for?"

"I promised I'd pay for everything," said Rilt. "Miryana seems the type to insist on your paying for her ribbons. That should more than cover it."

Kayle flushed pink. "Rilt, I can't-"

"Hey. I promised." Rilt grinned. He gestured for four skewers from the vendor and added quietly, "I'll ask Galena not to invite Miryana along for the next trip. She's so condescending to you."

"Just leave me out of your future dates, and I'll be very happy."

Kayle took two of the chikskewers from Rilt. "Thanks. I'll return you the change later."

The two pairs split up. Miryana appeared decidedly displeased about the prospect of spending time alone with Kayle, who was not enthusiastic about the idea either. Before her friend could complain, Galena took Rilt's hand and threaded her way through the throng of people.

"Miryana isn't too impressed with Kayle," she confided, with an amused gleam in her eyes.

Rilt scowled. "What's not to be impressed by? He's brilliant, kind and good-looking."

"He's short. Well, shorter than she likes her men to be," said Galena. "You're more her type."

"She's not mine."

"Hmm. What is your type?"

With a wry smile, Rilt pulled her closer so they walked with their shoulders brushing. "What do you think?"

Galena laughed, a rippling, lovely sound, and slipped her arm through his, then linking their hands again. "I could get used to this."

"Not because of the prospect of a title, I hope."

"Are you joking? I'm salivating for that title. Does it come with a coronet?"

Her hand was warm. She smelled very floral and feminine. Rilt said, "I believe my stepmother has a few that she would be more than pleased to give you if you do become duchess. One of them belonged to a Niekadian princess. Two centuries old."

"Ooh, now that is an incentive," Galena teased, bumping her hip against his.

They passed merchants selling almost everything Rilt could imagine: dresses and tunics of all colors and materials, assorted craft tools that looked vaguely menacing, stacks of books and stationery, and tons of accessories and imitation jewelry. Galena picked out a glittery gold-beaded purse, which Rilt bought her as a gift.

"Nice young man you got there, sweetie," said the matronly vender. She nudged her husband who was unpacking more goods from a box. "You never give me anything."

"I've already given my life to you, poppet," the husband retorted with a crooked grin.

Galena smiled and thanked Rilt prettily. She bought a comb herself, then said, "Let's take the other street back. That way you'll get to see more of the market."

They came across an armorer selling a breathtaking range of weaponry laid out like cutlery. Many of the customers were burly and muscular, but there were a couple of armored guards who looked twice as large as the biggest of those browsing. One of them hefted his axe in warning when he saw one of the potential customers picking up a sword; the customer quickly lowered it and muttered a sheepish apology.

Rilt was sorely tempted to purchase a dagger with a handle wrapped beautifully in blue and black. Its black scabbard was inlaid with a silver-and-blue serpent, and the cross-guard and pommel were bright steel.

"May I?" he asked the armorer, pointing to the dagger.

The wiry man nodded. "Keen eye, sir, that's a mastersmith's work you're holding. Early piece from Master Fandel himself. Got it from an estate sale two weeks ago, and I'm selling it near cost."

Drawing out the blade slowly, Rilt admired the design of the weapon and the feel of the grip. The mastersmith's sign, a stylized F, ws set into the base of the pommel. The dagger was heavy but well-balanced. Etched lightly on the blade were symbols that Rilt did not recognize.

Galena peered over his shoulder. "That's Ilyurshvic script. I've seen that in some scores; they usually have phonetic markings so we can sing them easily."

"Can you read it?" Rilt angled the blade so she could see the symbols clearly.

"I can pronounce it, but you'll have to ask someone to translate for you. Um…" She squinted at it and said, "It says, 'Ja-su-lik-va-lim'. I think."

"Jasulikvalim?"

"It's a phrase, I guess. Something about courage." Galena frowned at it. "It is beautiful, though."

Rilt sheathed the dagger. "Why would a mastersmith put ilyurshvic script on his weapon?"

The armorer shrugged. "Could be that it was the client's request.

Fourteen silvers and it's yours."

"Fourteen? Come now, mister, it's from an estate sale and it's only an early example of his work, as you said. Ten silvers would give you plenty of profit," Galena said with a sweet smile.

"Miss, if everyone tried that angle, I'd be beggared in no time. Fourteen silvers."

"Ten."

"Thirteen silvers and two coppers, fair bargain."

"Extortionate, you mean," Galena said. "Ten and five, or we go."

Rilt was baffled. He had not said he wanted the dagger, but Galena and the armorer were already busy bargaining. With an inward sigh, he got the money ready.

Galena drove a hard bargain, and the armorer eventually conceded to Galena at the price of eleven silvers for the weapon, with a dagger frog thrown in for free. Rilt secured it to his belt and tested the smoothness of its draw. The blade was beautifully well-balanced.

"You look good with that," she said, once they were on the way again. They could hear the food vendors once more, and a variety of savory aromas greeted them.

Rilt grinned and squeezed her hand. "I wasn't planning to buy it, but you had so much fun bargaining."

"If you don't want it-" She reached around him to take the weapon.

"I want it," he said, quickly catching her other hand. Then, disregarding a muttered complaint behind them for obstructing the way, he ducked his head and kissed her soft lips.

"Not here." She smiled, breaking the kiss. Catching her lower lip between her teeth, she led Rilt down a different aisle and then into a narrow alley. It was quiet here. Apart from two wagons chained together, a snoozing ginger cat, and the inevitable stink of all alleys, they were completely alone.

Rilt placed his hands on Galena's waist and tugged her close. His lips brushed hers as he said, "Sorry. Not very romantic."

"You're not romancing me," she countered cheekily. "This is all for fun, isn't it?"

"Yes, that's true, but I can still treat you to something nicer than this."

"Next date. Without Kayle." She tiptoed and pressed their mouths together, her hands sliding up his biceps to steady herself on his shoulders.

It was a warm, sweet kiss, tinged with a faint taste of the wine they had earlier. She was clearly used to kissing, but he was not complaining; confident kissers made confident lovers. Her lashes brushed his skin and her fingers tightened on his arms. Her breasts were soft and yielding against his chest, even though the buttons felt odd pressed against him. He felt himself respond to her and slipped his right hand down to explore her behind. She squirmed against him and giggled when he squeezed.

With a playful slap on his shoulder, she said, "Enough of that. Miryana and Kayle will be waiting for us."

Her hair looked deliciously tousled. He kissed her once more and reluctantly let go, discreetly adjusting himself. "Come on. Perhaps we can have dessert before we take a cab."

As they exited the alley, Rilt caught sight of a head of dark curls weaving into the crowd. He wondered if that was Kayle, and shook himself. There were plenty of people with dark curls.

When they got back to the vicinity of the komma stall, Rilt was surprised to see Kayle and Miryana sharing a spindly table with Gareth. They all had half-finished bowls of desserts in front of them, and Gareth was listening politely to the young harpist.

Kayle saw Rilt and Galena first and waved them over, grabbing two empty chairs from an adjacent table. Rilt snagged a place next to his roommate and helped to hold Galena's shopping.

"I got what I wanted," said Galena to her friend. "What colors did you get?"

"Kayle bought me these," said Miryana brightly in her breathy voice, showing off half a dozen lengths of pastel ribbons. "He's really good at picking out colors that go with my skin and hair."

"I learned by watching my neighbors back in Port. They always looked beautifully put together." Kayle smiled at Miryana. "You can pair any two together and they will perfectly complement your coloring."

Uninterested in ribbons and colors, Rilt took Kayle's spoon from his hand and tried his sweet bean soup. It was very creamy and thick, with a nutty aftertaste. He pointed his spoon at Gareth somewhat accusingly. "I wasn't expecting to see you here."

"I needed to see what sort of mischief you've dragged my best friend into," said Gareth, jerking his chin at Kayle, who ignored the little jibe.

Kayle plucked his spoon back out of Rilt's hands. "Well, it has been a lovely morning, girls. Thanks for showing us the market."

Galena shot Rilt an odd look, but didn't say anything. She tried to signal the vendor for another bowl to share with Rilt, but there were too many people in the way. They could hear a commotion somewhere in the near distance.

Gareth peered around. "I wonder what that is."

Miryana shrugged. "Someone must be in their cups. Part of the reason why we prefer to come here early is to avoid the violent drunkards and snatchpurses. They swarm around sunset, when most people are dull-witted from their dinners."

"Do you have a problem with gangs here?" asked Kayle. "We had a fair number of gangs in Port. They controlled the docks and the captains made sure they kept on good terms with the gang bosses."

"I wouldn't know," said Miryana with a disdainful sniff. She finished her dessert. "I don't associate with lowborn rabble. In any case, it's safer to stay in the university after nightfall."

Kayle and Gareth exchanged a thoughtful look.

Galena gave up trying to get the vendor's attention. "We can go down to the east bank another day when the weather is warmer. That's where street performers gather."

"What kind of ... Look out!" Rilt dragged Kayle off his chair and shielded him with his body as a black horse charged through the stalls and galloped straight at them. There was no time to run. Rilt heard the approaching clatter of hooves and ducked his head, bracing himself. Then there was sudden silence, a shadow, and a heavy thud of hooves on cobblestones behind him. The horse bolted away into the stalls, intent on escaping the furiously shouting men rushing towards them to recapture it.

Rilt pushed off the ground, worried that he'd hurt his friend in his panic. He had barely levered himself up on his elbows when Kayle shoved him aside. A man stumbled over them and there was a metallic clink. Rilt was about to ask if he was alright, but the man got up and squeezed into the watching crowd. Before Rilt could figure out what was happening, Kayle had scrambled to his feet and was giving chase. Unfortunately, there were too many people in the way, and Kayle soon returned to Rilt.

"Are you alright?" Rilt asked. He dusted dirt streaks from Kayle's forearms. "What was that about?"

Kayle looked pale, but he managed a faint smile. "I'm fine. We can talk about it in a moment. How are the girls?"

Rilt then remembered their dates. Looking around, he saw Gareth next to Galena, who was brushing dust and dirt from Miryana's hands. Both the young women were unhurt, but appeared pale and stunned.

"Are you both alright?" asked Rilt as he picked up the girls' shopping.

"That's it. I'm going back to the hall," Miryana declared, grabbing her bag of ribbons from his arm. She ignored his question entirely. "Come, Galena, it's late."

Gareth helped Galena up before he went to check on the runaway horse. Galena glanced at Rilt and then past him. Rilt followed her gaze. She was staring at Kayle, who was righting the outdoor furniture and reassuring the frazzled vendors.

"I was in more danger than he," she pointed out quietly, sounding a little hurt.

The young lord was momentarily robbed of speech, but he rallied to his own defense. "Gareth kept you safe well enough."

"I am your date, not his," she retorted.

Chastened, he scratched the side of his neck and said, "If we could see you back…"

"Not necessary, Rilt. I have to go. Miryana's waiting." She turned away and then paused, as though she was going to say something else, then left to join her friend.

Rilt debated going after her but decided against it. He wasn't sure what to say—or what he had done wrong. True, he should have been more chivalrous and made sure that the two ladies were protected, but everything had happened so quickly. Besides, it had been easier to shield Kayle who had been right next to him. Gareth had been sitting beside her. As unlikable as Gareth was, he wouldn't let a young woman get hurt right in front of him without intervening.

A few stalls away, the horse had finally been subdued and city wardens were making their way to the source of the commotion. Kayle was standing alone near the edge of the crowd.

When Rilt came back to him, he said wryly, "I hope I'm not included in your plans for your second date, because this is far too much excitement for me."

"I'll be sure not to rope you in the next time." Rilt draped an arm over his roommate's shoulders and hugged him briefly. "Assuming there is a next time."

"Why not? She seemed quite happy with you when you two came back."

"The part where I saved you instead of her didn't impress her much."

"She doesn't know what she's missing," said Kayle. He reached up and squeezed Rilt's fingers, his voice low. "Incidentally, you're missing a dagger."

Rilt's hand flew to his belt. The mastersmith's dagger he had just bought was gone, with only the sheath remaining.

"That man who stumbled over us stole it and tried to stab you while your back was to him," the Halim scholar whispered, and handed the dusty dagger to Rilt, handle first. The dagger's tip was notched. "Do you remember his face?"

"Only that he had sandy hair and a fairly large nose," said Rilt. "Half a hand taller than you, if that."

"The men who said they are trying to kill you are really trying to kill you, Rilt. If you don't report this, I will."

"I'll let the right people know," Rilt promised. From Kayle's expression, he knew that his roommate was not reassured at all. He wasn't lying, though; he was going to pay a visit to Pellit, and through his valet, he could alert their Arald contacts for information. There had to be a warden or wardenchief in the pay of his house.

Gareth emerged from the crowd. He stalked over to his classmates and said, "That horse is new-bought. The owner decided to walk it through the avenues instead of going around like a sensible man, and someone accidentally burned the poor beast."

"What are the wardens doing?"

"They forced the horse to its knees and roped it down. The owner thinks the horse should be slaughtered for all the trouble it's caused," said Gareth. His voice was even, but the tension around his eyes and mouth showed his displeasure. "Scorch Creation, some people don't deserve animals."

"Will the wardens kill it?" Kayle sounded concerned.

"No they won't," said Rilt. "Give me a moment."

He shouldered his way through to the wardens who were still try-ing to wrangle the horse, while the two scholars followed behind. The distressed beast's mouth was flecked with foam and its eyes were rolling with fear and confusion. On its flank was a blistered patch of skin, about a hand's width. Rilt grimaced. No wonder the horse had bolted.

The owner was a pudgy man who was braying about not being able to pay for all the damages. "Kill it for glue, I don't care. It's put me through enough today."

"It's not the horse's fault," Gareth snapped. "You should be killed for glue."

"I'll buy the horse," Rilt said to one of the wardens.

"And who are you?"

"Lord Rilt Arald."

"Well, m'lord, I'm going to need some proof that you are of the noble house of Arald," said the warden politely, his eyes skimming over Rilt's expensive clothes.

"I'll go with you and the horse to the Arald estate." He pointed at the owner and added, "Make sure he pays for the damages to the vendors. The amount I'm paying for the horse is to go to the city, not to him."

"The horse is too nervy to make a good working beast, m'lord."

Rilt slipped his hands into his pockets and raised his chin. "It's not going to be a working beast. Let me know when you are ready to lead the horse there."

While the warden relayed the news to his colleagues, Kayle sidled up to Rilt and whispered, "Gareth is annoyed."

"Why would he be?"

"He feels indebted," Kayle said. There was a mischievous glint in his eyes.

Rilt grinned. "Good."

* * *

After making sure Kayle and Gareth were safely in a cab back to Kaedin Hall, Rilt and the wardens went to the Arald estate with the horse. Pellit was more than a little surprised at the new addition to the estate's menagerie. The wardens thanked Rilt for taking the animal off their hands and left.

"Sir, what am I going to do with this mare?" Pellit led the horse round to the back. He ducked when the beast tried to nuzzle him.

"Put her in the stables, of course," said Rilt. Without looking around, he asked, "What news do you have?"

Pellit lowered his voice and said, "There's something going around about a new gang in the city. They seemed to be centered near the docks."

"And the locals are letting them stay?"

"They aren't causing trouble for the locals. Yet." Pellit glanced around. "I hear they're connected to Kaedin Hall in some way. They call themselves the Verashki."

"Is it a big gang?"

Pellit shrugged. "It's been hardly a week, sir, give me more time."

Patting the mare's neck, Rilt smiled slightly. "Good man, Pell. I've more news and this time, I need you to set my father's eyes and ears on me. I'll bring you some of Kaedin Hall's pastries the next time I come by. The head cook makes a fine cloudberry pie, though their tarts aren't worth an Endigo copper."

"If I told my mother that, she'd walk the whole way here to bake you all the tarts you could possibly want." Pellit grinned, but his smile withered and he shrank back when the horse whinnied. "What name will you give her, sir?"

"Nothing, for now. I'll let Ced name her."

* * *

By the time Rilt got back to Kaedin Hall, it was nearly dinnertime. The cafeteria was bustling with people but Rilt could not spot Kayle. He did see Gareth, who was chatting with Oledan and Terras; given the rapid gesticulating, the scholar was probably relating the incident in the marketplace.

Having little appetite, Rilt returned to his room and found his roommate in one of the chairs before the fireplace. They had recently stopped using it, barring the occasional rainy night. The Halim was thoughtful and a faint line creased the space between his brows.

Rilt took the other chair. "Kayle, are you alright?"

"I'd told Gareth about the conversation we overheard in the green-house." Kayle's mouth thinned into a worried line.

"Well, that does it. You might as well tell the entire school."

"Gareth's more discreet than you give him credit for," said Kayle sharply. "And why shouldn't you tell the entire school? Someone tried to kill you."

Rilt spread his hands. "I'm still here, aren't I?"

"And if I'd not noticed the assassin?" Kayle exhaled heavily and shook his head. "You are far too nonchalant."

"Trying to kill me in a crowded market is a stupid plan. Having a horse rampage through the market is a stupid plan. There are many other ways to attack me that wouldn't hurt other people."

Kayle stared at him strangely. "Your life is at risk and you're worried about other people being hurt?"

The young lord shifted in his seat. "I can defend myself."

"You big idiot." Kayle rubbed the bridge of his nose. "You big, kind idiot."

"I'm going to take that as a compliment."

"You are worth ten of me. Ten of any of them," Kayle said, his sapphire gaze in equal measure amused and exasperated. "You're the future duke of Enthin, Lord Rilt Arald. You have to be selfish about your life."

Staring at the flickering flames, Rilt shuffled his feet and mulled over Kayle's words. He could see the cold logic in them. He could see where Kayle was coming from, but he could not quite articulate why he disagreed with it. Eventually, he said, "I have a younger brother."

"Cedaran, right? What of him?"

"Cedaran looks up to me." Rilt chewed on the inside of his lip lightly. "I want to be a brother he can be proud of. If that means I die while protecting an innocent, then that's how it is. But I won't ever be someone Cedaran can't respect."

The sudden sound of water running in the shared bathroom broke into their silence. Kayle exhaled a soft laugh, and said, "You're a far better person than many I know, Rilt. Enthin is lucky to have you."

Feeling a dull flush creep up the back of his neck, Rilt swiftly diverted the conversation away from this topic. "Yes, well. We are cleaning the bathroom tomorrow, right? You'll have to show me how."

From Kayle's expression, it was clear that he knew Rilt had changed the subject deliberately. He grinned anyway. "You are definitely going to hate it."

SWIMMING

Dear Ced,

I wish I could have been there for the lambing; I suppose you got your hands dirty for once! I hope the village girls helped you clean up thoroughly. It's good that your new tutor takes you out and about to show you the practicalities of managing the land. Master Baelmin could have taught me a little more about the practicalities of living away from home, for that matter. Thanks to Kayle's patient guidance, I've learned to sweep the floor, hang up my clothes, and wash the bathroom. Can you even imagine doing that? Also, if Master Delon talks about the Dahl like Master Baelmin used to, ask him to describe the smell when the wind comes from the sea. It defies description. I heard from Terras that it used to be much worse, but in recent years there have been several fierce storms that have washed the worst of the river muck out of Izdahl. I suppose some of Enthin could use some storms right now; let's hope the dry weather doesn't turn to drought.

It has been very dull now that we've settled into a routine. I'm grateful for the dullness after the events of the market. The mare is now named Hedia, as you suggested, after our ancestor's favorite mount. She's a black beauty, all silk-sheen and muscle. Pell says she goes to him when she sees him. I suppose he's been slipping her redfruit and she associates him with sweet treats. Maybe when you and Mother visit, you can take her home with you. The estate is more suited to an animal of her temperament.

As I have mentioned, life is dull and thus very safe. You don't have to keep sending me lists of nobles who may want me dead. Even Pellit and Zarin haven't been able to find out much from their sources about these would-be assassins. I suppose the fact that their attempt failed and I'm aware of their existence has scared them into lying low for now.

One thing though: I can't believe you found the Bariths' pearl necklace and the thief. Now I have to apologize to Naelen. Have you any idea what trouble you've just caused me, Beanpole? Knock your own glasses off your nose for this inconvenience.

At least I'm not having trouble in my studies. Kayle's suggestion of roping Naelen and Gareth into a study group has paid off. He is full of good ideas. As he advised, I've not flaunted my rank and I've kept initiating casual conversations with other students. Now, hardly anyone reacts to 'Arald'. That could pose a problem in the future, but at this point I'm more than happy to blend in.

Do assure Mother that I won't be murdered in my sleep. Also, if I hear of her trying to get me out of Kaedin Hall one more time, I will physically chain myself to the building. I am not abandoning my studies just because some cowards are trying to take my life. If great-great-grandfather Subald could hold back an invasion of Ilyurshvan raiders by himself with a broken lance, I can survive a term in the university while our people investigate.

Take care of yourself, Ced. I miss you very much. Your journal is coming in handy—I've been exploring the city, and there are so many places to see and foods to try. Once you're here, we'll tick off the items on that list.

As always, your dear brother,
Rilt

* * *

The day after Cedaran replied verifying Naelen's account, Rilt forced himself to knock on the door of Room Five. He hated admitting he was wrong, but not apologizing was unthinkable.

Gareth opened the door. "What do you want?"

"Naelen."

"He's in the library. As usual." Gareth was about to shut the door, but stopped abruptly. "That horse. It's in your care now?"

Rilt nodded. "My younger brother named it Hedia."

"Alright then." The scholar closed the door, and leaving Rilt confused about why the mare had been brought up at all.

Naelen was indeed in the library, chatting amiably with Anya. To be more precise, he listened attentively as the leggy runner talked.

Rilt jogged over to the long table where the blond was and said, "Naelen, could I have a moment?"

"That's my cue to leave," said Anya perkily. She winked at Rilt. "Any more messages to run to 4304? I'm sure another handful would suffice."

"My business isn't for you to comment on, Anya," Rilt warned.

"Of course, Lord Rilt. I am but a lowly runner, far too common for one as lofty as you." Anya grinned impudently and strolled away to the librarian's office.

Rilt frowned after her. "That one needs to relearn her manners."

"And perhaps you need to remember that you are a student," said Naelen. "What was it you wanted? Kayle just went off a moment ago, if you were looking for him."

Now that he had to say it, Rilt felt uncomfortable around the collar. He sat down facing Naelen and blurted, "I'm sorry."

The other Enthinian cocked his head. "What for?"

"The girl. The necklace. I was wrong about you and I apologize for being presumptuous," said Rilt, a little stiffly.

"Oh," said Naelen. He considered the young lord for a moment, and nodded. "Alright. Apology accepted."

That's it? Rilt was a little offended. Did Naelen not realize how challenging it was for Rilt to admit his mistakes? Annoyed, he added, "My younger brother says he has found the pearl necklace and it's been returned to your mother."

Naelen brightened. "Really? I shall write Lord Cedaran and thank him for his kindness."

"His kindness?" Aware of how that had sounded, Rilt quickly said, "Definitely. It was all because of Cedaran's kindness."

"Am I supposed to thank you for the apology, Lord Rilt?" asked Naelen wryly. His lips curved in a faint smile. "I appreciate the effort. All of it."

Feeling like he'd made a fool of himself, Rilt hurried out of the library. He was not going to tell Ced about this.

* * *

Galena had apparently decided that Rilt wasn't worth the effort. More than ten days after the date and a dozen apologetic messages later, he finally got a reply from Galena: she was busy preparing for the King's Ball and was thus unable to meet up for future outings.

"She could be busy with rehearsals," said Kayle when he read the note Rilt thrust at him in a fit of pique. "If you're so in want of female company, why not go out with Anya? She's keen on you, if you haven't noticed."

The runner had made her intentions very clear indeed, but Rilt was not interested in her at all. "She's not my type. All leggy and flat-chested. It'll be like bedding a boy."

Kayle huffed through his nose. "She's very charming in her own forthright way."

"If you're so charmed, why don't you ask her out on a date?"

"I am not going to ask her out. She's not keen on me." The scholar put away the assignment and scrutinized his bluespine, checking it leaf by leaf. It had grown quite a fair bit, and Kayle took care to trim it so it would not overgrow its pot. Then he stretched, grunting as his joints creaked and popped. "I'm going to go for a swim. Join me?"

Still smarting over Galena's rejection, Rilt put away his half-finished work and grabbed two towels. "Let's go."

They were not the only students by the water. It was a Fifthday evening, after all, and the lake was very inviting now that the weather was warmer. Half of the first-year cohort were there, as well as many of the older students. Some of the seniors were showing off, racing across the surface like flying boats, and a few indulged in creating acrobatic displays with the water. Most, however, were content to splash about idly. Kayle led them towards a cluster of their friends.

"Hey, Kayle!" shouted Cammod, a plump student in Trae class. "Gareth says you're the best swimmer he knows in Port."

"He hardly knows any swimmers," said Kayle with a self-deprecating laugh.

Gareth showed him a rude gesture. "Come on. Felas and Ladmos are about to race. You might as well join them there, by the stone wall."

"I'll join," said Rilt. In response to Gareth's skeptical expression, he said, "I swam a lot back home in the river, alright? I am good."

Oledan yelled at Felas and Ladmos, telling them to wait.

"If you say so, lordling," Gareth drawled. By now the term was less of an insult. After Rilt had saved the mare from being butchered,

Gareth's attitude towards him had softened a little. He jerked his chin at Kayle. "Come on, Kayle. Show the landbound lubbers how it's done."

"Fine." Kayle rolled his eyes. He tugged off his shirt and tossed it in Gareth's face. "If it's to be a race, what are the stakes? Who's got the pot?"

"I've got the pot," said Oledan. "You'll get a share. Nice tattoo, Kayle."

"Thanks, Oledan. Hold on to the money for me," Kayle replied, grinning. Then he turned to his best friend. "When I win, I get half your winnings on top of mine."

Gareth looked outraged. "You're a pirate, Radieri."

"You know how my sails are rigged, so don't blubber."

"Anyone wants to bet on me?" asked Rilt.

"I will." Naelen, who was sitting on the grass with a book, took out two silvers and tossed them at Oledan.

"Thanks," said Rilt with a short laugh. He had not expected that.

"Go win me some money," said Naelen, not bothering to look up from his book.

With Cammod leading the way, Rilt jogged to the starting point with Kayle. Felas and Ladmos had already taken up positions on the low stone wall. Kayle and Rilt went to the far side. Felas told them that they were competing to swim to the pavilion and back.

"Let's add one more stake, just between us," Rilt said to Kayle as they bent over, ready for the jump. "Three favors, no questions asked. You in?"

Kayle flashed him a mischievous grin. "You're on."

Cammod shouted, "Ready! Set! Go!"

Rilt dove cleanly into the cool water. It felt wonderful to swim again, and for the first few minutes he paid scant attention to the race, so caught up was he in the joy of the sport. Whitesong petals were scattered over the water, like snowflakes on dark glass. Their delicate fragrance floated about them, light and breezy. For a moment Rilt was transported to his home where he used to race his younger brother. With a sharp pang, Rilt wondered if Cederan was spending his days stuck in the library or if he went swimming. He hoped Cedaran would be sensible enough to bring along his valet if he did go to the river. Then he spotted a head of dark hair in front of him, and Ladmos was right next to him. Reminding himself of the stakes, Rilt concentrated on the race.

It was much easier to swim in the lake than in the river Thinas. Without having to work against currents, Rilt was able to pull ahead of Ladmos and then Felas. Kayle seemed to sense his approach and put on a burst of speed. He got to the pavilion first, grinned wickedly at Rilt when he saw his roommate surfacing, and kicked away from the stony base of the pavilion.

Unwilling to concede defeat so soon, Rilt tried his best to keep up. His chest and belly ached, his calves burned, and it would take copious amounts of tea to wash out the taste of lakewater from his mouth. He had not swum this vigorously for a long time. To his delight, he passed Kayle about a quarter of the way to their goal. He was just about to relax his pace slightly for his legs to stop complaining when Kayle splashed past him again, followed by Felas.

Losing to Kayle was one thing. Losing to Kayle and Felas was another. He spurred himself on, kicking hard, and nearly caught the pitch of resonance in his head. Rilt nearly gave in to the temptation of using his resonance for an added boost, but ignored it. Try as he might, he could not catch up to the two in front of him.

Without warning, a sharp pain stabbed into his side. Both his thighs cramped up. Taken by surprise, Rilt tried to kick himself forward, but his leg muscles locked up and he went under. Instinctively holding his breath to stay buoyant, he swept his arms frantically, needing to burst out the surface for just a second, just to shout for help, but he had sunk too fast.

He could feel weeds touching his feet, and that triggered panic. His heart pounded desperately, his vision flashed black spots, and he clawed wildly at the few weeds that brushed against his calves and ankle. The need for air screamed at him to try kicking again, but he couldn't straighten his legs. He could not see the glittering surface of the water anymore. His mouth fell slack and water rushed into his throat, burning like acid and fire along his airway.

I don't want to die here, he thought. *Will Ced be angry with me?*

When his vision was almost completely gone, he felt a strong pull on both his wrists. And then there was welcoming darkness.

* * *

"Breathe, you idiot, breathe," Kayle panted. He sounded very far away.

Rilt felt someone's mouth close over his, blowing air into his mouth, followed by firm, rhythmic pushes against his ribs. The water that he had swallowed lurched out of him abruptly. He twisted to one side to throw it all up. His eyes stung and he could not control the retching.

"He's alright!" someone called out.

Kayle made a sound that was almost a sob. "Thank the Creators."

Coughing weakly, Rilt blinked at the dim shapes gathered over him. A sour film coated the insides of his throat and tears streamed down his cheeks. A few heartbeats later, he could make out Kayle kneeling next to him, Wolvam peering down on his other side, and behind them, a circle of his classmates, all looking worried.

Wolvam helped Rilt roll on his side and rubbed up his spine. "Cough up what you can."

Rilt reached out and grasped Kayle's hand. "Who ... who saved me?" he asked hoarsely.

"You're holding onto him." Gareth hunkered down and peered at him. "Healers are coming. And here you were bragging about how good a swimmer you were."

"Gareth!" Kayle snapped. That was the angriest tone he had ever taken with his best friend. He patted Rilt's hand and squeezed his limp fingers.

Wolvam stood up, looming over Rilt. His clothes were wet, though his hair was not; Rilt was too dazed to understand why. Later, he would learn that the adept had rushed down into the water the moment he noticed, using his resonance to help carry Kayle and Rilt to shore. The other seniors had not been paying attention until the first-years yelled for help. He waved to someone in the distance and then told the onlookers to back away. The healers appeared soon after.

One of them tutted at Rilt. "Best he stays in the infirmary for over-night observation. Water in the lungs doesn't always clear completely at first."

"May I sit with him tonight?" Kayle asked quietly as she and the other healer propped Rilt between them. Warmth spread through Rilt at the thought that his roommate cared this much.

She smiled and shook her head. "We'll be keeping an eye on him.

He'll be back tomorrow."

"But-"

"It's alright, Kayle," said Rilt. He sounded terrible. With a reassuring smile at his worried friend, he obediently allowed the two healers to take him to the infirmary.

* * *

Rilt woke up to the soft scrape of the door in the dead of the night. He had thrown up again in the infirmary—according to the healers, this was a good thing—and had woken up a few times from the discomfort in his throat. The bed was too soft. He had to smile at the thought. When he returned home, it would be an ordeal to get reacquainted with his huge bed and mountains of down pillows.

The lights in the healers' room were out, so whoever had come in was neither Oyedun nor Halon, the two healers on night duty. The slim figure who had slipped in was unmistakable once he slipped past the privacy curtain. He grinned and stretched a hand to Kayle as his roommate slid onto the side of his bed.

"Missed me?" Rilt teased.

Kayle snorted softly. He squeezed Rilt's hand and let go. "I kept worrying. I had to be sure."

There was a slight tremor in Kayle's voice that hinted at a story, but Rilt wasn't sure he was ready to hear it. Instead, he sat up and rested his hand on his friend's shoulder.

Kayle went rigid. "What is it, Rilt?"

"Thank you for saving me," said Rilt. "I didn't have the opportunity to say it earlier. If it hadn't been for you, I'd have drowned and died."

A silence enveloped them, awkward and strange. Kayle averted his gaze, wrapping his arms around himself. Finally he said, in a suspiciously thick voice, "You're welcome. Don't do it again."

"Kayle, what's wrong?"

"Nothing, I just … It's nothing."

"You're crying." Rilt gently but firmly turned his friend's face towards him. His hand was cool on Kayle's damp, warm cheek. "Why are you crying?"

The scholar sniffled and swiped at his eyes. "It's nothing. I'm glad you're alright. I really am."

A sudden burst of insight loosened the reins on Rilt's tongue. "Did someone you care for drown?"

Judging by the tension that snapped instantly around Kayle, the answer was obvious. Even so, Kayle didn't leave. He took a deep, shaky breath, and nodded. His features were masked by pools of shadow, but Rilt heard the thickened breathing, felt the teardrops pool between his palm and Kayle's cheek.

Seized with remorseful compassion, Rilt wiped the tears away as cautiously as though Kayle was made of fine porcelain. The other student stayed statue-still, even after Rilt slid his hand further behind to cup the side of his head, his thumb rubbing soothingly beneath Kayle's earlobe.

"It was a long time ago," whispered Kayle. "Today … today brought up memories."

Rilt leaned forward, pressing his brow to Kayle's. "I'm here. I'm safe."

"For now," Kayle sniffed. "There could have been an attempt on your life here."

"I am completely safe in Kaedin Hall," Rilt reassured him distractedly. Kayle smelled like salt and flowers, this close, and his accent made his words a sweet song.

"I snuck in here without getting caught…" Kayle did not even sound like he was paying attention to his words any longer; his hand rested on Rilt's knee, fingers kneading tentatively.

Their breaths mingled, warm and moist and sweet; Rilt could smell his friend's familiar scent, hear the click of Kayle's throat as he swallowed quietly. His pulse picked up.

"Rilt, I-"

The light in the healers' room flickered on and threw an orange glow onto the ceiling and walls. Kayle jerked back, startled. Rilt frantically signaled him to hide under the bed while he scrambled to get to a jug of water on the stand.

It was Healer Halon who peered around the privacy curtain at Rilt.

"I heard some noises."

"I was getting out of bed to pour myself some water," Rilt lied. "Nearly tripped over my sheets." *Don't look under the bed, don't look under the bed, please don't look under the bed…*

Halon nodded and turned to leave. "Well, you'll miss your morning meditations, but we'll send you back for breakfast. Try to get some rest."

"Yes sir."

It was another interminable ten minutes before the healers' lights were dimmed. Kayle emerged from under the bed and looked at Rilt who had crawled back under the sheets. The two shared a broad grin, and then Kayle ducked behind the curtains to disappear the way he came.

Rilt tried to sleep. Like restless pikefish, his thoughts circled ceaselessly. How warm Kayle's breath had been on his face. The tremor in his friend's voice.

* * *

"Look who's back!" Oledan crowed when Rilt strode towards the tables where his friends were gathered. "How are you feeling?"

"Worn out. The beds in the infirmary aren't comfortable at all," said Rilt, masking his fatigue with a half-truth. He caught Kayle's eye, noticed the dark shadows under them, and realized he wasn't the only one who had been affected by their conversation the night before.

Naelen pushed a plate of food over to him. "Wolvam said your group will be learning how to expel water from the lungs."

Rilt thanked Naelen. "Sorry I lost you money."

"It wasn't much," said Naelen, flipping open a book. Cammod lifted it to peer at the cover and was swatted away, but they had already seen the title: *Amalgamation of Alloys through Kae Shaping*.

"Do you ever read anything for fun?" Cammod asked.

A small crease appeared between Naelen's eyebrows. "This is fun."

"You need to learn what 'fun' means for regular people."

"Speaking of fun," said Oledan, "I've got something for us. Come by Room Nine tonight after dinner."

Ladmos looked crestfallen. "Oledan, I thought that was for us."

"We have a hero and a survivor, we have to celebrate!"

Ignoring the chatter, Gareth shouldered Ladmos aside and started on his own breakfast. "Did you hear? There's someone important coming into the city. The adepts are being drafted for security detail."

"Who's so important that the adepts are involved?"

"Not all of them, just eight or so. They've vying for the spots, apparently. Terras was complaining about it to Ubeko when I passed their table."

Rilt shrugged. "The Lords' Convene, perhaps? I remember my father and I being guarded throughout our stay last year. We only had two kingsriders, though."

The acidic look Gareth shot him was ameliorated by Kayle's smile. Before anyone could add to Rilt's comment, they heard Terras calling out for Kayle.

"Here, sir," said Kayle, standing up hastily and wiping the corner of his mouth with his thumb.

The first-year students fell silent and parted to give way to Master Midusel, who was trailed by Terras. The dean nodded absently at those who were still seated, and waved a hand to keep them from offering their courtesies. Kayle swallowed visibly and straightened.

"Kayle Radieri?"

"Yes, Master Midusel," Kayle replied, his gaze cast on the table.

"You saved your friend's life. Lord Rilt Arald—and Enthin—owes you a great debt. Very quick thinking. Well done."

Kayle flushed. "I-I did what needed to be done."

"I also heard from Terras and Master Jodius that you have remarkable control of your resonance. You're certainly setting a high standard for the royal scholars, not to mention the rest of the cohort." At that, Rilt darted a sly look at Gareth, who gave every impression that he was unimpressed. The dean went on, "I look forward to seeing you progress in your career, my boy."

Kayle nodded and kept his head bowed. "Yes, sir. Thank you sir."

Terras grinned and slapped Rilt on the shoulder. "You really should treat your roommate to a good meal, eh? He's earned it!"

"That's a good idea. Thanks, Terras."

The adept trailed after the dean, leaving the students to crowd around Kayle and Rilt again. Kayle waved off their teasing praise with a bashful smile.

After the other students dispersed, Rilt leaned across the table and prodded Gareth in the forearm. "You have to show yourself worthy of the scholarship like Kayle, or everyone will think you're a fraud."

"That is none of your business, lordling," Gareth snapped. He kicked Kayle under the table. "What's with you? You've gone paler than a seasick lubber."

"Excuse us." Kayle pushed away from the table, and grabbed Rilt's bicep. "Come on, I just remembered we forgot something in our room."

"What-"

"Now, Rilt!" Kayle hissed.

They did not return to their room. Instead, they ducked into an empty classroom.

Rilt leaned against the big table in the front of the room. "Kayle, what in Creation is going on?"

"Didn't you recognize the dean's voice?" Kayle demanded. "That nasal voice?"

Rilt then blinked in surprise. "The men in the greenhouse."

"It was him," said Kayle. "Master Midusel is one of the men who talked about killing you, Rilt." He huffed exasperatedly when the young lord had no response to this revelation. "Why am I the one who's more worried about your life?"

"Because I don't think Master Midusel is out to get me?" Rilt nibbled on his lower lip. "Kayle, calm down. If the dean wanted me dead, he just needed to, I don't know, make sure I was put in a dangerous situation. Send me out of the hall on some pretext. Set up an accident in the classroom. If it was him, I'd be dead by now."

The scholar rounded on him. "Have you forgotten the assassin in Central Market? I haven't."

"I have not forgotten it at all." Folding his arms, Rilt continued, "The fact is that I am still alive. That's proof enough. That assassination attempt was not from someone in this hall. They could've come in through the window if they were."

"No they couldn't."

"Kayle, all anyone needs is a ladder."

"I've dusted bluespine leaf powder outside the window frame. Anyone who tried to come in would get blisters on their palms." Kayle looked at his hands. "I apply it whenever you aren't in the room."

Rilt stared at his roommate with his mouth agape. When he found his voice, he thought he sounded like he was speaking from a great distance. "You ... you didn't tell me? I could have accidentally touched it. I could have been poisoned. We could have been poisoned!"

Kayle tried to appear penitent. "I wasn't going to risk your life, Rilt. But I had to try to make sure you were safe."

"You could've hurt someone!" Rilt hissed.

"They would've deserved it."

The young lord was aghast. "Kayle, you can't do things like that. Not to keep me safe."

If an artist needed a model to paint someone full of contrition, Kayle was, at the moment, the best candidate. He muttered, "I'm sorry. But in my defense, it was a very diluted dosage."

"Don't ever do it again."

"Fine." Kayle kicked his heels on the floor. "But I'm telling you, the dean is involved. He was at the greenhouse, Rilt. He was talking about killing you. Someone has to try to protect you, if you won't be vigilant yourself."

Rilt studied the subtle patterns in the stone floor. At last he said, "I'll have my valet dig up Master Midusel's past. Perhaps we can find out why he might want me dead."

Kayle didn't look convinced, but said nothing more.

* * *

Oledan Puros certainly had connections everywhere. He said gleefully as the small group made their way to his room, "I've got a case of linnis brandy from an associate. And a case of whitesong wine— first pressing, mind you—that just arrived in Izdahl, perfect for you Enthinians. Ladmos and the others are there already."

Rilt perked up. He loved whitesong wine.

"Thanks, Oledan." Gareth was grinning. Oledan had extended the invitation to him without any reluctance, even though Gareth wasn't on easy terms with most of the cohort. Rilt knew he wouldn't have done the same unless Kayle made him.

"Maybe you shouldn't, Gareth. You know how you get when you've had too much drink," said the Halim scholar.

Gareth rolled his eyes. "I'll be fine! Scorch it, Kayle, it's been months since the inn. That won't happen here."

Oledan laughed and threw an arm over Kayle's shoulders. "I'm sure he'll be fine. I just don't want Ladmos to drink it all, the scrawny little sponge. He drank me under the table last weekend at the Lute and Harp. Who knew, eh? Skinny runt holds his drink better 'n I can."

Rilt was pleased to see those who were already there—Felas, surprisingly, plump Cammod with his ever-present dimples, and big, shy Derone—while Ladmos was handing out cups of various sizes. He brightened up when he saw Oledan returning with Kayle and Rilt in tow, and blushed when he noticed Naelen entering the room. It was a running joke among the first-year students that nearly everyone had a mild infatuation with the blond. Rilt didn't count himself among them.

"Brandy or wine? Not you two Enthinians, I know what you'd prefer," asked Oledan when everyone had an empty cup in hand. He handed the wine to an eager Rilt, and poured a generous measure of brandy in everyone else's cups. "Don't mix the two though, I guarantee it'll be far too strong. Unless you're this sponge here, then you can mix all the drinks you want."

Ladmos poked his roommate in the ribs. "My uncle runs a distillery. I've been around brandies since I was a wee toddling."

Knocking back his first mouthful, Gareth winced and exhaled forcefully. "This is strong, Oledan. Whereabouts did you get such potent brandy from?"

"Ah, that'd be telling," said the plump student, winking again. "Anyway, my associate brought it in for his business partner but the sale fell through, so he had stock that he couldn't take out of Izdahl and asked me to assist. So, his loss, our profit." He drank his brandy more circumspectly and grimaced. "Wow, that is strong."

Kayle studied the clear amber brandy and sniffed it. "Are the city wardens looking for these, perhaps?" he asked.

"I'm not saying anything," Oledan replied breezily. He grinned at Kayle. "Come on, scholar. No one is going to be arrested for enjoying a good drink. But it should be unlawful not to finish them. Do me a favor, eh?"

Naelen and Rilt savored their shared bottle of whitesong slowly. It was a good pressing, clean and crisp, with a sharpness that rounded off to a silky smoothness in the back of the throat. The aromas of belldancer flowers and cloudberries wafted from the whitesong wine, bringing lazy summer weekends to mind. Rilt wondered if anything as good as these had been sent in to the estate back home; recent pressings had been too dry, in his opinion.

Seeing their appreciation, Oledan handed an entire box of five other unmarked bottles to them. "They're your responsibility now."

Naelen plucked one out. "I wonder if I could have one sent to my mother. She'd love it."

Oledan grimaced. "Best not to have these out and about, if you know what I mean? Questions will be asked."

The young men chatted about classes and gossiped about the seniors. Wolvam was a popular complaint, especially from Rilt, Ladmos and Oledan. They soon polished off the first and second bottle and were down to the third. The two Enthinians found themselves sharing stories of people they both knew. Rilt nearly gave himself hiccups when Naelen recounted Lady Therra's slip of the tongue that outed her affair with Naelen's oldest brother to none other than Naelen's sister-in-law.

"So, red as a heartblossom and spitting like an angry cat, Harlena grabbed the nearest bowl and overturned its contents on Therra," said Naelen, giggling, his face warm with good wine, "but, see, my second brother had been chewing tarballs all evening, and had been using it for his tar-spit!"

Rilt groaned theatrically while laughing. "That must have been disgusting!"

The others were also on their third bottle of brandy. It had put them all into a good mood. Felas was singing a Duntean song with Derone, both their voices wobbly but still lovely. The words were in a dialect unfamiliar to Rilt: the syllables slurred and joined together, the melody meandering like a wide, slow river. On the other side of the room, Ladmos, Cammod, and Oledan were arguing passionately about someone named Fior or Fiya. Rilt squinted, trying to figure out what they were saying, but all he understood was that Fior— or possibly Fiya—was someone they wanted to meet but had never found the opportunity to.

On his left, Kayle was sipping his brandy slowly. Outside of a bright sheen to his blue eyes, the Halim scholar showed no sign of being tipsy. He saw Rilt staring and smiled. "How's the wine?"

"Really good," said Rilt. He tapped his cup with Naelen. "Smooth on the tongue."

"Let me try some," said Kayle, draining his cup in a single swallow. Rilt tried not to pay attention at the throat Kayle bared to him, and of course could do nothing but stare at it. Kayle handed the emptied cup to Rilt, and when their fingers brushed, heat raced up the back of Rilt's neck.

He poured a measure of wine clumsily, slopping a little over his left hand. Passing the cup back to his roommate, Rilt licked the back of his hand and his fingers, sucking on the web between thumb and forefinger. When he next looked up, he caught Kayle quickly averting his eyes.

"You two are so silly," Naelen muttered under his breath, a small curl of amusement on his lips when Rilt glared at him.

Kayle breathed the wine in. "It smells wonderful."

"I first drank whitesong wine when I was … nine? Ten? My first successful hunt. A rollock fawn, but it was fast, and Father said he was proud that I'd managed to kill it. Father let me drink the wine as the men butchered the animal. We had a good meal that night." Rilt sighed and his head lolled back to rest on the wall. "Ced hates hunting, so he got his first taste when he perfectly memorized the five lists of houses Master Baelmin set him. Father never bothered to listen to him recite though. Mother and I were the ones who poured his first cup."

Naelen shrugged. "I had my first when I was thirteen. Helped Father close a deal with Port Halim when I beat Liria at a card game."

"I never knew whitesong wine meant so much to you Enthinians," Gareth drawled. His normally sallow cheeks were already blotchy and red, his eyes bright as his gaze skimmed from group to group. He could not hold his drink as well as Kayle, evidently. "Even for you, lordling. I thought you'd have feasted and wined since the day you were weaned."

"I wasn't ever hungry, if that's what you mean," said Rilt, too pleasantly languid with wine to take offense at the 'lordling' epithet. "I was born into fortune, I know, but there are so many times I wish I could just…" He threw his hands up. "Get rid of it all."

Gareth was skeptical. "Right, throw away your privilege and your house name and your wealth and your power. I believe you."

Rilt snorted and emptied his cup in a quick gulp, too fast to enjoy the wine. "I don't care if you believe me or not. What would you know of the duties and expectations that I have? It's not just fun and games, not if you intend to hold the line. The Aralds have been around since the days of Coleri Aleis, and I am not allowed to fail it."

Kayle bumped Gareth with his shoulder when the latter was about to speak. The quelling look Kayle gave his best friend seemed to be lost in transit, because Gareth remarked in a whisper loud enough for the entire room to hear, "That is what I say all the time!"

"Yes, Gareth," Kayle replied with a small, exasperated smile. "That's enough brandy for you, don't you think?" To Rilt, he whispered, "He's like this when he's drunk. Don't mind him."

Rilt wrinkled his nose. He wanted to mind it, but it would be petty now that his roommate had brought it up.

The singing grew louder as Felas and Derone transitioned to one of the popular airs now making its rounds in the University. Oledan dug out a deck of cards and called for the group to huddle up for a game of Fives. The stakes were rounds of brandy and wine. Oledan had one more bottle of brandy to work through and three more bottles of wine to clear. Despite knowing that he was not at his sharpest, Rilt joined in the game. The first round passed in a blur, with Oledan and Rilt interrupting each other when explaining the game to Derone and Cammod. By the time they were on the sixth hand, all of them were loudly accusing one another of hoarding the fives and laughing at the silliest comments.

Kayle was surprisingly good at the game. He deflected suspicion and was still able to suss out those who held the necessary cards for second swaps. However, when he picked Gareth for swapping out three in his hand, the latter started getting aggressive over—of all things—the way Kayle phrased his question. Rilt naturally took his roommate's side, and Gareth took offense at that too.

"You don't get to say I'm insulting when your tongue is sharper than a barnacle-blade," snapped Kayle. "And leave off Rilt, you're just picking on him for no good reason."

"Just because you are sharing his-"

"Yes, we're sharing a room, and thank Creation I'm not sharing with you, you rude, self-centered-"

"Rude? I have excellent manners!" Gareth prodded Kayle in the chest.

"Excellent for a plowhorse!" yelled Rilt, incensed by Gareth getting physical with Kayle.

All of them jumped when they heard the four solid thumps on the door. Ladmos, the closest to the door, struggled to his feet and opened it timidly. It was Terras, who smiled and wrinkled his nose when he saw the bottles inside the room, together with the red-faced students.

"Keep it down, boys, I could hear you from the third floor," said Terras amiably.

Oledan grinned. His greasy face was shinier than usual. "Join us for a drink, Terras. We've just begun a game of Fives."

"Not for money, I hope," said the adept as he stepped into the room and made for the gap between Naelen and Felas. "Gambling is not allowed in the hall. I'll have to report you."

The plump student waved off Terras' concern. "Just for drinks. Linnis brandy or whitesong wine?"

It should be awkward having Terras here with them, but once the adept joined in the game, Gareth and Kayle dropped their fight and the game went on. Rilt let himself lean nonchalantly against Kayle when he saw that Cammod was doing the same with Derone. It was comfortable, and Rilt's focus drifted from the cards, realizing only too late that he only had a six, an eight, two guardians and a crown of swords. Gareth grumbled about Rilt hoarding the crown card when he laid down his crown of cups and a two.

"Too bad you couldn't figure out that I had it," Rilt gloated.

The dark-haired scholar scowled at him. "Someday I'll fool you, see if I don't."

Terras was good at the game, with a flush of four through eight of dragons.

"I have an Imperial," Naelen announced when it was his turn to show his hand, beating all the others. "Uh … what do I do with the drinks?"

"Distribute as you like," said Oledan generously. "Or stuff them all in one person."

Already deeply pink with wine, Naelen frowned at the drinks like he was considering drinking them all himself, and then peered at all his friends. He passed five cups to Kayle and five to Terras.

"You two look the least inerib … inevibr … least drunk," said the blond. "That's not fair. Drink up."

Kayle sighed. "Of course Terras looks the least drunk, he just got here." Nonetheless, he didn't demur as he downed cup after cup, much faster than the adept. The others roared their approval when Kayle finished off a particularly full cup of wine and was shushed by Terras quickly.

"You all have morning meditation tomorrow," Terras reminded them. "One more game, and that's it."

"One game? Alright then," said Oledan, placing the half-finished bottle of brandy in the center of the group. His gaze was still steady. "Rilt, that bottle of wine. This time, the one with the weakest cards has to finish one of either, eh?"

Kayle tried to object, but Oledan was already dealing. Gareth rested his chin on Kayle's shoulder, looping his arms around Kayle's mid-section, and said, "I wish we did this more oftenerer. Often. Cards and drinks. Reminds me of the caravavanan days, right Kayle? And that time in that little inn after my father came and we had the place to ourselves." He sang a garbled snatch of verse, a somber tune that was somewhat familiar.

Laughing, Kayle ruffled his friend's hair. "You really should've stopped at four."

Rilt was put out by the two scholars showing affection openly, but even in his tipsy state, he knew better than to comment on it. Instead, he studied his hand. Three fours, one crown of swords, and a five. They went through the swaps, and Rilt's hand was improved to two fives. Sitting out the second swap, he watched Terras debate amiably with Cammod and then later with Gareth. It was nice of Terras not to send them off to their rooms with a warning or even a punishment, Rilt thought.

Cammod won the round. The two with the worst hands were Ladmos and Felas, so they had to down the entire bottle. Seeing that Felas was looking a little green, Kayle offered to take the forfeit and chose the bottle of wine.

"I'm surprised you're here, Lord Rilt, drinking with the common-born," said Terras as they watched the two students drink. Felas had escaped to the bathroom and they could hear him retching. "Guess you've really gotten used to being a student."

"It's fun," agreed Rilt. "I'm glad I came here."

"Only for you," muttered Gareth. He was ruddy and smiled hazily. It was a little disconcerting to see Gareth smile, as it was such a rare occurrence. "What about you, Terras? Why are you here?"

"Because I wanted to make my village proud," said Terras with a smile. "And you, Gareth? Why did you choose Kaedin Hall?"

"It's what I was born to do." Gareth closed his eyes and tightened his arms about Kayle's middle. "I mean, it's in the blood, being kaedine. My father wouldn't have let me done anythin' else. He can't disown me but I'm sure he'd try if I said I'd rather trade. Can't make a scorching choice for myself, everer."

Kayle nearly choked as he rushed to gulp down the last mouthful of wine. Wiping his mouth and chin with the back of his hand, he set the bottle down and apologized. "I should get Gareth back to his bed, he's already too far gone. Thank you, Oledan, the brandy and wine were both fantastic. Rilt, help me with him please? Naelen, if you could open the door to your room?"

Getting to his feet, Terras opened the door for the four of them. The other students were tidying up, while Felas was still busily being sick in the bathroom. The adept patted Rilt on the shoulder and said, "You four rest well."

* * *

"Move!" Wolvam bellowed at the handful of pale-faced students who had indulged a little too liberally the night before. Rilt grimaced from the volume. Kayle was annoyingly bright-eyed and alert, and so were Ladmos and Oledan. Felas still looked vaguely green, and Cammod and Derone kept squinting and rubbing their eyes. Gareth looked like a living corpse and visibly cringed when Wolvam shouted them into their places. The senior adept looked a little too gleeful, even straightening from his perpetual slouch as he harried the students into moving faster.

Instead of meditating in the central courtyard as usual, the adept had ordered them to take up places facing the lake. Rilt had wondered why Wolvam had insisted on that venue until he realized that they would have to stare at the rising sun and the glittering shards of light on the water. From the expressions of dismay on Felas' and Gareth's faces, it was clear that the others had discovered this too.

"He's evil," Rilt whispered to Kayle. The inside of his head felt like it was being scraped with slivers of broken glass. "Can't I just drown him or something? I'll make it look like an accident."

Kayle glanced behind Rilt with a placid smile. "Good morning, Wolvam."

Rilt cursed under his breath.

"Arald. Such a lovely morning for meditation, isn't it?" said the senior adept.

"Um, yes, sir?"

"SO WHY ARE YOU STILL TALKING?" Wolvam thundered. His voice ricocheted inside Rilt's skull. The student nodded meekly and breathed a sigh of relief once Wolvam stalked away. Oledan grinned in sympathy over his shoulder; he was none the worse for wear.

Kayle murmured, "It'll be over soon."

The rest of the session was punctuated with Wolvam talking loudly next to those who regretted imbibing too much the previous night. It was obvious the adept was punishing them for their drinking session and, from the stifled sniggering of the rest of the cohort, Wolvam's picking on them was met with approval.

When they were finally dismissed for breakfast, Gareth groaned and lay flat on the grass. "Someone scorching kill me, please," he pleaded in a low voice.

"I'll be glad to," said Kayle heartlessly. "Told you, didn't I? You shouldn't drink."

"Just because you have a sea-captain's liver…"

"Keep whining and I'll yell in your ear."

Gareth moaned and curled on his side. Rilt was glad he had better tolerance, although he really needed some food to settle his stomach. As he hauled Gareth to his feet to hurry him to the cafeteria, Wolvam strode over. Behind him trailed the other five, who arrayed themselves in front of him when he barked a command at them.

"Next time," the adept said, "I'll have you all standing in the School of History's bell tower for the entire day. This is a hall of learning, not leisure and certainly not liquor. Oledan, one more party, and I take you directly to the dean."

"Yes sir," said Oledan cheerily. He quickly feigned contrition when the adept narrowed his eyes in warning. Once Wolvam had strode off, Oledan mimed wiping his brow with the back of his hand.

Rilt grimaced. "He could have been a little more decent," he complained as they picked their way back to the school.

"No more than what you deserve." Terras was waiting at the main door with a broad smile. He held out a small pouch. "Hangover pills. Take two after food, and drink plenty of water."

"You knew Wolvam would be mean about this," Gareth grumbled, still pale and sweating a little. "Why didn't you stop us?"

Terras laughed and stuck his hands in his pockets. "Would you have stopped just because I said so? Besides, Wolvam likes his bit of fun. He may be a bit of an old builder's rule, but he has a sense of humor inside."

"It's buried deep down, then," Gareth said. "Someone plow him for it, please."

"Wolvam's a good man." There was no hint of laughter in Terras' voice now. "If there is anyone in this hall that I know will give his life to protect you, it's him. You may not like him, but you will respect him."

At that, Gareth apologized. Rilt was surprised at the real anger in the adept's tone, and it was so unusual to hear this from Terras that the students were suddenly ill at ease. Perhaps sensing their apprehension, Terras smiled and added, "He's always been surly, but he's kind when it counts. Now, go get yourselves lots of water. I'll see you later for the tutorial." He strode down the corridor towards the classrooms.

Rilt wondered if he was the only one who saw that Terras' smile had not reached his eyes.

SECOND CHANCES

Rilt was not one to give up, but he was close to it when another dozen messages were run to Galena with no response. He plucked up the courage to go to the School of Arts himself one afternoon, when Master Berras let the class off unexpectedly early.

When Kayle saw him wandering off alone, he caught up. "Where are you going?"

"To see Galena."

"You shouldn't be walking around by yourself," Kayle said, though he clearly did not want to intrude on what was certain to be a private moment. "People trying to kill you and all, remember?"

Rilt slung an arm over his roommate's shoulders. "Then escort me."

Laughing, Kayle shook his head, but kept walking with Rilt. "Galena won't be pleased to see me, you know."

"Why not? She knows you're my friend."

They walked leisurely to the other school, about a quarter of the lake's circumference away. The other halls around the lake gleamed like mounds of snow, topped with brightly tiled roofs. There were a number of students strolling about, the color of their belts or sashes indicating their respective halls. The whitesong trees were starting to shed their blossoms. In another week or so, there would be pale white berries clustered on the long, swinging branches, and over three weeks the berries would turn a delicate blush-pink. The first whitesong berries of the year in Enthin were always very sweet, with a lingering tartness. Then after the late summer blooming—never as many flowers in summer—would be the autumn crop, which produced less sweet, but juicier berries. Enthinian vintners liked using the spring harvest of berries for winemaking, while the cooks favored the autumn crop for jellies. Rilt wondered if that was the practice here, too.

A strong breeze stirred up the branches and white petals showered over them both. They shook off most of the flowers easily. Kayle giggled when a petal landed right on the tip of Rilt's nose and the young lord went cross-eyed to stare at it.

"You're one to laugh. You've got some stuck in your hair," said Rilt, reaching out to pluck them from his friend's dark curls. Kayle stopped laughing. It was only as Rilt was tugging two petals from silky hair and watching the curls spring back into shape that he realized how intimate this gesture was. He hurriedly dropped the petals and stuck his hands in his pockets. "I'm going to apologize to Galena and probably ask her out on another date."

"That's good," said Kayle, without enthusiasm. "I shouldn't be there. She won't want me tagging along a second time."

"No, I guess not. Anyway, I'm not going to the marketplace the next time. Just a walk by the river or something."

The wind stirred the whitesong trees again, scattering thousands of moon-white petals. Rilt dusted off those that clung to his arms and neck. This time, he didn't check if any had landed on Kayle.

* * *

"Galena Aedinal? She's in rehearsal. Last room on the right, that way." The second-year student they met near the main door pointed to a corridor. He smiled and added in a conspiratorial tone, "Wait outside for the break. If you interrupt the rehearsal, Master Tilfa will turn your hides into drumskins."

"Thank you for the directions. And the warning." Rilt started down the hallway, but Kayle lingered behind. He waved for the former to proceed without him. Evidently, he had appointed himself Rilt's personal guard, but meeting Galena was out of the question.

The rehearsals were ongoing and, mindful of the possibility of being skinned, Rilt waited patiently a little way down the corridor, listening to the rehearsal for about a third of an hour before the bell chimed and students streamed out of the classroom. Most of them paid him little heed, but a few cast him odd glances. It was Miryana who caught sight of him and tapped Galena's arm.

"It's your darling duke," said Miryana with a crooked grin.

That made a handful of stragglers pause, but Galena shooed them on. Miryana laughed and dragged two others along with her.

"What are you doing here?" Galena asked. Her hair fell in messy waves around her face and her nose was shiny. There was a small blemish on her chin. When she saw him looking at it, she covered it with her fingers and flushed. "It's been a stressful few weeks."

"So the rehearsals were the real reason you didn't reply to my messages?" Rilt said, opting for a flirtatious tack.

She rolled her eyes, but the smile on her lips was coy. "Alright, alright. I had a bad bout of blemishes. They've only just faded. Save for this one."

Rilt brushed her hair back. "You look fine. And in case it wasn't clear from my two dozen notes, I'm sorry about what happened during the previous date. Give me a second chance?"

Though she pretended to hesitate, Galena's smile grew wider. "Let me think. A duke-to-be is begging me to go out with him a second time. Should I? Should I not?"

"Of course you should. I'll see you next Sixthday? Just a leisurely walk along the canal. Something quiet. No horses."

Galena agreed, and they decided on a meeting time. She headed the other way, presumably for another class. Feeling much more cheerful, Rilt whistled as he sauntered back to meet Kayle.

He was surprised to see his friend already accosted by three young women at the stairs. They were flirting outrageously, batting their eyes and pressing themselves against the clearly uncomfortable Kayle. There was a brunette who was practically throwing herself at him, pulling a petal from his curly hair and giggling while he blushed furiously.

Rilt strode up to them and barged right into the conversation. He took Kayle by his elbow and steered him away from the girls. "We have to go. Sorry, ladies, another time."

"Thank Creation," Kayle whispered as they hastened down the path to the lake. "They cornered me and the only way to go was up the stairs. I didn't think that would have helped."

"Please tell me you didn't give them your real name."

"I told them I was Gareth from Cirnos," said Kayle blandly. "Small village on the border between Halimgor and Dunte."

Rilt tried to rein in his amusement, but he burst out laughing. His mirth set Kayle off too. Rilt laughed so hard he gave himself a cramp in his side, while Kayle ended up leaning on a nearby whitesong, rubbing tears from his eyes.

"If Gareth—ha—if he gets any notes from those girls, he's going to be so confused," Kayle said, grinning with genuine cheer, eyes curved like the crescent moon. A lock of dark curly hair fell over his cheek, bouncing when he tossed his head. "He'll know… he's going to know it's me … it's worth any prank he puts me through though, if I can see his face if they come looking for me … him …" He gave up on words and dissolved into guffaws again.

Watching Kayle, Rilt felt his heart skip into his throat. He wished Kayle laughed like this more often, free and relaxed. Until now, he hadn't paid enough attention to his friend or noticed how often he seemed burdened. It was only apparent when the weight on Kayle's slender shoulders was lifted momentarily. He smiled and stuck his hands in his pockets, saying, "Let's get back. We have those chapters to summarize for study group."

* * *

Oledan caught sight of the two of them from the opposite side of the court. "Hey, Rilt, you're going to love this! Come take a look!"

Bemused, Rilt and Kayle cut across the grassy court to a notice pinned up for first-year students. Across the top of the paper, in Terras' neat handwriting, were the words 'Practical Combat Training — Session Times and Partners'. The other students were checking the list below, so they couldn't see the details.

Coming over to the pair, Oledan prodded Rilt in the side. "Guess who your partner is."

"Not you, I hope."

"You'd be so lucky. No, you're paired with Krell."

"Gareth?" Rilt shouldered his way to the list and scanned the names. Indeed, his name was next to Gareth's. Kayle had been paired with Derone, whose broad, muscular physique belied a painful nervousness. The hulking youth literally flinched at even the mildest criticism. It was easy to see why the adepts had put friendly Kayle with Derone. He could be trusted not to tease Derone. Gareth, on the other hand, was certain to point out every mistake made by Rilt in the most obnoxious way possible. He squirmed out of the cluster and narrowed his eyes at Oledan, who was wearing a huge, smug grin.

Oledan shrugged. "You have the best luck, Rilt. Wolvam must have it in for you, eh?"

Kayle snorted. Rilt glared at him. "Traitor."

"I'm not frightened of you," said his roommate. "You'd never hurt me."

"As if anyone would ever hurt you," Oledan cut in, rolling his eyes. He perked up, his round face brightening. "Alright my friends, pleasure calls. Felas, Ladmos, and I are heading into the city for some left-handed fun."

"It's in the middle of the week," Kayle protested.

"All the more reason to unwind. Want to come along? There's time before curfew."

Kayle turned down the offer and strolled towards the dormitories. As they walked, Rilt could not resist his curiosity. "Left-handed fun?"

At that, his roommate stopped in his tracks and stared at Rilt, exceedingly amused. "You don't know what that means?"

Rilt frowned. "If I knew, I wouldn't have had to ask, would I?"

"They're visiting a brothel." Kayle giggled when Rilt turned pink with comprehension. "I mean, most of us have our fun right-handed, but…"

"Alright, enough, I get the picture."

Before Kayle could tease Rilt further, they saw Anya waiting outside Room Six. She tossed them a salute and handed a sealed letter to Rilt.

"I was explicitly ordered to hand this to you personally," she said, handing him a chit to sign.

"Thanks, Anya." Rilt smiled when he saw the seal. It was from Pellit.

"You know, for a lord, you're not as stuck-up as I'd expected," said the runner girl. She nodded at them both. "Ta, Lord Rilt."

* * *

Dear Lord Rilt,

As per your earlier instructions, I have made contact with those friendly to the Aralds. So far, no one has heard anything untoward. That new gang has seemingly dispersed; the locals say there has been no sight or sound of them ever since we began investigations. I may have roused the serpents when I stirred the grass, but their disappearance suggests that they are far too new to gain a proper foothold in Izdahl.

As for Master Midusel: Formerly known as Midusel Daller, the third son of the family. Entered Kaedin Hall in the tenth year of King Eldos. Made mastery in the seventeenth year of King Eldos. Became dean of Kaedin Hall in the third year of King Eram. Head of the Kaedin Council. Supports Duke Halden's proposals in the Privy Council most of the time, speaking out only twice: once against increased levies on textile merchants and once against the dissolution of the Kaedin Council.

Sir, I really don't think Master Midusel is one of the plotters. There is nothing he stands to gain from your death, and everything to gain for you to succeed. If you wish for more reassurance, Zarin and Jero will shadow you outside of the hall, as your escort.

Your loyal servant,
Pellit

Kayle put down the letter and raised his brows at Rilt. "I'm not fully convinced." He folded the letter and tucked it back between two pages of Rilt's red journal. Chewing thoughtfully on his lower lip, the scholar added, "Fine. Let's say your valet is right. I'm still worried that you are not more concerned."

"I don't need someone to be my personal guard, Kayle. I can protect myself."

"I'll keep that in mind the next time I rescue you from an assassin who's stabbing you with your own dagger." Kayle paused, and in a softer voice, asked, "Are you sure you'll be safe with Galena?"

"Look, we're only going for a stroll along the canal. I will have my house guards shadow us from afar, as Pellit proposed. The warden keep isn't that far and there are always wardens along that walk. I'll even let you walk me to the back gate. I will be safe, Kayle, rest assured."

His roommate rolled his eyes. "I will escort you there only because I'm supposed to meet Master Jodius for a tutoring session at the greenhouses around that time."

"For a royal scholar, you need a lot of tutoring."

"I'm learning more than what's in the syllabus. Master Jodius has had healer training, so I've asked him to teach me about medicinal plants."

Rilt frowned. "What's Master Jodius like? You hardly ever talk about him."

Kayle shrugged. "He's very thorough. Unlike you, I don't like to complain about my instructor after practically every lesson."

That was true, so Rilt could not return the goading. While the young Enthinian lord respected that Wolvam did know what he was teaching, he still felt that the adept was purposely picking on him. Wolvam would often have Rilt demonstrate new techniques, and often used his errors to instruct the others. Of course, Rilt was also among those Wolvam praised, even if praise came infrequently.

He flopped onto his bed. "You know, it'd be a lot easier if we had any clue what the plotters want from my demise."

"If they attack you during your date, maybe they'll tell you before they murder you." Kayle tossed a textbook onto his stomach. "Now get to work."

* * *

The following restday morning was spent largely in preparing for a test in Master Whitsam's class on Ethics, but Rilt remembered his date just in time to smarten up and shave. True to his word, Kayle waited until Rilt had fussed enough about his appearance and was ready to leave.

After Rilt bade Kayle goodbye at the gate leading to the greenhouses, he strolled to the meeting point where he was supposed to pick up Galena. She was dressed simply this time, her hair bound at the nape and her yellow dress fluttering in the faint breeze.

"Am I late again?" Rilt asked in dismay.

Galena smiled, flashing her dimples. "I'm early. Shall we go to Riverbank Park?"

"Lead on, fair maiden," Rilt said, gesturing with a courtly flourish.

She slipped her hand into his, laughing, and they ambled down the path. Lindene and oak trees lined the walk on the wall side. Narrow picker boats rafted down the canal, the pickers' broad-brimmed hats shielding them from the afternoon sun while they pulled flotsam from the water for sorting. Rilt glimpsed Zarin keeping well away from him and Galena, but drew no attention to the servant.

Galena and Rilt were not the only couple taking a stroll. Many other students from guild schools and the university were out and about as well. Rilt was more than eager to tell Galena about Cedaran's misadventure with a placenta while helping the shepherds in the high reaches of Westend.

"My father and younger brothers would never think about doing something as filthy as that," she chuckled. "Father likes wines, but we have entirely the wrong sort of land for vineyards. Didn't stop him from turning fifty hectares into a vineyard a few years ago."

"How was the wine?"

She grimaced. "Mother was the one with the bright idea to turn the wines to vinegar. Now it's in demand all across Dunte. Last year's blight really hurt the crop, so I don't know if it will produce as well this year."

They bought themselves sugared ices from a vendor and sat down on a stone bench to savor the cold desserts. Rilt said, "I can arrange something with our best vineyards. Maybe your viners can cross-breed something suitable for Dunte from our strains. Of course, whitesong doesn't grow well past the Sudahl, but our silfen grapes are very hardy in all types of soil."

"Oh, would you? That would be wonderful." Galena caught a syrupy drop with her tongue before it melted and dripped onto her dress. "My parents would be pleased. They've been distressed by the blight, I know, even if they try not to worry us. It's why Mother wants me married off."

Perplexed, Rilt tried to connect the blight to Galena's mother wanting her daughter to be wedded.

Galena rolled her eyes. "You're an Arald. Everyone's trying to marry into your house. There aren't that many houses who can claim an unbroken line all the way to the kingdom's founding, after all."

"Actually, the line of Arald began well before Aleis was founded."

"That's not my point." She shook her head and stood up with a sigh. "You have title, land, wealth, power. We Aedinals have our title, some land, not enough wealth, and certainly not much power. Take away the lands, and the wealth goes away even faster. I have to marry well to keep what we have now."

"That will also mean you don't have your title anymore, since you'd be out of the Aedinal house." he said. She rolled her eyes again and began strolling off. Rilt caught up to her. "What's wrong?"

"You just don't see, do you?" said Galena with a soft sigh. "Hear me, Rilt. You were born at the top of the heap. Where I am, being an Aedinal is just a step above being a commoner. A blighted crop may be a spate of bad luck for you, but it's catastrophe for us."

Rilt knew better than to raise the topic again. He could not fathom her casual dismissal of her house name, even if they were minor nobles. Much as Rilt resented his father, he recognized that the duke's beliefs and actions stemmed from a need to protect the house and their name. Even the Alcaronans and Awells, powerful as they were, could not match the history of the Aralds; only the Alwyths were anywhere near equals in their lineage and prestige. Giving up the Arald name was unthinkable.

Then again, she's a woman, thought Rilt. *Giving up her name is part of marriage.*

Riverbank Park was a circular space west of the palace grounds. There was a statue of the founding king of the Alcaronan dynasty at the entrance, kept scrupulously clean by the city. Galon Alcaronan and his greater ice hawk stood staring towards the west, his staff in his left hand angled in the same direction. Even though the statue was well cared for, vandals had still managed to carve graffiti into the base. Rilt saw a few crude words and some symbols that he supposed were gang signs. The freshest one was a square within a circle, with a small 'v' in the middle.

"That's new," said Galena, seeing what Rilt was observing. She pointed to another, a four-pointed star with red rubbed into it, and whispered, "That's the sign of the Crimson Compass, largest gang on the docks. I've heard that they've claimed the canals for themselves. All the picker boats are run by them, even if it's the city council who gives out licenses."

"Who tells you these things?" Rilt wondered with a grin, sliding his arm around her waist. She did not pull away, so he planted a kiss on her cheek. "You are full of surprises, Lady Galena."

She batted her lashes. "I have my sources. Also, musicians gossip a lot."

"You're a musician," he pointed out, laughing.

"Exactly." She winked at him.

At this hour, the park was still populated with young couples—all fairly wealthy, judging from their attire. Occasionally, some children would toddle by, with their nurses and house guards following. Rilt could see wardens walking around casually.

It was safe.

He had not realized how tense he had been until he was away from the hall, from remembered whispers of assassination, and from Kayle's stifling concern. Rilt finally felt his shoulders relax since the moment Kayle declared that Master Midusel was the man in the greenhouses.

They walked around the park, looking at more statues of kings and queens past and fountains decorated with dolphins and fantastically bizarre beasts. Squirrels feasted on lindene nuts and acorns, bounding back to the trees whenever someone approached them.

"Kayle looks like that when we have those tiny cheese rolls for breakfast," he said to Galena when a squirrel scampered past, its cheeks stuffed to bursting. He mimicked his friend's face, puffing out his cheeks.

Galena giggled and poked his left cheek with a finger. "I really should spend some time with Kayle."

"Why?" Inexplicably, Rilt found the idea unpalatable.

"Because he's important to you," said Galena, as if it were self-explanatory.

"He is. I've never had a friend like him before," said Rilt. "I mean, Ledon—he was a friend I made in Enthin—was nice but we didn't spend every day together, and I didn't know him like I know Kayle. Kayle is sweet and funny and, well, occasionally too much of a worry nit, but that's just him being concerned. I think … I think he's the best friend I've ever had."

For a long moment Galena just looked at Rilt. Then she smiled and caressed his cheek, tugging him down for a kiss. When they parted, she murmured, "You dense, lucky boy."

He wanted to ask her what she meant, but she kissed him again, more soundly, and the question slipped out of his mind.

* * *

Galena assured him that she was quite capable of walking back to her school by herself, so once they were back in the university compound, he jogged straight to the dormitories. Riverbank Park was pleasant, but there were not many places where they could be alone, and the arches that she promised him before were all occupied. He hoped Kayle had not got back to their room so he could have some time alone.

As he unlocked the door, he saw a freshly-scrubbed Kayle at the desk, gently touching the leaves of his potted bluespine. His slim hands shook and he clenched them into fists a few times, before scrubbing his face and rubbing the bridge of his nose. He was so preoccupied with his own thoughts that he hadn't noticed Rilt coming in.

Trying to hide his dismay, Rilt greeted his roommate. "Hello. How was your session with Master Jodius?"

"Enlightening," said Kayle quietly. He flashed a small smile at Rilt. "How was your date?"

"Good. We talked."

"I'm sure you did more than that," Kayle said, turning back to his plant. "You have her lip rouge on you."

Rilt blushed. "I'll take a shower."

"I'll make sure not to listen in," said his friend, but the tease fell flat. He touched his bluespine again, his jaw tense. Not wanting to break Kayle's focus, Rilt slunk into the shower and made sure he was very quiet.

SEA CHANGE

The whimpering woke Rilt from his sleep. The young man lay on his bed, blinking stupidly at the pattern of light and shadow on the wall. The dream he'd had earlier dissipated like mist under sunlight.

He could hear loud snoring from one of the seniors upstairs and the creak of the pipes in the walls, but he paid no heed to these usual noises. Then the whimpering came again, just behind him; it was Kayle. Rilt rolled up with a grunt, kicking off the blanket, and scrubbed a hand through his sleep-mussed hair.

Kayle was curled up like a fetus, every line of his body tense. His soft mewling made it sound as though he was in pain. Rilt shook his head clear of the remnants of sleep before he crossed the room, wincing at the icy floor, and shook his roommate's shoulder to wake him.

To his shock, Kayle flailed and jolted upright at Rilt's touch, nearly hitting him. His breathing was fast and erratic, his eyes wide and unseeing. Sweat beaded his face and even in the dim moonlight, Rilt could see that Kayle's nightshirt was soaked with sweat. When he reached out to feel Kayle's forehead for a fever, the scholar flinched and held up his arms, as though he was blocking a blow.

The sight sent a stab of sympathy through Rilt's heart. His friend had been there for him, and yet he knew so little of Kayle's worries.

"It's just me," he whispered. "Kayle, you're safe, you're alright. It's me, it's just Rilt." He had to say it a few times before his friend seemed to understand, slowly shaking off his fugue.

Kayle shivered and slowly unfolded his limbs. He swallowed and took a couple of deep breaths, his tongue darting out to lick his lips. Unsure of how to calm his friend, Rilt poured him a glass of water.

"I'm sorry," the scholar said. Wiping his brow and temples with the hem of his damp nightshirt, Kayle added, "Bad dream."

"I'll say." Rilt worried his lower lip. "What were you dreaming about?"

"It's nothing."

"Kayle, please." Taking the scholar's shoulder, Rilt squeezed lightly, the way Kayle had the night before. "Tell me."

It was a long time before Kayle could whisper, "My mother."

"You flinched. Just now, when I reached out for you." The young lord sat on Kayle's bed. Kayle's gaze was haunted and shadowed. "Why?"

Kayle glanced at him, and then his gaze flicked away to stare blankly at the shadows pooled in his blanket. When he spoke, it was with a tone of dull horror.

"I dreamed of my mother. Her death. She drowned."

Rilt's throat tightened. "I'm sorry."

"She didn't drown by accident. They … they shoved her. They shoved her into the tub, under the water, and I was there. I was there, Rilt, and they killed her in front of me. I tried to stop them. I tried and … and they laughed. They laughed and they kicked me aside while…" The words tumbled out breathlessly in disjointed phrases. "Too late. I tried, Rilt. I tried, and she was so cold and I tried, so hard…"

Kayle's voice cracked.

Filled with remorse for asking his friend to recount the memory, Rilt squeezed Kayle's hand to try to reassure him. The scholar's hand was cold and his skin clammy.

"You're safe now. You're here, and safe, and I am so sorry you had to go through that."

Apparently still unable to speak, the other young man nodded. Rilt forced aside the thought of embracing his friend, even though he ached to give Kayle comfort. He wasn't sure how Kayle would respond to that.

"You should change out of your nightshirt. You'll catch a chill." Rilt gently pulled his hand away and set the now-empty glass on the floor. He felt the rustle of Kayle's nightshirt as it was tossed past his head. When Rilt looked at Kayle again, he forgot what he was going to do.

The moonlight bathed the young Halim scholar, his pale skin nearly luminous in its pale glow. Kayle's hunched back offered Rilt a glimpse of his roommate's tattoo. Noticing Rilt's sudden silence, Kayle looked up. Wild curls framed a face both beautiful and sad.

His cheeks shone silver with undried tears. His lips, usually curved in a friendly smile, were now parted slightly, hesitant and wanting. His slender throat moved as he swallowed, and then one hand crept over to touch Rilt's fingers. The contact sparked a thrill down the young lord's spine, pooling hot in his gut, familiar and alien at the same time.

"Is this … unwelcome?" Kayle asked, the words barely more than a breath in the stillness of the night.

Rilt felt his mouth go dry. "N-no."

With his other hand, he swept his thumb over Kayle's cheeks, wiping away the tacky remnants of tears. A quiet, desperate fluttering began beating in his ribs, as though thousands of gauzewings were trapped within.

"I don't know what I'm doing," he confessed on an exhalation, and drew close to Kayle.

Their first kiss was shy, their lips barely brushing. A shiver danced through Rilt's body, his skin tingling in its wake. He could feel his heart thundering in his chest, and the delicious warmth of Kayle's breath. Kayle's lashes tickled his eyelids. They parted, barely more than an inch.

Kayle's eyes were closed. "Rilt, I…"

Without waiting for his friend to complete his sentence, Rilt kissed Kayle again.

He had kissed many girls before, but he felt like a complete novice as their mouths met once again, and was welcomed with Kayle's parted lips—soft, ripe, and warm, tasting faintly of salt. It was a heady rush, like fine wine from Eastwyn. Kayle's chin and cheeks were slightly raspy—they both needed to shave—and this reminder of their masculinity made Rilt's pulse beat a little faster. He grasped Kayle's forearm and tangled his other hand into Kayle's silky hair.

The kiss deepened into something heated, urgent. Rilt felt hot under his clothes and groaned as Kayle's teeth grazed his tongue. They separated for the unbearable few seconds to yank off Rilt's nightshirt, and then they were pressed together again, skin to skin, Rilt's hands sliding up Kayle's spine and over his shoulders. The slim scholar shuddered and moaned, low and soft, muffling it against Rilt's neck too late.

Rilt nipped Kayle's lip. "We have to be quiet," he warned with a teasing smile.

"Yes," Kayle breathed, ducking his brow against Rilt's cheek. "I know. But I've wanted this since I met you. By Creation, Rilt, you have no idea how hard it's been…"

"I can feel how hard it is," Rilt joked feebly. His heart hammered wildly against his ribs. Kayle huffed with amusement and squirmed against him.

It was a starkly unusual experience to map out a body so similar to his. Lightning danced under Rilt's skin, along his veins; it felt like quicksilver was curled taut beneath his gut. He pressed Kayle to the bed with little resistance. Skimming his hands over Kayle's pale, flat chest, he marveled at his own eager response. He loved girls: he loved the ample curves of their supple breasts; their sweet floral perfumes blending with the musk of desire; their long hair that feathered over skin and pillows in silky strands; their yielding heat. Kayle shifted under him, spreading his legs to fit Rilt between them. Rilt felt his pulse speed up in reaction. He pressed his nose to the juncture of Kayle's neck and shoulder and inhaled: briny and faintly sweet at the same time. When he sat up, he studied the slender form beneath him. Kayle was flushed from cheeks to chest, and he kept licking his lips. He was beautiful. Rilt had never applied that adjective to a man before, but there was no denying it. His palms skated up Kayle's waist, over his stomach, and then played over a flat chest. The first rub of his thumb over a nipple was accidental, but Kayle's surprised, half-stifled giggle encouraged Rilt to do it again. And again, until Kayle, panting, took hold of his wrists to stop him.

Kayle bit his lower lip and then covered his mouth with the back of his hand, as though suddenly bashful from Rilt's scrutiny. "Am I… You don't have to. I mean, I know I'm not a woman…"

"I want to," Rilt whispered, interrupting Kayle. He bore down, trying not to think about how odd it felt to have someone else's arousal pressed close to his own, focusing instead on the way Kayle wrapped his legs about him. Instinctively rocking his hips forward to seek that familiar, welcoming heat, Rilt was surprised at how good it felt, rubbing himself against Kayle's hardness. From the wide-eyed look on Kayle's face and the flush that darkened further, his roommate felt the same delightful frisson rushing through his slender body.

Rilt lowered his head to trail kisses along Kayle's jaw and under his chin. The salt of Kayle's tears was layered over the faint salt-sweetness of skin; Rilt wanted to taste all of it. As his mouth quested down the delicate jaw, Kayle rolled his head back against his pillow, his neck bared for Rilt to nuzzle and lick, while covering his mouth to muffle his soft, purring sounds of urgent need.

"Shh, hush," Rilt murmured, shifting up again, mouthing at Kayle's earlobe. "Do you want me to stop?"

"No, please, by the creators…" Kayle grabbed Rilt by his hair and kissed him on the lips again, "Don't stop. Unless you want to."

"I've never … I've only ever bedded girls," Rilt admitted in a harsh whisper, sliding his hands through Kayle's dark, sweat-damp curls. He was aching for more. "I want to, I've never wanted so much. I just don't know how…"

"Let me." Kayle sucked on Rilt's lower lip, lightly scraping his teeth over it. With a firm push, he rolled the young lord onto his back, but thanks to how narrow the bed was, Rilt collided against the wall. They both froze. For a few heavy breaths they waited, but there was nothing from Room Five. With a sigh of relief, they grinned sheepishly and then kissed each other. Kayle rubbed his cool hands over the noble's clothed thighs, his touch leaving tingles in their wake. The fabric stuck uncomfortably to Rilt's erection where it was damp.

Shifting away from the wall, Rilt propped himself up on his elbows, his throat tight with anticipation. If he'd previously thought his friend beautiful, he was spellbound now. Kayle's dark curls were a wild, shadowy halo. His nipples were hard, and Rilt could not resist leaning up to rub his thumbs over them. The touch made Kayle whimper quietly, catching his upper lip between his teeth in an increasingly futile effort to keep his voice down. He arched his back and rolled his hips in an undulating wave, trying to seek relief. Rilt shuddered with pleasure at the movement, and leaned in to kiss Kayle, sucking on his lower lip and worrying it with his teeth, just to hear the scholar's soft and desperate gasps. His hand now lingered on the small of Kayle's back and ventured down daringly over smooth, plump flesh.

With a sharp exhalation, Kayle gently pulled away. Sliding down the bed, he wasted no time tugging Rilt's sleep pants down to his knees. The cool air briefly sobered Rilt from his aching need, but the shock was short lived. With one more glance up at the young lord,

Kayle bent his head down and took Rilt into his mouth.

Rilt bit the inside of his cheek so hard he tasted blood. His elbows gave way. Covering his mouth with both hands, he focused on breathing steadily through his nose as Kayle licked and sucked eagerly. He wanted to thrust himself into that delicious mouth, but Kayle pinned him down with firm, smooth hands, fingers digging into his hips. All Rilt could do was ride the sensations, eyes squeezed shut as heat coiled tighter within him, and suddenly, it felt like blood was rushing inward from his limbs. He bit his knuckle as he crested past his climax. With the taste of copper in his mouth, Rilt trembled and shuddered as Kayle kept his mouth on him, tongue and throat still working, until the Enthinian protested with a vague murmur.

Afterwards, Kayle pressed a shy kiss to the corner of Rilt's mouth. "Was that good?"

Struggling to catch his breath, Rilt could do nothing more than nod. A lassitude melted into his limbs and he could barely lift them. Kayle looked smug at having reduced his friend to this state, and rested his head on Rilt's shoulder.

"It was fantastic," Rilt murmured after his heart had slowed its mad racing. He combed his fingers through Kayle's curly hair, trying to ignore a dark suspicion in the back of his mind. He kissed Kayle on his forehead and asked, "Do you want me to, um … I've never done it, but I can try…"

"It's alright," whispered the other student. He kicked off his own pants and slid a leg between Rilt's. "Just… May I?"

Rilt nodded, his arms circling around his friend. He tried to relax his face, revealing nothing of the relief and disappointment that battled within him, black and venomous. Burrowing his face against Rilt's neck, Kayle began riding the young lord's thigh, rubbing himself slickly over Rilt's leg. The sensation was bizarrely tantalizing. After a few minutes, Kayle muffled a long, breathy groan against Rilt's neck. His movement stuttered as he whimpered, his body going rigid, and then a wet warmth spread between them.

The two held each other for a long while. Rilt willed his heart to calm down.

"How in Creation," whispered Kayle, after he had got his breathing under control, "are we going to clean up without Gareth and Naelen hearing us?"

For some reason, that sounded funnier than it really was; Rilt shook with silent laughter, infecting Kayle with his mirth. After they had regained their composure, Rilt gently nudged Kayle off him and went into the bathroom with his towel. When he returned, Kayle had climbed off the bed and was frowning at their strewn clothing.

After Kayle had cleaned away the mess on his lower belly, Rilt swiped halfheartedly at the stickiness on his hip and thigh. Kayle turned to look at him, suddenly bashful and timid. "What happened just now…"

"You've done this before," Rilt blurted the first thing on his mind and then bit the tip of his tongue. He hadn't meant to say it. Not like that.

Kayle's smile disappeared. His fingers clenched on the rumpled sheets. The silence between them felt interminable until he nodded, looking terse and ashamed. He took a deep breath and then looked at Rilt. "Yes. I'm bent."

Rilt inhaled sharply. The tug in his chest felt like a hook ripping through flesh. "I'm not." All of Enthinas had thought he was, simply because he had developed a close friendship with Ledon, and by the time the visiting healer had left Enthinas, the damage to his reputation had been done. He could not care less about the opinions of the Enthinians, but Cedaran had had to bear the brunt of malicious gossip among the nobles. If this got out, what would Cedaran think?

Hurt, anger, and then cold resignation rippled across Kayle's face. He tugged on a nightshirt and his pants, and then lay down on his own bed, facing the wall.

"Kayle," Rilt began, not knowing how to continue. He didn't even know what he'd really meant to say.

"Good night," Kayle said, and threw the covers over his head.

* * *

The following day was an uncomfortable dance of avoidance. In their dormitory, Rilt and Kayle navigated around each other as though contact was deadly. Rilt felt guilty, but he wasn't sure what he was guilty about. In the end, he fled to the library, spending what remained of his Seventhday reading about wars and dynastic politicking. The only other person in the library besides the librarian was Naelen, who shot him an incredulous look and left him alone.

If he retained anything of what he had read, Rilt wasn't aware of it. Words buzzed and faded from his mind. The one constant thought was the memory of how he had ended the night before with Kayle. It had been so good, and then it had just gone … wrong. Horribly wrong.

Rilt had never suspected that Kayle was bent, or the extent of his affections. After all, the scholar had gone out on a double date with him, Galena and that girl—what was her name?—and he'd seemed to enjoy himself. True, Kayle often leaned against him when they sat together during their evening study sessions, but he was equally physical with Gareth and sometimes others, slapping them on their backs, draping an arm around their shoulders, or playfully elbowing them.

Rilt chewed on the inside of his lower lip. What about himself? He liked women, liked their curves and sweet-smelling hair, their soft, high voices, but when he kissed Kayle … Rilt's felt his neck grow warm at the memory. He'd kissed many girls and enjoyed those kisses, but kissing Kayle was different. Better. Thrilling. Time had slowed, the world had fallen away; it was just Kayle and him, on the bed, in that moment. It had been calm and perfect and beautiful.

And when Kayle had put his mouth on Rilt so eagerly … Rilt swallowed and shifted in his seat. The act itself was not new for Rilt, but the passion and eager skillfulness which Kayle displayed made it an astoundingly sublime experience.

Then Rilt had said what he said, even though that wasn't what he'd meant.

The sky outside was dull and overcast, the heavy-bellied clouds threatening rain; when Rilt stared blankly from the tall windows, all he could focus on was the bleak shadowy form of the lake and the front courtyard. A few second-year students were hurriedly alighting from cabs, while two masters walked along the bank, their kae staffs sparking and flaring with bright purple light as they gesticulated. Ahead of them, porters pushed a cart with a bulky item covered with a tarp. Idly, Rilt wondered what it covered.

"Hello. It's rare to see you here," said a girl, dropping into the chair next to him. "Usually it's Naelen or Kayle."

Startled, Rilt swiveled around in his seat. He was surprised to see that it was Anya, the runner. Vaguely annoyed by her intrusion, he retorted, "Why are you here?"

"Well, aren't we all high-and-mighty, Mister Lord Rilt Arald of Enthin?" The runner did not seem offended. "Anyway, I came to deliver a package to the librarian and I have to wait for his reply. What are you doing here on a Seventhday all by your lonesome?"

Rilt flushed. "Reading."

"I'd have thought you'd be out with that singer from 4304."

"What-" Rilt caught himself. Anya did deliver his messages to Galena. He rubbed the tip of his nose. "Not today."

Slinging her feet to rest on the chair opposite, Anya tilted her head and squinted at him. "Did you two fight?"

"We…" Rilt shut his book and took a deep breath. "That's none of your business, Anya."

"That'd be Miss Anya to you if you gon' talk to me like that."

"My apologies, Miss Anya."

"Accepted," she went on blithely and crossed her arms behind her head. "You did something wrong, didn't ya?"

"Who said I was in the wrong?"

"Given what you said to me just now," said Anya, "I'd hazard a guess that you said something you shouldn't of and she took offense. Not every woman's as magnanimous as I am, Lord Rilt. So, if you're feeling bad about it, you should say sorry, whether you're in the wrong or not."

A flash of lightning lit up the inside of the library. Thunder rumbled, as though to underscore the runner's advice. Rilt shifted in his seat. He seldom paid attention to the runners in Enthin, but he understood their reach. They had eyes and ears everywhere, and who was to say what they heard stayed unspoken?

"I did say something rather … rather stupid. I'm not sure how to go about broaching the topic."

Anya narrowed her eyes. "Are you asking me for advice?"

Rilt swallowed his pride. "Yes."

"A lowly runner?"

"Yes." He smiled as winningly as he could. "Please."

"Apologies are good. Apologize. Grovel, if necessary. Say that you didn't mean what you said. Though, if you did mean what you said, then maybe you should've said it differently, aye?" Anya smiled, revealing crooked incisors, and added, "You'd best do it soon, else what's bad'll get worse."

Rilt let the words sink in, and mutely nodded his thanks when she was called away by the librarian. Soon, fat raindrops began to splatter on the windows. Rilt watched the rain fall on the lake, sheet after sheet marching white over its black surface.

Someone tapped him on the shoulder and shook him out of his reverie. It was Naelen, peering down at him with a frown. "You seem troubled," said the Enthinian.

"I am." Rilt exhaled heavily and gestured to the seat facing him. He should not dwell any longer; it was unhealthy. All he had to do was apologize. He could do that. He would do that. He just didn't know what to say, exactly. Determined not to feel sorry for himself, Rilt nodded at Naelen. "Did you have plans for today?"

"Studying in the library," replied Naelen with a faint smile.

"Are you always in the library on restdays?" Rilt asked.

The rain made him think about rainy days in Enthin, when he and Ced, in their childhood, would run to their playroom and dig out toys to stage battles. He remembered the first time he consciously chose to lose to his baby brother, and how delighted Cedaran had been. Rilt really missed him.

Naelen shrugged. "I take a longer time to read than most people, and quiet places help me focus better. Kayle sometimes helps me with the denser text."

It was just like Kayle to help Naelen without telling anyone about it. Rilt reflected on his behavior again and was awash in shame. Master Baelmin would have chided him for his tactlessness were he alive to know about it.

"Could you show me where the section on the Warring Years is?" he asked, struck by a sudden thought. Master Baelmin had set him a task, after all. He wasn't ready to face Kayle yet, but that didn't mean he couldn't get something else done.

"Why? The Warring Years period isn't in the syllabus."

"Master Baelmin specialized in those years," Rilt said. "I think he'd be pleased if I continued my studies in that era."

Naelen nodded, recognizing the tutor's name, and then led the way to the stacks in the far corner, away from the tall windows. "These out here are recent books. The older ones are in the protected collection—they're just too fragile to be out where sunlight can damage them."

Rilt perused the shelves. Most of the books were written in the recent decades. He even spotted one by Master Baelmin, and a lump came into his throat as he ran a finger over the spine of that book. He had not read it before—Master Baelmin had brought some of his later writings with him when he began his employment under Halden, but his earlier works remained in the university. Setting Baelmin's book aside, Rilt browsed until he found a likely candidate.

"*Before Coleri: The Kaedine Struggles of the Warring Years*," Rilt read aloud. "Perfect." Then he scanned through the contents page and deflated. "Lack of uniform training, kaedin-to-kaedin conflict, poor understanding of resonance…"

Naelen leaned against the stack. He studied Rilt carefully. "What are you really looking for?"

The young lord hesitated. How far could he trust Naelen Barith? "Master Baelmin had confided in me something that needs verification," Rilt said at last. "If there is any truth to what he told me, it'd be in the records from the Warring Years."

The other novice frowned lightly. "In that case, you should ask the head librarian for access to the protected collection."

"What if I need to keep this secret?"

Naelen's frown deepened. Suspicion grew in his green eyes. "Why?"

How much to share? "Look, it's something that bothered him while he was alive. Master Baelmin thought that … he thought that this secret got him dismissed from the university. If I can prove that he was right, then he'll be vindicated. If I cannot, at least I can't hurt his name any further. I just need to know. Perhaps you could … retrieve the books for me. Without letting the head librarian know."

"You mean steal the books."

"Naelen, please. You and the librarians are on good terms. You can get in there easily."

"No, Rilt. You're suggesting that I help you steal. I cannot condone that." Naelen took the book out of Rilt's hands and put it back on the shelf. "If it is so pressing, you can ask the librarians to help. And you know better, Lord Rilt."

He walked away, leaving Rilt alone to seethe. He could hardly blame Naelen; the latter did not know Master Baelmin, and Rilt was reluctant to share the notion of there being kaedin with fire resonance. *Deyre breith wer flaume yn fir...*

He walked out from the stacks and spied Anya still waiting inside the librarian's office, two rows of keys behind her. Inspiration struck him. He quickly rounded the counter and rapped on the door, catching Anya's attention.

"Hey, Anya, glad you're still around. I've a question," said Rilt. He kept his expression casual, though his heart began pounding hard in his chest. He would have to move fast.

Anya brightened. "Come on in. The librarian's forgotten what he was supposed to send. Can't believe he's kept me waiting this long."

Racking his brain for a question, he strolled in and perched on the edge of the table facing Anya. He remembered what she had advised earlier and said, stumbling over his words, "I don't know what—how else to make it up to Galena. What do you think she'd like?"

Anya smirked. "A lord not knowing how to win a lady's forgiveness? How rare." She then went on to deliberate the meaning of various gifts and how Rilt could present them. While she prattled on, Rilt scanned the keys while half-listening. They were usefully marked with letters, and he caught sight of one marked 'HLO'.

"Yes, I agree," he said when she paused. "Flowers are a great idea. Rosales, you said?"

"Yep! Yellow ones. Those mean forgiveness, after all."

Rilt smiled at her. "I should go write a letter of apology to go with the flowers. Thanks, Anya, I'd never have thought of this without your help." He went over to give her a brief hug and, very quickly, swiped the key marked 'HLO'. His heart thundered when he realized that Anya had not noticed. "Think you can help me out by ordering a bouquet? I'll have the letter ready tomorrow evening, so you can send the message and flowers over together."

"Sure thing, Lord Rilt." Anya grinned, and flicked him a neat salute. "Oh, and next time, ask a girl before you hug her. I coulda kneed you in the jools."

* * *

When he went to dinner, Kayle was already sharing a table with Ladmos, Cammod, and Felas. They were talking and laughing, although Rilt noticed that Kayle was paler than usual. The scholar glanced at his roommate when he came in, but turned away quickly when Rilt took a step closer. The message was very clear. Gareth was nowhere to be seen, and Naelen was only just getting his own tray. Grabbing his own share, Rilt sat alone and finished his meal in hasty gobbles, hardly noticing the taste of the carochik, and rushed back to the dormitory.

"I'm sorry for what I said, I'm sorry for what I said, I'm sorry for what I said," he repeated as he paced the room. Fireplace, bathroom door, chest of drawers, bed, desk, and back. During his fourth circuit, Kayle returned.

Rilt froze. He raised an open palm, and then lowered it when he realized how awkward it looked. "Hey."

"Hi," said Kayle, his tone carefully casual. He tugged off his belt and shucked off his tunic, studiously avoiding eye contact. "You went out today? I didn't see you around."

"I … I was in the library."

"That's rare. Found anything interesting?"

"No. Not really. Just, uh, Naelen and Anya." Rilt's heart pounded with nervousness. "I—I've to … I'm sorry. For what I said. About. For what I said last night."

Kayle raised his eyebrows. "Why do you need to apologize?" He exhaled heavily through his nose and smiled, brittle and understanding. "I was upset, you came over to comfort me, things got out of hand."

"I didn't mean-" Rilt stammered. What did he mean? "Kayle, last night was—last night was unexpected. It was special."

"Sure. But it's not something you want." The dark-haired student shrugged. "I'm bent, you're not. I understand. You were very kind last night, Rilt. I only ask that you don't let others know, please. Only Gareth is aware and … I don't know how the hall will respond should the dean find out. And the other students … Not everyone accepts people like me. I want to stay on. I can't risk my scholarship."

Before Rilt could gather his words again, Kayle went into the bathroom and locked the door. The noble stared at where Kayle had been standing, and wondered why he felt as though he had just killed something innocent.

Dear Master Baelmin,

I know. You're dead, and I am writing to no one. But you've always given me good advice. Maybe something you've said before will come back to me, through my letter to you.

I've made a mess of things with Kayle. He's the best friend I've ever had and I slept with him. It wouldn't have been so bad, except I said that it wasn't his first time doing this, which of course he took offence to, and then I added wood to the fire by insisting I'm not bent— I am not, but he is—and now he thinks I slept with him out of pity. I apologized and he apologized too, but I don't know if we can remain friends. I don't know if I've ruined the best thing I have here in Kaedin Hall. And he's being nice about my stupid blabbering mouth, by Creation, and I'd be mad about it except I feel really guilty.

I'm sorry, I know I'm not making sense. I don't understand. I'm happy with Galena. I should be content with Galena. She's friendly, smart, and warm, and I feel good when I'm with her. I can talk about nearly anything with her.

But with Kayle, it's different. I want him to be happy. I want his full attention as often as possible. He makes my heart race. I can listen to him all day and when I'm with him, I'm not the future duke of Enthin. I'm not from the house of Arald. I'm just Rilt, his friend. I want him as a friend and now I want him in my bed too.

Maybe I am bent.

But I can't be, if I want to be with Galena too, right? Sorry, I would never have said that to you if you were here, but you're not. I suppose that should be fine.

I'm really afraid Ced will find out. He was harassed over Ledon when there was nothing between me and Ledon at all. What if someone found out about Kayle? Ced would be ashamed. I don't want him ashamed of me, ever.

I wish you were here and you could smack some sense into my head, the way you used to with that wooden rule of yours. I don't know what to do. He's now at his bed and deliberately not looking at what I'm doing, when a couple of nights ago, he'd have come over and peered over my shoulder. I miss the easy closeness we had, and I want it back, but if I speak now I just know I'm going to mess it up even further.

Perhaps I'll wake up with an idea. I hope I do. Sleep on my troubles, like you used to say, and maybe something will untangle the knot I've found myself stuck in. It will look better at sunrise. I hope.

Your stupid, stupid student,
Rilt.

SPARK

Even without the thought of what he was going to do that night, Rilt would not have nodded off. As it was, he waited until he was certain Kayle had fallen asleep. He crept from his bed and dug the key from his pocket. His heart was racing. He had never stolen anything in his life; he could hardly believe he'd gotten away with swiping the key from the office in the first place. Now that the theft was done, he had to see it through. With a deep breath, he tiptoed to the door, his palms sweating as he unlocked it. He nearly yelped in shock when he opened the door to find Naelen already standing there, waiting.

"I know you wouldn't take my advice," said Naelen. "You filched the key, didn't you? The librarian thought the head librarian took it with him."

"Naelen, I just need to take a look."

"No, Rilt. Give it to me."

Desperate, Rilt said, "Come with me. I won't damage or remove anything." He swallowed his pride and added, "Please, Naelen. He was my tutor—the only way I can possibly repay him is to prove that he was right, and he was wrongfully dismissed from his post. I am begging you, let me do this for him."

Naelen hesitated, then dropped his outstretched hand. "Come on. The porters will be on patrol, though. We should go up by the library's back door."

"You know a lot about the library."

"I do spend nearly all my free time there, Lord Rilt, in case you hadn't noticed."

Rilt snorted. "You're spending too much time with Gareth, Naelen. You've picked up his sharp tongue."

"And you haven't spent as much time with Kayle as usual today. Did something happen?"

Rilt had to bite back his retort. It was none of Naelen's business what happened between him and Kayle. His silence was answer enough for Naelen.

"Whatever happened, you should not be risking yourself," Naelen chided. "What if you were caught?"

What if he was caught? Rilt hadn't considered the consequences. He was a lord, when all was said and done, and the hall would not humiliate him by making his crime known. Duke Halden would certainly seize upon the chance to drag Rilt home and keep him in Enthin forever. The thought sobered him a little. He didn't want to spend his life sighing over how small his world was.

However, he knew he should at least try to find out the truth for Master Baelmin. The old man had not asked for much when he was alive, just a small room with space for his books and plenty of rosales tea. In return for those few courtesies, he had opened Rilt's mind to possibilities of seeing the kingdom. The sheer joy in Master Baelmin's face when Rilt asked for his aid to prepare for the aptitude tests, the gleeful satisfaction on both their parts when Rilt took the examination in disguise, the pride he would have felt knowing that Rilt was here, in Kaedin Hall…

No, he owed Master Baelmin validation.

"I'll just have to make sure I'm not caught, then," Rilt replied, with a cockiness he did not feel. Naelen sighed and led the way around to the back of the teaching block.

Some of the rooms in the upper levels were still lit, and occasionally a snatch of conversation would drift out into the night. Rilt made sure to move with catlike stealth, fearful that someone would poke their head out a window and spot them.

They had to go up a flight of steps and take two turns down a long hallway to get to the back door of the library. It was completely dark, so the two had to fumble for the stair banister and keep a hand on the wall. In the walls, the pipes groaned and creaked. Every little sound made Rilt's skin prickle, and the back of his neck tingled with nerves.

Just as they got to the back door, they heard the thumps of heavy boots climbing the stairs and a moment later, a pool of light washed up the far end of the hallway, casting strange shadows on the wall. Rilt and Naelen both froze. One more turn, and whoever was coming this way would see them.

There was nowhere to hide: this used to be a servants' hallway, before it was used as a teaching hall, so there were no convenient alcoves or arches for two young men to duck into. Nor were there thick curtains to hide behind, since there were no windows on this side of the building. With their backs pressed to the wall, Rilt tried to come up with a solution. All he could hear was the rumbling pipes behind him.

"If I'm thrown out," Naelen hissed, "I swear to Creation I'll break your nose again."

An idea flashed into Rilt's mind. Ignoring Naelen's threat, he squeezed his eyes shut. Perhaps it was the panic distilling a sharp taste of metal into the back of his mouth that added a boost: Rilt attuned himself to the water in the pipes between one breath and the next.

Naelen stared at him. "What are you doing?"

"Shut up," Rilt gritted out. He thought of the water, felt the shape and joints of the pipes in the walls, and pushed all the volume he could gather to a weak point down the pipe.

A moment later, there was the unmistakable sound of water spraying out from a narrow aperture. Then came a solid round of cursing from the people holding the lantern.

Naelen turned to glare incredulously at Rilt, who put a finger to his lips.

"Scorch this," grumbled one of the men. "I'll go wake old Gambin up, you go look for a bucket or something."

"They really should rebuild this place," said the other. "Everything is falling apart. Did you remember the beam in the workshop, the one that was rotted all through? Fine lot of kaedine who don't even see what's going wrong in their own hall…"

The first one snorted a laugh but his response was not audible by then. Rilt tried to open the back door, but it was locked.

"Rilt, you damaged school property!" Naelen hissed.

"The pipes were going to leak already. I just gave them a reason to repair it."

"You are incorrigible."

Ignoring the other's nagging, the young lord fiddled with the lock and gave up. He had not realized that the library would lock its doors. Then he remembered that Naelen was metal-resonant.

"Naelen, come on, you should know how to unlock this," Rilt pleaded. "Just give the parts a little push."

The other student looked rebellious, as though he was about to stalk off, but he bent to the keyhole and cocked his head, one hand to the door's lock. Rilt chewed his lower lip, trying not to bounce on his heels. He kept listening for the return of the other men.

"Got it." The lock clicked and opened. Rilt and Naelen hurried in and shut the back door just as they heard boot heels coming down the other passage again. Once it was clear that they'd made it without being caught, relief flooded Rilt. He had to stuff a hand in his mouth before he could start giggling.

The blond sagged against the door and shook his head with a sigh. "What in Creation am I doing?"

"You're being an accomplice," Rilt whispered, a huge grin coloring his tone. "Fantastic job."

Even in the dark, Rilt was sure that Naelen's expression would have stripped paint. The two students got away from the back door, navigating the aisle between two of the stacks, and emerged into the main library.

The library in the dark appeared sinister instead of impressive. The feeble light outside the tall windows helped little. Rilt navigated by memory to the librarian's office, feeling slightly guilty about doing so. Naelen followed him like a disapproving shadow. The head librarian's office was in the back, and the key slid into the lock soundlessly. With his ears pricked for angry yells demanding what he was doing there, Rilt pushed open the door.

The roomy office had no windows. Once the door was shut, Rilt lit the lamp inside the office and turned to the shelves lining the walls. This was the protected collection. The shelves were glass-fronted. He peered into them, trying to infer what their contents might be from their titles.

"Aha, here we go," he muttered, seeing a pair of leather-bound tomes marked with the disused crest of the house of Aleis: the tusked lion. The cabinet was locked, but the head librarian had left the keys in his desk, and it only took Rilt two tries to find the right key.

"I don't feel comfortable about this," Naelen said, rubbing his left elbow. "All this sneaking about."

Rilt paid him no attention. The books he had selected were records from the first ten years of the Aleisan dynasty. He opened the first, skimming for references to flame or fire. No luck there; he moved on to the next, and then gave up both to try other books. By the seventh volume—an unassuming cloth-bound book titled *Battles of Northwyn: A Record*—he had found something. His finger danced down the page as he read.

"What does it say… 'We founde a town sorowful yn discoraged… it had of men many hundreth, al wer deiy sore yhurt from flaume-bre-ithe… the men wythoute call insultes on the town, that the men be as wymmen yn the chillen be as swayne… Our General Keyron Arralde shall marche us alle in the morning to cerche abouten ther troth of deiyr fir, yn seek to douse deyr breiths yn lifes'." Rilt covered his mouth.

Naelen had been listening. "What does that mean?"

Too caught up with his thoughts about Master Baelmin's final let-ter to be discreet, Rilt translated aloud: "We found a town sorrowful and discouraged. Men in the hundreds were hurt from flame-breath. The men without—I guess that meant outside of the town—called insults on the town, calling the men women and the children swine. Our General Keyron Arald shall march us all in the morning to seek out the truth of their fire, and try to douse their fires and end their lives."

There it was, in written text: evidence that once there were men who breathed fire, and that kaedine of Coleri Aleis' day had fought them. Rilt felt numb. His tutor had found evidence of this, and had then been dismissed from his post. Did the masters know about fire-resonant kaedine? How many knew?

What did they do with the knowledge? And how were the Aralds involved?

Naelen took the book from his unresisting hands and turned the pages carefully, making sure not to tear the fragile paper. Then he paused on another page. "Rilt, look at this."

"I didn't know you read the old tongue."

"I don't," said Naelen. He thrust the book at Rilt. It was open, displaying two pages with illustrations. Random pencil sketch-es peppered the margins of the page. Black earth and a pale sky, with skeletal frames of buildings in silhouette. Small illustrations of things that did not look disturbing in themselves, but chilled Rilt to the core: a box that looked melted, half a shoe, the remnants of a building. One corner showed the remains of a doll clutched in a small, blackened hand, drawn exquisitely, as if that was all the artist could bear to focus on. A third of a doll, and a tiny hand burned to blackened bone.

Rilt stared wordlessly at the drawings then shut the book. "We have to go."

Once they had all the books back where they were supposed to be, Naelen helped him lock the cabinet and return the keys to their original places.

They sneaked back out of the library, careful to peek out from the back door to see if there was anyone in the hallway. There was some light, but it was on the far side, and from what Rilt and Naelen could hear, they were discussing how to best repair the leaking pipes throughout the building. The two did not speak as they exited, Naelen giving the lock a soft tap that presumably locked the door once more.

Once they were safely back inside Naelen's dormitory, Naelen whispered over the snores of a sleeping Gareth, "First, that was too close for comfort. No more night jaunts, Rilt. Second, whatever was in that book about… about whatever it was, you shouldn't tell other people." Seeing Rilt's dubious expression, the blond hissed, "I'm serious, Arald. You best be careful with the knowledge. Your Master Baelmin was fired for it."

"Fine. No more outings, I promise," Rilt said. Then he added hesitantly, "Thank you. For helping me."

"You're welcome. You are also going to tell me everything tomorrow."

Rilt chewed on his lower lip. "I don't know if I should."

"Rilt. What we found earlier … None of the history books I've read has mentioned even the slightest hint of it. Why would anyone hide the existence of such … atrocities?" Naelen exhaled and added in a low voice, "And the illustrations … What in Creation could've led to such destruction?"

"You said it's best not to tell other people."

"I've already seen the pages. Since you've involved me, I'm definitely helping you to dig out answers."

Rilt shook his head. "I've more questions than ever, and I don't think I like where those answers will lead us."

They both heard the rustle of blankets as Gareth sat up groggily. His hair stuck out at weird angles. "Lordling? What in Creation are you doing here in my room?"

Rilt flicked a quick glance at Naelen, then said, "I needed a word with Naelen. I didn't mean to wake you from your beauty sleep."

"Eat weed, lordling," said Gareth without any heat, flopping back down in bed. "Talk tomorrow. Your chatter is too scorching loud."

Rilt resisted the urge to snarl a retort. With another nod of thanks at Naelen, he slipped back into his own room. To his surprise, Kayle was sitting in one of the chairs by their little fireplace, nursing a steaming mug.

"Where did you go?" Kayle asked.

Trying not to sound flustered, Rilt answered, "I needed to clear my head. Think about some things."

The scholar narrowed his eyes and then returned to sipping his drink. "Hope the walk helped."

"It clarified some matters for me, yes."

"Good for you." Kayle stood up abruptly and pushed past Rilt to enter the bathroom. He shut the door a little too firmly.

Rilt clenched and relaxed his fists. He had to mull over what he saw, and he also had to decide what to do about him and Kayle. There was too much to sort through. He kicked off his shoes and shucked off his shirt, opting to attempt grabbing as much rest as he could.

When the bathroom door opened, he pretended to be asleep.

* * *

The next day, Rilt tried to act normally, although he was second-guessing himself at every juncture. It didn't help that he was exhausted from lack of sleep. His inattention was called out a few times in class, but Rilt couldn't focus at all during the lessons. His mind flitted between the things he learned in the library the night before and the tension between him and Kayle.

If Kayle felt differently about Rilt, he showed no outward sign of it when they were among their friends. He still laughed and joked, still sat with Rilt during their common lectures, still shared a table at mealtimes. The only difference was that he kept his hands to himself. Rilt marveled at how well Kayle was acting. He himself was having difficulty maintaining a facade of normalcy.

The last lesson of the day was their first hand-to-hand combat session. They were practicing basic holds and throws. Wolvam and Terras had demonstrated the moves, and now the small group of first-year students were spread out in assigned pairs around the gymnasium. Rilt stepped onto the thin, firm mat, readying himself for the first practice, though his head was groggy from sleep. His partner was Gareth, who was radiating anger.

On Wolvam's whistle to begin, Gareth stepped close to Rilt and hissed, "You filthy rat, how dare you hurt Kayle?"

"What?" Rilt blinked, and then comprehended. Embarrassed anger unfurled in his chest. "He told you?"

"Yes, he told me," Gareth confirmed in a low, even tone. His eyes flashed with icy fury. "How dare you?"

"I didn't mean to," said Rilt, the phrase sounding weak even to himself. He squared his shoulders and tried again. "It was a mistake. I already apologized to him."

Wolvam shouted for them to get into position.

Gareth strode forward and grabbed Rilt by his wrist and shoulder, his bony fingers digging painfully into Rilt's flesh. He muttered, "You took advantage of him, scumbucket. He was upset and you took advantage. Don't even think of denying it."

"I didn't-" His words were cut short as Gareth levered him over his back and shoulder, slamming him hard into the mat just before Wolvam whistled for them to begin, and kicked him in the side just below the ribs. The adepts were standing at the other end of the gymnasium, so Gareth's assault went unnoticed, except by their neighbors. However, when Gareth's mouth twitched in a smirk, the other students took it as a taunt between friends.

"Go easy, Krell," said Heldin, who usually avoided speaking to Gareth. "It's only practice."

"He's already been taught by his house guards," said Gareth. "I'm sure he can take it."

Rilt coughed and sat up. Kayle and Derone were four mats away, so his roommate was not a witness to this. Heldin and Doren were now watching them, so he could not retort as he wanted. With a quick grimace, he got to his feet and faced Gareth.

"I shouldn't have said what I did," he whispered, "but it's not your place to tell me off."

"Someone has to." Gareth's nostrils flared. His usually sallow complexion was ruddy, and his upper lip curled in a sneer. "He would never think of doing it himself."

It was Rilt's turn to grasp Gareth's wrist and try the same throw. On Wolvam's shrill whistle, he stepped forward and threw the scholar over his shoulder with bruising speed. Unnoticed by the adepts, he twisted his hold and Gareth gritted his teeth at the abrupt, sharp pain in his wrist.

When he was sure his point had been made, Rilt let go. "He should've told me, right from the start. I'd have known-" He wanted to say that he would have known to be warned against Kayle, to be wary of his roommate, but the words got stuck behind his teeth. The wrathful look in Gareth's eyes made something flare vicious and hot in Rilt's belly. On the pretext of helping the scholar to his feet, he snarled under his breath, "You're just upset he chose me instead of you."

Gareth pulled free and punched Rilt in his left eye, who instinctively retaliated with a well-placed kick to Gareth's knee. The scholar yelled in pain and then leaped at him, both of them punching and pummeling wildly, the rest of the class completely forgotten. The noble jabbed and kicked, feeling darkly pleased with every hit that connected, even though his left eye was swelling shut and he could taste blood in his mouth. Someone was shouting at them, but Rilt paid him no heed. Gareth needed to be taught a lesson. He wanted to punch Gareth's face until that young man was crying and pleading, to erase that perpetual air of superiority, to make him bleed.

The combatants were forced apart by their classmates, Rilt and Gareth still straining to kick each other. Rilt could see Heldin and Oledan dragging the scholar away; he had no idea who was holding him back.

Wolvam stepped into view and slapped him, hard and stinging. Without pausing, he strode over to Gareth and did the same. The ringing sound of the slaps silenced the two combatants. Rilt's chest was heaving, but the red haze of fury faded to a low buzz and his limbs felt chilled. His fingers and knees shook.

"I don't give a goat's arse about who started it," Wolvam growled, "but you are both confined to your rooms for the rest of the week immediately after lessons. No dinners. Who are your roommates?"

Rilt blinked. He ran the tip of his tongue over the inside surface of his teeth, tasting blood from one of his back teeth, and tried to ignore the anger surging through him. His left eye was swollen almost entirely shut and throbbed with pain.

Kayle stepped forward meekly. "Sir."

"You're rooming with Arald, right? You and Barith are not to bring your roommates any food, is that understood? Otherwise, I'll extend the punishment to two weeks, and it will include all four of you." Wolvam glared at the offending students. "Go back to your rooms this instant, both of you. Terras, walk them there, please."

"A whole week, Wolvam?" Terras asked as he came over.

"I spoke clearly enough."

"They need food," the stout adept reminded Wolvam. "They're still growing boys."

Wolvam's keen gaze stabbed at Rilt and Gareth. "They should have thought of that before they started brawling like drunk cutpurses. Go on, Terras. I can continue here. Norwan, you'll help me demonstrate."

With a sigh through his nose, Terras shooed Rilt and Gareth ahead of him. Their boots clicked on the stone tiles in counterpoint, but neither student looked at the other. Rilt's shoulders tensed with ire and he balled his fists so tightly his knuckles hurt.

How could Kayle tell Gareth about us? his thoughts growled. Betrayal tasted sour and bitter on his tongue. *How dare Gareth accuse me of taking advantage? What does he know?*

A tendril of doubt crept to the forefront of his mind, bringing with it an acrid taste at the back of Rilt's tongue. He darted a sidelong glance at Gareth and studied him, the angular, pallid face set hard as stone, the fire in his gaze earlier when Rilt mocked him… He bit the inside of his lower lip, wincing when a small cut opened up. An uneasy suspicion crawled down his spine and whispered in the spaces between his heartbeats, but with Terras present, he couldn't address his doubts. He could not demand a response from the scholar, not without revealing that Kayle was bent.

"Both of you should know better than to fight in front of your classmates," said Terras sternly. "You are supposed to set standards for your peers. Gareth, you're a royal scholar. Rilt, you're an Arald. It's disgraceful. What sort of leaders are you going to be if you can't control yourselves? If neither noble blood nor outstanding intelligence can rein in your tempers, what will it take?"

It was a short walk from the gymnasium to the dormitory block. Terras kept an eye on them as they went into their respective rooms.

"If you wish to fight, at least do so where you won't be caught," Terras chided. "What's so serious that you can't talk about it in a civil manner?"

"Nothing."

"Well, 'nothing' has got you barred from dinner for a week." The adept sighed as he watched the two glumly unlock their doors. "Do remember you can talk to me, boys."

Rilt shut the door and counted to twenty under his breath. Every count strengthened the assumption until it was a belief until it had to be fact; there was no other explanation. He eased the door ajar to see if the adept had gone. Once he was sure Terras was no longer around, he stormed into Room Five through the shared bathroom.

Gareth was in one of the armchairs, prodding tenderly at a bruising patch on his cheek. He flicked Rilt a cold look. "What do you want, lordling?"

"Are you in love with Kayle?" Rilt asked bluntly. His face felt hot, blood racing with anger and embarrassment. "Are you jealous? What has he told you?"

"What he told me is none of your scorching business," snapped Gareth. When Rilt bristled, Gareth's tone turned sly and mocking. "He's my best friend, has been for years. I've watched over him and cared for him, and you've just strolled into his life, share his room by sheer chance, and you think you have the right to question me? Lordling, you have no idea what Kayle and I have together. I've told you from the beginning."

Before Rilt was aware of what he was doing, he had dragged Gareth up from the chair and shoved him against the wall. Gripping the scholar's tunic by the collar, he hauled Gareth to the tip of his toes.

"Are you," he gritted out his question, "in love with Kayle Radieri?" The words burned like hot wax on his tongue.

Gareth bared his teeth, his thin fingers digging into Rilt's wrists. "Are you?" he mocked.

"Answer me!"

The scholar's response was to knee Rilt in the stomach. Wheezing from the surprise attack, Rilt dropped Gareth, who did not follow up on the retaliatory blow.

Gareth sniffed scornfully as Rilt got his breath back. "I warned you right at the start. He's my best friend, Arald. Use that puny little brain that supposedly exists in that thick head of yours." The scholar grabbed Rilt by his elbow and pushed him into the bathroom, slamming the door shut after him.

Despite his sore abdomen, Rilt wanted to keep going after Gareth until he got a direct answer, but he knew that if the adepts or a master heard of their scuffle, the two students would be in serious trouble. Halden would be more than pleased to pull Rilt from the hall. Gritting his teeth, he checked on his injuries in the bathroom. The bruise over his left eye was already starting to bloom pink-purple, and his lower lip was ripped. He gingerly nudged the torn bit with his tongue and grimaced.

"Let's hope Father never finds out," Rilt said to his reflection.

After a lukewarm shower, he slunk to his study desk with a textbook on Aleisan geography and an increasingly bad headache. Other than the wounds on his face, his stomach hurt, and he couldn't shake Gareth's expression of smug scorn from his mind.

The more he thought about it, the more he was certain that Gareth held a torch for Kayle. Right from the start of the term, he'd been guarded and possessive of Kayle, and clearly hadn't wanted Kayle to be too friendly with Rilt. His barbed comments and snide observations took on a different meaning as Rilt revisited each of them.

Even as he mulled over his recollections, Rilt could not avoid wondering what all this meant about his own feelings for his roommate. He was certain he did not share the same inclination as Kayle: he had bedded several girls, after all, and enjoyed every experience. He was not sure what prompted him to respond to Kayle's advances that night. Perhaps it was compassion for what Kayle shared about his mother. Perhaps it was the intimacy that came from living in close quarters.

Perhaps I love him.

The thought was a bitfly that refused to be waved aside. It pestered Rilt until he was forced to examine it.

He liked Kayle and admired him. He couldn't deny that Kayle was remarkably attractive; how many times had Rilt found himself watching his roommate, enchanted by his grace? The times his pulse raced when he and Kayle were caught in a moment of strange intimacy? That time in the infirmary when Kayle sneaked out of bed to check on him, and that time by the lake, when he plucked petals from Kayle's hair?

By Creation, I think I love him.

Chewing nervously on a knuckle, he tried not to think about what might happen if his father were to hear about it. Halden would not raise a ruckus, but he would do everything to get his son out of the hall or—Rilt tightened his grip—threaten Kayle and his scholarship. Being bent was as good as being a criminal, in Halden's eyes. Rilt wondered if Izdahlis would accept Kayle if they knew. Was that why Gareth was so possessive of Kayle? Because he wanted to save Kayle from the censure of the student populace?

He let his gaze fall on the page for perhaps the tenth time, the words barely making sense to him. There was important information here for their survival challenge, and he had to pick out the main points of the assigned reading. Taking a deep breath, he shook himself and got down to work.

* * *

The firm knocking on the door roused Rilt from his morose contemplations. It was already late in the evening, Rilt finally noticed, having been lost in thought for well over two hours. His left eye was more tender to the touch now and he wondered how bad it would look in the mirror.

Naelen was at the door with a book tucked under his arm while Ladmos had a covered plate in his right hand. "May we come in?"

"You do realize we share a bathroom, right? You could have come in from there," said Rilt to Naelen, stepping aside for his classmates.

"Kayle wanted to talk to Gareth," said Naelen. "Possibly yell at him."

Ladmos handed him the plate. "Here's your dinner."

On cue, Rilt's stomach growled. "I thought Wolvam said we're not allowed dinners."

"Kayle said that Wolvam's exact instructions were that we couldn't bring our roommates dinners. Ladmos isn't your roommate." Naelen took one of the chairs by the fireplace.

The scrawny student nodded at the plate. "Go on."

Rilt thanked him and started on the slices of roast and bread rolls. As he chewed on a pickled lomet, he said, "You'd better not let Wolvam know about this."

"He already saw us."

"All he did was raise his eyebrows," Ladmos supplied quickly.

Rilt raised his brows in mimicry. "Like this? I hope it was a sign of approval."

Shrugging, Ladmos took one of the chairs at the desk, his heels perched on the edge of the seat precariously. "I can never tell whether he likes us or not. Sometimes I wonder if he was forced into teaching us. I mean, Terras is fun to chat with and always helps when I'm stuck with assignments. I never feel like I can go to Wolvam."

Rilt paused in mid-chew. "Wolvam's not too bad as a teacher, you have to admit. He explains the principles to us very well. I just wish he'd stop asking me to demonstrate. Heldin is perfectly capable of being the group dummy."

"True. But you have the strongest resonance in the group. If only you had better stamina, like me. Then you'd be the best in class."

"Go plow yourself, Ladmos," Rilt said with a smile.

Ladmos unfolded from the seat. "Once you're done, I'll return the plate. The kitchen staff was very adamant that we don't hoard dinnerware in our rooms after that incident with Cammod and Derone. I think the staff thinks we're going to try to cook in our rooms and set all of Kaedin Hall on fire, and we'll all end up like the candlers down Hangs Row last month." Ladmos crossed his legs and stared at the potted bluespine on Kayle's table. "Nice punch you landed on Gareth, by the way."

"To be fair, he got me too," said Rilt, pointing to his left eye. Then he frowned, somewhat gingerly. "The candlers? Wasn't that the one…"

"Where a three-year-old toddler was the only survivor, yes. I heard the candlemakers' guild took him in, so he'll be raised as a foundling. Small mercies, I guess."

"At least he has somewhere to go." Rilt made a mental note to send over some gold to the guild, mark it for the child's care. He ate briskly and thanked Ladmos for his help. The thin youth waved aside his thanks and hastened down the hallway to get to the cafeteria.

Naelen hummed tunelessly. "Wolvam isn't really all that terrible, is he?"

"No, he isn't," said Rilt with a grin, then winced when the expression tore his lip open again and reminded him of the bruised eye. Then they heard their respective roommates yelling.

"Scorch it, Gareth, I don't need your help!"

"Really? You didn't use to say that back in Port!"

"This isn't Port anymore, in case you haven't scorching noticed! I can take care of myself!"

Then there was an angry slam of a door, followed by Kayle storming back into Room Six through the bathroom. He stopped when he saw both Naelen and Rilt. His cheeks were flushed a dull, blotchy red, and his curls were wild, as though he had run his hand through his hand multiple times.

Seeing Kayle's discomfort, Naelen rose gracefully from the chair. "I'll go back to my room."

"Thanks, Naelen," said Kayle in a small voice. His gaze flicked from him to Rilt. "And Gareth's in—he's in a mood. Sorry."

"I can deal with him. I think you and Rilt might have some things to deal with too," Naelen said with an arched brow. Then he smiled and jerked his chin at Kayle's bed. "Also, I would appreciate it if you shift your bed a couple of inches away from the wall if you plan on sharing it again."

At that unexpected remark, both Rilt and Kayle blushed deep pink. Neither of them said a word as Naelen left for his own dormitory.

Kayle sucked in a breath through his teeth and swung his arms front and back awkwardly. "I guess that means he doesn't disapprove."

"I suppose." Still, he had no clue how to broach the topic of their tryst. He was a coward for trying to hide from this, he knew, and that knowledge soured his stomach. Then again, they couldn't continue their mutual silent treatment. The past two days had felt peculiarly surreal and prickly. Rilt hated it. Though their friendship had only begun this spring, it was now an important part of Rilt's life, and no matter what had transpired between them, he intended to keep Kayle as a friend at the very least.

"Kayle, I…"

"It was my fault." Kayle said abruptly. He was curled in one of the chairs by the fireplace. "I initiated it. So don't beat yourself up over … over what happened. And I know-"

"That's not true," Rilt interrupted. In the pit of his stomach, there was a deep and hollow yearning for Kayle to smile at him again, that slightly crooked smile that made his impossibly blue eyes twinkle with mischief. He made his way to the other chair and sat on the edge, hands clenched together.

Kayle looked at him, his gaze clear and inscrutable.

Rilt rubbed the back of his neck, then said in a low voice, "I kissed you. I wanted you. Even if—even if I don't share the same proclivities as you do, I liked it. I … I wanted you, that night." He took a deep breath, unaccountably shy and nervous. The truth perched on the tip of his tongue and he set it free. "I still want you, now."

"You can't want this; you're the firstborn of the house of Arald," whispered Kayle, his voice wavering. "If your father finds out…"

"Then we'll keep this a secret," Rilt decided. Emotion surged from deep within and he closed the gap between them, standing before his friend. The scholar took Rilt's proffered hand and stood. They were mere inches apart.

"You've so much to lose." Kayle shook his head. "You cannot want this."

Rilt held Kayle in an embrace. Defiance and desire blended into an unshakable belief that he could have this, that he should protect Kayle with everything he could use.

"Just two days of us not talking and … and being apart, and I am already about to go mad. We can do this, Kayle. We'll keep it secret and safe, and it'll be just us. You and me."

Rilt did not realize how he'd ached within until he felt Kayle return the hug, and then the tension that had wound him up since those stupid words left his mouth relaxed.

He held on more tightly. "I'm sorry for what I said. I was … I was shocked by what I felt after. I was rude and dumb and I am a dimwit. And I'm sorry. I'm so sorry, Kayle."

To Rilt's gratified relief, Kayle clung to him. "Don't be sorry. There's no need to be sorry. I'll be your secret. I don't care how long you keep us secret, if this is real. I want this, I want you. I want you and I trust you."

Rilt had to pull away slightly. Brushing Kayle's curls from his brow, he steeled himself to ask, "Is … is Gareth in love with you?"

The answer was swift and certain. "No."

"How do you know?"

"If he wanted me, he's had plenty of chances," said Kayle. He smiled at Rilt's disbelieving expression. "Gareth thinks that he gets to decide how I live my life because he knows my secret. He's trying to protect me, but he takes it too far sometimes."

Pointing at his black eye, Rilt said wryly, "I noticed."

The other student chuckled and gently brushed two fingers over the sore spot. Rilt winced but did not duck away from the tentative touch. He could feel the minute shifts of Kayle's muscles as Kayle slid his hand from Rilt's left cheek to his chest, and then the soft, moist warmth of Kayle's breath as they kissed once more.

The contact stung and Rilt hissed at the pain. He had forgotten the cut in his lip. They parted, grinning like children. Rilt tried to ignore the lurch of his heart, but he could not help nuzzling into Kayle's dark, silky curls.

Kayle rested his temple against Rilt's right cheek, his arms looped loosely about Rilt's waist. "I do mean it," he murmured. "I'm willing to be your secret, as long as you want me."

"Of course I do. I'll want you all my life," Rilt declared.

The scholar only exhaled heavily in response and pressed a quick kiss to the side of Rilt's jaw. They stood that way for some time; it was the deep breath before a dive, and Rilt wondered how deep the waters were.

Slowly sliding his hands down Kayle's arms, Rilt caught his roommate's—his lover's hands in his own. He squeezed the slender fingers and said, "I can't promise you anything, I know this. I know nothing about how—how it is, how things are done between men. But if just one day without you made me feel as though a hole had been dug through my body, I don't want to picture never having you ever again."

A small smile wavered on Kayle's lips. "It hurt so much, keeping away from you. I thought you were … that you were disgusted by what we did."

"Not disgusted, surprised. I've never bedded another man before. You're my first."

A low chuckle, and Kayle squeezed Rilt's fingers in response. "I'm honored, truly. Anyway, I should fill you in on the two lessons you missed today. Tomorrow we'll resume study group. We need to prep for our term challenge."

Rilt wrinkled his nose in distaste. "I want to punch Gareth in his face, I don't mind telling you."

"You won't."

"I want to."

"Try it and I'll add another black eye myself." The dark-haired scholar shook his head and let go of Rilt's hands. "Both of you are important to me. I don't want to have to choose between you. He's my best friend. You're … you are my lover."

The bashful look Kayle gave him from lowered lashes warmed Rilt. He was about to say something, when he remembered what he'd brought along with him.

Ignoring Kayle's urging to review the lessons, Rilt rummaged through his chest of drawers, shoving aside old letters, his father's seal ring, and his red journal until his searching fingers closed around a small velvet box.

Eagerly, he opened it and slid it across the table. "I'd like you to have this."

Kayle gaped at the starsilver ring nestled in its black velvet cushion. The sapphire sparkled in the lamplight, the star in the blue gem rayed in brilliance. Rilt smiled when he noticed that the stone was the exact shade of Kayle's eyes.

"What? Rilt, I can't take this, it's much too valuable," the scholar protested, color high in his cheeks. "I… There is no way someone like me could own something like this."

"Yes, you can," Rilt demurred. He covered Kayle's hand around it. "It was my mother's, something she wore when she was a girl. I want you to have it."

"Rilt…"

"You don't have to wear it. Or I can get you a long chain and you can wear it on the chain, or you can lock it up somewhere safe. I just

... I want you to have it." Rilt pushed his tongue at the cut in his lip. "I want you to know that you are important to me."

Kayle put a hand over his mouth and stared at the ring, his eyes suspiciously bright and wet. Eventually he nodded. "Put it on me. Let me see if ... I'll wear it on a chain when the challenge is over."

Taking Kayle's left hand in his, Rilt plucked the ring from its cushioned box and slipped it onto Kayle's forefinger. The ring slid on with hardly any trouble, and against Kayle's smooth, pale skin, it looked very elegant. It looked like it belonged there.

"It's beautiful," Kayle murmured. His eyes were dewy and he blinked rapidly. "Are you sure I can—that I deserve this?"

"Of course. I'm giving it to you."

The Halim scholar pressed his lips to the gem, and then took the ring off and put it in his desk drawer reverently. "Let's get to work. I have to meet Master Jodius in an hour."

"This time of the night? Why?"

"He's teaching me how to make bluespine antidote, now that my project is advancing so well. This is the only time he's available after his own studies and research." Kayle pulled out two textbooks from his satchel and his notes. "Here. We'll start with history."

* * *

By the time Kayle got back from Master Jodius, Rilt was already in bed. The sound of the door closing roused him from a vague dream of turbulent waters. He opened one eye and yawned, before propping himself to a half-sitting position. "You weren't joking about being back late."

"Go back to sleep, Rilt," Kayle said quietly and went into the bathroom.

The room was cool. Outside, a soft pattering of rain fell on the window, a serene drumming of water on glass. The wind rustled the trees lightly; Kaedin Hall was well sheltered from all but the worst storms, located behind the bulk of the palace and near to one of the main canals.

Lying down again, Rilt gazed dreamily at the ceiling, his mind drifting with the ebb and flow of the raindrops on the window and the sounds of Kayle taking a late shower. It felt like a gentle melody was playing in the back of his mind, a soft tinkling of strings. Back home in Enthin, when it rained at night, he would listen to the water drumming on the immense windows, or sneak out to the attic at the top and listen to the sound of rain on the roof. When Cedaran was toddling around, he would run pattering into Rilt's room should there be lightning and thunder, and Rilt would comfort his baby brother until the storm abated—although he was not that much older than Cedaran.

Kayle had said something about vicious storms before. He wondered what a storm at sea was like. In his mind, he pictured surging mountains of seawater crashing together. White-tipped waves, just as they were described in the stories, spitting foam into an iron-black sky. Ships tossed about like toys thrown by a bored child. He imagined huge billows smashing into steep stony cliffs, tearing down hundreds of cliff roses and drowning their scarlet-tipped petals.

Perhaps, his drowsy mind supplied, *one day I'll be powerful enough to command a storm. Ride one across the sea and explore the world. Aleis isn't all there is out there.*

By the time Kayle returned from the bathroom, rubbing his hair with a thick towel, Rilt was almost asleep. Still, he flipped down a corner of his blanket drowsily and patted the mattress.

Kayle hesitated by the side of the bed.

"I'm not going to do anything," Rilt said. "I would like to hold you, that's all."

After another moment's pause, Kayle slid into Rilt's bed. His hair was still damp, but Rilt was oddly comforted by Kayle's salty-sweet scent. The Halim scholar turned to face him. Even in the darkness, he could tell that Kayle was studying him.

"What is it?" Rilt whispered.

"Nothing."

A touch tickled his lips. Kayle brushed his fingers over Rilt's mouth and then shifted closer, his exploring hand curled between their chests. Rilt draped an arm over his waist and murmured for Kayle to rest. Kayle shuffled and rolled so that he was facing away from Rilt and their feet were not fighting for space.

Rilt's mind was still suspended in the fog between sleep and wakefulness. The rain lent a faint percussive beat to his hazy thoughts, filling in the spaces between with meaningless noise. He nuzzled closer to Kayle, his lips just touching the bared neck before him. The smooth warmth of Kayle's hand covering his own was the last thing he registered before he drifted into sleep.

* * *

Kayle was dressed in a sleeveless turquoise tabard with splotches of murky red and rust-brown, and his hair was much longer, sweeping to the floor in a cascade of dark brown waves. The surroundings were dim, except for the young Halim scholar, and Rilt walked over to him. Kayle was staring up at a tall black tree, so tall that its crown was within the red clouds overhead. Ice hawks screamed overhead but their cries were distorted.

"We can't go up there," Rilt said, grasping Kayle's shoulder. "It's too high to climb."

"I'm not climbing it," said Kayle. His voice echoed strangely, layered over itself again and again into an echoing distortion. "I am going to live within its roots."

Rilt looked at the base of the tree and had to step away. Instead of roots, a mass of gold and black serpents twined and writhed. "They will bite you."

"Yes," Kayle answered, completely unconcerned.

"You'll die," Rilt pleaded. He grabbed Kayle's elbow; it was cold as bone.

Kayle turned to him and cupped his face. His free hand was cool as polished marble, but Rilt found himself arrested by his eyes. No longer were Kayle's eyes the brilliant, clear blue that he knew; they were milky white, dead and unseeing. The dark-haired scholar tilted his head and then smiled sadly. Rilt felt a tremor of undistilled terror shiver down his spine.

"I know," said Kayle, his Halim lilt coloring his words sweet and melodious. "Do you?"

Rilt took a step back and stumbled. When he struggled to his feet, he was next to a golden ram as large as a horse. It regarded him, its slit-eyed gaze terrifyingly familiar, and then trotted across a bridge towards a bright sphere, half-buried in the earth. In it, a flame flickered and wavered, almost like a dancer twirling.

"We're not supposed to touch that," Rilt called out to the ram. The animal waited by the sphere, pawing the ground impatiently. Rilt hesitated. He took one step, and whispered, "We're not supposed to touch that."

The brilliance of the sphere expanded and engulfed the ram soundlessly. It continued to grow and Rilt had to shield his eyes from the light. Then the world trembled and shattered like thin glass.

* * *

"Rilt, wake up," said Kayle, shaking his shoulder. "Come on, I don't want to be late for morning meditation. Wolvam will throw a fit."

"Kayle?" Rilt frowned.

The other student sounded exasperated. "Yes, Kayle. Come on, Rilt, you're already in trouble, let's not add tardiness to it."

Rilt sat up and shook his head. The inside of his skull felt fuzzy and thick. He groped for the images that had passed through his head and came up empty. "You died. And there was … there was a light." He licked his dry lips. "And I was sad."

Kayle huffed through his nose and levered himself off the bed. "Of course you'd be sad if I were dead. Anyway, if you're not getting washed and dressed in the next ten minutes, I'll leave you to Wolvam's tender mercies."

He crossed to the other side of the room and deliberately messed up the sheets, before he put it back in a careless manner. After Kayle had gone to the bathroom, Rilt sat up and tugged his sheet straight.

Precautionary measures, he thought. Stretching, he winced at the pop in his left shoulder. For the life of him, he could not recall what Kayle had told him in his dream.

THE PROPOSAL

Though by the third day it was clear that neither Gareth nor Rilt was going hungry, they were not punished. Terras must have persuaded the other senior adept somehow, because Kayle swore that Wolvam saw him leaving the cafeteria with a covered plate and made no comment.

Gareth was giving Kayle and Rilt the cold shoulder, which suited Rilt just fine. Kayle complained a little about Gareth's attitude whenever he returned from delivering dinner to Room Five; Rilt simply listened to his lover muttering irritably about Gareth's pettiness while he plotted schemes that would let him have Kayle without compromising the house name. From childhood, he had been instructed in this, after all: the fine art of planning for the worst and strategizing to avoid it.

He had meant it when he declared that he wanted Kayle. However, after the initial rush of jealous passion that prompted his declaration, he had recalled that his father had eyes and ears all over Izdahl. Halden probably had spies in Kaedin Hall too; it would be naive to assume otherwise. To deflect any attention from his new intimacy with Kayle, he would need to draw their eyes elsewhere. The only way he could achieve that was to enlist Galena's help. He hoped she would be amenable. After all, she had everything to gain if she played along.

"Rilt?"

The noble blinked. "Yes?"

"Bed?" asked Kayle, his cheeks pinking. They had been sharing a bed ever since they made up, though they always messed up the sheets of the other bed the next morning.

It had been difficult keeping their voices down while they learned the secrets of each other's bodies, so they had taken to burying their faces into the nearest pillow. Kayle was obscenely good with his mouth. Rilt was more than happy to reciprocate with his hands, and both of them enjoyed kissing. They were careful not to leave any marks, just in case; the kae training in Aega class had by then progressed to them entering the lake clad only in short pants. The last thing Rilt wanted was to rouse the curiosity of the rest of the Aega group.

In itself, the furtiveness was a sort of joy. To find out what Kayle responded to and how he cleaved to Rilt was an endless source of delight; in the darkness, Rilt's palms memorized the texture of Kayle's skin, his fingers traced the lines of his lover's tattoo, his lips and tongue teasing soft, helpless breaths from his lover's mouth. Kayle seemed determined to map Rilt's contours by tongue, and though they turned in before curfew, they seldom slept until it was well past.

That night, after they were sated, Rilt whispered, "I'll have to keep dating Galena. I don't know if that's wise."

"She's not stupid," said Kayle, catching on immediately. His slender fingers trailed an aimless design over Rilt's left shoulder. "If she knew the truth, would she tell?"

"Maybe I can make it worth her while to be our ally," mused Rilt thoughtfully. He pressed a kiss to the corner of Kayle's mouth, nearly missing it entirely.

Kayle sighed and nuzzled closer. "We can hope."

* * *

Rilt felt uneasy about having to deceive Galena. He wondered if any other men in the Arald line had ever been bent. Obviously there would be no clear record of it, but he could read between the lines in the entries. Copies of records from the previous members of the Arald line were stored here, duplicates of those from Enthin. He could identify the ancestors he was suspicious of. There were a few who'd never married or had maintained intimate friendships with their own sex that—from his new perspective—seemed suspect. Kayle had wanted to accompany him to the estate, but Master Jodius had asked for Kayle, so Rilt went alone. With his seal ring in his pocket—he would need it to access the vault—he had a cab drive him there. He made sure to bring along some cloudberry pies for Pellit, having charmed the head cook into making half a dozen for his valet. However, when no one answered his knocks at the front door, he grew irritated. He pounded hard on the door again, annoyed that he was being made to wait.

Pellit's look of relief upon seeing Rilt was unexpected. "Sir, I was about to send a runner to you," he said in a rush. "Her Grace told us to prepare for a guest, not for a party. I don't even know how I'm going to explain the mess." He gestured vaguely at the inside of the house, babbling about stains and breakages.

"Pell, what are you talking about … *what in Creation happened here?*"

The moment he stepped into the main hall of the mansion, he was stunned. It was a complete mess. There were far too many half-dressed people asleep on various pieces of furniture or on the rugs, some still entwined. A few rugs bore still-sticky wine stains and the air had a decidedly sour, smoky tang to it. One wall sconce dangled from the wall, and a few paintings had been knocked askew. The maids and footmen stood in the doorway to the servants' quarters, as though they were waiting to clean but were too embarrassed to wake the sleepers up.

"Mother said there would be a guest?" asked Rilt, incensed at the state of the mansion. He left the pies on a sideboard. "Who is this guest? Where are they?"

"It's Lord Evvas of the Alwyth house, sir, and he's in the guest room. I assume he's with company," stammered Pellit. "I apologize, sir, we thought it'd just be a dinner party and prepared for that, but more and more people arrived and things got out of hand. We'd only just cleared out the leftover food and… "

Ignoring Pellit's stuttering, Rilt stormed into the main hall and waved the servants to follow. "Draw the curtains and open the windows," he ordered. "All of them. I want this stench out of the house. Zarin, wake up the guests. You, send for cabs. These ladies and gentlemen are all leaving right now."

Some of the sleepers stirred and complained at the bright lights streaming in. Rilt ignored all of them and took the stairs two at a stride. Pellit hurried up behind him. Rilt flung every door open and Pellit hurried to part the curtains and invite fresh air into the rooms. The young lord even bodily hauled a naked youth out of the study, and throwing his pants after him as he scurried down the stairs, while the young woman who had woken up with a shriek scrambled after her paramour.

Rilt felt boiling, white-hot rage at the sight of the disarray of his estate. It was rude of Evvas to throw a party in someone else's home, let alone such a decadent one. He was going to order a complete inventory check after this. Eventually, Rilt made it to the guest wing and he shoved the double doors open.

A lanky young man was splayed over a large bed, with two naked women snuggled up against him. The young man had to be Evvas.

"Open the windows, Pellit," Rilt commanded loudly. "See the ladies into cabs."

The noise woke Evvas. He groaned and rolled over, unabashed by his nudity. He first saw Pellit and shouted, "Who let you in here? Get out. You're a servant, you should know better."

"He does," said Rilt coldly. He was glad he had brought his father's seal ring today. He slipped it on and strode over to the bed, picking up clothes from the floor as he passed. Throwing the garments at the three naked forms, he said, "Get dressed."

One of the women with dark red curls scowled. "Who are you again? I don't remember seeing you last night, bossyboots."

"I am Lord Rilt of the Arald house, and this is my estate. Get off my property. There should be cabs waiting for you by the time you manage to be decently dressed. Tarry longer and you'll be seen off without your dresses." The edge in Rilt's voice woke the two women up more thoroughly, and they pulled on their clothes.

Evvas languidly straightened up in bed. "Rilt? How lovely to finally meet you. Aunt Selvina mentioned you in her letter when she offered me the use of this place. Sorry about the state you find me in, and I think my friends got a little rowdy last night. Nothing the servants can't clean up, I'm sure."

Rilt glared at him. "I'd prefer to talk to you with your pants on, Evvas."

"What, you don't see cocks hanging about in Kaedin Hall? You're all lads over there, aren't you? Bet there are more than a few bents living in the dorms. If you've never tried a bent, you really ought to. Tighter than the sweetest virgin," Evvas drawled as he pulled on a pair of trousers. "Plus, they won't ever talk about it, you know. Not when they could get sent to the mines if some noble lodged a complaint."

Already at the end of his patience, Evvas' remarks about bents sparked Rilt's ire. The Arald lord grabbed Evvas and dragged him out of the bed, pinning him to the floor rug with a hand at his throat. He flashed the ring on his other hand, the twin rams glinting golden, and then pressed the ring into Evvas' cheek. He almost wished the ring was a branding iron.

"You are a guest because of my mother," snarled Rilt. "But I have the seal ring of the house. In the eyes of the law, I am the head of the Aralds in Izdahl. I have every right to throw you out after the stunt you pulled. This isn't Halimgor, Evvas Alwyth. You are not spending my house's money on your depravities. The only reason I have yet to hound you out is because of my mother's regard for your father. My hospitality extends only as far as your courtesy, Lord Evvas Alwyth, and if I get wind of any more of such 'parties', I will have you driven out to beg like a dog. Do you understand?"

The other lord's eyes were wide and his breathing was rapid. Rilt squeezed Evvas' throat more tightly. "Do—you—understand?"

Evvas nodded.

Rilt let go and stood up, looming over the other lord. "Good. Pellit, neaten up the room. Come, Lord Evvas, put on a shirt and we shall breakfast. Zarin makes excellent bacon and eggs."

* * *

Rilt ordered Pellit to take stock of the contents of each of the twenty rooms, in case anything had been taken by Evvas' guests. "The next time, inform me before the party. You and Zarin are senior here. What do you think I would have done?"

"I apologize, sir. Her Grace did say to offer every courtesy-"

"My mother is not here. I am. And while I am here, I am the head of the household." Revealing the seal ring on his finger, Rilt added, "I'm going to look through the house records. There may be something in them to tell me about those targeting me. Is there any way you can get Evvas away from the manse?"

Pellit's brow creased. "Lord Evvas likes Hedia a lot, sir. He likes to go into the stables and talk to her, pet her a bit. Perhaps he would like to take her out for exercise."

"Good. If he likes her all that much, she is his for the duration of his stay." Once his valet had scurried off, Rilt took a deep, steadying breath, with Master Baelmin's voice counting to ten in his mind.

He should not have laid hands on Evvas. It was rude and certainly not something Selvina would be pleased to hear about, even if Evvas deserved a far worse beating. While it had been satisfying earlier to see him cave, Rilt suspected that Evvas would find some way to get back at him for the humiliation. Perhaps he would inform Selvina about Rilt's discourtesy. He shrugged off the thought and made his way to the private study, where Zarin was already waiting for him with the vault key and a book of records.

"I have the staff cleaning the first and second floors, my lord," said Zarin while Rilt skimmed through the record entries. It was a detailed list of what had been put in the vault over the years. "I will personally oversee the inventory check with the Izdahli housekeeper."

"Send me the final report, including damages. Tomorrow evening, by sunset."

"Yes, my lord."

"You may leave now." Rilt waited for Zarin to leave the study before he unlocked the heavy door. It was not the only barrier, of course; Rilt had to press the seal ring to a device designed by a master locksmith which then opened the vault itself.

The vault was designed as a small library, holding papers and notebooks. The smell of old paper settled over Rilt like dust. He put the ring in his pocket and, with reference to the records, picked his way to the back of the vault. Fragile papers dating back five centuries were carefully preserved between sheets of clear glass.

Cautiously, he lifted one sheet. The ink was only slightly faded, and the page yellowed and browned in spots, but it was otherwise in good condition.

'My swéteu Gwynna,

The dæg hath cyme when the beornpréat face kaedine. The fooe will fall yn home I return, wyth tressu yn glorie…'

Rilt scanned through it, struggling a little with obscure words, and then set it aside for the next. It took him ten before he discovered something of interest.

'I saw his face. His hewe was salow yn pale as wex, but he breithen. Malencolik his speech, spoken he of fyr yn flaume unceising. His words werr so caytyf yn felle that mine owne men qualled in deyr boots. Wrecched kaedyn! In the even he was wyth us, yn by the morne he yn half myn soljiers desert. See hym again yn I sleen him! Fyr yn fluame! I will se yt wtyh mine eyen yet.'

A quick check showed that it was a letter from Rilt's ancestor, Keyron Arald, who rode to war against the then-general Coleri, before the Aralds joined forces with the Aleis. Later letters confirmed that Keyron had indeed battled fire-resonant kaedine. The more experienced fire kaedine could attack with bursts of intense heat, while lesser fire kaedine hurled fireballs repeatedly. Some of the letters were lovey-dovey nonsense, and some relayed information about the battles Keyron had seen or fought in. The losses, the wins. Rilt was on his twenty-eighth letter when he found it. What he read nearly made him drop the glass panels.

"The four other elements of kaedine closed ranks against their brethren," he translated under his breath. His finger left smudges on the glass, but he paid no heed to that. "They had seen the ruins of Golrak, the mighty city reduced to ashes and blackened bones, and what was once flowering and rich was now … death. Peace—no, a pact was made … to silence all kaedine of flame."

He set the letter down. Cold chills prickled over the back of his neck. He had come looking for an idea on how to keep Kayle as a lover without hurting the Arald name. He had found something of far greater import.

Guilt gnawed at him. Master Baelmin had entrusted him with the task, and he had all but forgotten it. He slid the glass panels back into their original places, his mind heavy with worrisome thoughts. Perhaps he should discuss this discovery with Naelen. In the meantime, he would need to deal with the more practical problems raised by his new relationship with Kayle.

I want him. But to have him as a lover openly would be dangerous for him. Father may find out through his spies. As Rilt surveyed the vault and consulted the list of his ancestors' writings, a plan came to him. He was of high breeding, after all was weighed and measured; his value was in his bloodline and heritage. Though he was loath to deceive Galena, she had everything to gain.

* * *

"You have got to be joking," said Galena when they met up on Seventhday. They were again taking a leisurely stroll along the canal to Riverbank Park. "A week without dinner? This Wolvam is horrible!"

"My friends were very kind and smuggled food to the rooms."

They stopped at one of the many stone benches. Rilt brushed off the seat for her and sat down next to the singer. He offered his right hand, palm up; she regarded him for a moment before taking it. Squeezing lightly, he kept their hands between them. He hoped this would be enough for now; his stomach was lurching uneasily at doing this with Galena, even if it were only to protect himself and Kayle from being found out. It was odd how he no longer wanted to be intimate with her, though he still found her attractive.

"Your eye has healed well." She rubbed her thumb over the edge of his palm, a slow and deliberate caress. Before Kayle, Rilt would have taken up the unspoken invitation. Now, he pretended he did not understand the game that was supposed to end with them behind the trees or under one of the arches in the wall around the university. When he looked at her now, all he noticed was how her eyes were not the right blue, nor was her smile charmingly crooked, and there was a depressing lack of faint freckles over her cheeks.

Rilt surveyed the length of the riverside walk. There were very few people out walking, which was surprising. Galena and Rilt headed away from the Red Bridge leading to the palace, choosing instead to head upriver, where white-walled and black-tiled mansions glittered at them from the facing shore. In fact, if Rilt squinted, he could see the roof of the Aralds' Izdahli mansion. He hoped Evvas was behaving himself. Cedaran mentioned in his last letter that the duke and duchess were about to come to the capital for the King's Ball.

That reminded him. "Will you be performing a solo at the ball? You've been rehearsing a lot lately."

"I'll be playing the harp for an ensemble performance before the

King's Table, and a solo piece afterwards," she replied, breathing in with a broad smile. If they had gone downriver, the air would be a lot less fresh—the docks would be teeming with activity, with picker boats unloading their cargo and the bigger carriers downriver to the sea.

"I look forward to your playing then," said Rilt with a bright smile.

"I wish I'd got the singing part, but Thera's range suits the role better." She sighed. Carefully, she leaned against his shoulder and said, "You don't have to pretend, you know."

"Pretend?" He glanced at her and then patted the back of her hand. "I don't know what you're talking about."

"You're a terrible liar, Rilt Arald," said Galena. She tapped his nose with a long, painted finger. "You're involved with someone else now, aren't you?"

Rilt's grip convulsed.

She winced and slipped her hand from his grasp. With another sigh, she continued, "You're not the first I know of. These halls are full of young, virile people rooming together. I've a friend who had to abort because her young man was already engaged to someone back home."

"I need your help to keep it secret."

She scrutinized him for a while, and then asked, "What's in it for me?"

That was not the reply Rilt had been expecting. He'd thought he would have to lie to her, and use her as a mask without her knowing about it. He looked at her and really studied her for the first time. Beyond the pretty face, he saw the determined glimmer in her eyes, and the firm set of her lips. "Are you going to blackmail me?"

"No, not exactly," said Galena. "I have no grudge against you. But I don't wish to play your mask without some compensation. My teachers have taught me one thing: know your worth. I want to know how much my charade as your lover is worth to you."

"That's blackmail."

"That's employment." She shrugged and put her hands demurely in her lap. "Regardless of your answer, I won't tell others. However, if you want my assistance, I deserve something in return."

He gritted his teeth. "What do you want?"

"An engagement."

"Excuse me?"

"I want to be engaged with the future duke of Enthin," said Galena calmly, as if she was commenting on the weather. "I'm from a minor house, and if my parents have their way, I'll be married off to a merchant next year—as long as he has a decent tract of land, lots of gold, and can provide them the lifestyle they're used to. I don't want to be a jumped-up farmer's wife. If you're going to use me as a shield, then I want something out of it."

Rilt considered the proposition. This was his original intention, after all. He just wished he had been the one to come up with it. "You want us to be engaged?"

"If you can accept me looking for my own lovers—I'll be discreet, of course—while you dally with your own," she said, playing with one of her dark curls. "I'm pretty, I'm talented, and by the time I leave the university, I'll be a fairly accomplished musician. You can show me off to our peers. Our first meeting outside the city gates, you and I falling in love at first sight… They'll just lap up our perfect marriage like fresh cream."

"You," Rilt breathed, suddenly seeing the image she was preparing to present to the rest of the world, "are a cunning, devious woman."

"I'm ambitious and smart," Galena corrected pertly. She smiled. "Do we have a deal? Make me a duchess, and you can do whatever— and whomever—you want. I'll find my own entertainment."

Chewing on his lower lip, Rilt mulled over her requests. He doubted that she would tell anyone even if he were to reject the proposal; she had no proof, after all. It would be her word against his, and she did not know who he was involved with. As an Arald, his voice carried more weight. However, the fact that she would support his affair was already surprising, and if she was willing to be a wife only in name in exchange for the title, he had no compunctions about using her.

"I need you to promise you'll never talk about this again," said Rilt.

She glared at him, though she was smiling. "My word is as good as yours, Lord Rilt, and I swear by the Creators that I will keep your secret."

"And in return, I will make you a duchess," said Rilt, leaning forward to kiss her on her lips. Soft and yielding and perfumed, but ultimately wrong; Rilt drew away and brushed his thumb over her lower lip. "I'll get you an engagement cuff before the King's Ball. You'll meet my parents and brother too."

"In the meantime," she said, running her knuckles along his jaw, "You and I are going to run Anya ragged with messages and love letters. Make them scandalous, my dear."

"As your grace-to-be commands," Rilt teased, taking her hand to kiss her fingers. Then his tone softened as he said, "Thank you."

She huffed in amusement. "I'm the one gaining all the benefits here. You're not the catch in yourself, Rilt, you know that." Her words were so warm and friendly that he had to laugh, and they grinned cheekily at each other.

Quietly, he murmured, "I'm glad you're taking it so well."

"Be glad that I am your friend," she whispered, and pressed a kiss to his cheek. Skimming her mouth to his ear, she went on quietly, "I've been asked about you by a few too many people, some of whom wouldn't give me the pitch to start a song."

Rilt angled his head so his lips touched her cheek. "I'd appreciate names."

She recited a few, none of which Rilt recognized, but he committed them to memory regardless. Galena added, "I can't confirm a thing, but we should be wary of the runners."

"Runners are sworn to secrecy."

She levelled him with an arched look. "You of all people should know that a mouth opens when gold glitters before the eyes."

He smiled broadly and got to his feet. "We'll just have to date every Sixthday then." He held out a hand to assist her.

Galena matched his smile and kissed him lightly on the lips. "I'm looking forward to it." Then she looped her arms around his neck and tugged him down so her mouth was close to his ear. "Give Kayle my congratulations on his fine catch."

Rilt nearly choked on his tongue.

* * *

Kayle was reading with his feet propped up on his side of the desk. He barely looked up from the book when Rilt ruffled his hair. "How did it go?"

"She wants to be the duchess of Enthin. And she knows it's you."

"Told you she isn't stupid." Swinging his feet to the floor, Kayle marked his page and set the book aside. He raised an eyebrow at Rilt. "You agreed, I suppose."

"Mother is going to be so thrilled. She loves to plan parties." Rilt dropped into the other chair and placed a hand on Kayle's knee. "You're not surprised that she guessed it was you?"

"I'd be surprised if she didn't figure it out after your first date."

"You really don't mind?"

Kayle shrugged. His fingers traced a random pattern on his desk, swirling invisible circles as his gaze flicked from Rilt to the dull blue sky outside and back again.

"Who am I to mind?" he asked. "I am grateful. You should be too. We should be on bended knee, thanking her for helping us. She's willing to play her part, and I have to thank all the Creators that she's intent on making this work to her long-term benefit, instead of selling you out."

He blew out a long breath; his eyes were suspiciously bright. Patting Rilt on the shoulder, he said, "I'm going for a swim."

"Kayle-"

"I don't want to have to play a jealous and whining little lover just to soothe your ego, Lord Rilt of the house of Arald." He dug around his closet for a towel. "It's not as though I'm not prepared to live in the shadows. I know what I have to sacrifice."

If Kayle shut the door a little too firmly, Rilt tried to ignore it. He had his doubts about Galena, but it was too late to switch trails now. Certainly the lords and ladies of various houses had affairs. In fact, Rilt was fairly sure that his stepmother had been Halden's mistress before Rilt's own mother died, even though he could never ask and no one in the house would dare gossip about the duchess. Selvina's family was a distant branch of the Alwyths of Halimgor who had settled in south Enthin, of much lower status than Rilt's birth mother, who was of the house Adbel of Izdahl, close relatives of the ruling Alcaronans.

A daughter was of value to a noble house only in terms of the marriages she could make, and those who could not nab a good title would want their daughters marrying into wealth. The merchants, despite not being of noble stock, were often richer than some of the lower houses; having a lady as a wife satisfied their commoner ambitions to rise above their station. Rilt could empathize with Galena's shrewd decision to make use of this opportunity, even if he resented her a little for seeing through his ploy before he could even execute it. As for his closeness with Kayle, no one would ask, since he would have a lovely, accomplished wife as proof, and Kayle was too sensible to flaunt himself.

A tremor crept under his skin and into his bones. The scale of his deception dawned on him and made him cold, like he had been hung on a rack of antlers and left to bleed out. His sham engagement aside, Rilt finally had to absorb the truth of the matter: he was bent.

There were mines in the north of Enthin, in the foothills of the mountains. Sometimes, people suspected of being bent were sent there, condemned for some minor crime, to live out their days toiling in rock and darkness. Rilt wondered if any of them had actually been guilty of the crimes they were accused of. The main criticism of those who were bent was that they bore no offspring and were thus violating the essence of Creation. If Rilt and Galena married and had children, would that take them off the butcher's hook?

He exhaled shakily and covered his mouth. They were safe in Kaedin Hall. In a hall full of virile young men, it was tacitly understood that they had needs and a helping hand could ease tensions. It was not as though he had not heard stories about the seniors, and at night, sounds carried quite well. Rilt and Kayle had been discreet thus far, at least.

"We'll be fine," he muttered under his breath. "We'll be fine, Rilt. Focus on what you need to do."

They had drawn up a list of necessities to prepare for their survival challenge, and Rilt was to gather their basic medical supplies. It would be essential—a splinter or a cut could get infected. While Rilt was amenable to the idea of Gareth being pricked by thorns and bitten by swamp mitches, he knew that a small discomfort would lead to an unpleasant stay out there in the woods. All their bandages and cotton packing were sealed in waxed bags to keep out the wet, and he mentally calculated if there was a need for more.

"Kayle, you there?" Gareth poked his head out from the bathroom. His brow deepened immediately into a scowl when he saw Rilt. "Where is he?"

"Swimming."

Gareth started to leave, but suddenly returned. Glaring at the noble, he crossed his arms over his chest and said, "I'm going to make this very clear. Regardless of your feelings, what you have with Kayle isn't going to last."

"That's not for you to decide."

"I know him. I know what he's like, what he'll do. You can make all the plans you want, they're not coming to fruition."

Feeling the sharp bite of anger, Rilt took a deep breath and slowly counted to ten. Eventually he said, "We'll see. Time will tell."

After another long, calculating look at Rilt, Gareth stalked away. He did not slam the door shut as he returned to Room Five, but it was plain that he had wanted to.

* * *

"What's that stack of envelopes?" Kayle asked after his bath, his curls damply sticking to the back of his neck. "They weren't there when I left."

Absorbed in his resonance practice, Rilt glanced at the letters. "Those? Letters to Galena. I figured I might as well write a whole lot and run one over every few days. Make it believable that we are serious."

The words tasted ashy in his mouth. Rilt ignored it and returned his attention to the basin of water in front of him calm as ice. The note in his mind wavered in and out of focus. He did not notice Kayle going over to read them silently. The surface of the water rippled and then subsided. A few more tries later, he managed to lock on the note of resonance and carefully altered the shape of the line in his mind. He watched as a ribbon of water snaked upwards, hovering and flowing ceaselessly.

Kayle watched, grinning. "That is amazing!"

Rilt released the resonance and winced as a sharp pain sliced through his temples. "That was tiring."

"You're still holding your breath when you tune?"

"Bad habit, I know. I'm trying to break it."

"Come here," said Kayle, setting down the letters. When the Enthinian strolled over obediently, Kayle made him face away from the window and close his eyes. "Now hold out your arms to the height of your shoulders—that's right—palms up."

Rilt frowned, his lips twitching with amusement. "I feel stupid."

"That's the least of your concerns. Now I'm going to place two drops of water in your palms, and you're going to make them hover." Kayle did so quickly, and then stood behind Rilt. He splayed a hand over Rilt's chest and placed the other hand just below his belly.

"This is the oddest embrace I have ever been in."

"Shush. Move this hand when you breathe," the scholar said, laughing quietly as he flexed the fingers of the hand on Rilt's belly, "and this other hand stays still. Breathe in."

With Kayle's hands on him to guide him through, Rilt found it easy to go through the breathing exercises, and the resonating note rang shrilly in his mind. It was much simpler to tune now. He floated the two drops of water in his hands, and, just to flaunt, reached for the water in the basin with his mind. Carefully, he levitated the entire mass as a spinning sphere.

Kayle chuckled. "No one likes a show-off."

"You like me enough." Rilt deliberately ignored Gareth's words from earlier. The intimacy between him and his lover was real and grounding. Gareth didn't know what he was talking about.

"Oh, really?" The scholar grinned and slipped his hands under Rilt's light tunic. "I'll just show you how much I like you."

The sphere Rilt had been levitating splashed back into the basin and water slopped over the floor, but neither student took any note of it.

* * *

The morning sun woke Rilt from a deep sleep. Rolling over with a grunt, he was displeased to find that Kayle had already gone. He got up, noting the deliberately disheveled state of the unused bed on the other side of the room, and grinned—they had been alternating beds, and been very careful with their messes. Heat rushed up Rilt's face as he recalled exactly how Kayle had cleaned him up last night.

And he's mopped up the water too, Rilt thought, slightly guilty that he hadn't done it. After he got out of bed, he tidied up around the room, putting their books away. It was Seventhday, so he had nothing to do other than two assigned chapters to read and a report on the development of kaedin-craft in Enthin to finish. Before he straightened up Kayle's side of the table, he gingerly turned the bluespine a quarter of the way around on its spot on the windowsill, the way Kayle did it whenever he sat down to work.

The little potted bluespine had grown about a hand taller since Kayle first got it. The spines were a dark, inky blue, stark and dangerous against the pale green stem. Rilt seldom paid much attention to it, but in the morning light, he could see why Kayle liked it so much. There was an eerie beauty to it, and knowing just how poisonous it was made it seem that much more innocuously threatening.

The secret between him and Kayle was eating at him like venom in a wound. He knew Gareth and Naelen were aware, but didn't trust them enough to confide in them about his fears. He could not tell Cedaran, because Selvina might find out. Besides, Cedaran was a lousy liar. Galena knew and she was exploiting this situation for her own benefit, so he had no intention of giving her more leverage. He wanted to confide in Master Baelmin, but the old man was dead. Regardless, he needed to unburden himself. After mulling over his words, he began writing.

Master Baelmin,

I miss you. I miss having access to your advice, I miss your scolding, I miss your encouragement. I just wish I'd been there in your last days. I could use you here with me right now. Remember Kayle Radieri? We've made up. I wish I could tell Ced but I can't know if Mother (or worse, Father) would find out through him.

Kayle is beautiful and intelligent and kind and so sensible, Master, you'd have loved him. He forgave me for my stupid words and told me he was willing to be my secret. When I'm with him, I feel fierce and strong and protective, like a graywulf with his mate. I want to keep him safe with me, always, but how am I to achieve that?

I know you would not have disapproved of my being bent as long as I fulfilled my obligations to my people and the kingdom. I've a fiancee now. Galena is sharp as steel shuttles, and she's willing to be my duchess even though she knows about me and Kayle. I am so grateful and yet I'm suspicious.

Now would be a good time for you to help me figure all this out. Words can't convey how much I wish for you to be here.

Forever your student,
Rilt

He sealed the letter in an envelope and tucked it in the last few pages of the red journal. It made him feel a little better. Even if Master Baelmin could not offer advice, Rilt could confide, and that was enough.

* * *

Rilt dear,

Yes, I did receive a letter from Evvas with his side of the story. You really should have sent Pellit out from the room before talking to Evvas. Was there really a need to embarrass him in front of his guests or in front of the help? I thought you'd know better than this. I will of course write to Evvas as well. It has been a difficult time for him, having lost his birthright to his sister, and so please do be more understanding of his pain.

I'd hoped that both of you would be good friends. Evvas is one of the few people in the kingdom who understands the burden that's been placed on your shoulders. I suppose a friendship is out of the question now. Given that neither of you seem to have left a good first impression on the other, is it too much to ask that you behave cordially whenever you do have to meet?

Your father and I will be coming to Izdahl soon. Do check in on the staff and make sure they have freshened the carpets and tapestries. We will be hosting quite a few guests while we are there and it won't do for the estate to be less than perfect. We'll have a family dinner the night before the King's Ball, so do invite anyone you wish for us to meet. How about your roommate, Kayle? He sounds like such a delight in your letters, I'd love to meet him.

With all my love,
Selvina

* * *

Rilt folded the letter and tossed it onto his desk. He wondered if Selvina knew just how little free time he truly had, now that they were preparing for the term survival challenge. Time between classes was spent memorizing lists of edible plants and how to construct snares, along with hand-to-hand combat practice. He and Gareth were still performing their throws and counters with more force than necessary. Wolvam was eyeing them with suspicion, but neither Gareth nor Rilt had done anything to cross the adept's line yet.

Naelen glanced up from Rilt's journal when he heard Rilt sigh a second time. "What's bothering you?"

"My mother wishes to meet Kayle."

"I assume you've written about him to her." He closed the journal, a finger keeping his place in the slim volume, and added, "Do you think that's wise?"

Rilt wrinkled his nose. "I know she'd love him. It's just—I don't want Kayle to meet my father."

Naelen nodded slowly. He opened the journal again and pointed to the translation Rilt had jotted down. "This bit about silencing fire-resonant kaedine sounds dire. I suppose they succeeded."

"Why do you say that?"

"Seen fire-resonant kaedine around lately, have you?"

Naelen's sense of humor was sometimes so dry Rilt had to wonder if it was humor at all. He leaned back in his seat and blew out a long breath. Kayle and Gareth had gone out to get tents and cooking gear for their survival challenge—Gareth's parents lived in a trading caravan for some time, apparently—and Rilt had taken the chance to have Naelen go through what he discovered in the vault. Though he was loath to admit it, Naelen's perspective was invaluable. It was Rilt's nature to charge ahead and think of consequences afterwards, if he thought of them at all, so Naelen's more circumspect approach was needed if the investigation was to get anywhere.

"But if the fire-resonant kaedine were as powerful as the records say, how would they go about silencing them?" asked Rilt. He drummed his fingers on the table thoughtfully. "And how do you silence all the kaedine of one particular element? Silencing just one adept takes five master kaedine."

"Killing them would be easier," Naelen said slowly, as if drawing silk through water. The blond student's tone was devoid of emotion.

"It would be harder to kill those who had mastered the element, but easy enough for those new to tuning or shaping. A sudden fluctuation in concentration would make them lose control. It would be just another fire. If you could incapacitate them beforehand…"

Unease and suspicion bloomed dark in Rilt's mind. He was about to speak when the door to the room flung open and the other two staggered in with large packages.

"Did you hear? The bakers' guild caught fire!" Kayle exclaimed.

Gareth dumped everything in his arms onto Rilt's bed. "It was a smoking wreck when the cab took us past it. Smelled like ten thousand pies put too long in the oven."

"How many people were hurt?" Rilt cast a glance at Naelen, whose stoic demeanor did not entirely hide his acute interest.

"We didn't ask," said Kayle apologetically. "The wardens are going through the wreck still. The fire spread to neighboring guilds too, and their dormitories. The main healer hall is overwhelmed; I don't know where the apprentices are going to stay."

Rilt stood up and headed to the door once he had the Arald seal ring on his finger.

Gareth called out, "Where are you going?"

"I have a mansion with fifteen empty rooms," said Rilt, looking over his shoulder as he tugged on his boots. "It can easily hold sixty apprentices, more if they don't mind sharing beds or sleeping on the couches."

A quick message via the runners to Pellit later, Rilt was on a cab trundling towards the bakers' guild. Indeed, the large compound and two neighboring buildings were blackened husks. Thin streams of smoke snaked lazily into the sky while onlookers gathered around, muttering to themselves. Wardens were herding crying apprentices to one side, away from the passers-by, and journeymen conferred in hushed tones with masters.

Staying away from the crowd, Rilt sought out one of the masters and made his offer. He discreetly revealed his seal ring to prove that his offer was real.

Master Frades shook his hand vigorously. His cheeks were black with soot. "Thank you, my lord. I don't know how we can repay your generosity."

Feeling quite discomfited by the gratitude, Rilt said, "There isn't any need for that. Go on and gather your apprentices and journey-men. The house can easily put up to sixty to eighty people. You shouldn't have to sleep rough tonight. My staff will see to your comfort, and the cooks have been notified to provide meals for all of you until you can find other accommodation."

"Lord Rilt, you are too kind."

"It's the least I can do, Master Frades," said Rilt, cheeks heating up. "It's really no trouble."

With a word to the wardenchief, Rilt left the organization to the master baker and some wardens. Not wanting to be thanked again, he slipped into the guild compound and disappeared into one of the blackened buildings so as not to be seen. The cries of relief and delight floated into the air and he was glad he was not there. It would be embarrassing if they all came up to thank him.

He looked around at the ruined space. From the looks of it, this used to house the great ovens where the master bakers produced thousands of loaves of bread for the city. Metal trays were warped and the tables were charred to ashes. The smell of burnt bread coated the insides of Rilt's lungs. Thankfully, there was no scent of burnt meat; Rilt remembered far too well how the air had smelled at Master Baelmin's cremation.

"What are you doing here?"

Rilt nearly lost his balance as he swiveled around. There was nobody in the room, and once he calmed his racing pulse, he realized that the question was not directed at him. It was someone outside speaking to somebody else.

Aware that he was not supposed to be in the room, Rilt tiptoed across the kitchen to hide beside the massive blackened door that still hung from its hinges. Peeking through the gap between door and wall, he was astonished to see Wolvam carefully picking his way through the debris. The adept was wearing a thick coat and a worried expression, the latter of which was directed at Terras.

"Terras, you know it's better for you not to be here right now," said Wolvam, sounding gentler than Rilt had thought possible.

Were the two adepts...? Rilt bit the inside of his lower lip. He knew there was no way to tell for sure, but it would explain a lot.

Terras shook his head. "Every time, Wolf. It happens again and again and again. Why does it have to happen?" Terras didn't sound like his usual self; there was no humor or warmth in his tone. Instead, his voice was full of rage and sorrow. If Rilt hadn't been watching, he would not have known it was Terras speaking at all.

The other adept placed a hand on Terras' left shoulder. "You know it is not yet our time."

"Then when, Wolf?" Terras shook off Wolvam's hand. "He was only three, Wolvam. Three years old. And he will never get older."

"The Kaedin Council won't be renewed for another four years," said Wolvam quietly. "Four years, Terras. We can do this."

"Or we can stop doing this." The stockier adept gestured to the devastation around him.

"Who's going to believe us, Terras?" Wolvam sighed, and then grabbed Terras' shoulders to shake him gently. "I've not given up. I need you to have patience, Terras."

Terras stepped away. "You always counsel patience. I don't know if I have any left."

"But do you trust me?"

"…with my life."

"Then trust me. I will make it right. I am trying to make it right." Wolvam shook his head and sighed once more. "Go back to the hall, Terras. This is not a good place for you to be."

Terras' shoulders slumped and he ran both hands over his face and neck. "Yes, you're right. Don't stay too long either. The masters wouldn't want us caught." He seemed a lot calmer than before Wolvam spoke with him, but the rigid set of his back told Rilt otherwise.

Rilt pressed the back of his hand to his mouth. The Kaedin Council was second only to the Privy Council in its influence, and from what the adepts said, there was a link between them and this fire. Pellit had also mentioned that the Verashki had links to Kaedin Hall.

He had to get out of here before Wolvam discovered that he'd overheard their conversation. Naelen would want to know about it, but Rilt did not want to share with him as yet. Some threads were coming together and he needed to sort through his own thoughts. As he slipped away from the burnt shell of the kitchen, he could not help shaking the sensation that Terras' fury had not been assuaged in the least.

* * *

Word of Rilt's generous offer to the bakers' guild spread, and the embarrassment of praise was worth knowing that Evvas had been forced to share rooms with five burly journeymen bakers. There already was talk of setting up an oven with the Arald crest as a gift for Rilt when the guild was rebuilt. Rilt would have to find some way to talk them out of it.

He wished he could feel more pleased about doing good. Instead he obsessed over the child who was killed in the fire. He had not been able to find out more about the cause of the fire from Wolvam afterwards, who curtly told him to leave the matter alone. Rilt had poked at the wardens too, but they had little to contribute.

There was an ugly suspicion that Rilt did not voice. He dared not say it, until one late evening Naelen accosted him outside of the cafeteria as they were about to go back to their rooms.

"I went to the Hall of History's library yesterday," he said. "I found something interesting."

"What? About…" Rilt lowered his voice, glancing around, "about fire-breathers?"

Naelen shook his fair head. "No, but the masters of history keep detailed records of hangings and unexplained deaths in the kingdom. It was rather morbid. But I discovered that every year, there are at least three to five deaths by fire from 'unknown circumstances'."

Rilt could swear his blood ran colder in his veins. "Every year?"

"Every year." Naelen lowered his voice further and cast a wary look about them. "I've also looked up adepts' mastery journeys from our library, those that were available. Many of the journeys terminated where the fires were … and when they returned, they were made masters."

"Naelen. Naelen, you're—you are saying that the master kaedine are…" Rilt covered his mouth. His pulse was racing and thoughts jostled around his mind. "That can't be true. Kaedine are sworn to protect."

"And serve the king," said the other Enthinian solemnly. "Look, it's a theory. And you're in a position to speak up about it. You can raise your suspicions at the Lords' Convene. There will have to be an open inquiry then."

Rilt swallowed the lump of unease in his throat. He remembered Wolvam and Terras' conversation at the bakers' guild. Meeting Naelen's clear gaze, he murmured, "I can't raise my suspicions. Not yet. The Kaedin Council will shut down any inquiry. They'll find an accident … oh, scorch it. By Aega, Naelen—Wolvam and Terras."

Naelen was confused. "What about them?"

"They were there, at the bakers' guild. They were talking and … it wasn't an accident. The journeying is an excuse for adepts to prove their loyalty to the hall and to the king. They know the signs, I think, of fire resonance, and then they make these accidents happen somehow." Rilt's head swam. "But Terras… And Wolvam may be a strict and demanding plowhorse, but I don't think he'd do anything to hurt innocent childen. Don't tell anyone about this, Naelen."

"I won't tell," said Naelen quietly. "It's only a guess, and I could be wrong. Coincidences do happen."

Neither of them seemed to believe that.

* * *

Now that he suspected the master kaedine were capable of such nefarious schemes, Rilt was more determined than ever to keep his title. Master Baelmin had entrusted him with something of great import, and for the sake of his old tutor's reputation, Rilt could be patient. Four years until the Kaedin Council was renewed, and by then Rilt would have returned to Enthin. He could take on more of Halden's duties and then, then he could ask for an inquiry.

Galena and Rilt went out a few more times, spending their time strolling along the river or in the city and gossiping about their classmates. On the off-chance that they were followed, the two spent some time in the shadowy groves, cuddling together and kissing, appearing to all Creation that they were a couple.

Kayle never remarked on these dates; after all, he and Rilt spent the nights entwined. They didn't become more intimate outside of what they had already explored, but it was a secret they reveled in, something they delighted in keeping hidden from their peers. No shared glances throughout the day, no overtly familiar touches outside of friendly bumps with their elbows. At night, after the lights went out, they would select a bed and indulge in all the caresses and kisses and fond gazes they abstained from when others watched them.

It was thrilling and dangerous and foolish. It was absolute bliss. Rilt could not help the swoop of his stomach when Kayle murmured sweet nonsense against his bared neck, nor contain the lurch of his heart when Kayle applied soft lips and slick tongue to naked skin. In all his affairs, Rilt had never felt as strongly for his lovers as he did for his roommate, and the fact that Kayle reciprocated his affections made this a secret worth twice of any title or fortune. Their trysts kept him from feeling overwhelmed by the monumental task of unraveling what Master Baelmin had set out for him to do. Rilt wished he could include Kayle in his investigations, but he did not trust his roommate not to tell Gareth, and that was the single consideration that kept him from sharing his other secret.

SURVIVAL

Rilt had just handed in a late assignment to Master Whitsam when he remembered he had to return a library book which he'd left in his room. When he got to the door, he heard an ongoing argument inside.

"…remember what you promised me? I'm holding you to your word."

"Have I broken a promise to you yet? Gareth, it'll be fine."

"Fine? You know what's at stake here. I'm not allowing you to risk it all on some whim-"

"Rilt isn't a whim-"

"No, he's a danger. His very existence in your life is putting years of planning at risk, and what's worse, you don't care. You could be blubbering to him in bed for all I know."

"You can choose to trust me or you can throw me to the fishes. And if you trust me, *then trust me*. I haven't forgotten my debt or my promise. And you know what I'm already doing for you."

This was not a conversation Rilt wanted to barge in on. Retreating a few steps and running up to his room, Rilt opened the door swiftly, pretending he hadn't overheard anything earlier. He scowled at the sight of Gareth gripping Kayle's wrist. "What are you doing?"

"Talking to my friend," Gareth retorted. With a final glower at Kayle, he let go and stalked through the bathroom to his own dormitory.

Rilt stared at the shut door. "We ought to put a lock on that."

Kayle laughed, although it sounded forced. "He gets protective."

"He gets possessive, and he doesn't have the right," Rilt corrected. Absently shifting some dirty clothes off his chair, he retrieved the book he needed from his drawer.

Kayle shrugged and sat in the other chair. "How ready are you for the term challenge?"

"On a scale of one to five? Maybe two." Rilt blew out his breath in a rude sound. "I've never slept without a roof over my head. It will be difficult."

"It's quite fun if it doesn't rain," said Kayle. "Gareth and I have lived rough before, with his parents." He spotted the dagger Rilt bought on his date with Galena on the table, half-hidden by a messy stack of papers. "Bring that along."

"I'm supposed to use a mastersmith's dagger to cut branches and skin animals?"

"That is a dagger's function. I know my belt knife is shorter and probably duller than that one. An additional blade would come in handy."

"My pack is full. Put it in yours."

Kayle rolled his eyes but did so, tucking it into the side pocket so the scabbard would not show. Then he kissed Rilt lightly on the cheek, fond and sweet.

Rilt smiled at him and his gaze softened.

"What?" asked Kayle, the tips of his ears reddening.

"I like this."

"Like what?"

Rilt brushed his knuckles lightly over Kayle's cheek. "This. As if this is something ... something we could have every day. Talking behind Gareth's back, about our lessons. Being affectionate."

Kayle exhaled and laid his hand over Rilt's. "What we have, we can only have here, in our dorm room."

"I know. I just wish—I wish everyone else could see how much I love you." Rilt leaned forward and kissed his lover's lips softly. "I don't enjoy the deception with Galena at all."

"Never thought you did," murmured Kayle. He was about to say something else when there was a rap on the door. Kayle wrinkled his nose and got up to open it.

Anya was standing just outside. "I've got something for his lordship. A package from your valet."

"Thanks," Rilt got up and went to sign for the flat, thin roll.

Anya peered over his shoulder at Kayle and wagged her fingers in greeting. "The book on charas cultivation has just come in today. I delivered it to the librarian earlier."

"Thanks Anya, I'll go pick it up."

Kayle waited until Rilt closed the door and then hooked his chin over Rilt's shoulder, his arms wrapping loosely around the young lord's waist. "What's in here?"

"If Pellit sent it, then he's done his digging." He unwrapped the package and plucked out a tight roll of thin papers. "And here's the information I asked him to procure."

They skimmed through the sheets, crammed with Pellit's thin, spiky handwriting. Kayle exhaled heavily. "Nothing obviously incriminating on anyone in our cohort or among the adepts. This is ridiculous."

Rilt turned his head slightly and nuzzled against his lover's cheek. "Now will you believe me when I say that I am perfectly safe in Kaedin Hall?"

"The sails will tell when the wind blows." Kayle nipped playfully on Rilt's earlobe, making the latter shiver in delight. "Come to bed."

Rilt wrinkled his nose. "I have to return this book first." Noticing Kayle's mock-forlorn expression, he pressed his mouth to Kayle's cheek and whispered, "I'll pick up your book and be back as soon as possible."

* * *

The warm weather suddenly snapped into a week of torrential storms. Rain poured down relentlessly and the river Dahl raged, its water boiling gray and brown as it hurtled through the city's canals. Lower Izdahl was flooded and the dock was shut down. Several Aega kaedine were dispatched to manage the flood situation.

Luckily, Upper Izdahl was not affected by floods. The worst that the students at Kaedin Hall suffered were chilly classrooms and persistent damp. Oledan complained to anyone who would listen that the rains were unseasonal. Kayle insisted on lighting a fire in their room every evening. They kept each other warm at night, cuddled under two blankets, while rain sheeted down outside and masked any sound that they inadvertently made. These nights were wonderfully intimate and timeless, secret jewels stolen while the rest of Creation trudged on. It was perfect until Rilt caught a cold.

Much to his chagrin, he fell sick about a week after the storms began. At least he wasn't the only one; the infirmary was inundated with students. Kayle promptly moved back to his own bed and warded off the illness with noxious herbal concoctions that he also foisted on Rilt.

To Rilt's annoyance, Gareth wasn't bothered at all by the storms. If anything, Gareth's sallow complexion had improved. Nevertheless, they had to prepare for their upcoming challenge, and there was no time to slack off.

"Are you sure we can't just leave him here to wallow in his snot?" said Gareth the evening before the challenge after Rilt suffered through seven explosive sneezes in a row.

Naelen shook his head. "Four in a team."

"At least we're not the only team with extra baggage." Gareth shoved his foot into Rilt's side.

Rilt replied with a rude gesture. "Go plow yourself into a swamp."

Grinning, Kayle rolled up an extra fleece coat and stuffed it into his bag. "Almost all of those in the Aega group are sick."

"Must be something in the water," said Gareth snidely.

Rilt repeated the rude gesture, this time with both hands. Kayle and Naelen ignored their roommates' childish squabble, conferring over their list and checking that they had all they needed. Eventually they pronounced the team ready for the challenge.

With a sigh, Naelen sat back on his heels. "At least I won't miss meeting up with Liria. She'll only arrive after we get back."

"Are you two…" Rilt trailed off, unsure how to pose his question.

"Like I said, we're friends. We played cards together. Sometimes we went for walks around Enthinas or a neighboring town."

Gareth stared incredulously at the blond student. "You mean— you're really just friends?"

"Yes." Naelen frowned at his roommate, perplexed. "Why would I lie about that?"

"Because she's considered to be one of the most beautiful women in the kingdom?" Kayle remarked in an offhand manner. "Half the kingdom wants to bed her."

Naelen snorted. "Her beauty. That's all they talk about. Liria is so much more than that."

Now Rilt was curious. Wrapping his blanket about himself, he asked the other Enthinian what he thought of Liria. It took Naelen a few minutes to pick his words. His frown deepened, as though he was working out a difficult equation. Eventually he said, "She is wily and a keen politician, and far too quick at cards. She might beggar a tradesman with clever bargaining and buy out everything that you own before you realize it, but I trust her to do the right thing."

That was perhaps the most anyone had ever heard Naelen say about something that was not academic in nature. Kayle smiled softly and said, "She sounds fascinating."

"We understand each other perfectly," said Naelen. He stilled his movements, as though he felt a burden settle on his shoulders. "There is so much that people misunderstand about her."

Kayle placed a hand on Naelen's elbow. "I look forward to meeting her, Nael."

They discussed the likelihood of the rain abating before the challenge, but Gareth was openly scornful of that possibility. In the end, they stuffed an additional fleece blanket into the rucksack as well as waxed matches.

"I doubt any of us would be able to start a fire in this deluge," said Gareth, rather too cheerfully. Kayle grunted and went to poke at the fire in the little fireplace. Gareth rolled his eyes at his best friend's grumpiness. "Two nights of cold won't kill you, Kayle."

"It's not just the cold that bothers me," he replied with a grimace, "it's the damp."

* * *

The following morning was dreary, with rain still coming down in heavy gray sheets. The ground was soggy with mud, and about a dozen students were sniffling and wiping their runny noses. Everyone bore a look of disgust at having to take their survival challenge in such horrendous weather.

"I swear to Dagas, Gareth thrives on our misery," Heldin grumbled raspily when the scholar sauntered past them, whistling.

Oledan agreed with a noisy sniff. "Maybe he absorbs all our health to boost his own."

It was a day for staying in and being waited on hand and foot, but the first-years had to walk to their challenge sites. The survival challenge served as a test of their practical skills, so none of the first-years begged out of it. Rilt doubted that the instructors would have let them off anyway. He sneezed so hard that his ears rang, but other than Kayle solicitously offering a kerchief, there was no one who cared. Periodically, they would hear a bout of coughing from someone in the back, or a few sneezes, scattered about the group. Wolvam was surlier than usual, and even Terras' perpetual stout cheer had been dampened.

They were all marching towards King's Head Bluff, which was five miles from the west gate of the city, and they had been walking the foot trail for a good hour after a predawn breakfast. Rilt's feet were sore, his head felt stuffed with wet cotton and his boots full of mud, and Gareth's vindictive brightness grated on his nerves.

"Why is it called the King's Head Bluff anyway?" Kayle asked Terras, who flanked the cohort. The downpour had slackened off to a steady drizzle, and they could finally see into the distance.

Terras shouldered his pack and pointed to a dark smudge ahead. "Rumor has it that after the last Aleis was beheaded, his head was buried there. Legend says that the trees on the bluff grow strong and tall because they leech off the kae that was present within the king's brain."

"Can trees do that?" Rilt asked Kayle.

"Only in the sense that flesh and bone decay and feed the earth," Kayle replied. "The vegetation here is very dense; this place has good earth. I'm surprised there aren't farmlands here."

"The bluff and the lands around it are ranger lands." Terras again shifted the pack on his shoulder, as though he could not settle the weight evenly behind him. "They use it for training. We get special dispensation to use it for our challenges, but Wolf—Wolvam—had a headache of a time, shifting the dates forward. The rangers weren't too pleased about that, but I guess with the rain and all, they're happy not to be out here shooting crossbows and longbows at one another."

Rilt darted a disapproving glance at Terras. This was not information the students needed to know, after all. Instructors were not friends with the students, and even though what Terras had said about Wolvam was innocuous, Rilt had a feeling that Wolvam wouldn't have appreciated the students knowing about it.

Over the past few weeks, he had come to grudgingly admire the taciturn Wolvam. Though their initial encounter had bruised Rilt's pride, Wolvam never mentioned it a second time, and never used Rilt's rank against him. He was a good teacher too, helping those who were slower through repetitions and giving the faster students challenges to push them. With a wry sniff, Rilt had to admit that he felt a sense of loyalty to his instructor.

Gareth asked Terras more questions about the terrain. The adept pointed southwest, saying, "The stream that feeds these woods come out from there and crosses Izdahl all the way down to join up with the Daogh in Dunte. If you can get to the stream, you'd find plenty of game."

"I always thought this would be a better place to site the capital," said Gareth thoughtfully. "Good earth, clear lines of sight all around."

"I suppose Coleri Aleis had his reasons for putting the city where it is." Terras chuckled. "Look, there's King's Head Bluff."

Off to the north, they could all see a rise of thick woods. Mainly needleleaves, judging from the silhouettes, and Rilt was thankful. Needleleaf trees held sweet sap that was both nourishing and flammable, not that anyone could start a fire in such damp conditions.

Naelen had obviously come to the same conclusion. "If we can find a cave or burrow, we won't be cold tonight."

Wolvam halted the group. Three other second-years had been roped in to assist. While the first years got into their test groups, the seniors and the adepts conferred.

Terras strolled over to Rilt's group. "Naelen's four, Cammod's four—you boys come with me. I'll drop you off at your sites, and then you'll just have to stay alive till Fourthday morning. Good luck."

* * *

The undergrowth was densely carpeted by fallen needleleaf leaves, and every step squelched. Overhead, raindrops fell on them as though there was no shelter at all. They were placed in a clearing near running water, much to Rilt's delight. They couldn't see it, but they could hear the rushing waters. The river hummed brightly like a symphony in Rilt's mind, and isolating a single note to tune to was tough. Judging by the vaguely distracted expression on Kayle's face, he was probably overwhelmed by all the greenery around him. If one river was a symphony to Rilt, to Kayle the forest was possibly multiple orchestras playing at the same time.

They chose to set up camp on the north side, where there were two fallen trees—each was at least as wide as two of Rilt—and a large mossy boulder provided a shelter of sorts.

Gareth put down his pack on a log and stretched, grimacing when his shoulders popped. "That was a trek and a half."

"Makes you appreciate horses," said Naelen. He wiped the wet from his brow and peered around them. "Let's get our shelter built, shall we, Gareth?"

"I hate it when you volunteer me."

"Kayle and Rilt have other duties."

Busy untying four leather waterskins, Rilt agreed absently with Naelen's remark. He touched Kayle's shoulder. "Come back to us, Kayle."

"Hmm?" The other student blinked rapidly, alertness returning to his eyes. "Oh. Right. Duties."

Rilt almost leaned in to kiss his lover, but remembered just in time that they had an audience. Glancing around, he saw Gareth's venomous expression, but Naelen was utterly unconcerned. Kayle touched his wrist surreptitiously before grabbing Rilt's dagger and a coil of rope.

"Food, the two of you, and don't get distracted by each other," Gareth remarked with an upward quirk of his eyebrows.

Kayle grinned as he handed Rilt his dagger. "We're not animals in rut, Gareth. You'd better set the shelter up by the time we're back. I'm tired of this rain."

* * *

"What—happened—to not—being—animals—in rut?" Rilt grunted and clutched desperately with his right hand at the tree trunk behind him. His other hand had tangled into Kayle's curls.

They had been on the way to the river, Rilt reasoning that he could fish for their dinner instead of trying to track animals. However, the moment they were sure that they were out of Gareth's and Naelen's hearing range, Kayle had set upon Rilt in a frenzy of kisses and caresses, shoving him hard against a nearby tree and showering them both with loose leaves and rainwater.

Kayle was unable to answer Rilt's question, his mouth being otherwise occupied, but his amused hum sent tingling shocks racing over Rilt's skin. It did not take long for Rilt to finish, and after the latter had tucked the young lord in properly he stood up and kissed him. Rilt held his lover close, tasting himself on moist, warm lips. It was decadent and debauched.

"We won't have the opportunity tonight," Kayle murmured, brushing his knuckles along Rilt's jaw, "And that didn't use up much time. Can't say if we can grab a chance tomorrow, so I thought I might as well."

Rilt palmed the front of Kayle's trousers, making the scholar suck in a harsh breath. "What about you?"

"You may watch," Kayle replied with a grin. Rilt did not limit himself to just watching, of course, but they did not linger; it was still uncomfortably damp and they needed food.

After they had cleaned off, Kayle shook himself and stepped away from his lover. "This is going to be a hard three days." When he saw the stains on his knees, he grumbled and swiped ineffectively at the rough fabric.

"You don't say," Rilt said dryly. He swept his hair back from his brow, wringing it out at the nape, and exhaled on a grin. "Still, more reason to celebrate when we get back to our room."

They heard the sound together, the soft scuffling of an animal moving through undergrowth. Kayle tensed. Rilt kissed the other student on the nose.

"I'll head on alone to the river, see if I can get any fish. You hunt, but be careful."

"Of course."

* * *

It was not a river, but a stream with a fast current. Rilt carefully navigated a path down a slick, rocky slope. The water was bitterly cold, and the rains had stirred up the gravelly bottom. He let his mind grow still and tried to resonate with the stream, but Wolvam hadn't taught them how to tune with fast-moving water yet. With a frustrated grunt, he filled the first of the waterskins and waited for the sediment to settle. He would have to transfer clear water to the other skins and leave the bits of gravel in the first.

As he waited to complete his task, the drizzle stopped. For the first time in many days, he felt sunlight on his skin. It was weak and mild, but still better than the incessant rain. When he saw that the clouds weren't massing again, he tugged off his boots and did his best to wick the wetness out of them. It was slow going, but he wasn't in a rush. He was sure the others would be basking in the tepid sunshine.

The forest around him woke up, tentatively and then in a rush. He spied a few bluetails fluttering about—they were not more than a mouthful each, but they tended to congregate near honeycombs— and some speckled roslings, wagging their plump bodies free of moisture as they emerged from the undergrowth. He could set up some snares for tomorrow. Roslings were good eating.

He filled the waterskins quickly after he dried his feet and pulled on his boots. After he returned the water to the campsite, they could come back and fashion a few fish traps. They could even bathe here the next day. Picking his way back up the slope, he focused on levitating the waterskins partially so that they wouldn't weigh too much on his shoulder and didn't pay much attention to his surroundings.

The first bolt whistled out from the forest and punctured the right side of his waist. Startled, Rilt doubled over, dropping to his knees. Pain didn't kick in until a second bolt whizzed past, and his body reacted on instinct. He let himself topple to his uninjured side, his left hand uncorking one waterskin. It was not a deep wound, but it hurt a lot with every movement Rilt made.

Kayle was right about the assassins.

The assailant emerged. Gritting his teeth, the kaedin student tried to regain the resonance he had with the water in his waterskins. The other party—Rilt assumed it was a man—strode forward, wary and silent.

Not a professional killer, Rilt thought with some relief. A professional would have shot him in the head on the first try, when he had not been on guard. That, or the assailant wanted him alive.

That made two of them, then.

The masked man was about five paces from Rilt when the latter smashed a globe of water into the man's strange wooden mask. The impact shattered the mask and the man staggered back. Behind the mask was a square-jawed face with skin like tanned leather, nose bleeding from Rilt's counterattack, and narrow beady eyes set too wide on a weathered face. Rilt gathered a fist-sized globe in his palm again and sat up.

"Who sent you?" he demanded.

The assailant raised his small crossbow. To Rilt's amazement, the tip of the bolt caught fire without the man placing any naked flame to it. Before the man could shoot, Rilt enveloped the man's head in water. The bolt careened wildly from the bow into the wet foliage overhead as the assailant flailed. He clawed at his face desperately, trying to push the liquid from his nose and mouth.

Rilt bared his teeth. His wound was beginning to throb and burn; he had no time for this when his friends could be in danger. Kayle could be fighting for his life. Rilt squeezed.

He could feel water surging into the man's nose and followed its progress into his airway. He kept it there, one hand on his oozing injury with the other hand clenched into a fist to help him stay focused. The assailant started to choke. His eyes rolled to whites.

The realization that he was about to commit murder slammed through Rilt, like a charging stallion suddenly faced with a wall. He released his hold. Never in his life had he wanted another person dead. He could feel a burning under his ribs, the first sign of overexertion. "Will you talk?"

The man glared at him and nodded, coughing up fluid from his throat and gasping hoarsely for air. Eventually he rasped, "You're not the target."

"That's not good enough." Rilt stepped closer. Two fist-sized globes of water hovered around his shoulders. That was all Rilt could manage at that point, but it was important to keep up the threat. "Who is the target, then?"

The assailant coughed again and smiled grimly. "He's dead by now. My brothers are stronger than I am. Our cause will advance and there will be a reckoning, lordling."

Fear drowned out all other considerations. Quick as a snake striking, Rilt stepped on the man's right hand as hard as he could, breaking the fingers, and kicked away the knife in his other hand. The man grunted, cutting off his own scream. Hunkering down, Rilt drew his own belt dagger and held its razor-sharp tip to the man's heaving throat, pressing just hard enough to feel the skin give.

"Who sent you?" Rilt asked a second time.

The man abruptly kicked both feet into Rilt's abdomen, sending him sprawling backwards into a tree. Rilt loosened his grip on his dagger. The assailant clambered to his feet and plunged forward to grab the blade. Though Rilt tried to hold on, the man managed to wrench it free from Rilt's hand and tried to jab it into his side, the blade slashing viciously across his abdomen.

Panicked, Rilt's mind rang with a loud, shrill note. The assailant halted as he was about to pull the dagger out. His eyes widened and he gasped, "Sto-"

He never finished the word. Blood burst forth from the man in a fine mist, a hot, stinking spray landing all over Rilt. The young lord froze in place, mouth agape, before he scrambled up on both feet, his jerky motions sending down a cold spray of water and needles.

All around him, the wildlife had fallen silent. Rilt could only hear his rapid breathing and his pounding heartbeat; his face and hands were wet and sticky, and he could smell the man's death. Books and stories never mentioned the smell: the cloying, coppery sweetness of blood, the stench of human waste, blending together to form a horrifying scent memory of this moment.

Rilt had hunted before, but he had never drawn blade or bow against a person. His stomach, unable to hold down what remained of his breakfast, lurched unsteadily. Falling to his knees, he retched until all that came up was sour fluid. Even then he wanted to vomit further, until he could pass out and forget this ever happened.

"He's dead by now." The dead man's words echoed in Rilt's mind until he struggled blindly to his feet. No matter how he felt, he had to make sure Kayle was all right, and Gareth and Naelen. With a hand pressed to his waist to staunch the bleeding, Rilt staggered away from his first murder. He tried not to look at the corpse as he passed.

He knew he would never be able to forget the malicious grin on that square-jawed face, and the tackiness of the blood that clung to his skin.

* * *

Rilt could not find Kayle. He debated calling out for him, but it would be risky. If Kayle heard him while fighting, he might be fatally distracted; if Kayle had managed to hide away from other assassins, it was stupid to let them know that there was another kaedin student out there.

He ignored the bleeding in his side as best as he could while he stumbled back to their campground in a haze of adrenaline and nausea, keeping close to tree cover and ears pricked for sounds of combat. Sweat gathered at his nape and under his armpits. Every motion that jarred his waist made him wince, and he had to stop for breathers more than he would like to admit.

When the wind changed, he heard it: the clang of metal against metal. He pushed on, gritting his teeth. As he moved, he gathered up tiny droplets of water clinging to leaves and twigs in a long thin stream flowing behind him like a line drawn in air. It was all he could do right now. Whatever he could do would be a mere distraction, but hopefully a distraction was all the others needed.

He saw the fight before he broke cover from the trees. Gareth stood over Naelen, wielding an oddly-shaped disc, shielding them both from flaming bolts fired from someplace off to Rilt's right. Naelen wasn't moving. Rilt bit down his alarm: he couldn't act rashly. Not now. *The assassins were in the trees, then*, he thought grimly. He could try to find them. His first step made him shudder with pain; his wound wasn't cooperating with his plan. There was nothing else to do but brace himself and push through it.

Before he could take a second step, he felt someone touch his left shoulder and whisper, "Are you alright? You're covered in blood."

"Kayle!" Rilt could faint from relief. His breathless exclamation earned him a brief smile. "I'm fine. Only a flesh wound in my side. The—the rest of the blood isn't mine."

"Good. I was afraid you'd been hurt." Kayle did not seem injured at all, which was indescribably reassuring. "Stay here."

The scholar crept forward, almost blending into the vegetation— was that part of his skillset as a Trae kaedin?—and disappeared from view. Then, Rilt heard two heavy thumps. And the one single scream that was cut off abruptly. There was no second scream.

The chill that shrouded Rilt had nothing to do with the wind.

Gareth dropped the shield and dropped to his knees. He swayed dangerously before he toppled over. Rilt scrambled out from his hiding spot and, clenching his teeth, staggered to his friends.

Naelen had a bolt in his ribs. Rilt could hear the gurgle of fluid in every inhalation. He needed immediate healer aid. Gareth wasn't injured, thankfully, but he seemed to have used up his reserves of energy; he was paler than usual, and his gaze appeared to go in and out of focus. Rilt stared at his friends helplessly.

Kayle emerged from the treeline and ran to their bags, where the adepts had given them two flares. He sent them shooting high into the air, the second one three counts after the first: that was the emergency signal. Then he sprinted over, skidding a little in the mud, and propped Naelen up.

"Don't you dare die on us, Nael," the scholar urged. "Help will be here soon, I swear. In Trae's name, you're not going to die on us."

Gareth breathed heavily, still lying on his side in the mud, and muttered, "Assassins. Of course there would be assassins. We're exposed. I should have known."

"Rilt, try to stem the bleeding," Kayle said briskly. "I need you to keep Naelen steady. Don't move the bolt at all. I'll secure our perimeter. Gareth, slow your breathing. I need you up on your feet as soon as you can manage it."

Only partly listening to his lover snap out orders, Rilt stopped up his wound. He felt lightheaded. How much of that was from the shock of killing, how much from the loss of blood, and how much from Kayle's seemingly unaffected state although he'd just murdered two assassins? Rilt sat behind Naelen and let the student rest against him. Naelen's every breath was labored and rattled with fluid. If Rilt had the finesse, he'd be able to pull out water from Naelen's drowning lung. As it was, he could only hold on to his friend and hope that help would reach them in time.

* * *

Wolvam was the first to arrive, and immediately did what Rilt had wanted to do. It wasn't a task for the squeamish; the fluid that Wolvam drew out was tinted pink with blood. The healer Wolvam had brought with him immediately got to work on Naelen once he was no longer drowning himself. Gareth hovered near them; pallid, shaky, and being a general nuisance until the healer ordered him to sit down before he fainted.

Terras and another healer turned up not long after the crossbow bolt was removed from Naelen. The second healer, Hoshad, cleaned and bandaged Rilt and gave him a fortifying drink. Terras tended to Gareth, who was apparently teetering on the edge of burnout. Kayle told Wolvam what happened, and Rilt wished he dared to reach out to clasp his lover's hand. Then he remembered he was still covered in blood. In the dead man's blood.

He nearly threw up again.

Once Hoshad was done with Rilt, Wolvam helped the student to his feet. "How many attackers came after you?"

"One," said Rilt. His hands and feet were like ice. "I killed him."

His horror must have shown in his eyes, because Wolvam clasped his shoulder and said, firmly and calmly, "It was self-defense, Arald. You did what you had to."

"I killed … I killed a man." Rilt took a deep breath. Then he glanced at Kayle, who was watching Gareth, and wondered how his roommate was not more affected.

Wolvam exhaled heavily. "Master Midusel is not going to be happy about this."

"I should hope not," Hoshad said. "I'll have Naelen sent back immediately. There's no more time to waste."

"I need you and Radieri to show me where the other assailants are."

Rilt pointed to where the final scream had come from. "There are at least two there. They were firing bolts at Gareth and Naelen."

Wolvam nodded, and when Kayle joined them, motioned to the two students to lead the way.

With their help, Rilt could walk without putting too much pressure on his injured side. When they got to the assassins that Kayle had dispatched, Rilt felt that same deadly chill from before sweep through him.

He had struggled to kill one. Kayle had slayed three of them without fear.

Kayle had used the trees to strangle them. Boughs thick as two of Rilt's arms wrapped about each head and neck. The last one had been crushed around his ribs. Kayle released the tree branches and coaxed them back to their original positions. The corpses he let fall in a heap at their feet. Rilt felt sick at the sight of the mangled men.

Wolvam patted Rilt's shoulder and said nothing. The adept went over to look through their pockets and clothes, but there was nothing obviously incriminating. The body of Rilt's assailant was similarly lacking in evidence when they found him. Rilt couldn't go closer than fifteen paces; nausea clutched at his throat, threatening to claw out his stomach. Kayle flashed him a quick smile, almost approving, and this made Rilt feel even worse.

Wolvam studied the corpse for a while. "Blood forced out of his orifices. Arald, while I'm glad you're alive, you have to control yourself."

When they got to the spot where Kayle had killed the man who attacked him, there was nothing left but a bloody pulp in a pile of clothes. Rilt threw up behind a tree and refused to look in that direction at all, while Wolvam poked through the mess with a long branch.

"He took me by surprise," said Kayle, ostensibly to Wolvam, although Rilt knew it was directed at him. "I was already in tune with the trees and reacted on instinct."

"Your instinct must be tempered also, Radieri," Wolvam warned. He sighed. "Nothing significant on him except this." He held up a blood-soaked bit of cloth with a symbol that Rilt remembered seeing before, but could not recall from where. It was a square set inside a circle, with a 'v' in its center. "Did they speak? Did they have an accent?"

Rilt waited until they had left the remains far behind to speak. He leaned on Wolvam when they climbed up a slope, flinching when Kayle tried to support his weight. "The one I k- The one who came for me didn't reveal who sent him. He sounded like an Izdahli."

Wolvam did not say another word until they got back to the camp site. Gareth and Naelen were already gone. After sharing what they had found, Wolvam told Terras to monitor the remaining students while he and healer Hoshad escorted Rilt and Kayle back to the hall.

Trying not to show how relieved he was, Rilt looked down at his hands. Blood had crusted under his nails. For a moment, he could again hear the man's final plea, see the sudden spray of crimson, feel the last heat of a dead man's blood on his skin.

"Rilt. You alright there?" Terras peered at him, kind brown eyes exuding worry beneath a furrowed brow. He helped Rilt into the saddle of one of the horses and passed him the reins. He paused, then strapped Rilt's calves and thighs into the riding gear to secure him.

The young noble blinked rapidly and his lips twitched in an approximation of a smile. "I'm … I'll be fine. I'm just really tired."

Wolvam whistled sharply. The horses began to move. Their gait was exceedingly smooth, and this made Rilt want to cry with relief. He had been expecting a jarring, agonizing ride out of the forest.

"The healers' wagon would have gone ahead with Barith," said Wolvam. "I'll run a message to Jenn's Mound for another."

Hoshad agreed that would be wise. "Once we have them at our camp, I can clean out his wound and sew it up. It'll sting like a grybel even with deadening salve, but…"

Much as he would like to know what Hoshad had in mind, Rilt's mind was flickering in and out of consciousness. He kept his eyes on the pricked up ears of the mare he was on, and was only dimly aware of the passage out of the forest.

UNVEILED

"We didn't fail the challenge, did we?" Naelen asked three days later, when he was finally moved to the same ward as Rilt. He was as white as the sheets he lay on, and his voice was as weak as a child's. Every inhalation seemed to drain him of strength. His torso was bandaged, and the healers had only just allowed him to sit upright that morning.

"I doubt it. We did survive an assassination attempt." Gareth peeled a dunefruit and shared it among them. He had recovered with unfair speed, for all he was nearly burned out. Two days of bed rest had put him back on his feet. Rilt was very much put out about that. "Be heartless for them to fail us."

Rilt snorted. He was getting annoyed at not being able to lie on his left. At least Kayle had walked away from all the carnage without taking any harm. Kayle and Gareth were already back in the hall, none the worse for wear. As for Rilt, he had Pellit arrange for him and Naelen to stay in the best ward, away from the general hustle and bustle of the lower floors. Rilt missed Kayle. It was odd sleeping alone in a bed now.

Apparently sensing that Rilt was thinking of him, Kayle slipped into the ward, laden with a large basket of bread, cheese, a covered pot, and more dunefruit.

"Hands off," he told Gareth when the latter reached for the pot. "That soup's for Naelen."

"He can have it," Naelen murmured.

"Come on, Nael." Kayle pouted. "I made it for you."

Rilt raised his eyebrows. "You made it for him?" He squashed the flare of jealousy in his gut. No one was fooled, of course.

"You can have some." Kayle pinched Rilt's ankle playfully and sat on his bed, shifting his legs out of the way. "I've been interrogated by Masters Whitsam and Midusel. Creation bless them, but they were longwinded! They kept rowing the same channel at least fifty times."

"I assume that means they kept talking about the same thing," said Rilt, his calves resting against Kayle's hip.

"Yes, it does, you landlocked numb-brain." Kayle's tone was entirely too fond.

"Did they say why we were attacked?" Naelen asked slowly, with deep breaths punctuating his short sentence.

If Rilt hadn't been watching his lover, he would have missed the look that Kayle and Gareth exchanged. The young lord nudged Kayle with his leg. "You two know something. Spill it."

Instead of responding to Rilt, Kayle nibbled his lower lip and studied Gareth. Eventually he said, "They nearly died, Gareth. They deserve to know."

Gareth looked conflicted. He worked his jaw for a moment, and then said to the two Enthinians, "You must not share what you hear from us, do you understand? It's not just our lives at stake, but the entire kingdom."

"Sounds dire," said Rilt, attempting to be lighthearted, but he was curious about what the two scholars had been hiding which was of such great import. Could it be related to what Master Baelmin had him investigating?

Gareth cleared his throat. "Kayle isn't who he seems to be."

Kayle straightened and stared at the other scholar. "Gareth, wh-"

"He's actually Prince Kirzan."

At any other time Rilt would have found Naelen's expression comical. As it was, his own jaw had dropped in shocked disbelief.

Kayle Radieri, the prince of Aleis? I've fallen in love with the man who will be king? His mind raced and looped his thoughts upon themselves. His false engagement to Galena. Kayle's promise to be his secret lover. Their passionate nights.

"Are you serious?" Naelen whispered and winced when his still-healing lung protested. "Kayle?"

"Gareth, you…" Kayle's face was oddly flushed.

"You said they should know," Gareth argued impatiently. "I'm telling them now. I mean, our deception couldn't have lasted forever."

Rilt was still trying to absorb the announcement. The idea was too enormous, too strange to parse.

The prince and I are lovers, he thought wildly. *He's been lying to me*

right from the start. His poverty, his background. His mother, by Cre-
ation. He lied about his mother. I'm sleeping with Kirzan Alcaronan,
the man who will one day sit on the throne. The man who will rule all
of Aleis. We've kissed and touched each other. We've been intimate. I've
promised to be engaged to Galena for nothing! Does anyone else know?

"I apologize for the lies," Kayle said into the silence that had fallen over the ward. The words seemed to be dragged from him. He took a deep breath, and went on quietly, "But we needed to be discreet. We weren't sure whom we could trust, and lives were at stakes."

"Are both of you," Naelen struggled briefly for air, "really scholars?"

Kayle nodded. "Yes." His left hand tightened on Rilt's ankle. "We didn't lie about that."

"We took the examination and earned our scholarships. So far, only Master Midusel—and you both—knows the secret," said Gareth in a hushed voice.

"Tell us about the group that wants to kill you," Rilt said, struggling to sit up. Half his mind was still going wild over all the things Kayle had told him about his life in Port, and the other half was contemplating the ramifications should Kayle—Kirzan—perish. A bloody and prolonged civil war between the greater noble houses would erupt. Enthin's forces were well-positioned to take the throne, far better than the houses in Dunte or Halimgor. There could be an Arald dynasty. Rilt pushed the thought away with revulsion. He had no desire to wear the crown.

After making sure no one was at the door, Kayle came back to the group and began. "We first heard rumors of kaedine traitors a year ago," he said. "It became necessary for us to enrol. Apart from looking for the traitors, it was time. The future king of Aleis had to be a trained kaedin."

"These bastards aren't working alone, we know that," said Gareth, picking up effortlessly where Kayle had left off. "Otherwise we'd just have Master Midusel interrogate everyone. What we don't know is the extent of their reach nor their exact plans."

Rilt chewed on his upper lip. "Are we sure it's not the greater houses plotting to take the throne?"

"The one likeliest to benefit is your house, Rilt," Naelen pointed out.

Gareth smirked. "Now that we've gotten to know each other better,

I think it's safe to say that you're not smart enough to plot your way to the crown."

"And given that you're my lover, I don't think you'd want to kill me," said Kayle nonchalantly. Rilt nearly choked on dunefruit. The other three looked curiously at his crimson face.

"Scorch it, Rilt, every person in this room knows about you two," said Gareth, rolling his eyes. His tone became more somber. "We don't know exactly who the traitors are, but now that they've made their move, we have more clues."

Rilt snorted and then winced. "Well, their move has nearly killed us."

Kayle absently patted Rilt's ankle. "One of the assassins who attacked me had burn marks, the sort you get from metalwork. The scrap of fabric that Wolvam found had a symbol on it." He drew the shape in the air.

"I know I've seen that somewhere before," Rilt said with a frown. "I just can't remember where it was I came across it."

"It's a local gang's symbol," Kayle supplied. "They call themselves the Verashki."

"How did you-"

"I asked Anya."

"You told her everything?"

Kayle stared flatly at his lover. "Rilt, I'm not an idiot. I drew that on a clean sheet and asked if she's seen it before, that's all. Runners see lots of interesting things out and about the city."

Naelen closed his eyes. "Difficult for a new gang to grab turf in a city as old as this."

"Stop talking," Gareth admonished. "Be a silent ornament."

"Careful, Gareth," Rilt teased. "If someone heard that, they'll think you actually care."

"Go plow yourself, lordling."

Kayle stroked Rilt's foot idly, deep in thought. Rilt admired the way sunlight brought out golden highlights in dark brown curls that fell in waves about his lover's head. The famed master artist Valdon would have loved to paint Kayle's portrait. His gaze moved to the sleek lines of Kayle's neck, smooth and enticing.

His cheeks flushed hot and he decided to change the subject before his thoughts ran away with him. "Wolvam. Do you trust him?"

"With my life," said Kayle. He smiled at Rilt. "Wolvam was the one who let us know about the kaedine involvement. He hasn't been able to identify the plotters though."

Naelen leaned back, already covered in a sheen of perspiration from the exertion of conversation. "I can't believe I thought … I thought Gareth was the prince."

"Me? Please. I can't stand any of them noble types. I barely tolerate Rilt as it is. I didn't know who Kayle was until much later, and by then it was too late." Gareth stood up and jerked his head towards the door. "Come on, Kayle. We have to get back to the hall before dinner."

After the two scholars left, Rilt sat up gingerly. He stared at the closed door, mulling over the entire conversation. Then he asked, "Do you believe them?"

"Not entirely," said Naelen after a long while.

"Me neither." Rilt brushed his fingers over his mouth, remembering how it had felt to kiss Kayle, and all that his lover had said to him before. So many things made sense now, from Kayle's smooth hands and fair skin to his bright intellect and incredible resonance. No one who worked at a port could have escaped the sun or kept their hands so free of calluses. His ruthlessness when confronted with enemies was another clue. The Alcaronans had ice in their veins; the kinslaying that gave them the throne was a taboo topic in history. Taboo as it was, somehow, everyone knew about it.

Rilt wondered what other things Kayle might be keeping from him, and why.

* * *

When Naelen was finally allowed to walk around, it was a relief for him both figuratively and literally. Rilt was equally glad, for he'd been the one assisting his fellow Enthinian to the bathroom for the past week. It had been embarrassing for them both, but that embarrassment served to break down the last few reservations Rilt had about Naelen.

There was an ugly horizontal gash on Naelen's chest, but Naelen was not bothered by the unsightly scar. Rilt supposed that Naelen, being more good-looking than most, did not mind a few physical blemishes. Rilt's wounds were much smaller and—since the dagger had missed his vital organs—he was recovering well.

The private ward helped them recover more quickly. Other than pre-approved visitors like Master Midusel, Wolvam, and Terras—as well as Gareth and Kayle—there were few to interrupt their rest. Pellit and Zarin had both visited with Rilt's permission, bringing with them concerned letters from both Selvina and Cedaran. Naelen had no letters from home, but there had been a note from the runners, and he had only smiled when Rilt asked him about it.

Given the relative privacy of the ward, Rilt found himself discussing the attack with Naelen as well as theorize further about Rilt's recent discoveries about the Kaedin Council.

"Thank the Creators that we hadn't told them about the fire-resonant kaedine," Naelen murmured. His eyes were shut and his breathing labored, merely from walking to the bathroom and back. "They might've told … might have told Master Midusel."

Rilt nodded sagely. "Please, stop talking. Anyway, 'silencing' was mentioned only in Keyron's letter. Maybe it was nothing."

"You don't believe that."

"No, I don't."

Naelen mused aloud, "There's only one thing we can do."

"We'll have to ask all the master kaedine about it until we get an answer."

"No!" Naelen was appalled. "You won't get anywhere that way. How in Creation did Master Baelmin think someone like you would be able to investigate this?"

Rilt glared at his friend. "I've done alright so far."

"Through luck and sheer coincidence," snorted Naelen. He winced as a twinge of pain shuddered through him. "No, what we need to do is become master kaedine ourselves. Then we'd have access to the information that's locked away."

Rilt was incredulous. "You do remember that I have to return to Enthin and learn how to manage the lands, right? My father would never allow me to continue beyond two years of study. I doubt I can take the adept badge, let alone take up mastery."

"In that case, I will." Noting Rilt's surprise, Naelen said, "My father won't care if I stay here for the rest of my life. I have no head for business and I'd only be in the way back in Enthin. My brothers are more suited to it, and they'd be happy to fund my learning. Having a master kaedine would be great for the house name."

Rilt wondered if Naelen's relationship with his father was similar to Halden's relationship with Cedaran. Did all fathers treat their later-born children with the same dismissiveness and casual cruelty?

His thoughts must have shown on his face, because Naelen smiled ruefully and added, "That's how it is, Rilt. I've accepted that this is as good as it is likely to get."

Before Rilt could challenge that statement, someone knocked on the door of the ward. A junior healer hurried in before Rilt could give permission.

"I apologize, Lord Rilt, but Lady Lira requests access and she is very adamant-"

"I'm not requesting anything, healer, I told you to inform." A beautiful woman dressed in violet silk and decked in purple gems swept in imperiously. She waved off the sputtering junior healer and instructed her personal guards to shut the door and keep watch. "Naelen Barith, who in Creation did that to you? Oh, and you must be Lord Rilt Arald! We've taken far too long to meet, given that we're cousins. How is Aunt Selvina?"

"She's fine, Lady Liria," said Rilt with a broad smile. "Please, call me Rilt."

"I intend to, and just Liria," Liria said. She pulled up a chair and plopped into it with as much grace as a colt. "What happened to you both?"

Naelen exhaled slowly and shook his head. "I already told you. We were attacked by bandits."

"Bandits that managed to hurt four kaedine."

"We're students, Liria."

"Still, Nael, you're kaedine. You should be ashamed that you couldn't defend yourselves against common bandits."

"Those were ranger lands, too."

"I'm going to have to tell off the rangers, aren't I? I'll put on my best duchess face when I see the Chief Ranger."

Naelen chuckled and groaned. "Don't make me laugh, Liria. Please."

Rilt watched the two banter. They were both far too good-looking to be allowed in close proximity to each other; he resented being the homely one in the room. Liria's beauty lay in her vivaciousness and warmth. Her large eyes were spaced just a touch too far apart, her nose a little too strong, her mouth a touch too wide, but when she smiled, he could not help staring at her. There was an easy casualness in their speech that reminded Rilt of himself and Kayle, and for a moment he ached for his lover and friend to be there.

Liria patted Naelen's foot and turned her attention to Rilt. "I hear my dear brother is putting up at your place. I'm sorry for all the trouble he's caused."

Rilt grinned. "You're sure he's created trouble?"

"He's Evvas. Trouble follows him like stingflies to rotting meat." Liria shrugged. "I doubt he's mended his sails since he fled Port."

"How long has it been since you saw him?" asked Rilt.

"Seven months, give or take." Liria cocked her head at him. "I'd love to see my dear brother today. Are you amenable to a trip out of the healer hall? I promise to have you back here before sundown."

Rilt glanced at Naelen. "Do you want to come along?"

"Not when I still feel like a side of beef that's hung out to dry," said Naelen. "You two go ahead. Bring back some komma, will you? The food here tastes worse than that okrai pea soup back in the hall."

"Ugh, yes. Komma and maybe some tangs. I'm sick of dunefruit."

"I'll tell Kayle that you've gone out."

A flush crept up Rilt's neck. He stuck his hands in his pockets and mumbled something about returning to the hall soon. Liria peered closely at his face and then grinned cheekily.

"There's something going on," she sang quietly. Rilt's wide-eyed denial made her smile widen. "Don't worry, I'll be discreet."

Once they left the ward, Liria carried herself differently. There was a more pronounced sway to her hips, she lifted her chin up more, and bestowed flirtatious smiles at the healers while Rilt informed them on duty that he was going to his mansion with Lady Liria.

"But sir, your wounds-"

"I'm fine," Rilt interrupted before they could flutter about him and find ways to prove he was on his deathbed. "I'll be back before sundown. If not, send people to the Arald estate, or look for Lady Liria Alwyth."

"Don't worry," said Liria sweetly, slipping an arm through Rilt's and pressing a kiss to his cheek, "I'll take very good care of him."

As she dragged him off, he hissed, "Now they're going to assume…
things!"

"As if you could possibly bed me in your state, Rilt," she said pertly,
poking him lightly in the side. He yelped in pain. Liria patted his
forearm in apology. "Now, what say we visit my dear brother, hmm?"

* * *

"Lord Evvas has returned from riding, my lord, Lady Liria, and is
in the stables at the moment. He is aware of your visit," said Zarin
respectfully as he set down a silver tray with tea and some pastries. "I
apologize for the state of the walls; we are readying the mansion for
the duke and duchess."

Rilt nodded. "Mother specifically mentioned that the tapestries
have to be in top form, so use only those that are not too worn or
faded," he said. "And since they will be entertaining guests for a few
evenings, do ensure we have sufficient wine."

"Certainly, my lord."

"You may leave us." Liria poured herself a cup of tea and waved
Zarin away. Her gaze swept around the room once the servant had
gone. "That's very fine woodwork you have here. Timat wood?"

Rilt was bemused. Why was Liria asking about the architecture? "I
don't know wood all that well."

Liria cast an impish grin at him. "Well enough, I'd gather. What's
Kayle like? A hot handful, perhaps?"

"Wh- No, there's… Lady Liria, I've not… Kayle is a friend," Rilt's
sputtering amused Liria greatly, as she threw her head back and guf-
fawed. Rilt took a deep breath and said with some heat, "Kayle and I
are good friends at the hall, that's all. He's my roommate, and one of
the loveliest people I have ever had the privilege to meet."

The mischief in Liria's face softened. "Sounds wonderful. I'd love
to meet him some day. Nael likes him too, and Nael doesn't like
most people." She sipped her tea, apparently content to wait for her
brother to show.

Rilt studied her. Outside of her beauty, Liria was vastly different
from the girls and women he had met in Enthinas. For one thing,
she was far more assertive and confident in how she addressed him
and how she dealt with those of lower station. Away from strangers,

she was almost boyish in her mannerisms. However, once there were onlookers, she emphasized her femininity.

That could not merely be a quirk of personality, he mused, as he drank his own cup of tea. The Alwyths were a sprawling lot, with many lesser houses that were ready to usurp the place of the main house with the title. Evvas and Liria were the only two full-bloods, but outside of the direct lineage, there were dozens more in line for the title and the lands. Her behavior had to be deliberate and calculated.

"People are quick to assume that a woman is weak for being a woman," she suddenly said. Her long lashes lowered for a moment as she contemplated the painted tiles on the floor. "You've the luck of birth and sex, Rilt, and I the misfortune of being secondborn and a girl."

"Nothing wrong with being either."

"Everything wrong with both, if you know you can be better than the one born to the role." Liria smiled. It was not an expression calculated to charm, but a hard, appraising expression. "There are very few who are pleased with my usurping Evvas' place. Isn't that right, brother dear?" she trilled to the door.

Evvas sidled in, a bland smile plastered to his face. "Most of them assumed you resorted to underhanded means, sister dear, though of course you and I both know the truth of that matter. How have you been?"

The tension in the room could be cut with a sword, despite the Alwyths' smiling faces. Rilt kept quiet, observing the two siblings. They resembled each other closely, especially around the eyes and jawline, but where Evvas exuded sleek, silken charm, Liria was lush and smooth. Evvas's shoulders were tense and a tic twitched in his cheek. Even though Liria was younger, she held herself as regally as a queen, amused at her brother's impotent rage.

She fluttered her lashes coyly. "I'm doing as well as can be expected after your departure, brother dear. Father will be pleased to know that Duchess Selvina has taken you in. She's always had a soft spot for strays."

"The duchess has compassion, sister dear. I'm sure you'll benefit greatly from spending some time with her," said Evvas, his smile brittle around the edges. He turned his attention to Rilt. "Lord Rilt, you must be tired. Perhaps you should return to the healers. Thank you for indulging in my sister's whimsy, even if she tends to get her way far too easily."

"That's my dearest brother, always looking out for me. Come, Rilt darling, you do need to go back and rest. Good day, Evvas dear. I do wish you'd come home soon and stop imposing on others, but I guess that is entirely up to you now." Walking over to Evvas, Liria kissed her brother lightly on the cheek. "I'll let Father know that you're doing just fine."

"I'm sure you will," Evvas sneered. "Good day to you both." The Alwyth lord turned on his heel and left.

Rilt raised his eyebrows. "I am very glad that while Cedaran is related to you by blood, he has none of your temperament."

Laughing, Liria said, "He has Alwyth blood in him, Rilt. It will show. Aralds may stand their ground, but we Alwyths are the ones who seek out the cracks and dig in."

* * *

Much to Rilt's disgust, he and Naelen had to sit for their term examinations in the healer hall a mere three days after Liria's visit.

"We nearly died," he protested when Wolvam delivered the papers the first day of the examinations.

The adept raised an eyebrow. "And yet, you're alive. If you're well enough to complain, you're well enough to take the examinations."

"Naelen, your injuries are more severe. Tell him not to test us."

"I studied," Naelen said with a small smile.

"This is precisely why I hate you," Rilt informed him.

Wolvam rustled the examination papers under his nose. Rilt took it with a glower. The adept pulled over a chair and settled into it to watch the two students.

An hour and a half later, Wolvam collected the papers from the two patients. He stood there next to Rilt's bed, his sharp gaze taking in the state of Rilt's recovery and the way Naelen was trying to breathe without wincing.

"I heard that you've been let into the secret," he said in a low voice. "Imprudent of them, but I suppose you are trustworthy enough. Don't allude to it at all, not to anyone: family, friends, lovers. The peace of the kingdom may depend on your discretion."

"You were the one who found out there were kaedine involved," Rilt said. "Do you have suspects?"

"That is not your concern." The adept slipped the examination papers into the envelope it came in and sealed it. "Master Midusel and I have it well in hand. You just keep watch over your friends."

Rilt wanted to protest, but Wolvam's forbidding glare shut him up. It did not deter Rilt from making plans to search out more information on his own. He wasn't one to skulk about, however, and if Kayle really was Kirzan, Rilt felt uneasy about leaving him all alone.

Exhausted, Naelen fell asleep as soon as Wolvam had left. Rilt slipped out of bed and sat down at the chair by the window. The rainy weather had cleared up in the past few days while they were in the healer hall. The floods in Lower Izdahl had receded, so Rilt supposed the citizens were busy clearing away the detritus. The healer hall was a large rectangular building encasing a lovely garden in the middle. Rilt gazed at it, two floors below, but he was not looking at the garden at all.

When it came to politics, Master Baelmin had told him to always follow the money. "Those who take action are people who have nothing to lose, or everything to gain," the old tutor had said. "It's a cynical view, and it has yet to fail me all these years."

The ones who stood to gain the most would be the noble houses—particularly the Aralds. Rilt could not imagine his father coming up with a plan to assassinate the ruling house, however. No matter how domineering Duke Halden was with his children, he was not a greedy or ambitious man. He hadn't even wanted Rilt to come to Izdahl, because others might think that he wanted greater influence among the houses in the capital. That left the other dukes.

Not the Alwyths: they had just sorted out their succession problem, and Liria was not so stupid that to crave the throne when she had had to overcome so much opposition to her taking the title from Evvas—and there was still the issue of the lesser houses of the Alwyth line to contend with. Her hands were going to be very full for the next few years.

The Awells of Dunte kept mostly to themselves, but from what Rilt could remember from their brief meeting, Duke Ingros did not strike him as a particularly avaricious man. His clothes were well-made but plain, with the signature vine patterns of Dunte, unlike the other lords and ladies who favored richly embroidered brocades and fine silks. In fact, it was hard to recall his appearance: Duke Ingros was neat, his expression placid, and the only thing that stood out about his features was a mole above his left brow. He had hardly spoken in the convene. It made little sense for the lesser houses to try, either, given that the Aralds, Alwyths, and Awells were still holding power.

Follow the money…

If the king and the prince were killed, what was likely to happen? Civil war would be the outcome. Rilt was the only kaedin in his generation among the three greater houses—the people would back him if they had no other option—but there were other, older, more experienced kaedine among the lesser houses. Kill the king, kill Kirzan, and then get rid of Rilt, and there would be no kaedine among the four greater houses. The thought was sobering.

He bit the inside of his cheek. He was overthinking this. With a pang, he wished Master Baelmin were alive, ready to provide his expert opinion. There was nothing for it but to progress faster in his training and be watchful, not just for the sake of his own skin but for Kayle's, too.

Kayle Radieri, the prince of Aleis? Rilt tried to match the name 'Kirzan Alcaronan' to his lover's face and failed. He knew the way Kayle's eyes crinkled up when he laughed, the habit he had of pushing his hair back from his brow, the texture of the raised skin of his tattoo. He knew the sound his lover made walking back to their dormitory, the scent he exuded after a shower, the taste of his mouth in the middle of the night.

How could Kayle be Kirzan? What about the story of his mother? Kayle's nightmare had not been feigned, that much Rilt was sure of. How much of what Kayle had shared with him were lies? How much was truth? Why had Kayle been so insistent that Master Midusel had been one of the men in the greenhouse, plotting his death? The young lord scrubbed at his cheeks and leaned back in his chair, wishing he had answers, yet fearing to ask.

* * *

"I'm surprised your family hasn't written to you," he said to Naelen that afternoon when they were having lunch together. "Given your injuries, I'd have thought they would be more worried."

"My father might not even grieve if I died." There was no bitterness in Naelen's tone, which made Rilt uneasy. Naelen saw the expression on Rilt's face and added, "My mother will write at the end of the month. She always does."

Rilt chewed on the bland meat they'd been given. "Don't they care?"

"Not really," said Naelen. The corner of his lips twitched. "He has my two older brothers to inherit the business. I'm the unnecessary and unexpected child. Becoming a kaedin isn't a matter of house pride, it's just a way for me to earn my own keep."

"That sounds lonely, I guess."

"Could be worse. At least I'm not beaten or starved." Naelen shrugged with his uninjured side.

They lapsed into silence after that as they picked through their tasteless healer hall dinner. Rilt supposed that Naelen, having grown up in that environment, would view things differently, but he thought it was unfair that the Bariths had Naelen as a son, yet didn't appreciate him.

Duke Halden was similarly neglectful of Cedaran, while he piled criticism after criticism on Rilt. Master Baelmin had been there to soften the instruction, but the more Rilt thought of his father, the more he realised that Halden had never had a good word for either of his children. If he spent more time reading, he was 'becoming soft'; if he ran about and played outside on the estate grounds, he was 'neglecting his studies'. Rilt had to be wise, prudent, daring, restrained, courageous, stern, and dozen other conflicting things all at the same time. It had begun to feel unbearably stifling when the Kaedin Hall entrance examinations came up, and Rilt decided to risk Halden's displeasure. Now, as he looked back on his father's attitudes, he marveled that it had taken so long for him to push back against his father's expectations.

"Don't feel sorry for me," Naelen remarked unexpectedly. His eyes were warm and gentle. "I don't feel sorry for myself."

Rilt made himself scoff. "Oh please, get over yourself. I was thinking of Galena. I should invite her to the ball, though she'll be performing."

"Too bad you can't invite whom you want to really invite," said the other student, closing his eyes.

Rilt shut his own eyes. "Too bad."

In his mind's eye, Rilt pictured Kayle dancing with him. Kayle would look good in a blue tunic embroidered in silver, the starsilver ring glittering on his finger.

CONTROL

It was another week at the healer hall before Rilt and Naelen were both allowed to return to their rooms. Gareth grumbled half-heartedly about having to share the room again, but the other students were delighted when Naelen and Rilt joined their friends for an assembled lesson outside the lecture hall just after breakfast.

"Good thing the bandits didn't know who you were, eh?" Oledan said with a laugh, clapping Rilt on his back. "The ransom for the future duke of Enthin would bankrupt Enthinas' coffers!"

For a moment Rilt was baffled, and then he understood. That must be the story the adepts and masters had circulated to cover up the fact that Kayle had been the target of the attack.

"It certainly surprised us," he agreed. "Good thing Kayle kept his head."

"Good thing you're hard to kill," Kayle interjected.

Gareth snorted. "Yes, like a housebug."

Ladmos asked Naelen exactly what wounds he'd sustained. Apparently, Gareth had been embroidering the tale whenever he was asked, so if Naelen had experienced all that Gareth said he had, he would have lost all his limbs, been gutted, half-strangled, and nearly decapitated twice over.

"I only had a punctured lung," explained the blond with a small smile.

"Only, he says," Oledan said with jovial disbelief.

Wolvam strode up to them at that point, scowling darkly, and told them to get to their places. Sensing the adept's black mood, the students scurried to their seats as quickly as they could.

"What's crawled up his pants?" Oledan whispered mutinously, just behind Rilt and Kayle. Wolvam slammed a sheaf of papers onto the table, making the first row of students jerk back in alarm.

The adept spread the papers before him. "Your examination scripts for kae theory are here."

Rilt bit the inside of his cheek. Had he done poorly? Then again, he had been laid up in the healer hall. Surely Wolvam had been more lenient?

What am I saying? This is Wolvam. Leniency is not in his nature.

"There are only four students who performed up to standard. The rest of you were appallingly mediocre. On the subject of tuning, some of you managed to confuse resonance with the potentiality of tuning kae." The rest of the session comprised the adept berating the common mistakes the students had made.

Eventually, Wolvam stopped his scolding. He folded his arms over his chest and said, "Norwan, you're the top of the class. Krell, Radieri, I suppose you've been distracted by the incident, but I expect better from you two the next term. Derone, Jeras, well done. You tied for second."

Rilt was disgusted. Being nearly mortally injured was only *distracting*. While Wolvam distributed the papers, Kayle leaned into Rilt's side and murmured, "Derone'll top the Trae group in tuning. I bet anything."

"You're more powerful than he is."

"He has more finesse."

Wolvam started distributing the scripts. Rilt dreaded looking at his scores, but to his relief, it wasn't as bad as he feared. Asking around, he gathered that he was eighth or ninth place in their cohort. Naelen had three marks fewer than Rilt, but he accepted the middling grades with equanimity. Poor Ladmos was nearly in tears when he realized he'd placed last in the subject. After the bell had gone, Wolvam had a quiet but intense talk with him, in the back of the room, and Rilt noticed how Oledan hovered nearby, pretending he wasn't straining to hear every word.

* * *

The rest of the day was spent in much the same way, though the other masters and Terras didn't lecture them as Wolvam did. Gareth topped History, much to Rilt's disgust; the latter thought he had understood the material better since Master Baelmin had been tutoring him in that subject long before he got to Kaedin Hall. Still, he was in second place, which assuaged his pride somewhat. As for the other subjects, he was pleased to have passed decently in all of them.

It was a race between Kayle and Felas for who had more firsts. Felas always squirmed in his seat when he lost to Kayle, his face flushed nearly as red as his hair. Rilt also found out that—contrary to Kayle's prediction—Derone had not topped his group; instead, Kayle had that distinction. Ladmos did the best in Aega class, earning one of Wolvam's rare smiles. Felas did the best out of the Terai class, and Naelen—much to Gareth's disgust—had beaten him in the Dagas class.

"You were in the hospital," groused the sallow-faced scholar when they were sprawled on the banks of the lake after dinner. "How could you possibly have completed the project?"

"I completed it before the survival challenge," murmured Naelen, his eyes closed as he rested against the trunk of a whitesong tree. The gardeners had trimmed the draping branches somewhat, but there was enough shade for the still-convalescing student. His brow was beaded with sweat from the short walk from the classrooms and Gareth had ordered him to sit and rest.

"I didn't see it," Gareth said, almost accusingly.

"It's in there," said Naelen, pointing to the thick pillars on the far side of the lake. There was a faint smile on his lips. "Master Berras' project, remember? The one about storing lightning."

Stretched out on the grass, Rilt vaguely wondered why anyone would want to try to store lightning. He supposed it was Master Berras' idea; he had designed the water heating system after all. Perhaps he could ask Master Berras to set up a similar hot-water system in the Arald estate. That had to be better than housing dangerous boilers next to the bathrooms.

The sun gave everything a faintly golden-pink halo, and the food weighed heavy and happily dull in his stomach, making him drowsy, too. Insects buzzed about them and over the water. The sky would be bright for another half hour yet.

Gareth prodded him in the ribs. "Where's Kayle gone to?"

"He said something about Master Jodius wanting to see him at the greenhouses. A healer hall apprenticeship, I believe."

"Inter-hall apprenticeships are only allowed for second-year students," Naelen said. Suddenly he straightened with a grunt of pain and alarm, his eyes wide. "They're only for second-year students."

Rilt did not understand the implications of Naelen's statement until he remembered who Kayle was. Even though Gareth had said that no one else knew, how could he be so sure? Stunned by the extent of his complacency, he leaped to his feet and took off running, the faint twitch in his injured side barely noticeable. Naelen would not be able to follow him, not with his still-healing lung.

He wasn't surprised to find Gareth keeping pace with him. They raced past the cafeteria hall, vaulted over the gate, and then careened through the orchard. The greenhouses had never seemed so distant or ominous before.

Rilt was frantic, wondering which of the greenhouses Kayle and Jodius were in, when Gareth shoved him to head to the one on the west side while he entered the larger one on the east. The west greenhouse was where some truly exotic plants were cultivated, and it was usually locked. However, the door was ajar.

Rilt crept in, feeling an odd sense of nervousness. Palms dominated the central dome, and dark green foliage formed partitions. The sand masked his footsteps. There were shelves mounted against the walls, where pots stood with little name cards propped up in front of them.

He hoped to Creation he was wrong, that Jodius really was only talking to Kayle, that Kayle was still alive. He got to the end of one row when he noticed movement in a far corner. That would be where the work stations for the gardeners and herbalists were, if it mirrored the layout of the east greenhouse. As he got closer, he heard an arrhythmic thumping and soft moans. Then he realized what he was hearing.

He froze, every fiber of his being rejecting the evidence of his ears. A strange tingling sensation buzzed in the tips of his fingers, and he thought he heard a familiar hum ricochet in his skull. He had never felt so cold before in his life.

"Well then," said Jodius, sounding slightly winded once the other noises stopped, "you've certainly earned my discretion. Your secret is safe with me."

"You're despicable," Kayle retorted. There was a rustle of fabric. "If any word gets out-"

"I promise I won't tell anyone. So long as you keep up your end of the deal, my beautiful boy, my lips are sealed." Jodius laughed, an unpleasantly smug sound. "Think about the friends you're protecting."

Their conversation registered only as background noise to Rilt, making hardly any sense. He could only stand there, trying to comprehend what Jodius had apparently just done to Kayle. With Kayle.

He was still standing in the middle of the narrow path when Jodius turned the corner, still doing up his belt. The master halted in his steps. "Arald. I was not expecting you."

"Rilt?" Kayle appeared behind Jodius. Whatever he saw on Rilt's face made him blanch. He jogged up to his lover and pleaded, "Rilt, wait-"

The young Enthinian lord didn't say a word as he shoved Kayle aside. The humming in his head grew to a roar, deafening him to everything else. It felt like his whole body was vibrating with the sound. He reached out a hand to the young master, not quite sure of what he intended. There was a sudden rush of movement in the foliage and then Jodius fell to his knees abruptly. He opened his mouth as if to speak, but he couldn't make a sound. Rilt was vaguely cognizant of Kayle tugging on his other arm, trying to get him to leave, but he planted himself more firmly into the ground. He let the hum crescendo in his head and tremble down to his outstretched fingers, and pulled.

Blood exploded from every pore of Jodius' body and sprayed over Rilt and Kayle.

The taste of copper and iron shocked Rilt out of his wrath. He lowered his hand, staring at Master Jodius. At the corpse of Master Jodius. He suddenly felt out of breath.

"By Trae," Kayle whispered. He sounded as stunned as Rilt felt. "Rilt. By all the Creators. Rilt, what have you done?"

"I just—I didn't mean to—Kayle, I don't know..." he trailed off, feeling sick. The world was askew. Master Jodius was more mangled than the assassin in the forest. "This wasn't supposed to happen."

"It wasn't supposed to happen? Rilt, you just—you just murdered Master Jodius! You could be hanged for this." Kayle's lovely blue eyes were wide with disbelief and anguish. He covered his mouth and stared at the blood dripping off the leaves, as if trying to will the gore away.

Rilt could not even wipe the blood off his face although it was trickling into his eyes. He blinked, tearing up. "I didn't mean to. I heard … and I wanted to make him pay, and I…"

"We need Gareth." Suddenly efficient and detached, Kayle swiped quickly at his own bloodied cheeks. "But how are we going to get him without other people seeing us covered in this?"

"He's in the other greenhouse." Rilt was shaking now, feeling cold to his marrow. He was terrified. He had lost himself to anger before, but not like this. Not to the extent of killing anyone.

It had been over so quickly. Far quicker than that assassin in the forest. No one had told Rilt it would be so easy to kill a man. Or that it would be so hard to breathe afterwards, when every inhalation smelled of death.

Time become inconsequential. He didn't even notice Kayle disappear from his side, but he did react when Gareth turned up.

"By Dagas, lordling, what have you done?" The usually acerbic tongue was reined in now as Gareth studied the scene and looked at Rilt in horror.

"Will they hang me?" Rilt asked. He sounded as lost as he felt. "Will it hurt?"

Kayle shook his head. "No, no they won't hang you," he said fiercely. He straightened his shoulders and added, "They won't hang you. I won't let them."

"Not the problem right now." Suddenly, brutally efficient, Gareth went around the corner to the storage shed, returning with a few burlap sacks. "We'll have to toss him into the river after we weigh him down with rocks. Since someone is bound to notice his absence tonight—tomorrow if we're lucky—we have to do it as soon as possible."

"These sacks aren't big enough," Kayle commented. He could have been talking about the weather.

"Then we'll have to cut him up." Taking in Rilt's horrified expression, Gareth snapped, "There is nothing else we can do for him. He's dead, because you didn't control yourself, and that's because you," here he turned on Kayle, jabbing a finger into his chest, "began sleeping with the lordling. I told you he'd become possessive. I told you it was a bad idea to sleep with him, and even worse, to fall for him. Now look at what your lover has done. Look at this!"

Kayle swatted Gareth's accusatory finger away. "If Jodius hadn't …

Rilt didn't know."

"No, but *you* did! I'm trying to save both your bent hides right now, do you understand? Now help me, or confess to the murder and hang!"

A silence fell on the three. Finally, Kayle hunkered down by the corpse. "What do you need?"

A trowel from a pot nearby changed shape into a wicked-looking knife in Gareth's hand. "Hold up the left leg."

Rilt watched, morbidly fascinated and repulsed, as Gareth methodically cut off Jodius' pants and then began dismembering the legs below the knees. The pants were a stinking mess; Kayle bundled the garment up into one of the sacks with barely a grimace. There was hardly any blood flowing from the cuts, since practically all of it had been expelled from the body. It wasn't until the two scholars had gotten to the elbows that Rilt shook off his paralysis. He took Jodius' hand and removed two rings.

"These should be destroyed," said Rilt quietly.

"I can do that." Gareth paused. "He can still be easily identified. Suggestions?"

"Take off his face."

"Kayle!"

"It's the fastest way."

"We don't have a lot of time," Gareth said briskly. "Naelen should be here soon. Kayle, if you could... Could you?"

Kayle took the short knife and sawed at the dead man's jaw. Slowly he peeled off the master's face. Once he could slice it off at the hairline, Kayle stabbed at the skin until it was nothing more than a bloody mess.

Trying not to gag, Rilt exhaled slowly through his mouth. He wished he could look away.

Strange, thought Rilt, that he could look so much like nothing. Like a life-sized mannequin, the sort the dressmakers and tailors used. Only the head needed to be cut off now.

It was Kayle who reached out and grabbed the dead man by his hair to hold it up for Gareth to cut through the neck. Rilt had to look away from the dead man's eyes. The miasma of death hung over the scene.

"Toss the parts into the sacks and leave them outside the window over there," said Gareth briskly. "There is a barrel of water in the back of the shed, use that to clean yourself off. I'll get Dagger to help tonight. Let's hope Naelen has not alerted anyone else."

Rilt followed Kayle and Gareth in a daze. He was not certain why they should follow Gareth's orders, but the scholar had more confidence than Rilt could muster at that moment. Kayle didn't make eye contact as they cleaned their faces and hands before rinsing out the spray of blood from their tunics as best as they could.

Just as they exited the greenhouse, Rilt and Kayle sopping wet, they met Naelen, who was panting heavily. Perspiration dripped off him.

"Are you safe?" Naelen asked breathlessly when he caught sight of them. "What happened to you two? Why are you wet?"

"Three guesses why," Gareth drawled. He rolled his eyes and added, "I stumbled on them doing what they do after they let me search the east greenhouse all by myself. What took you so long?"

Naelen wrinkled his nose defensively. "I can't move fast, you know that. And Terras caught me by the cafeteria block to check on my injury."

"You didn't tell him about anything else, did you?"

"Of course not." Naelen looked at Kayle curiously. "Where's Master Jodius?"

Amazingly, Kayle barely flinched. "He had an appointment in the city, he said. Told me I had a good shot at the apprenticeship if I assisted with certain extra projects."

Naelen was about to ask more questions when Rilt interrupted, saying that he needed to get out of his wet clothes. He let Gareth mock him and Kayle for the entire walk back to their rooms, but he couldn't take his mind off the gruesome sacks they'd left outside the greenhouse.

MIDNIGHT

Sleep would not come.

When they got back to their rooms, Rilt feigned fatigue and turned in early. There was nothing that did not feel like blood on his skin.

He tossed and turned. How much had Naelen seen in the orchard? Would he have noticed the smell of blood on them? He wondered how Gareth was going to do what he said he would without getting caught—and if he were caught, what would he say to the authorities? At the time, the scholar had sounded so sure of himself that Rilt's doubts hadn't had time to surface.

Kayle hadn't voiced any of his own doubts either. Did he trust Gareth so completely? What lay between the two scholars that Kayle could place his and his lover's entire life in Gareth's hands with no hesitation?

His lover. Right. They could be celebrating Rilt's return instead of agonizing over Jodius' murder, but neither Rilt nor Kayle wanted to touch each other. In the shower, Rilt had scrubbed and scrubbed and scrubbed, but the sensation of blood clung to every pore. He needed to get clean, he needed to feel whole again, but most of him was still in the greenhouse, so in tune with kae, to the exclusion of everything else, that he could still hear the humming in the back of his mind. Now that the rage had passed, the young lord could clearly see Kayle's panic and horror when he…

Rilt felt the bile rise and he dashed for the bathroom. Even throwing up in the toilet till he had nothing left in his guts didn't ease the churning nausea.

He heard the bathroom door open.

"I'll make you some tea, if you want," said Kayle.

Rilt wanted to slam the door shut. He wanted to bury his face in Kayle's chest forever and ever, and never do anything else again. He wanted to feel clean.

Nodding, he got up and rinsed out his mouth. Even the tepid water tasted like blood.

His face in the mirror was that of a scared, lost boy. He was about to lean his forehead against the mirror when he jerked back from his reflection, thinking he saw another pair of red-rimmed eyes looking at him from over his shoulder. But there was no one there.

* * *

Kayle already had their small kettle on the fire. He was unnaturally still as he stared into the flickering flames. The golden-red light cast him in bronze.

Sitting in the chair next to him, Rilt had never felt further from his lover than this instant. He kept his gaze on the black kettle, trying to ignore the tantalizing song the agitatedly boiling water within was singing to him, and clenched his fists so hard that his knuckles cracked.

"You didn't stop," Kayle said, his voice dull as a knife to the heart. "I tried to stop you but you wouldn't listen. Why didn't you listen?"

There were so many things Rilt could say to that, but what came out of his mouth was, "I didn't want to."

"Because you heard us? And for that you murdered him?"

Rilt could have argued that he was protecting Kayle, that Jodius assaulting him was punishable by death anyway, that Rilt had lost control because he had been shocked. The truth was far simpler: he had been blinded with jealous rage. He could still feel it curling in his chest, hissing like a cat.

"Your hands are no cleaner than mine." Rilt swung the kettle away from the fire and poured the scalding water into their mugs with the waiting teabags. Steam curled accusingly between them. "Yours are bloodier, if we're comparing. Remember the assassins?"

"I killed them in self-defense."

"You could have trapped them, or bound them with vines. You crushed their skulls instead." Rilt wished he could take the words back, but he could not. In the long stay at the healers, away from Kayle, the thoughts had festered and now the accusations spilled out, foul and poisonous. "I'm not proud of what I did, but I did it for you, and I'm really sorry, I truly am, it went too far and I wish I could take it back!"

He realized he had raised his voice and choked it down. With a deep breath, he pressed himself back into his chair and covered his mouth.

Kayle took his tea and sipped it without comment. Rilt noticed his lover's shaking hands and was viciously pleased that he had provoked that reaction. It wasn't until Kayle had finished his tea that he stood up and upended Rilt's untouched tea into the fire.

"For me?" he hissed, teeth white in the darkness of the room. "If you'd spared even a thought for me, you'd have stopped when I asked you to-"

He paused. Both had noticed the unmistakable sound of pebbles rattling against the window. Rilt rose to his feet, already tuned to the scalding water in the kettle. He heard the potted bluespine shrub shiver and rustle as Kayle peered out the window, shoulders tense.

"Calm your sails, Kayle, it's just me. We're ready."

Rilt joined his roommate at the window and looked down. Gareth's gaunt features appeared even sharper in the dim moonlight. "Rilt, you're up too? Of course you are. Why wouldn't you be?"

Rilt thought the other scholar's garrulity odd, and then realized Gareth was probably as disturbed as he was over the whole affair. "Who else is with you?"

Gareth glanced into the darkness behind his left shoulder. Something moved in the shadows. He exhaled sharply and told the two to join him by the back gate that led to the river. Then he darted out of sight.

* * *

After they crept out of the dormitory block, and slipped along the shadowed path to the back gate to the hall, Rilt and Kayle met Gareth and a broad-shouldered man who looked vaguely familiar. By the gate was the porters' little station, lit with a small wicker lamp. The man nodded gravely at Rilt and Kayle when the two students joined them.

"This is Dagger," said Gareth. The scholar looked thinner than usual next to Dagger, though they were about the same height. Oddly-shaped sacks were piled next to the wall.

Rilt frowned. "Aren't you one of the porters?"

"I am, sir." The man tapped a thick knuckle to his forehead. He was entirely average in appearance; Rilt thought he had possibly spoken with the man before in passing, but he did not make it a point to identify the hired help on sight.

Kayle folded his arms around his middle protectively. "What are we going to do?"

"The Dahl is running fast and full," said Dagger. The man jerked his jaw at the blackness beyond the light from the porters' hut. "There's been storms upriver. The Dahl can move him out to the sea, easy."

Rilt bit his lower lip, tasting the sick under his tongue. There would be an investigation, surely; a master kaedin missing, with no one who saw him leave—Kayle's lie would be ripped apart like antique lace. They would all hang. Probably not the prince, but Rilt himself would swing from a noose.

Kayle shook his elbow. "Rilt, focus. Dagger knows what he's doing."

"They'll ask around when they notice he's gone. They'll ask the man on gate duty if he saw Jodius," said Rilt. "They will know you lied."

"No lie, sir, since I was the man on duty at the gate. And indeed, I saw Master Jodius on his way out the gate in a hurry."

And this is how my crime becomes nothing. For a moment Rilt thought he would burst into hysterical laughter. He took a deep breath, counted to ten, and asked, "What would I do without my friends?"

The other three men looked at him strangely.

"I killed a man," Rilt said. His head ached. "I killed Master Jodius. And instead of apprehending me, you're helping me get rid of the body?"

"Because I want you alive," said Kayle. Wisps of hurt shimmered in his voice. "I don't want you dead, Rilt, I don't want you to be silenced or hanged for this. Not for Jodius."

Gareth folded his arms and stuck out his jaw. "He was blackmailing Kayle."

"I don't need..." Rilt swallowed his shout. "Does no one see that I've done something terrible? That I took a life, not in self-defense?

That's wrong, Kayle, you know this!"

"I don't care!" Kayle snapped, his voice cracking. "I don't care that it's wrong. I don't care if you kill one man, ten, a hundred, a thousand! I love you and I want you alive and if I have to bury a thousand Jodiuses I'd do it myself!"

His breath caught in a sobbed gasp and he covered his mouth, aghast at his outburst. The shout carried a little in the still night, but they were far enough from the teaching and dormitory blocks to be safe. Kayle swiped furiously at his eyes and nose.

An awkward silence descended on the group. Gareth cleared his throat. "I don't approve of it, lordling, but Kayle knows what's at stake. In the long run, it's better for us to hide this."

"Think of the big picture, right? Because that is what my father always says. Big picture. Long run. And the little people can go straight to the midden."

"Rilt, do you want to hang?" Kayle asked, exasperated and upset.

That was all that Rilt needed. True, he had killed Jodius, but the master kaedin would have been executed for the blackmail attempt anyway. Furthermore, he suspected that his father would have made similar arrangements, were he to have committed this crime on Enthin lands. Since he would not have to lie in the ditch he had plowed himself, he had no reason to be upset.

Other than the fact that this went entirely against everything he had been taught by Master Baelmin, and against every principle in his marrow.

He could tell Kayle meant exactly what he said, and this time, he was terrified. He had just proven that he was willing to kill for Kayle, while Kayle was willing to hide a murder for him. They barely knew each other outside of the hall, and the fact that Kayle had willingly slept with him, knowing that as the future king, he was risking his very throne, should the knowledge become public.

He had to let this go, for now. The deed had been done and nothing could be changed. Following Dagger's lead, he picked up two sacks and plodded after them, feeling as though a dead man was staring at him from over his shoulder.

* * *

The trees were dripping with fruit, but it was too dark to see. Rilt felt like he'd been walking for ages. Fog swirled about his feet.

"Hello?" he called out. His voice was muted.

Eyes glittered at him in the shadows, and he thought he could hear footsteps behind him. He wanted to turn around, but his body kept moving forward. The fog parted before him as he came to a monolith. The stone stood almost three times as tall as himself. As Rilt looked up, the sky lightened and the clouds parted.

Then the stone started to crack. Red tongues of flame spurted from the fissures, but the fire didn't burn Rilt, even as he reached out to touch it. The fire licked up his arms and wrapped about him. He stared, transfixed, until someone pulled him back from the monolith and he fell on his back.

"Don't go," Kayle said, sitting atop him. He was dressed in furs of deep gray and snow white, and he was crying. He was bleeding along his jaw, staining the fur crimson. "Don't go."

"I'm not going anywhere," Rilt said, sitting up and cradling Kayle's face. "I'm not going anywhere."

He watched as blood flowed over his hands and down his forearms, putting out the fire. In a daze, he trailed his fingers along the wound along Kayle's jaw and chin.

Someone behind him whispered, *Take that off.*

He knew that voice, though for the life of him he had no recollection of who it belonged to. He dug his fingers into the cut and peeled his lover's face up and over. Inch by inch he tugged, fighting to pull the skin off entirely.

Rilt pulled Kayle's face off. Jodius tilted his mutilated head and stared lidlessly at him, showing far too much teeth. "Like what you see?"

Rilt screamed.

* * *

"Rilt, Rilt wake up."

"No, no get away, get off me don't TOUCH me!"

"Rilt! It was a dream," Kayle said firmly, shaking him by the shoulders until the young lord stopped babbling. "Just a dream. You're safe, I have you."

Still gasping for breath, Rilt could only gape at Kayle's shadowy form. His skin felt tacky and cold with sweat. When his lover reached out to wipe his brow, he flinched. To his numbed shock, he was crying.

The bathroom door popped open and someone peered in. "Is everything alright?" Naelen asked.

"He's alright," said Kayle, not turning around. "Thanks, Nael. It was just a nightmare."

The door shut.

The brief interruption shook Rilt out of his trance. He stayed still this time, as Kayle gently swept his hair from his face. It was as though his skin had been flayed; he felt over-sensitive to even the minute currents of air, to every faint sound. He could feel the water in the pipes, which made tremors dance through his frame.

"Nightmare," he repeated in a hoarse whisper.

After pressing a soft kiss to Rilt's cheek, Kayle went to get a towel and came back to dab the sweat and tears from his face. Rilt pulled off his nightshirt and dropped it on the floor. Vaguely, he recalled the night when he was the one comforting Kayle, and how that night had changed their relationship.

He didn't want Kayle to comfort him now.

"Do you want to talk about your dream?" Kayle asked softly. This close, his face was a blur of gray and black, and his warm breath was jarring.

"No." Rilt swallowed and covered his face. "I think… I think it'd be better for us to sleep in separate beds tonight."

He could imagine how hurt flickered over Kayle's features, but at this moment, he just wanted to be away from the scholar.

The prince. Whomever he was.

Blood all over his hands.

Jodius grinning at him.

Peeling Kayle's face off.

The blood.

All over his hands.

He did not realize he was muttering under his breath until Kayle hugged him, murmuring, "I'm sorry, I'm sorry you had to. I'm sorry about everything."

"I have to… You… you had… You were bleeding," Rilt mouthed

the words into his lover's neck. "You were bleeding and I took off your face, I took it off, it felt so real, and it was… It was Jodius underneath that, he was smiling at me, he was smiling at me. The blood, I can still… Kayle. I can feel the blood."

The Halim scholar held him and rocked him gently, soothing him with quiet assurances. When Rilt could breathe more calmly, Kayle asked, "Do you still want us to sleep in separate beds?"

The young lord bit his lower lip. "I don't know. I don't… I don't think I can sleep. I don't want to."

Kayle brushed his palms over Rilt's cheeks and cupped the back of his head, resting their foreheads together. They breathed together, until their rhythms matched up, and then Kayle whispered, "Try. I'll watch over you."

Rilt pressed his nose against the side of his lover's face before he lay down on the rumpled bed. His eyes were sore and his throat felt raw. He skimmed his fingers over Kayle's skin and wished he could forget the images in his dream.

"I love you," he said, feeling the truth of the words down to his bones as his hand wrapped loosely around Kayle's wrist.

With a soft sigh, the scholar leaned down to kiss Rilt's cheek and nuzzled him. "I know. Go to sleep."

As Rilt closed his eyes, he heard Kayle singing softly, a song about a gentle breeze over the wide sea.

REVELATIONS

Someone should have noticed Jodius' absence in the morning, but since it was barely a week to the King's Ball, most of the instructing masters and adepts had suspended lessons while the hall was being set up for the event. No one knew for sure where anyone was. Many of the masters made themselves scarce while the students and adepts busied themselves with cleaning and decorating. The entire hall was a flurry of activity.

The usually jovial Terras seemed to be less affable than normal, as he rushed about to assist in putting up torches and lanterns in the central court. Wolvam was supervising the first-years as they scrubbed floors and wiped windows. Rilt would have been absorbed in his very first experience of cleaning like a servant, if not for the guilt consuming his thoughts. Every moment, he expected to be hauled up and accused of murder.

At noon, the news arrived via the runners. A mutilated corpse had been found by a picker-boat. A man, they said, whose face had been sliced off and his entire body chopped up. The city wardens wanted to know if anyone was missing.

"Wonder who the poor chap was," said Cammod, stretching to work out the kinks in his back. He added, "The murderer must have been a cold-blooded monster."

Rilt nearly dropped the scrubbing brush. He hoped that his guilt didn't show on his face. Gareth, who was just a few paces away, said, "I'm sure they'll find out who the killer is."

"Sooner the better," grunted Cammod.

Rilt resumed his work.

He did not sleep well that night either, but Kayle was there to hold him until the tears stopped choking him.

* * *

The next day, all of Kaedin Hall was in an uproar. The dismembered corpse had been identified.

"It's Master Jodius," whispered Oledan over breakfast. The first-years huddled closer. "The wardens posted drawings of a tattoo they found on the dead man, and I heard from Lyren last night that Wolvam identified him."

"Wo-Wolvam?" Rilt's fingers went cold. "Wolvam identified a tattoo on Master Jodius? How would he know about it in the first place?"

"Could he be mistaken?" asked Kayle.

Oledan looked exasperated. "Kayle, you're from Port. You know about Halim men and their tattoos; you even have your own."

Rilt could not swallow another bite of his bread. He pushed it aside. He wasn't the only one who had lost his appetite; most of the senior students were simply sitting at the tables, ashen-faced and waiting for more news.

Finally, Master Berras strode into the cafeteria. "I know you've heard the rumors," he said in his booming voice. "All students are to remain in their dormitories today until further announcements are made. Lunch will be delivered to your rooms. Adepts, gather in the library. Master Midusel wishes to speak to all of you."

One of the junior adepts raised a hand. "Master Berras, will the King's Ball be cancelled?"

"At this point, no. The wardens will let us know if that changes. Now, students, to your rooms. Adepts, to the library."

Rilt followed his friends numbly. He caught a glimpse of Wolvam seated at the adepts' table, staring into empty space, his hands wrapped around a cup. Terras was beside him, a hand on his shoulder.

* * *

Rilt thought he would not be able to handle being confined to his room, but oddly enough, not having to put up a facade helped. Though sorely tempted to write to Master Baelmin in his journal, Rilt knew better than to leave incriminating evidence lying around. Instead, he wrote down the rumors circulating the hall. At the end, he scribbled: I don't know why Wolvam knew about Jodius' tattoo.

Perhaps they had been close. I wish it hadn't happened at all. I'm sorry.

Someone knocked on their door. It was Terras, along with two wardens. Rilt froze in his chair, blood draining from his face, but Kayle greeted them calmly.

"Radieri, I heard from some of the other students that you met Master Jodius the evening before last at the greenhouses. Could you show the wardens in which part of the greenhouse you met?"

"Certainly. Let me put on my shoes."

Rilt struggled to master his racing heartbeat and walked over to the door as Kayle was about to leave with the adept and the wardens. "Is—is everything alright?"

Terras smiled faintly. "The wardens are just retracing Master Jodius' steps."

There was nothing Rilt dared to say. He watched his roommate walk away, down the hall. When they turned the corner and disappeared from view, Rilt shut the door and leaned his brow against it, feeling like a failure. Hot tears stung his eyes and he took a deep, shuddering breath.

"I'm sorry," he murmured almost soundlessly to nobody. "I am so sorry."

* * *

"They checked my story with the porters," said Kayle later, when Gareth asked over dinner. "Apparently, someone down in Lower saw him going to the courtesans."

The look exchanged between the two friends revealed more to Rilt than it should have. This 'someone' had to be a person they had paid to lie to the wardens.

And so my crime gets buried further and further beneath layers of lies. Torn between relief and loathing, Rilt could not decide if he resented Gareth and Kayle for stepping in when they did, or hated himself for not being strong enough to confess to his crime.

What would Cedaran say if he knew? What would Master Baelmin say?

* * *

He left to meet Galena in the midst of all the furor, needing to get away from the heavy atmosphere in the hall. He forgot to account for Galena's curiosity and intelligence, however. She wanted to know more, and he began to wonder why he'd agreed to the charade of the engagement at all.

"He wasn't my instructor, how would I know?" he snapped finally, yanking his hand from hers. Onlookers stared at the couple, and some whispered to one another when they saw the kaedin blue on his uniform. He glared at all of them until they turned away.

Contrite, Galena sat down beside him and called for drinks. She reached out to touch his clenched fist. "I'm sorry, dear. Perhaps we should talk about the ball. I do have my performances but we'll dance after the king's dinner."

"That would be good," he said, grudgingly. Her smooth hands reminded him of Kayle's, and that brought to mind the deception he'd fallen for. He forced himself to smile at Galena. "Do you wish to meet my parents? I'm sure it would be great for you to meet them over dinner. Before the ball, I mean. All the lords and ladies in Izdahl will be dining with the king and the scholars."

Galena blinked. She dimpled very prettily when she smiled. "I would love to meet the duke and duchess, Rilt. But perhaps you should get me something special to wear before I do."

It took a moment before Rilt understood what she meant. He finished his drink, stood, and offered Galena his arm. "Come with me," he said. "I know just where to go."

* * *

'Where to go' turned out to be the Aralds' Izdahli mansion. It was already bustling with activity.

Pellit hurried out to greet Rilt. "My lord, I wasn't aware you were coming by today."

"It was a spur-of-the-moment decision. I'll bring you some pies the next time. Are my parents here already?"

"No, my lord, Elais is here in advance of his grace. He's in the pantry, checking that we have stocked up adequately. Good afternoon, Lady Galena. What would you like to drink? Should I inform the kitchen staff to prepare dinner for two?"

Rilt waved the suggestion aside. "We'll go back to the university in a moment. Tell Zarin to meet us in the oak drawing room. I need the keys to the safe."

The mansion was sparkling after a thorough cleaning. Even the rugs had been beaten free of dust. Servants were busy polishing furniture and wiping ornaments; two footmen were struggling to put up the heavy brocade drapes that usually remained in storage. The few nicks and scrapes from Evvas' debauched party had already been repaired, and the Alwyth lord was nowhere in sight.

The servants bobbed and curtsied as he and Galena passed. They knew better than to speak to him out of turn, of course, but he noticed the maids exchanging delighted, cheeky grins.

Eight footmen were struggling with a massive tapestry. Rilt watched as the heavy material was unrolled, revealing a scene depicting the Arald-Aleis treaty that had brought Enthin and Izdahl together. The tapestry was easily as large as his dormitory in Kaedin Hall. In the middle were Keyron Arald and Coleri Aleis, tall and broad-shouldered, their right hands clasped about each other's forearms. Their forces were arrayed behind them in formation. Ice eagles soared in the skies above—the luster of kaedin blue had not gone out of the tapestry—and golden rams stood below, horns stained with blood. On the right was the familiar shape of the palace tower, the Eye of Aleis; to the left was the ancient Arald fortress in the Wyn mountains. Rilt had not seen it personally, but its likeness was found in many of his ancestors' portraits.

"Where are you putting this?" he asked.

"Lord Rilt, we've been told to hang this in the banquet room," said the oldest footman.

"Have Elais contact the weaver guild. This needs some repair right there, in the corner."

"Yes, my lord."

Rilt was about to leave when he caught sight of a thick band of red color high up in the background, behind a thick border of trees. "Hold on. Leave it for a moment."

The footmen stepped aside as Rilt paced up the edge until he got to the red horizontal line. He thought it had been a trick of the eye or that age had discolored the tapestry, but the weavers who made designed and woven this had included small black skeletons, smothered in the red.

Blackened bones. His breath caught in his throat. He suspected that the weavers had included the detail as part of the narrative of the treaty, but that story had been lost to the ages.

Lost … or silenced.

He would have doubted the efficacy of lies and deceit, had he not experienced it himself. The truth of what happened to Jodius would not be revealed to anyone outside of those who had been there. All people believed now was that the young master kaedin had gone out after sundown, was waylaid, and then murdered.

A tightness wrapped about his ribs. He nodded curtly at the footmen and guided Galena up the stairs to the drawing room.

"How lovely this is! I wonder if that chair is comfortable enough for two?" Galena asked with a coy flutter of her lashes, indicating a lone love-seat upholstered in deep green velvet in the corner.

Rilt snorted. "Very comfortable, but not right now." He took down one of his ancestors' portraits. Behind it was a safe.

"You asked for the keys, Lord Rilt, and I have them at present," Elais said, standing at the door. He bowed deeply. "I beg your pardon, I should have been at the door to greet you and your guest."

"You were counting cheeses and wines, so I won't hold that against you." Rilt gestured at the safe. "I want my mother's engagement jewelry. Open the safe."

"My lord, surely this has to be permitted by his grace."

Rilt held up the seal ring. "No, it surely doesn't. Open it."

Elais shut up and quickly unlocked the safe, his nimble fingers barely jingling the keys. Rilt took a box out and had Elais lock the safe again.

"Tell mother what I took. Now get on with your duties." Elais nodded and disappeared, as quietly as he came.

The box was square, the length of one hand on each side, and when Rilt opened it, Galena's mouth fell open.

"Rilt," she breathed. Her face went pale before her cheeks flushed bright pink. "Rilt, I cannot possibly accept that."

"Yes, you can," he said firmly. "You're going to be an Arald. I promised you that."

In the box was a necklace set with diamonds and sapphires. At the center of the necklace was a blazingly blue gem the size of a rosling's egg, flanked by rubies, each as large as Rilt's fingernail and red as the finest rosales. Along with the necklace were two cuffs for the wrists, glittering just as madly as the necklace. The jewels were of the finest quality Enthinian mines could produce, and had been in the family for at least seven generations.

"This is what you will wear when we make our formal announcement," Rilt murmured as he draped Galena's neck with the jewels. "But the cuffs—you are to wear one of the cuffs from this day on, Galena, and when your parents agree to the match, you will have the other to wear for the wedding."

He stepped back to gaze upon her. The blue of the sapphire was too strong for her coloring. It washed out her eyes, even if the rubies set off her milky complexion beautifully.

"Rilt, this … this is …" Galena looked like she was about to cry. "I didn't mean … Rilt, you don't have to…"

"I want to," he said, and he was surprised that he meant every word. "I think you deserve all the good things you can get, Galena, in exchange for what you're willing to do for me."

She sniffed and tears rolled down her soft cheeks. "Believe me, I was not thinking about these when you asked me to be engaged to you. Not something as… extravagant as these, anyway."

After picking out one of the cuffs for her and returning the rest to the box, Rilt gathered her close and kissed the corner of her mouth. "My mother is going to adore you."

∗ ∗ ∗

When he got back to the hall, he found Kayle turning the starsilver ring over and over in his hands.

"Something wrong?" he asked as casually as he could.

Kayle smiled, but there was a shadow in his eyes. "I have something to ask you."

"What is it?"

"I'd like to wear this on the night of the ball," Kayle said in a small voice. He bit his lower lip. "I know your father would be there. I don't—I don't to cause trouble."

Kayle was holding himself around his middle. His face was pinched and unhappy, and now that Rilt was observing his lover closely, he saw the shadows beneath his eyes. Kayle had been watching over him while he struggled with his guilt. Kayle, who had been violated by Jodius, protected him and kept him safe from the law.

Rilt's throat tightened. For a fleeting moment, he wished that he could announce to the kingdom whom he loved.

He loved Kayle. The depth of his conviction about his feelings both scared and bolstered him. It didn't matter that Kayle was also Prince Kirzan Alcaronan, the future king, or that Rilt was the future duke of Enthin. Yet for all that it didn't matter, it did, so much that they could never make their love known.

"Wear it," Rilt said, sudden and fierce. So what if Halden recognized the ring? If the Duke made a scene, he would be the one risking the house's reputation. No one else would know the ring's significance. He would have announced his engagement to Galena by then, obscuring any chance of gossip, and it would mean the world to Kayle if he could wear the starsilver ring in public.

Kayle brightened. He looked so glad that Rilt had to kiss him. His lover's mouth was soft and warm and yielding, opening to him with a small sigh. Rilt drank him in, holding him close with one hand tangled into dark curls.

Pulling away when their breathing became labored, he murmured against Kayle's lips, "You saved me, and you loved me, and you lied for me, and yet you ask me if you could—do you even contemplate what I would do for you? For this? Kayle Radieri, you could order me to walk into the Seas of Kedhros and I would do exactly that. I would do anything for you."

"Rilt, you-" Kayle's words were crushed by another devouring kiss. He whimpered and clung to Rilt, his fingers digging into flesh. Finally, the two students parted enough for the Halim scholar to say, "I don't deserve you. By Trae, Rilt, I don't deserve any of this. I don't want you to hate me when you realize…"

The two students broke apart when someone knocked on the door. Hastily tidying himself up, Rilt called out, "Who is it?"

"It's Anya. Lord Rilt, you've a message from His Excellency, His Grace, the Duke of Enthin."

Father. Rilt cursed fluidly under his breath before he opened the door. The lanky runner handed him an envelope sealed with the red wax favored by the Aralds. Her eyes rove over him and she even tried to peer into the room. When Rilt raised an enquiring eyebrow, she shrugged. "In case you have a message for them, m'lord."

"Not today," he said, and shut the door in her face.

Kayle watched as Rilt ripped the envelope open. "Your father's here?"

Rilt gave a sharp nod. "We are to have dinner together before the King's Ball." His stomach clenched unpleasantly and he wondered if their relationship would be any better after the few months' separation. He doubted it.

"Is your father really that…" The Halim scholar considered a few synonyms and eventually settled for, "Strict?"

Rilt took a deep breath and rubbed the back of his neck with both hands. How was he to convey the antagonism between himself and the duke? The fact that he had no memory of any affection from Halden, that praise had been given so sparingly and even then, only for achievements that his father deemed important.

"You'll be alright," Kayle said, touching his lover's forearm hesitantly.

Rilt made himself smile at Kayle, before he kissed him on his cheek. "Of course I will be." He sighed and embraced Kayle. Somewhere in the dark of his mind he recalled again that hot copper-iron spray over his skin. He forced away the horror of what he had done, in favor of loving the man he had in his arms.

* * *

If Kayle and Rilt seemed a little preoccupied with each other the next morning, no one caught them at it. Gareth was absent from breakfast, though he turned up after morning meditation and whispered a few hurried words to Kayle before rushing off again.

"Is something wrong?" Rilt asked under his breath when they were on their way to an assembly called by Master Midusel.

Surreptitiously, Kayle squeezed Rilt's fingers and shook his head. "The wardens say they have a suspect. Dagger will handle it."

In spite of the easy reassurance in the scholar's voice, Rilt could see that Kayle was concerned. However, this was no place to discuss this; all the students and adepts were gathered in the largest lecture hall. Rilt spied Wolvam slouching against a pillar right at the back of the hall. His dirty blond hair fell over his eyes, and his arms were crossed in front of him. He seemed more haggard than usual, his usually alert gaze now distant and unseeing. Next to him was Terras, whose friendly, open face bore signs of strain. He muttered to another adept and then hugged Wolvam's shoulders. Surprisingly, Wolvam didn't shrug Terras off, as Rilt expected.

After most of the audience had settled into their seats—some students perched on the stairs—Master Midusel took the podium. Everyone fell silent instantly. His voice carried easily through the room.

"You know why we have gathered here," he began, and for a moment he seemed to lose his line of thought. Rilt felt his heart hammering in his chest. Surreptitiously, he brushed the knuckles of his hand against Kayle's thigh, and the latter nudged him with his shoulder, as though leaning over for just a second.

Clearing his throat, Master Midusel went on, "Master Jodius was brutally murdered a few evenings ago. As of this moment, we do not know who killed him, or for what reason. However, the Kaedin Council and the City Ward are resolved to locate the murderer and have them stand before the justices as well as the King. We will find them, and they will hang for this … this heinous crime."

"All of us knew him. He was your student, your peer, or your teacher," said the dean. His voice shook. "He was one of the brightest masters to walk these halls, and to venture beyond it. He added to our repository of knowledge the indigenous herblore of the Kiwok islanders, and also helped grow in Aleisan soil the invaluable marial shrubs, without which the healer hall would have lost at least five hundred Izdahlis to the plague three years ago."

Rilt stirred in his seat. His fists tightened involuntarily. Kayle nudged his foot and glanced at him, but whatever he was trying to convey with his eyes was lost on Rilt. The young lord bit the inside of his cheek, wishing he could stand and confess to his crime, but his entire body felt frozen and numb. A sardonic voice murmured in his head, *Aren't you glad you have Gareth and Kayle to take care of such things for you?"*

Looking frail and worn, Master Midusel sighed deeply. "Despite the tragedy, the King's Ball will still be held, though it will be delayed for a day. We will all bear gray bands on our right arms for the rest of the week. Adepts, distribute them please. Master Jodius will be cremated and sent home to Dunte the morning of the ball, and we will see him off from Kaedin Hall one last time."

* * *

That evening, Rilt opted to forego dinner. He was skipping pebbles into the lake when he sensed someone coming up behind him. A quick glance over his shoulder allowed him to relax fractionally. It was only Naelen.

Rilt exhaled heavily and selected another flat stone. "Nothing better to do than shadow me?"

"Which of you did it?" Naelen asked.

The blunt question stunned Rilt. The tension that had bled out earlier slammed right back into his gut and gripped his heart and lungs. He didn't turn around; nevertheless, he could feel Naelen's gaze piercing into him.

"Did what?" he eventually managed. Already there had been too long a pause; it was clear he knew what Naelen was talking about.

Naelen walked forward to stand in front of him. "I have not mentioned my suspicions to anyone else," he said in a low, measured tone, "but I can put cattle and plow together, Rilt. One of you murdered Jodius."

Rilt felt his throat close. "There's no evidence."

"I don't plan to expose any of you. If I wanted to, I'd have done so. Who was it, Rilt?"

The young lord could feel his fingers trembling. In spite of the encroaching summer, he felt chilled to the bone. "He violated Kayle."

"That doesn't answer my question."

"That's all you need to know." Rilt forced himself to take a deep breath. The water of the lake sang out to him and he reached for the comfort of tuning. "Any one of us would have done it."

It was as good as a confession. Rilt wished he could name the expression painting Naelen's features. Horror? Disgust? Anger? Pity? The blond student turned away, blinking, pale and tense. The two Enthinians stood at the lake as the sun set and darkness invaded the sky, leaching heat out of the air.

"It's a good thing there isn't any evidence, then," Naelen said at last.

Rilt nodded. What else was there to say?

FAMILY DINNER

"You look fine, Rilt."

"You're not the one having dinner with my father."

"I'm sure you're exaggerating about how bad it's going to be," said Kayle gently. He straightened the shoulders of Rilt's clean tunic and leaned in to kiss him lightly on the lips. "Good luck."

Taking the chance to hold his lover, Rilt buried his nose in Kayle's hair. The Halim smelled of soap and that familiar, slightly briny scent, as if the ocean flowed through his veins, just under his skin. The fragrance grounded Rilt in the moment. That morning, he had woken up with the feel of tacky blood over his face and hands, frozen in place by guilt and fear; it had been Kayle's sleeping presence beside him that had soothed his pounding heart and slowed his panicked breathing. He wondered if the nightmares would plague him to the end of his days.

"I wish I could take you with me," he admitted in a whisper.

"I don't think you ought to inflict a Port Halim commoner on the Duke and Duchess of Enthin," Kayle teased.

Rilt huffed in amusement. "Mother won't mind in the least."

"But your father will, and you want this dinner to go as smoothly as possible, so let's not. Besides, Galena is going to be wonderful company." Kayle stepped back and smoothed down the tunic again unnecessarily. There was a faint sadness underlying his smile, but Rilt decided not to ask. Instead, he kissed Kayle again, hoping that the warmth and love would sustain him through a very trying dinner.

* * *

"Do I look presentable?" Galena asked breathlessly at the foot of the stairs leading to the School of Music. She twirled a little, letting her dress flare out. In the evening sun, Rilt could not rightly tell if the color was white or pale orange, but the sinuous design of vines on the hem and collar stood out. Galena's dark hair was loosely curled, and she wore yellow ribbons around her neck. The jeweled cuff was on her right arm.

He smiled, aware that the expression did not reach his eyes. "You look fine. Come, we don't want to be late."

The horse pulling the open-top cab trotted at a neat pace. Rilt lay back against the seat and watched the pink and gold clouds overhead. His left arm draped over the seat and Galena rested against him.

"It's still bad in the hall, isn't it?" she said.

"No one knows what to do or say," he answered.

Galena sighed and squeezed his knee. "It's worse because you're not used to feeling like victims," she said quietly. "Kaedine are so … so powerful, and to meet such a brutal end is just horrifying. I mean, first they got you and your friends, and now a master kaedin."

Unwilling to hear more, Rilt pressed his lips to her temple. "Let's not talk about it, alright? I don't want to worry Mother."

* * *

Cedaran was the first to greet Rilt and Galena once they had entered the house. The younger Arald careened down the stairs and pulled Rilt into a tight hug, which the latter gladly returned. Already, Cedaran was less scrawny than he remembered.

"I suppose you did miss me, Beanpole," Rilt teased.

"Of course I did," said Ced. Then he noticed Galena standing off to the side and immediately straightened and bowed. "I … I apologize. Um, I … Hello. Good evening."

Galena smiled, her eyes bright with amusement. "Good evening, Lord Cedaran. I'm Galena Aedinal, at your service."

"Lady Galena, pleasure to make you, I mean, to meet you. Rilt's mentioned you a few letters. A few times in his letters," Cedaran said. The tops of his ears were pink.

Rilt covered his mouth so he would not giggle. He hadn't forgotten how awkward his brother was around girls, but he thought Ced might have grown out of it. Clearing his throat, he asked, "Where's

Mother?"

"With Evvas in the green sitting room." Cedaran's gaze flicked at Galena. Rilt was not sure if that was meant as a warning or a signal. "Father is in his study."

Custom would dictate that Rilt introduced Galena to Halden first. He took her hand and squeezed her fingers. "You should know that my father did not approve of my studying in Kaedin Hall. And he made his disapproval extremely clear."

Comprehension dawned in Galena's pale blue eyes. "I understand."

"Thank you."

Not willing to subject Galena to Halden for any longer than necessary, Rilt led her to his father's study. Cedaran stayed at the end of the hallway and kept fiddling with his glasses.

"Come in."

Despite the intervening months apart from his father, Rilt still squared his shoulders instinctively once he heard Halden's voice. With a steady breath, he led Galena into the study.

Perhaps the time away had done some good, after all. To Rilt, Halden no longer looked as imposing. The duke was still powerfully built, but he did not fill up the space with his presence the way he used to in Rilt's memory.

"You're early," said Halden. "And who is this? I wasn't aware you were bringing a guest."

"This is Galena of the house Aedinal," said Rilt evenly. "I informed you in my reply yesterday."

"Good day, your Grace. It's an honor to meet you," said Galena, curtsying with a perfect dip of her knees. She had the sense not to speak more than that.

Halden peered at her. "Aedinal? From Dunte? A lesser house, thrice removed from the Awells." He set aside his pen. "Good day, Lady Galena. Pleasure to make your acquaintance. He mentioned that he was bringing a guest, but I have no idea why he has invited you."

Rilt took Galena's right hand in his left. He had to fight to keep his grasp firm and not crush her slender fingers. "I wish to marry Galena."

The only response from Halden was silence. The two young people watched the duke rise from his seat, his movements slow and deliberate. He studied their faces and their joined hands, and then nodded.

"Lady Galena, if you would give my son and me a moment alone."

Galena glanced at Rilt and squeezed his fingers, before curtsying again and leaving the room. Duke Halden's face was inscrutable even after the door had clicked shut. Wondering what his father wanted, Rilt fought for balance and calm within. Again, he heard Master Baelmin admonishing him for impatience.

"At last you are stepping up to your responsibilities," said the duke. His voice was heavy with recrimination. "After the trouble you got into, this would at least prove to the Enthinians that you have not forsaken your duties. And the whole debacle with that Ledon fellow would be forgotten."

"Nothing happened between me and Ledon. How many times do I have to ... never mind." Rilt inhaled sharply and squared his shoulders again. "Do I have your blessings?"

"I suspect," said the duke, his tone almost fondly resigned, "that whatever I say, your mother will insist on making your engagement public by the end of the week. She is not from a house I would have chosen, but in this case, I have no objection."

Rilt wanted to be angry, that even now his father could not summon any happiness when his firstborn had found a spouse. That he could not even give his approval. He wanted to be furious, but he wasn't. He thanked Halden and exited the study.

Cedaran was worrying his lower lip when Rilt walked over. "How was it?"

"Good enough," said Rilt, mustering a smile for Galena and his brother. "He's not opposed. Now, let's meet my mother."

* * *

As suspected, Selvina was rapturous once she heard about Rilt's intention. She also tutted at Rilt's choice of engagement gift.

"We are Aralds, for Creation's sake," she scolded with a broad smile on her lovely face. "I will commission a brand new set for your engagement party, my dear. It's a good thing we are here in Izdahl and I can meet with the master jewelers. That old thing will have to do in the meantime."

"Old thing, she says," Rilt said, shaking his head in amused disbelief. "It's an antique, mother."

Selvina flapped her hand at him. "We can do better. Now, Galena, tell me everything about yourself."

"Oh, but your Grace, don't you wish to hear more about Rilt and his studies?" Galena said, helplessly charmed by the duchess' warmth.

Selvina laughed and clasped the young woman's hands. "Rilt writes regularly. Come, I want to learn about you. As for you gentlemen, out of here. We'll see you at dinnertime."

Thus banished from the drawing room, Rilt found himself walking towards the den with Cedaran and Evvas. Evvas trailed his fingers over the ornately carved picture rail on the wall ahead of the two brothers, whistling. He paused just before they got to the den and whirled around to face them.

"Congratulations, Rilt. She's beautiful," said Evvas with just a hint of a leer. "Your offspring would, of course, displace Ced from his place in inheriting the title and the lands. Such a shame."

"I've never-" Ced began, incensed, but his older brother stopped him with a hand on his shoulder.

To Evvas, Rilt said coolly, "Cedaran will be invaluable when I take the title, and I know he will stand by me. We may not be full blood-kin, but we're brothers in heart and mind. I trust him with every-thing, even with the lives of my yet unborn children."

The subtle dig at Evvas' relationship with Liria was not lost on the Halim lord. He raised his chin. "You have a lot of faith. Let's hope it's not misplaced. After all, betrayal by a sibling does sting."

With that, Evvas ambled away. Cedaran made a rude sound under his breath and Rilt squeezed his brother's shoulder once more.

"Why did Mother insist on showing him hospitality?" Cedaran grumbled.

Rilt smiled thinly. "He is of her house, after all. Come, talk to me about the happenings of Enthinas and your tutor. You write too little."

He had his suspicions about Evvas' presence. Halden was not one to suffer fools or leeches, and while Evvas was not stupid, he was also not the sort of person the duke would keep around willingly, what-ever Selvina said. There was something in this for Halden.

"Is Evvas going to be at the Lords' Convene?" Rilt asked after Cedaran recounted an accident at a mill.

"I suppose."

Father is going to speak for Evvas. Rilt tucked the thought aside for further consideration in private. Liria was canny, but she was a woman, and if Halden actively opposed her taking the title, Evvas would have a decent chance of reclaiming it. What good would it do for Enthin, having such a man as Duke?

* * *

Nearly an hour later, Pellit popped into the den to inform Rilt and Cedaran that dinner was ready. He furtively handed Rilt a thin, narrow pouch, bound with brown string.

"What's this?" Rilt asked, after he told his brother to go ahead to the dining room.

"Sir, information. Master Jodius was involved with the new gang, the Verashki," Pellit murmured. "I paid for those copies of a report from the healers in the morgue. They found the Verashki's brand on the corpse."

Rilt narrowed his eyes and tucked the pouch into his pocket. This was unexpected. Had Kayle been aware of this, then? There was no time to quiz Pellit privately; Rilt hurried to the dining room where everyone was already seated.

"Sorry," said Rilt.

Halden did not acknowledge the apology, but Selvina smiled and chided him gently for tarrying.

"I hope you like Enthinian food, Galena," the duchess told the young woman. "It's nothing as sublime as Duntean cuisine, of course."

"I'm sure the meal will be fantastic," Galena demurred.

Rilt smiled across the table, pleased that his stepmother had taken Galena under her wing. He wondered if Galena cooked; it was not uncommon for Duntean ladies to be skilled in the kitchen, he had heard, because Dunte was proud of its culinary heritage.

Elais signaled for the dishes to be served. The cooks had outdone themselves. The first course was a clear tomato soup, with colorful cubed roots in it, and over the tartness of tomatoes, Rilt could taste the savory richness of strained blood. Across the table, Galena described to Selvina how they would add Dunte herbs to enhance the tartness of the tomatoes. Rilt noticed with quiet glee that even

Halden was interested in Galena's words; he hoped that it meant that Halden had a higher opinion of the match than he'd let on.

The thought of getting married just to avoid future gossip soured his appetite abruptly. Kayle was going to be king, so neither of them would be able to meet frequently. It would be a miracle if Rilt could even come to Izdahl for two weeks in a year, and how much time could he and Kayle—Kirzan—devote to each other, truly?

At least Rilt did not detest Galena. Whatever happened, he believed he had found a woman who could manage the demands of being a duchess far better than some of the tittering, vacuous girls back home. Galena had ambition, talent, and passion: good traits to pass on to children.

Children. Rilt nearly choked on the thought.

"Something wrong with the fernut-stuffed rosling?" Evvas asked mildly. "I find the lemon sauce delightfully piquant, myself."

"Nothing wrong with it," said Rilt, gulping a mouthful of water.

Evvas sliced off another bit of the game fowl. "I wondered if perhaps your tastes have changed, being stuck in Kaedin Hall for the past few months."

"A season and a half is too short a time to alter my tastes, Lord Evvas." Rilt caught the implied meaning in Evvas' words, and hoped no one else did.

"Possibly, but we never know. Izdahl is full of temptations and delights unknown to Enthin."

Halden waited for the second course to be cleared before he spoke to his son. "I hear there has been a vicious murder in Kaedin Hall. I want you out of that place as soon as the ball is over."

"The murder didn't happen in Kaedin Hall," Rilt protested. "And is this something we should be discussing over dinner?"

The serving girls had already set down the third course. Roasted lambs' tongues, from the looks of it, cupped in baked pastry shells spilling over with garden herbs and fried slices of loa. This was one of Rilt's favorite dishes, and he knew that his stepmother must have instructed the cooks to prepare it especially for this night. He wished he had the appetite to savor it.

The duke sliced up the tongues. "Why not? This will affect Cedaran and your future wife. Once you have left the hall, we can make arrangements for the wedding."

"I'm not leaving the hall before my studies are complete."

Duke Halden glared at his son pointedly. Rilt straightened in his chair, fighting the instinct to get to his feet. He did not need to loom over his father to stand up to him. It seemed to Rilt that his father had never entertained the thought that Rilt would resist him in this matter.

"The hall cannot protect you," said Halden. He set aside his fork and knife. "I will not have the future duke of Enthin traipsing about while a murderer is on the loose in the campus."

"I am safe there as I am anywhere," Rilt argued. He clenched his fists and added, "And I won't let something like this force me to cut short my studies."

"Your studies? Your duty is to Enthin. Your studies are inconsequential."

"Inconsequential? Inconsequential? I am learning how to help the people of this kingdom-"

"The only people you need to worry your head about are Enthinians!"

"Enthinians, Izdahlis, Halims, Dunteans, what does it matter? We are all Aleisans, and as a kaedin-"

"You are NOT a kaedin!" Halden bellowed. "My son is the heir to the house of Arald! Not some lackey to be summoned and chivvied about by an Alcaronan!"

Incensed, Rilt slammed his fists on the table. "Kaedine are not lackeys! Just because you don't dare to step out of Enthinas without ten house guards doesn't mean I can't go out and see the kingdom for myself. My friends know more about this kingdom than I do!"

"Those commonborn swine have turned you against your own-"

"My friends are not swine, don't you ever-"

"ENOUGH!"

Both Halden and Rilt stopped their tirades. Selvina was glowering at them both, her hands flat on the table. Beside her, Galena kept her eyes on the table, her shoulders rounded.

The duchess glared at her husband and her stepson. "Sit down, both of you. This is a dinner for family. We have wonderful news that Rilt has found himself a sweet girl to be his wife. I will not have yelling at the table. I will not, do you hear me?"

Selvina was seldom this forbidding; Rilt felt shame creep up his spine. He lowered himself to his seat and drank more of his water.

"Rilt had the right idea," the duchess said. "Murders are not appropriate topics for a dinner table with guests. Elais, the next course, and top up the wine."

Rilt had not even noticed that he had toppled two goblets of wine. The deep red liquid was soaked into the white linen tablecloth, resembling blood. He had to tear his eyes away from the stain and tried not to scrub at his fingertips.

While Elais hurried to the kitchen, Cedaran muttered something and excused himself.

"I'll go talk to him," said Rilt in a rush, unwilling to remain any longer at the table. Without waiting for either of his parents' agreement, he fled the room. As he exited, he heard Evvas drawl, "I suppose Galena and I will have to enjoy their desserts then."

* * *

After some poking around, Rilt found Cedaran in his bedroom.

"Thank you for giving me a reason to leave the table," Rilt said outside the door. He knocked again. "May I come in?"

"You never asked before."

"Living among others have taught me that privacy is important."

Cedaran gave his permission. The sixteen-year-old boy was sitting in the middle of the bed, knees tucked and arms wrapped around his legs. He looked very young at that moment.

Rilt sighed and his smile turned rueful. "I really should keep my tongue reined in. I'm sorry."

"You never used to apologize either," Cedaran said. It was unclear if he was teasing his brother, or just making an observation.

Taking a seat on the edge of the bed, Rilt decided to let the comment slide. He poked Cedaran in his arm and asked, "Are you alright? Notwithstanding my idiocy, of course."

"I will be. I just—I don't like it when you and Father argue." The younger boy's cheeks flushed. "I hate it when people yell, and it was... While you were gone, there wasn't any shouting. I missed you, but I didn't miss that."

Guilt flooded Rilt. Somehow, he always forgot that Cedaran had witnessed too many raging quarrels between his father and brother.

It was clear to Rilt that Cedaran conscientiously tried to emulate the best qualities of both himself and Halden, but when Rilt faced his father, only the worst in both surfaced. He had hoped to avoid such scenes tonight, and he had failed miserably.

"I'm sorry, Ced," he said again. "I wish I had more control over my tongue. I'm trying to curb my temper, I truly am." He held out a hand. "Forgive me?"

Cedaran looked at the hand and then flicked his gaze up at his older brother. "You know I always will. And I'm on your side, whatever Father says."

Rilt smiled and tousled his brother's hair. "I know, Beanpole."

* * *

"Is every dinner with your family this riveting?" Galena asked as they returned to the university.

"Do they all include a shouting match? Yes, ever since my father knew I was going to Kaedin Hall." Rilt had little need for discretion, since Pellit was driving them back to their respective halls. "I'd thought that we could set that aside tonight, but obviously, that didn't happen."

She pressed into his side. Anyone who saw them would assume they were a couple, and he supposed they were. He had announced his intention to marry her, after all, and Selvina would invite the Aedinals to Enthin once the duke and duchess returned home. The streets around the nobles' estates were quiet at this hour. Life for the rich and powerful happened behind thick walls. Only commoners lived together, sharing spaces.

"You're right about that," said Galena. Only then did Rilt realize he had spoken aloud. She sounded thoughtful. "I wonder if they are envious of us, or if they pity us."

"Depends on whom you ask, I guess," he answered, closing his eyes. He wanted Kayle with him. Kayle would be able to tell him more, having lived rough for a time, away from the trappings of the palace. Rilt wondered why the king would send his son away, but now he thought he understood. "Those who envy us wish to be free of the worry of money and hunger. Those who pity us know that most of us won't ever have real friends."

Laughing, Galena agreed. She entwined her fingers with his and whispered, "You don't have to go through with the agreement if you hate it, you know."

"I like you," he said simply, and kissed her on her brow.

When the carriage rolled to a stop at the School of Music, Galena kissed Rilt fondly on the lips. "I'll see you at the ball."

"Good night, Galena," said Rilt, tucking a stray curl of dark hair over her ear.

On the way to Kaedin Hall, Pellit stopped the vehicle. "Sir, if we could speak privately for a moment?"

"Sure." Rilt opened the window to the front seat. "What is it?"

"Lord Evvas has spent a lot of time outside of the estate in recent evenings," said Pellit. "He's been going to the pubs by the docks, the ones held by the Crimson Compass."

"You think he's up to no good?"

"Sir, Mother always says that a first impression is seldom right, but a gut feeling is seldom wrong." Pellit hesitated. As a valet, he should not be criticizing his betters, let alone make vague accusations. "I think that it's best to be on your guard against any potential threats, sir."

Rilt hummed noncommittally. The carriage started again, the horses' hooves clipping neatly on the path. When they got to Kaedin Hall, he said, "He's related to Mother, so I cannot personally take action, but I'll be on guard. Do let Lady Liria know that I need to speak with her about Father, before the Lords' Convene. Make sure Ced has a weapon hidden on him before he leaves the mansion. Even a dagger would be useful."

"Yes, sir."

"My regards to your mother, Pell. And keep our Izdahli eyes and ears open. Run me messages should you get wind of any goings-on."

"Yes, sir."

THE KING'S BALL

"How did it feel, listening to your lover fooling around with another?" Jodius asked, idly wiping the blood from his face and neck. The cuts were still there, jagged and unskilled.

Rilt paused. "You forced yourself on him."

"Did I, now? How do you know that?" The master gazed into the center of the massive greenhouse. The plants within stretched far into the blue sky, impossibly tall. Their foliage obstructed the view beyond.

"I know Kayle. He wouldn't betray me like that."

Jodius gestured and suddenly, all the trees collapsed. Behind was Kayle, naked and displaying every sign of enjoyment as Jodius mounted him. Rilt froze.

The Jodius beside him sneered, "Or perhaps you didn't know him at all."

"Rilt, I love you," said Kayle as he rolled onto his back. It was no longer Jodius between the scholar's legs, however. Gareth pinned Kayle down, and then with a sharp, feral grin, Gareth bit down on Kayle's throat. Blood spurted thick and black over Gareth's mouth.

"No," Rilt whispered. He should be trying to save Kayle, but he was rooted to the spot. Gareth's face became less sharp, his gray eyes flickering to blue, and Rilt was now staring at Kayle atop Kayle. "You killed yourself."

"I didn't mean to," Kayle said quietly behind him. Rilt felt slender arms wrap about his chest. His heart pounded like the hoofbeats of a stampeding herd. Kayle murmured, "I am sorry, Rilt."

The Halim scholar reached into Rilt's chest and carefully pulled out a fist-sized organ. It pumped slowly, and Rilt knew it was his heart.

"You don't need this," Rilt said. He was utterly calm now, as if the anger and fear were all in that organ.

Kayle smiled and pressed a kiss to it. His lips were stained wine-red from the blood, the brightest red Rilt had ever seen. "I'd like to have it, all the same."

"But I won't have one if you take it," Rilt explained.

"Let me borrow it for a little while, then," said Kayle, his eyes wide and pleading. "I promise I'll return it."

* * *

"Rilt? Rilt, wake up. We have to assemble at the front court in an hour to send Master Jodius off," said Kayle, shaking the young lord's arm.

"Promise you'll return it?" Rilt murmured.

"Return what?"

Getting his bearings, Rilt blinked and sat up. There was a nasty coppery taste in his mouth. He must have bitten himself in his sleep. Kayle was already dressed in a somber deep blue tunic with the requisite ash gray armband.

Rilt smiled faintly. "Nothing. I'll get ready."

The face in the mirror was his, but Rilt could hardly recognize himself. He shaved off his stubble, all the while contemplating how he had changed since he arrived at Kaedin Hall.

He could not shake the sense of failure clinging to him. What had he accomplished, really? He hadn't made much headway in the matter Master Baelmin had entrusted him with, he was about to announce a false engagement to hide his relationship with Kayle, and he had killed people. He had murdered a master kaedin and was now lying to save his own neck. Whatever good Master Baelmin had seen in him was clearly an error on the late tutor's part.

He could not stay in the bathroom forever. Washing his face once more in the tepid water, he braced himself for the day.

* * *

It was bizarre, sending off the remains of the man he had killed. The first-year students stood right behind the masters, who each laid their kae staff on the ground as the urn was carried past them. Wolvam was openly crying, his hand covering his mouth as tears streamed down his face. That sight alone was too much for Rilt to handle. He stared at his feet instead. At the end of the procession, Master Midusel veiled the urn bearer and the urn. The sheer gray linen fluttered briefly in the breeze.

Once the urn bearer and his horse were out of sight, the masters picked up their kae staffs and walked away. Most of the students dispersed too.

"Do you want to come back to the room?" Kayle asked.

Rilt shook off the concern and said that he needed time by the lake to clear his mind. There would never be enough time, he mused, but he would take what he could get.

"It's over now, Rilt. Don't brood on it," Naelen said, not unkindly.

Rilt shrugged. Then he remembered something Naelen mentioned. "Nael, will you be able to see Liria before the ball this evening?"

The blond stopped in his tracks. "Yes. I'm meeting her now, in fact."

"Tell her Evvas will be attending, and that… that she should be prepared." Rilt could not risk saying more than that, not where others were listening.

* * *

Rilt was not the only one by the lake. To his consternation, Wolvam was already there, idly tossing pebbles into it. Drops of water hovered and zigzagged like jewelwings over the ripples. When Wolvam saw that Rilt was watching him, he let go of the water droplets. His eyes were red-rimmed and puffy.

"Feeling pensive?" the adept asked. His voice was rather hoarse. "Plenty of space to do some thinking alone, if you want to. Or you can join me. I promise not to chew you out for that shoddy essay you submitted for the review. I should, but I won't."

Despite himself, Rilt had to smile. Wolvam motioned to the patch of grass beside him and Rilt took the offer. He waited until the ripples died down before he spoke. "Were you very close to Master Jodius?"

The adept went still. A cool breeze rustled the surface of the lake and Rilt kept his eyes on the bank of clouds gathering in the distance. There might be a storm that night. The rainy season had yet to stop battering Izdahl. Wolvam exhaled heavily through his nose and pushed his hair back from his brow. This close, Rilt could see the tear stains and faint freckles on Wolvam's face.

"Don't noise it about, but Jodius was my former lover," he said bluntly.

Rilt gaped.

The adept raised an eyebrow. "Are you surprised? We shared a room in our second year as adepts. I broke it off when it was clear he was going to make mastery before I could."

"I … I didn't think you'd admit to…" Rilt bit his lower lip before he inadvertently insulted Wolvam.

"I'm as bent as they come. Does that bother you?"

"No, not really."

"It shouldn't, should it? Seeing as you and Radieri are together."

"Wha- How…" Rilt gulped. "Nothing is going on between us."

Wolvam's smile was faint but understanding. "If you say so, Lord Rilt."

After another long, awkward moment, Rilt muttered, "I'm very sorry for your loss."

"He wasn't the man I fell for anyway. Being a master changed him. It changed him so much I couldn't see why I liked him before." Wolvam skipped a pebble across the lake. It touched the water surface six times before it sank. The older kaedin's voice was rough when he added, "Even so, I'm going to miss him. When we were together… it was good, for a while. And for the first time in my life, I could be whom I really was."

Rilt's guilt stabbed even more deeply. He cleared his throat and got to his feet. "I should-"

"Go. Get ready for the King's Ball. You first-years ought to enjoy yourselves. Try to grab a dance with Radieri if you can. Before you sleep, perhaps." Wolvam rubbed the heel of his palm over one cheek and skipped another pebble across the water. This one did nine hops before it sank without a trace. "Don't miss out on your chance, Rilt. You won't be here forever."

* * *

Gareth was mid-gesticulation when Rilt walked into his Room Six.

He paused when he saw Rilt.

"Fantastic. You're finally back. Please tell this waterlogged, rum-addled lubber that it's a bad idea to wear that tonight," snarled Gareth.

Rilt frowned, befuddled. "Wear what?"

"I told him I want to wear this," said Kayle, holding up the starsilver ring Rilt had given him. "We're all dressed in our finest. It won't stand out."

"You're going to meet the dignitaries. That includes his father. We may even be sharing a table with him. Do you really think he won't notice that your ring came from Rilt?" Gareth threw up his hands in despair. "I give up. I give up. You are intent on ruining everything, Kayle, all because of some misplaced affection for this lordling!"

A thrill shivered down the young lord's spine. He ignored Gareth's dramatics and caught Kayle's hands in his. "You still wish to wear this?"

Over Gareth's sarcastic sighing by the bed, Kayle nodded. "I'll whisk it off if I'm in your father's vicinity, but otherwise, for the main part of the evening, I'd like to wear it in public—even if it's just this once."

Rilt smiled and pressed his brow to Kayle.

Gareth mimed throwing up. "Why did I even hope you'd be helpful?"

"Why are you still here?" Rilt asked, not taking his eyes off Kayle. "Go back to your room, Gareth. Kayle and I have something to do."

"Bed each other, you mean."

"Precisely."

Kayle tucked himself more snugly into Rilt and waited until they heard the bathroom door slam shut. Then he whispered, "Are you really sure it's alright for me to wear your mother's ring? I don't want to cause a scene for you."

Rilt ran his hand through his lover's dark hair and pressed his lips to a soft cheek. "Father pays scant attention to a commoner. As it is, he barely pays attention to those from lesser houses. Unless you're going to reveal your identity tonight, I doubt it's going to be a problem. I'd like to introduce you to my brother and stepmother, regardless. Cedaran will like you, and I'm sure Selvina will too."

Kayle hugged him tightly. "I'm scared."

"Why? Your father is going to be there."

"I'm not- It's not about the king, it's about all the lords and ladies who will be there. I don't know if I could … everyone is so fancy, and I've never learned the correct etiquette."

Rilt frowned. "But you're-"

"I was sent away when I was very little, with a pair of kingsblades pretending to be my family," Kayle said quickly. "I was raised as a commonborn citizen, Rilt, remember? And if I make a mistake, everyone's going to talk about it."

The young lord smiled softly and kissed Kayle soundly on the cheek. "They won't mention it in the future, my dear Prince Kirzan. It'd be beyond rude."

Blushing, Kayle pushed away from Rilt. "Don't call me that."

"That's your name."

"Someone might be listening." Kayle took a deep breath and nodded, half to himself, and then strode to the closet where he hung his few clothes. Reaching in, he took out a richly-embroidered tunic. Its sky-blue fabric instantly brightened Kayle's eyes, and the material held a sheen that whispered of luxury. Silver embroidery traced geometric patterns in the cuffs and hem. The scholar chewed shyly on his lower lip and motioned to the outfit. "What do you think?"

"It's perfect," Rilt said sincerely. He took the tunic and set it reverently on the bed, then kissed his lover. "You're perfect."

You're not for me to have. We can never really be together.

Kayle reciprocated the kiss and deepened it. Rilt forced himself to focus on the moment. He was ashamed and guilty about killing Jodius, but he had protected Kayle, and if he kept thinking that, perhaps he could someday absolve himself of the blame. Someday.

* * *

"Coming!" Rilt hurriedly brushed through his hair and secured his belt before opening the door.

Kayle and Gareth had already gone to the great hall to be briefed by Master Midusel about dinner, and Rilt had lost track of the time while sorting through his notes about the Verashki, including the information Pellit had passed him. There hadn't been much in the end, just a note that the master had a brand on his skin linking him to the new gang. Rilt supposed that was where the rumor of the

Verashki being in Kaedin Hall stemmed from.

Naelen appeared at the door. The other Enthinian was already dressed in a leaf green short-sleeved tunic with gold and ivory accents, and looking far too handsome in Rilt's opinion. Naelen did not notice Rilt staring at him, but entered the room immediately.

"I've relayed your message," he said, peering at Rilt's plain maroon tunic. "Shouldn't you be at the great hall?"

"What? Why?"

"You are of the house of Arald. Remember? You are to sit at the king's table." Naelen frowned as he explained, as though speaking to a particularly obdurate child.

Rilt grimaced. He had forgotten about that. After some hectic rummaging, he located his seal ring—his father's seal ring—and jammed it on his forefinger before dashing off to the door of the great hall.

He made it to the foyer of the great hall just before his parents were announced. The duke and duchess were both resplendent in deep red rich as blood, with gold embellishments. Selvina's dark curls were caught in a fine net of gold thread with small rubies scattered across it. The jewels glinted like sparks from a fire. Cedaran was in the same hue, albeit with far less gilt on him, and looked quite uncomfortable in his attire. He scurried over to join them, sharing a cheeky grin with his brother. With a start, Rilt noticed that the footman announcing the guests was Dagger.

"His Grace the Duke of Enthin, Her Grace the Duchess of Enthin, and the Honorable Lords Rilt and Cedaran." Then, with a pause, Dagger added, "The Honorable Lord Evvas of Halimgor."

Rilt noted that he placed an emphasis on the final syllable for Evvas' name, and cleared his throat before he succumbed to laughter and disgraced his parents. Master Midusel came over personally to greet the Aralds.

"Good evening, your Graces." Master Midusel bowed over Selvina's hand and smiled at all of them. While the dean had clearly made an effort to dress up, he was unfortunately the sort of man who looked scruffy no matter what he had put on. The russet shade of his robe made him look paler than he had this morning. He tilted his head at Halden. "I believe this is your first visit to Kaedin Hall, Your Grace?"

"Indeed. I had no reason to come here before," said Halden. He scanned the room and raised an aristocratic eyebrow.

Evvas tucked his hands behind him, mimicking Halden's stance. "Not too shabby."

"No, it isn't at all," agreed Master Midusel. He returned his attention to the duke. "I'm sure you're proud of your son's achievements this term. He was one of the four who foiled a vicious bandit attack. Adept Wolvam tells me that Lord Rilt has a lot of potential and we have high hopes for him."

Selvina patted Rilt's head fondly. "I am very proud of him. Master Midusel, I would love to speak with you further, but we simply mustn't monopolize you. Come along, Cedaran. Halden, dear?"

Once the dean had left and the party was inside the foyer, Rilt could no longer safely ignore the duke. He had not bidden his father farewell the other night, having left the mansion with Galena after curt goodbyes.

"Good evening, Father," said Rilt, stiffly.

As though Rilt was invisible, Halden looked around at the foyer. "Not as large as I'd thought it'd be," he sniffed.

Selvina shook her head slightly. "You can't compare a five-century-old building with our own estate, dear. And they've done a lovely job with the decorations. That chandelier is absolutely exquisite, and the carved banisters are superb craftsmanship. And the flowers! I must bring some cuttings back to Enthin, I've not seen some of these before."

Indeed, the foyer had been scrubbed clean and lavishly decorated. The enormous chandelier overhead held more than a thousand glassfires, each one hand-blown by a master glass-smith. There were tons of hothouse flowers bound with yards and yards of kaedin blue ribbons, the colorful blooms brightening the stone stairs and plain walls.

"We'll speak to the master in charge of the greenhouses." Halden smiled at his wife fondly. Then his expression grew stern. "Rilt, your mother and I have people to meet. Do show Cedaran and Evvas around."

"Of course, Father," said Rilt. "Where is Evvas, then?"

"Still loitering by the doors." Cedaran jerked his chin at the handsome young man talking to two young women who looked identical. Evvas cut a dashing figure in slim-cut trousers and a fine orange brocade tunic that clashed with the Aralds' red.

Once both Halden and Selvina were out of earshot, Cedaran exhaled forcefully and murmured, "It won't be soon enough for him to leave. I can't wait for the Convene."

"Did you find out if Father is speaking for the lout?"

"Yes. It's stupid. What does Father see in the leech that he's speaking for him, I'll never understand."

Rilt threw a companionable arm over his brother's shoulders and gestured at the huddle of nobles congregating around their parents. "Brother mine, what do you see?"

Cedaran frowned. "Izdahli nobles? You know I don't recognize them."

"Bees to honey, Ced. And the Arald name is the honey." Rilt then jerked his chin at Evvas, who was still busy flirting with the girls. "That leech has latched on to our house. If Father does get him confirmed, Evvas will be indebted to the Aralds, and that means the Aralds have stronger support in the Convene when we submit proposals." That was his theory, at any rate. He hoped Liria would turn up soon.

Cedaran snorted. "You and I both know he'll turn on Father once he deems it expedient to do so. Gratitude fills no bellies."

Proud of Cedaran, Rilt ruffled his brother's hair and took the lead in walking to Evvas, who saw them approaching and grinned at the girls. "Ladies, I present Lords Rilt and Cedaran Arald. Rilt, Ced, these lovely visions are Ladies Feyora and Ereda of the house Aramint, both first-year students at the Hall of the Sciences."

"How wonderful for them," said Rilt with a pleasant smile. "Evvas, come on inside. Father and Mother are making the rounds and I'm sure you wish to be made known to the other Izdahli nobles. The ones you haven't met at that party you threw in my home, anyway. Lovely to meet you, Feyora, Ereda."

Evvas shot him an irritated look. However, with his title on the line, there was precious little he could do but follow the Arald brothers. Cedaran was grinning, his hands behind his back.

There were not many who recognized Rilt. Some had seen him greet Halden and Selvina, and might have had a clue, but no one approached them as Rilt showed his brother around the hall and pointed out where the teaching and library wings were. Evvas followed at a saunter, yawning. As expected, Cedaran wanted to know if he could visit the library.

"I'd have to ask permission, Ced, but I'm sure one of the Masters would allow you to go in under my supervision," Rilt said, apologetically.

Cedaran looked wistful as they made their way back to the foyer. "It must be so tranquil, reading and studying in the library with the lake for a view."

"Bah, books. They get in the way of learning," said Evvas dismissively.

Rilt was about to make a cutting remark when the footmen at the doors announced, "The Honorable Lady Liria of the house Alwyth of Halimgor!"

It was almost funny how nearly everyone turned to look at the latest arrival. Liria had shown up in a jet-black gown with a sprinkling of white gems all over her bodice and full skirt. Her black hair was swept up and held with a pair of ivory combs, and an ivory fan dangled from her wrist. Naelen stood by her side, as she held on to his arm. Nearly everyone in the hall was staring at the beautiful couple; the only exception was Evvas, who had taken one look at his sister and turned away contemptuously.

"Slutting around with an empty-headed pretty boy not of any noble house…" the Alwyth youth muttered.

Rilt warned, "That is Naelen Barith, a student of Kaedin Hall, which makes him much more than an 'empty-headed pretty boy'."

"And the son of Merc Barith, the merchant chief of Enthinas," Cedaran piped up loyally.

Evvas stuck his hands in his pockets and shrugged, dismissing both Arald siblings. His gaze returned to his sister, taking note of the various nobles who chatted with her. It was evident that he was tallying up names of those who would not support him in his bid to reclaim his title. The hard, bitter set of his mouth was immediately replaced with a brilliant smile when she caught sight of him, but Rilt noticed that the smile never touched Evvas' gaze.

Liria responded with a beaming smile of her own and approached them, towing Naelen along behind her. "Evvas! Brother dear, I wasn't expecting to see you again so soon after our little chat at the

Aralds. That outfit… that's the one you always wear to impress the ladies, isn't it? It still fits you as well as it did when you first had it made two years ago. Rilt, darling, you should've dressed up. Such a waste of that classic Arald jawline. And who is this dashing young man?" She laid a slender, graceful hand on Cedaran's upper arm and fluttered her lashes at him.

Cedaran blushed and stammered his name. He nearly dropped his glasses when he nudged them up his nose, and his face reddened when Liria reached up to pat his cheek fondly.

"Cedaran? You are our blood cousin, then. Look at you! You've inherited your mother's looks and your father's physique." Liria smiled coquettishly at Rilt and added, "I bet you're miles smarter than your brother, Cedaran. You know better than to leave home for some piffling education."

Naelen shook his head, smiling. "Thanks for putting down my school, Liria. I truly appreciate that."

"You could've come to Halimgor for nautical studies."

"I've no interest in that."

"Pfft. Interest. My dear brother here didn't need interest to learn the ins and outs of Port Halim," Liria said, her Halim lilt more pronounced than Kayle's. "In fact, I think he knows all the salacious secrets of the port better than I do."

Evvas tilted his head and shrugged again. "Given how often you dirtied your pretty silk slippers in the fish markets, sister dear, I'm sure you have the greater bounty."

"I never wear silk to the fish markets, brother dear. I always dress for the occasion."

"And undress for all occasions too." Evvas bared his teeth, leering.

Laughing, Liria smacked Evvas playfully on his shoulder. "Brother dear, let's not be crude. You should know by now that I choose my occasions very carefully."

"I am well aware of the fact, sister dear. I am very well aware."

"Too bad there's not a dice table in sight," Liria continued blithely. She bestowed a dazzling smile upon the other three young men and confided, "Dice is Evvas' game. The risk gives my dear brother such a rush."

Evvas' smile had disappeared now. "If you're not rushing off after the ball, sister dear, we could play some dice. High stakes."

Liria met his glare with a lovely, soft smile. "Oh brother dear, you have forgotten. I prefer playing cards. Much easier to observe people's tells than rely on mere fortune. I mean, both of us need all the luck we can get, don't we?"

Watching from the side, Rilt was perversely pleased that Cedaran was his brother. While it was clear that Evvas was outclassed by Liria, observing how her verbal jabs landed their mark repeatedly made Rilt feel a little bad for the former. Had Ced turned out to be like Liria… Rilt shook his head. He was lucky to have his scholarly, devoted half-brother.

Looking a little uncomfortable, Naelen cleared his throat. "Liria, there are other people you wanted to meet. Shall we?"

"Oh, of course! See you later, Rilt, Cedaran. Evvas dear, you really should come stay in our own Izdahli estate, hmm? A guest who outstays his welcome is as good as three-day-old fish, after all."

"I'll wait for the duke to tell me to leave, sister dear. Wouldn't want him thinking I'm finding fault with his hospitality."

"I'm sure he knows his hospitality is flawless, brother dear. Cedaran, won't you introduce me to your father? I've not had the pleasure of meeting him."

Once Liria's back was turned, Evvas' smile snapped into a scowl. He flicked a glance at the departing Cedaran and Liria, then eyed Rilt critically.

"I know what you're thinking," he drawled in a low voice. Rilt frowned. Evvas went on, "If my own younger sister can turn on me, who's to say your half-brother won't turn on you?"

"I do." Rilt returned the look with cool indifference. "I trust Ced with my life. I'm sorry you can't say the same with Liria, but I suppose she has her reasons."

"She's a conniving little fen wasp, and someday, you'll find out just how poisonous she is," hissed Evvas. "You think she'd be content with managing Halimgor, when there's an entire kingdom open for the grabbing?"

"I think she'll be far better at managing Halimgor than you. I'll deal with her ambition to claim Aleis if it happens," said Rilt.

Evvas' face darkened further. His nostrils flared and his lips thinned with anger, but instead of saying something insulting, he stalked off in the direction of a waiter bearing a tray of drinks.

Rilt and Cedaran joined their parents. By then, Liria and Naelen had swanned off to another cluster of nobles. Just as Rilt was about to ask Selvina about Liria, the head porter of Kaedin Hall, dressed in blue-and-white livery, stepped out of the banquet hall and rang a bell to invite them to dinner.

Inside, three long tables had been laid out, with seven students were standing at the side of the table. Rilt saw Kayle as well as Gareth and waved at them. Kayle waved back cheerfully. There was no sign of a ring on his fingers, but Rilt knew Kayle had it on him. Later, after dinner, when they could join the main party out in the front court, the Halim scholar could slip it on, and no one would be the wiser. He took Selvina's hand and led her to the royal scholars. Cedaran trailed after them when Rilt beckoned for him to follow.

"Mother, Cedaran, this is Kayle Radieri," said Rilt eagerly when he got to the small cluster of students. "My roommate and best friend."

Kayle flushed prettily. He looked very good in his blue tunic with its silver embroidery. "Your grace, my lord, it's an honor to meet you both."

"You're Kayle? How lovely to put a face to the name. I've read quite a bit about you from my son's letters," said Selvina. She smiled gently at Kayle and asked, "Has Rilt been a good roommate? He's never had to share quarters with anyone, and he certainly never did chores himself. He must've left messes everywhere."

"Mother! I did try to pick up after myself," Rilt interrupted, his ears growing hot. He put a finger to Kayle's lips when the scholar was about to speak. "You are not allowed to tell my mother anything embarrassing."

Selvina frowned at her stepson momentarily before turning back to Kayle. "In case there isn't time for us to talk, do come to Enthinas and stay with us over the term holidays. It's the least I can do to thank you for looking after my son."

"Oh! Th-thank you, ma'am. I mean, your grace. Rilt's looked after me as well, to be fair."

"Well, well, what do we have here?" An unwelcome voice insinuated itself into the conversation. The equally unwelcome owner of the voice sidled up. "Hello."

If Rilt had not been watching closely, he would not have noticed Kayle's eyes briefly widen, nor would he have taken note of the nervous swallow. He wondered if Kayle had ever run into Evvas personally before back in Port. It would not have surprised Rilt if Evvas had left a bad impression. He made the introductions again, with much less enthusiasm than before, hoping that Evvas would take the hint and leave.

Of course, Evvas remained, a deep burgundy drink in hand. He leered at Kayle and said, "Your face is very familiar. I've seen you around someplace before."

Rilt shifted so he stood next to Kayle, one hand on the small of the scholar's back when he sensed that Kayle was shrinking away from the Alwyth lord. "Kayle was originally from Port Halim."

"Ah, I see. A passing face in the night, perhaps," Evvas drawled, glancing slyly at Rilt. "We should take our seats. I hear the king will arrive shortly."

Was that a smirk of triumph on Evvas' face? Rilt could not understand what that odious man could possibly feel victorious about. Liria was already at her place, listening attentively to Duke Ingros Awell, whose dour face and somber gray tunic contrasted with the young woman's vivacious manner and exquisite dress. Evvas strolled to his place on Liria's left, which meant he would sit next to Cedaran—who looked dismayed and resigned.

To the Alwyths' left were places marked out for the Aralds, and facing them were the royal scholars. Much to Rilt's delight, Kayle was in the seat opposite him. Gareth was seated next to the king, and between the two friends was Felas Norwan, looking distinctly uneasy at being among so many notables. The other guests were chattering away. Rilt peered around and spotted Naelen. His role as Liria's escort did not extend to a place at the king's table, but he had been granted a seat at the table nearest the doors, along with very minor nobles and the untitled escorts.

The musicians struck up a soft melody and the chatter died down. Rilt spotted Galena on the stage. She was intent on her playing, however, and did not notice him.

"Who are you looking at, dear?" asked Selvina.

"Galena," Rilt said with a quick grin. He pointed out the brunette girl playing the harp. Galena's silvery dress complemented her fair skin, and the engagement cuff glittered like a band of stars on her arm. "Doesn't she look pretty?"

Kayle looked over his shoulder and smiled at Selvina. "She's a lovely person too, Lady Selvina. A wonderful conversationalist, and quick-witted."

"I agree," said Selvina. "Well, Rilt, you've picked a good girl. Your best friend and your mother approve of her."

"There's one more opinion I must have. What do you think of Galena, Ced?" Rilt asked, only half in jest.

The tops of Cedaran's ears pinked. "She's pleasant enough." Changing the subject, he whispered, "The king's late."

Just then, a blare of trumpets heralded the arrival of King Eram. Everyone rose to their feet, and twelve heavily armed men with black capes strode in from the main door, parting to form an aisle for the king.

In person, King Eram was stern and slender, with a long, thin nose and high, broad brow over dark gray eyes. His long hair flowed down his back; it was graying at the temples and added gravitas to the man. He reminded Rilt of somebody familiar. Stealing a glance at Kayle, he was surprised to see his lover averting his eyes. This must be the first time Kayle was seeing his father in public.

The armed guards took up places at the doors, their heavy boots thumping across the tile floor. The king took his place at the head of the table. "Be seated."

The musicians left the dais, ducking behind the curtains to a small antechamber to wait. Once everyone had taken their seats, Master Midusel stood to address all the guests. "Tonight we honor our best and brightest, by introducing them to the noble houses. For they are the ones who will take over leadership of this great kingdom. First, our royal scholars-"

Abruptly Evvas began to cough as though he nearly choked. When Master Midusel glared at him, he raised a hand in apology. "Wine down the wrong tube," he said, clearing his throat. "Sorry, Master Midusel. Didn't mean to interrupt."

Master Midusel looked nonplussed. "As I was saying, our royal scholars. I present Gareth Krell, Felas Norwan, Kayle Radieri, Ginia Orwes, Polana Eldaton, Wenneth Logdi, and Laran Essa."

The scholars stood up and bowed to the king. Rilt noticed that Kayle was pallid and tense, entirely unlike his usual demeanor. His fists and even his jaw were clenched. He was avoiding Rilt's gaze as he sat down.

The king smiled genially at the scholars. "You came from vastly different backgrounds, but will now forever be counted among the elite. The alumni of royal scholars have all been instrumental in making Aleis safer, stronger, and wealthier. I look forward to your contributions to the kingdom in the future." Raising his glass, King Eram toasted the scholars. "Enjoy the feast, everyone."

As the wait staff served up the first course of cheese and honey arpell medallions, Evvas commented, "It's wonderful that the royal scholarship is open to so many in the lower classes. Don't you agree, Kayle?"

Looking surprised that Evvas would address him, Kayle dropped his fork to the plate and hastily picked it up. His cheeks flushed dark pink. "Yes, indeed."

Rilt studied Kayle, and then looked at Gareth, whose sallow face was starting to turn paler. He leaned forward to look at Evvas and remarked, "I didn't know you were so interested in opening opportunities for the lower classes, Lord Evvas."

"What can I say, I like to give even the lowest of the low a chance."

Rilt could feel a tight ball of unease growing in the pit of his stomach. Kayle kept his eyes on his plate, as if trying to shrink in on himself. The second course was served, but Rilt barely tasted the burro, even though the fish had been poached in whitesong wine and smelled divine. He watched his lover warily, and noted that Gareth was also keeping an eye on Kayle. As the meal progressed, nothing happened, so Rilt's vigilance decreased.

When the fourth course of venison rolled around, Evvas spoke again. "Sister dear, since we've not dined together for such a long time, shall we place a wager?"

"A wager? Brother dear, what do you possibly have that you can use as a stake?" Liria laughed, the sound bright and delightful. "As you well know, Father is adamant that we don't squander the house fortunes. Your stipend doesn't come in till next month, brother dear, but I'll see what I can do."

It was clear to all within earshot that Liria was reminding Evvas who held the real power. Rilt let his lips curl in satisfaction and turned to look at Liria. "I imagine, Lady Liria, that you usually win any wager you place, small or large."

Evvas narrowed his eyes and his nostrils flared. Then his smile turned viciously cheerful. "How about I wager something with you instead, Lord Rilt?"

"Liria just said you've nothing to wager with, Evvas."

"Just a copper, Rilt. That much I have," said the Alwyth lord. He fished it out of his pocket and placed it on the table. "Come on, for a lark."

"Rilt, don't," Cedaran murmured, tugging on his brother's tunic under the table. "He's up to something."

The conversation between Rilt and Evvas had drawn the attention of his parents, the king and Master Midusel as well. The scholars were looking at one another, except for Kayle, who was resolutely focused on pushing a sprig of daffi around his plate. Gareth was scowling, while Felas looked bewildered.

Rilt folded his arms. "I'll play. What's the bet?"

"I wager that your royal scholar Kayle Radieri isn't who he says he is," said Evvas.

That got Kayle's attention. "Rilt, don't-"

Rilt grinned and said, "I'll take the bet. You go first."

"Kayle Radieri isn't his real name," said Evvas slowly, sliding his gaze over to the stricken Kayle. "Or maybe it is. But he used to go by the name Endel Kaile. And he was a whore. A porthole for sailors or anyone with enough coin. Right, Endel? There was a scandal with you and, what's his name, Lord Verat. I thought you'd been hanged. I heard such great reviews of your skills, Endel. Especially your pretty mouth. Pity I'm not of that inclination."

It was preposterous. Rilt was about to laugh when he looked at Kayle. His amusement fled. All color had left the Halim scholar's face, leaving his wide, shocked eyes staring bleakly at Evvas. Silence spread like ink in clear water. Everyone was staring at Kayle, whose face had gone as white as the tablecloth. Rilt was still wearing a half-smile tinged with disbelief.

"Kayle, tell them who you really are," he urged. When Kayle made no response, he turned to the scholar beside him. "Gareth? Tell them the truth. Kayle? You're not ... You're not what he says you are."

Instead of speaking up in Kayle's defense, Gareth looked like he wanted to stab Evvas with all the knives at the table. It was then the pieces clicked into place. In an instant, Rilt felt as though all his breath had been stolen from his lungs.

"Blending in is a matter of survival."

"If you stand out, you become a target."

Kayle's expression when Gareth said he was the prince.

Gareth ordering Dagger about.

The attacks in the market square and the forest.

Kayle making sure he demonstrated more potential.

Gareth's infuriation at Rilt and Kayle's affair. He must have thought Kayle might tell the truth.

The thoughts coruscated through his mind and turned his spine to ice.

"You were … You were a prostitute," he whispered. "You lied to me."

Kayle could not look him in the eyes. "Rilt, I'm sorry-"

"Don't talk to me, you filthy, lying whore. I can't believe I trusted you." Hurt blinded Rilt to the rest of the table. He wanted to reach across the table and shake Kayle, or perhaps to punch him. Maybe scream at him. He stayed motionless, not even trembling. He knew Cedaran was gripping his clenched fist, but he could feel nothing.

Evvas' voice reminded him that they were not alone. "All you can trust in a whore is that he's always open for business." He snorted. "Parts of him, anyway."

The king frowned at Evvas. "Such talk is not suited for this table."

"I humbly apologize, Your Majesty, my tongue runs away with me sometimes." The triumph in Evvas' voice turned Rilt's stomach. "Sorry, Lord Rilt, perhaps we can finish the wager later."

Liria rose to her feet in a single graceful motion. "Your Majesty, I don't feel too well. Brother dear, won't you escort me outside for some fresh air?"

"Yes, go with your sister, Evvas," Duke Halden said abruptly.

The dismissal was obvious. The obnoxious man had to follow her out. His air of victory lay over the guests like a sour miasma. Rilt would have been pleased that Evvas was gone, but he hadn't torn his gaze from Kayle, who couldn't meet his eyes.

Master Midusel lifted his hand. "When we leave the banquet table, no one is to speak of this. Kayle Radieri earned his scholarship and has proven himself to possess the potential of an honorable kaedin. His past does not define his future."

"Enough talk, Master Midusel. You, serve the dessert now," said King Eram, gesturing at a servant. His sonorous voice seemed to break the spell, and every other guest settled back in their chairs.

Pushing his chair away from the table, Kayle muttered a hurried apology and bolted out of the banquet hall. Gareth followed instantly, calling for him.

Rilt remained frozen and numbed in his seat. Around him the chatter rose, as though the volume could mask the awkwardness of Evvas' disclosure and Kayle's exit.

Cedaran asked meekly, "Rilt, are you not going after your friend?"

"I told you, you should have befriended the Barith boy instead," said Halden. "Your judgment of character is simply atrocious."

"My judgment?" Already upset, Rilt exploded. He shoved his chair back to stand and face his father. The chair toppled over with a heavy thud. "My judgment? You were the one who brought Evvas Alwyth to Izdahl. You brought him here, and he humiliated the man I love in front of the king, on a night he was to be honored. And I'm the one who has atrocious judgment of character?"

"That boy was a prostitute!"

"He is a Royal Scholar. He's amazing and intelligent and kind, and I love him!" The words raced from his mouth, unstoppable and inevitable. "If anyone has atrocious judgment, it's you, Father. How dare you think you know him? That you can judge him? You know nothing about him!"

Then he remembered that they had an audience. They were lapping up the drama hungrily; gossip was the favored currency of the noble houses. Halden's face was deep red, and the corner of his eye twitched erratically.

"Sit down, both of you!" Selvina hissed. "You're embarrassing the house."

"No, mother. I'm going to look for Kayle." Rilt was breathing heavily through his nose. Somehow, he gathered enough composure to turn to the king. "Your Majesty, I apologize for the scene. But I hope that what transpired earlier will not lead to Kayle's scholarship being revoked."

"Of course not," said King Eram. A little smile hovered over his lips. "I personally vetted him. Find him and my son, Lord Rilt, and tell him I desire to speak with him later, after the meal."

"Yes, Your Majesty. Thank you."

"Unfortunately, no one is going anywhere."

The main doors to the banquet hall opened to admit a dozen masked men, each bearing a lit torch. Four of them proceeded to the side doors and shut them.

King Eram rose to his feet slowly. "What is the meaning of this?"

"This, your Majesty, is the changing of the times," said the stoutest one at the main door. His voice carried easily across the room. Rilt and the other kaedin students exchanged glances of confused recognition.

Master Midusel stood as well. "Terras?"

"I guess my mask isn't really necessary," said the man, and took it off. Terras smiled pleasantly at everyone in the room. "Good evening, lords and ladies. I hope your meal has been satisfactory so far, given that it's your last."

Rilt cast a quick eye around. The glass windows would be the easiest escape, but how could he leave when the king and other nobles were in danger? He had no weapon on him either—it would have been the height of discourtesy, bringing weapons to the king's table—and he knew he could not hope to beat Terras in a fight. Who were the men Terras had with him? Why would they try this unarmed, knowing who was in attendance? What did they want?

The king's personal guards didn't hesitate. Each of the dozen guards drew swords and charged the men at the side doors. To Rilt's surprise, none of the masked men withdrew.

Deyre breith wer flaume yn fir.

"No, stay away-" The words had barely left Rilt's mouth when each of the masked men held their lit torches before their faces and twelve gouts of fire issued forth, engulfing the king's guards in flames.

The lords and ladies scrambled from their seats, screaming. The burning men fell to the ground, rolling to try to put out the fire, but the fire-breathers kept up their attacks until the guards were no longer twitching. The scent of burned fabric and flesh filled the room. The masked men let go of the torches. Each man now had a fireball hovering over their upturned palms.

"Unless you are fireproof, my dear lords and ladies, do stand aside." Terras said amiably. He gestured and drew a tongue of flame from a dead guard, which curled into a fireball and hovered over his palm.

It looked like a miniature sun at dusk, orange and pretty, but Rilt could not stop the dread spreading through his body. The fireball burned steadily, bobbing over the adept's fingers, and he began advancing on King Eram. The terrified guests scuttled to the far end of the tables as Terras walked up the aisle with a purposeful tread. Rilt stayed close to his brother but caught Naelen's and Felas' attention with a brief nod.

Without flinching, Master Midusel reached under the table and took out two kae staffs, one of which was a plain iron rod, and handed that to the king. He held his own across his body. Its carved tip was glowing purple-green, pulsing steadily in time with the dean's breath. "Stand down, Terras. You cannot hope to come out of this unscathed."

"That is not my hope, Master Midusel. Please step aside. You have been a good teacher to me." Terras ducked a bolt of purple light from Master Midusel and returned a bolt of fire. "I don't want to kill you, sir."

"That makes two of us," replied the master kaedin.

While the adept and the dean faced off, Rilt sidled close to Cedaran and whispered, "Where's your dagger?"

"Dagger? Is this why Pellit wanted me to… Wait, Rilt, what are you going to do?"

Rilt squeezed his brother's hand and let go. There was no time to explain. Desperately, he focused on the goblets of wine on the table. The instant he could hear a hum in his mind, he locked onto the note and gathered all the liquid into a large, wobbling globe. Then he began creeping towards the king.

"Very nicely done, Rilt," Terras called out. He continued his fight against Master Midusel, a head-sized ball of flame balanced before him. "Verashki, kill that one."

The other masked men unleashed their fireballs at Rilt at the same time. The blast hit the table, shattering it into splinters. Rilt felt the right side of his face struck by several pieces, but Creation bless him, nothing hit his eyes.

He had to draw the Verashki away from the others. He darted towards the side door on the other side of the room, ducking streams of flame, and blasted the globes of wine at the three closest. Out of the corner of his eye, he spied Naelen melding all the silverware into a shield and running towards him.

"No! Keep them safe!" Rilt yelled, dodging a fireball nearly a heartbeat too late. He slapped at his chest to beat out the small flame before the Verashki could make use of it, then ripped off the thick jacket when it continued to burn.

"Behind you!" Felas shouted. He punched a fist into the floor. Tiles cracked as the ground beneath lurched, tripping Rilt over, and unbalanced the men about to attacking Rilt.

Terras stomped as well, just before the quake reached him. "You need more power behind that, Felas. I've taught you better th- No!"

While the adept was distracted, Master Midusel waved his kae staff. Six jets of purple light flared out, shattering one of the stained glass windows and hitting five masked men right in the chest. The moment the purple light hit the men, vines exploded and wrapped around them tightly. The fireballs that the Verashki been hovering over their hands caught on the vines, igniting them. Their screams felt unnaturally shrill; Rilt averted his eyes and focused on getting to the doors. If he could get them open, the guests could flee.

Terras shot a ferocious barrage of flame at the dean and King Eram, but was thwarted when silverware flew in front of them and wove together into a dense netting. Terras' flame bounced off the net of metal harmlessly, though some of the sparks fell on the assembled guests near the front. Rilt saw Halden stamp out a spark that had fallen on the train of Selvina's dress. The other masked men gave up trying to kill Rilt, and ran to bolster Terras in his assault.

Rilt grabbed the door handles and immediately regretted it. The metal had been heated to burning; his palm screamed with searing agony as he tore his hand from it. He rammed the door with his shoulder instead but it wouldn't budge. Felas dashed over and plunged his arms into the floor. When he pulled them out, a thick layer of cracked tile and stone covered his limbs like armor.

"Duck," he told Rilt, and swung his limbs into the door. It shuddered once. On the second strike, it opened.

With his wobbling globe of wine, Rilt blocked stray fireballs from the door and from the nobles cowering on the other side of the room. Naelen, using his makeshift shield, hurried the guests towards the open door. Right at the back of the group, Halden pushed Selvina and Cedaran to go ahead and flee, and then pulled out his short beltsword.

"Father! Come on," Rilt called out, heart hammering. His scorched hand throbbed rapidly in time to his racing pulse. "Father!"

"Get them to safety, or don't call yourself an Arald," Halden replied. He grabbed a large serving platter and smacked aside a fireball lobbed at him.

Felas kicked Rilt on the shin before the young lord could rush back to his father's side. "Our classmates can help. See if any adepts are around."

Rilt licked his lips. "If you two can hold them, I'll run and grab everyone."

"Go," the redheaded scholar urged. "Don't take too long."

* * *

Outside was a scene of chaos. Rilt told Cedaran which hallway to go to get the masters from their studies; the others he escorted to the combat training room, with its thick metal-reinforced walls and door that could be locked.

"For the love of Creation, do not open this door to anyone but an Arald," he told Selvina. "I have to save my friends."

"Go," said the duchess. She was pale but not shaken. "I will keep us safe."

As Rilt raced down the corridor, he began to feel worried. There were scorch marks on the walls, and the trees in the courtyard were on fire. A few bodies lay on the ground but there was no time to check if they were alive.

Where are all the other adepts? The masters? Wouldn't they have heard the screaming from the banquet hall?

As Rilt turned the corner approaching the front yard, someone jumped out at him and he reflexively punched the person in the face. The assailant kicked him in the solar plexus and he doubled over, wheezing, rolling aside just in time to avoid a club to his skull. Before Rilt could get his bearings, he saw twin flashes of white stab into the man's neck. Blood sprayed like fountains when the white blades were removed.

To Rilt's amazement, Liria was the one who had dropped his assailant. She was holding onto two sharp daggers that looked bone white.

Blood dripped from her hands and the blades. Her hair was loosed about her face, her gaze fierce.

"Ivory daggers in my fan and comb," she said when she saw him gaping. "Evvas ran when he saw them marching towards the school from around the lake. He knew they were coming, the bilge rat. Many of the other schools are on fire; I think most of the other masters and adepts have gone to assist. Let's hope they haven't been waylaid. Kaedin Hall seems to be their target, so they'll converge here and there won't be reinforcements on their end. On the other hand? We're probably on our own."

"How many are there?"

"Easily fifty of them. They're breathing fire. Throwing fireballs. Someone is going to have to explain that. All the non-kaedine students have been corralled into the library by my house guards. The kaedin students should be able to hold the library for a while longer, but unless we can douse their flames, we can't survive this. There are three adepts out there keeping them at bay, but they'll tire eventually." Liria shook her head. "Who are these attackers?"

"They call themselves the Verashki," said Rilt. He led the way to the front court by one of the lesser-used passages. Pressing themselves to the stone walls, Rilt muttered, "The other nobles are safe. The king and Master Midusel are holding their own so far, but the only other kaedine in there are Naelen and Felas. They cannot hope to outlast the Verashki. Terras must have brought the strongest of his fellow conspirators in there."

"Nael will outlast them." Liria peeked out. "You have a plan?"

Rilt licked his lips. "No. I also need to find Gareth and Kayle. The Verashki are after them too."

"I'll lead the support back to the king, you look for your friends."

"Be careful, Liria."

Liria grinned at Rilt. "Don't worry. I didn't win Halimgor to die here." She slipped ahead of him to get to the main entrance. "I'll wait here. You grab them."

Rilt thought about his father, still in the banquet hall, and made a run for it. It was not until he had gone through the massive arched doorways that he saw what they were up against. Outside of the shelter of the passage, it was apparent that the students had defended themselves admirably, though he saw a handful of fallen bodies, blackened and smoking. Selfishly, he hoped those bodies didn't include any of his classmates. Dozens of men were hurling fireballs ceaselessly against hastily constructed earthen walls.

Overturned kegs of ale near the base of the steps gave Rilt some liquid to defend himself with, and he wet his clothes for good measure. He spotted Wolvam leading the defense along with two other junior adepts, but the rest of the kaedine students were doing their best to throw whatever they could at the attackers. It was haphazard defense, at best. The lake glimmered orange around its edges, reflecting the burning halls of the university. Smoke plumed like gray snakes into the overcast sky. Rilt realized that the masters would not make it back in time to rescue them.

Dodging flaming debris raining down overhead, Rilt grabbed the first student he saw. It was Oledan. "Tell Aega and Terai classes to stay and bolster the adepts! Everyone else, to the banquet hall—the king needs us! Terras has gone renegade!"

"Terras?" exclaimed Oledan in disbelief.

"Not now. Survive this, I'll explain later."

Oledan's greasy face was ruddy with heat and exertion. He nodded and relayed the instructions in a bellow.

"Derone, there are helmets in the archives with mesh face plates. Use that to shield your faces from the fire. Grab shields and whatever weapons you can use. Follow Lady Liria's lead. Be careful!" he hollered at the rapidly retreating backs.

Ladmos and Oledan, along with others who were water-resonant, gathered around Rilt. The young lord cast an eye at the three adepts and hoped to Creation they could hold back the fifty attackers for a while longer.

"Terai class, walls. Force them to our left. We need a path to the lake. Keep us covered. Oledan, you and Ladmos have the strongest push. The rest of us will bring the lake to you. Heldin, you and I will tune and shape. Douse their fires!"

The Terai students ran right up behind the adepts. As one, they plunged their hands into the earth. A thick wall sprung up, twice the height of the tallest of them, cutting the adepts off from the attackers. Their short-lived reprieve was over when the Verashki started lobbing fireballs over the wall.

"Quake!" someone in the group shouted. The students responded by stomping on the ground in a repetitive beat, led by one of the junior adepts. The earth trembled, wave after wave rippling outwards.

"Now!" Rilt charged, trusting that his classmates would protect them. To his amazement, they made a roof that kept them sheltered all the way to the water's edge. There was no way for the Verashki to get to him, and no way for Rilt to see what was happening beyond the wall. He had to trust that they would all hold up their end.

Rilt ordered them into line. "Get your clothes wet. Ladmos, you first. Oledan, switch when he's tired. Terai class, open a window for Ladmos!"

As the rest of his classmates spread out, Rilt forced his breathing to slow. He found the familiar hum in his mind, focused on it, and amplified it. The surface of the lake rippled and then surged up overhead into a thin column. With his eyes closed and his breathing steady, Rilt imagined a large globe hovering in his hands, and when he opened his eyes again, he saw the globe before him, exactly as it had been in his mind.

"Take it," he told Heldin, the next in line. "Quickly!"

The knowledge that he could not fail helped to Rilt to concentrate. Again and again, he hefted globes of water as large as his own torso. Sweat and water blurred his vision by the time he'd shaped the fifteenth globe, and he swapped places with Heldin. Transferring was easier than tuning and shaping. They had already taken out more than a dozen of the Verashki, Rilt noted, even as he returned to take over from the flagging Heldin. He was about to keel over when a hand between his shoulder blades kept him from falling.

Soot-streaked, Wolvam nodded at him. "I'll tune and shape. Help Ladmos and Oledan. Only two dozen or so left. Direct the counterattack."

Rilt was relieved. He ran to the window to help Oledan and Ladmos, panting, and watched his classmates knock out Verashki after Verashki. Only about half of the number he had seen earlier were still attacking.

Amazingly, they were holding their own. Finally, with only about ten of the fire-breathers left, they were ready to let down the wall and capture the rest. That was when the remaining Verashki decided to launch a full-blown attack. A fireball, larger than any Rilt had seen, rolled and boiled like a star fallen to earth.

"Drop the wall!" Rilt bellowed as the fireball shot towards them. "Give them all we have!"

The Terai class collaped the barricade, while the Aega class swept all the water they had with them forward. The wall of water engulfed the fireball and a huge cloud of sizzling steam exploded. A handful of students were thrown back by the blast and someone shrieked. Thick jets of water shot forward from the lake and smashed into the remaining Verashki with a vengeance. The attackers were swept off their feet and then into the side of the stables, knocking them unconscious. Wolvam grinned fiercely at Rilt, panting. He had unleashed the final shots.

"Well done," Wolvam said. Sweat was pouring off him. "It's not over. Wader, Minas, bury those men up to their necks. Don't kill them. The Kingsriders will want them. Those who can move, come with me. We have to save the king."

* * *

Rilt was terrified of what he would witness by the time he stumbled back to the banquet hall. When the group careened into the hall, he was so relieved that his knees nearly buckled. The doors had been twisted open by a huge tangle of vines and roots, and a few students were standing by them. Their faces were soot-stained and alert.

Rilt ran in, looking for his father. He saw his brother and mother first. Cedaran was sitting in a corner, helping to bandage Naelen's left arm. Relief made Rilt's knees weak. His baby brother was safe. His stepmother was hugging a hysterical lady in a turquoise gown, while Liria was questioning someone in a black tunic.

The smell of charred meat and burned silk was overwhelming. Rilt fought the urge to gag as he followed Wolvam past overturned tables and chairs, trying his best not to see the bodies that were scorched and smoking. The Dagas class were armed not only with the mesh helmets, but also with steel-plated leather armor. Derone was there at the end of the hall, his helmet under one arm.

King Eram was seated on a chair, eyes closed, a hand to his chest; Master Midusel was by his side, listening, and Halden was there as well. The duke's face was bloodied and his right arm was bandaged from shoulder to fingers. However, everyone's attention was on the king.

"You are not allowed to die," Master Midusel said harshly. "Especially not if you die defending me! You're the king, for Creation's sake!"

"My … my son," gasped the king. Only then did Rilt notice the terrible burn in the man's abdomen, as well as the thick stone slab thrust through his belly. The fact that he was not dead was a miracle. "Where's my son?"

"Where's Terras?" Wolvam asked Derone.

"I can't find him," said Derone, in tears. "I've been all over the building, I can't find him. We're still looking."

"Find Kirzan," the king whispered. "I owe … apology. My son."

Cursing, Rilt swiveled about and ran for the door, Wolvam following close behind. They nearly collided with Cedaran and Naelen.

"Where are you going?" Naelen asked.

"Terras," Rilt gasped. "He's not here. Gareth and Kayle still … not found. He's not here."

Cedaran shook his head. "We've searched all the masters' studies and the library. I found the other students."

"Where would Kayle have gone?" Wolvam demanded. "Think, Rilt. You know him best."

Rilt's mind raced. Kayle had been upset, and he would have wanted to be alone… "The greenhouse. No, not the greenhouse. That's where I…" He caught himself before he admitted to murder. "Our room."

"Lord Cedaran, tell the other kaedine to follow us," said Wolvam. "Arald, are you certain- Rilt!"

Ignoring the summons, Rilt bolted down the corridor, already picturing the horrors that could have befallen Kayle. Gareth was the prince, he had to be, there was no other explanation—Kayle would fight to the death to protect Gareth. It all made sense now. Kayle was not Kirzan, he was the one Kirzan picked to pretend to be Kirzan should someone suspect the prince was in the hall… Whomever Kayle Radieri was, really was, he was not the prince.

Naelen caught up despite his injured arm. "You focus on holding back Terras," said Naelen, breathing harshly, "I'll get the other two to safety."

It was already full dark. The wind picked up, howling like a wild creature. Lightning slashed across the sky, painting the surroundings in flashes of black and white. Thunder growled like a ravenous beast, bringing the promise of rain. Rilt's heart lurched when he saw that the door to Room Six had been ripped from its hinges. Beside him, Naelen slowed down, holding his metal spike ready like a throwing spear. Rilt raced past him and skidded to a stop inside the room. He had barely taken in the chaotic mess that his room had become when Wolvam barged in and grabbed him by the shoulders.

"What would you have done if Terras was still here?" Wolvam bellowed, shaking Rilt roughly. "You could've been killed instantly! For Creation's sake, Rilt, get a hold of yourself! Where's the strategic and thoughtful leader I saw earlier?"

"It's Kayle!" Rilt screamed back. "It's Kayle, and the last thing I said to him was to accuse him of being a lying whore! If he dies, it's all my fault, I'm to blame-"

Wolvam slapped Rilt across the face. Stunned into speechlessness, Rilt could only take big gulps of air. The adept shook him again, less roughly.

"The king is dying. We need to find Gareth. I need you to remain calm. This is not the time for panic, do you understand?"

Numbed with shock, Rilt nodded.

Naelen called out to them. "I see some tracks down there," he said, pointing to the ground six feet below the ledge. "More than two persons from the looks of it. Rain's coming. We'll lose the trail if we tarry."

Wolvam let go of the young lord. "Naelen, go around the block. Meet us at the back gate, but be careful. Rilt, roll once you hit the ground, the way you were taught in hand-to-hand."

"Yes sir." Rilt climbed onto the sill, watching where he put his feet, dropped and rolled. Mud stuck to his clothes and arms, but he had not broken anything.

Wolvam was much more graceful in his landing. He helped Rilt up. "Can you continue? Are you alright?"

"You were holding off the attacks earlier nearly single-handedly, are you alright?"

"I'll be alright when this is over." His lips twitched before he loped off ahead. Even though the adept had brushed off Rilt's concern, the latter could see that Wolvam's gait was off-balance and that his face was more pinched than usual.

Naelen met up with them as they reached the back gate. "I found the bodies of two porters behind the block," he said. He looked a little green. "They weren't burned to death; their throats were cut. Small mercies."

Wolvam directed them through the orchard. "Come. Move quietly, keep to the shadows."

Lightning lit the way in infrequent bursts. Thunder rumbled overhead again, masking their steps. With Wolvam in the lead, the three crept silently along the path. Rain began to splatter on them, making their feet squelch in the mud. It was only when his hand got wet that Rilt felt the pain from the seared flesh on his palm.

The gate was warped and twisted, as though giant hands had torn it open. The ground was broken, with tall pillars of stone jutting up at intervals. Wolvam snarled something rude under his breath. Rilt could feel his pulse pick up.

"There," Rilt said, when he saw red flashes in the distance. As they approached, the rain got heavier. The lamps on the bridge provided meager light, but it was enough to see by. The rain made the note of resonance in Rilt's head fizz and sputter, like there were too many notes tinkling and not enough time to concentrate on any one of them.

Terras and three other Verashki with lit torches were facing off against Gareth and Kayle. The fire from the torches guttered and hissed, but the flames held. Kayle was battered and bloody, and his right sleeve looked as though it had been burned off. His forearm was red and peeling. Gareth was only marginally better off. He gripped lengths of black metal, their pointed ends dripping.

"I trusted you, Terras," said Gareth, loudly enough to be heard over the rain. "All those times I chatted with you—why didn't you kill me then?"

"I thought it was Radieri. And Wolvam kept a close eye on you both," said Terras. Lightning illuminated the scene briefly, enough for Rilt to see the bleeding welt across Terras' back. "Radieri, step aside. You can't hope to take another hit from us a second time."

Kayle smiled and wiped away the blood running down his left cheek. "If you could kill me that easily, you would've. You want Gareth? Over my dead body."

"If you wish." Terras advanced, drawing a stream of fire to his hand in a familar gesture.

Instantly Wolvam rushed him from behind, tackling the other adept to the ground. Caught off-guard, Rilt watched the two tussle, before he ducked a fireball lobbed at him by one of the masked men. Cursing himself for not grabbing a weapon before he came after Kayle, Rilt dodged behind the nearest tree and snapped off a low branch to use as a club. It would have to do. Charging out from behind the tree, he brandished the club at the man who had tried to burn him. The rain was pouring now and it was overwhelmingly difficult to ignore the water pounding different notes in his head, making the most terrible din. It even drowned out the throbbing agony in his hand.

"You can't beat me with that," sneered the Verashki. He fired another volley of flame but Rilt was quick on his feet, nearly slipping on the wet flagstones. Once he was close enough he swung his makeshift weapon at the back of the Verashki's head even as the latter readied for another fireball.

The club connected with a satisfying thud, and the man stumbled forward. Rilt danced out of the way and circled around him for another blow. This one connected even more powerfully and sent the man tottering back, his face broken and bleeding. He reached for the canal's guardrails and missed. Flailing, he fell over into the water. Rilt rushed forward, skidding the last few steps, but the water below was already churning white. He couldn't see the man at all.

A yell of pain brought Rilt's attention back to the fight. Naelen was standing by Kayle, Gareth behind them. The cry came from one of the men who had been pierced through with one of Gareth's spears. Unfortunately, it hadn't been enough to incapacitate him. He pulled it from his side and flung it into the river.

As one, the Verashki raised their torches to their mouths and gouts of fire burst forth, more fearsome than ever. Kayle dragged Gareth away even as a thick wall of tree saplings sprung up between them and the attackers. The saplings caught on fire almost instantly.

"Oh well done, Kayle, more fuel for the fire-breathing assassins!" Gareth hollered.

Rilt could practically hear Gareth's snide comment of "All this rain and you can't help?" but common sense kicked in. The strongest and steadiest source of water was the canal. He hadn't learned how to connect with running water, but within two breaths, Rilt had found the resonating note and latched onto it with all his might.

Water spiraled out from the canal in a thick column. It was filthy with mud and debris, but it did the job. Rilt crashed the heavy snake of water into one of the Verashki and then into the burning trees.

"Run!" Terras suddenly shouted. "Take him and go! The Ward is coming!"

Take who? Where's Wolvam? Distracted, he let go of the water column which washed over the flagstones, leaving behind a thin coating of mud. He grappled for control, and again called up a large globe of dirty canal water in case Terras tried to burn his friends. When he looked at the stocky adept, he saw that he was already wrapped in a cocoon of vines.

"You can't expect to get through this alive, Terras. Surrender," said Gareth, stepping out from the shelter of the smoking saplings.

Terras smiled. If the expression was sinister or cold in some way, Rilt would have felt better. Instead the adept looked as friendly and approachable as usual.

"This wasn't about my survival, Prince Kirzan," Terras said. "It never was."

"I suppose you're going to tell us what it was about," said Gareth.

Terras' smile vanished. "No."

He stamped hard on the flagstones. A strong quake rippled out, three times as powerful as the one Felas sent out in the banquet hall. Gareth lost his footing and staggered back into the guardrail. Rilt hurled his globe of water at Terras, but the adept deflected it with a wall of earth that appeared with another stomp of his foot. Then he sent the wall crashing into Rilt and buried him under it; only his head and one arm were free. The quake also sent Kayle skidding, which loosened the young scholar's hold on him. Terras wiggled out of the vines easily and pulled out a dagger.

"Sometimes, the most direct ways are the best," he said to Kayle as he passed. "It'll be over quickly, Prince Kirzan. Painless. Unlike your father's death."

Rilt struggled, clawing and kicking to free himself. The downpour helped, washing away some of the earth into mud. His ribs hurt—he'd probably cracked at least one of them. Out of the corner of his eye, he could see Terras nearly reaching Gareth. Just as Rilt pushed enough of the wet earth away from him to sit up, he saw Naelen wrench off the top bar of a guardrail with his good hand and swing it around like a whip. The metal connected with the adept and then wrapped around Terras' torso, binding his arms to his sides. Then Gareth sent another guardrail to tangle around the renegade adept's ankles.

"You and your accomplices will die as painfully as my father, then," snarled Gareth.

Kayle came over to help Rilt up. "Are you alright?"

"Are you?"

"Could be better," said Kayle with a small smile.

Rilt gripped Kayle's hand before the scholar could turn away. "We have a lot to talk about, after all this."

"Yes. Yes we do." Rain plastered Kayle's curls flat to his scalp, and Rilt could see that bruises were beginning to bloom over his face even in the dim light. The skin on his right forearm was blackened and blistered.

Rilt thought Kayle had never looked more beautiful than at this moment.

They returned to Gareth and Naelen, Rilt using what remained of the guardrail to support himself. The burn on his other hand started stinging again. Kayle stood behind him, a hand between his shoulder blades.

"Gareth, your father wants you back at the hall," said Rilt. He was feeling twinges of pain from his ribs, and fatigue reared its head.

"He's alive?" Relief blossomed over Gareth's thin, pale face. Rilt was shocked to see that his classmate was just a scared and exhausted young man. "He's alright?"

He's dying. Rilt could not say the words aloud, for fear that it would be true, but he had to tell Gareth somehow. He could not find his voice, nor could his mouth form the words.

His silence was a sufficiently eloquent response, apparently, for the relief in Gareth's face hardened to an inscrutable mask. He stared at Terras again. Terras met his gaze fearlessly. Close to, Rilt could see blisters on various parts of the adept's face. Courtesy of Kayle's bluespine leaves, he suspected.

"Why were you nice to me, Terras?" the prince asked. For the first time, Rilt could hear a faint shimmer of hurt in Gareth's voice. "What have I ever done to you to deserve your wrath?"

"Ask your father what he has done. What all the kings have done since the days of Coleri Aleis," said Terras, still smiling, though all warmth had leached from his expression. "Your house is the reason why Aleis is in a mess. Why droughts and blights and storms sweep through the land, why the common people suffer. My death means nothing. The spark has been lit, prince, and in time the kingdom will burn. The reckoning has begun. It will not end until there is no longer a king on the throne."

Gareth raised his chin defiantly. The downpour was easing. In the dim lamplight from the bridge behind him, Gareth looked every inch the son of King Eram.

"I will not allow my kingdom to burn, Terras. But I will see you burn, once you have been tried for treason."

The adept smiled. "Your father would be proud of you: a true Ice Eagle of the Alcaronans. I hope he lives long enough to tell you this, but I doubt it."

Gareth did not even flinch. "If my father allows himself to die from a third-rate assassination plot, then he deserves it."

"Oh, you are cold-blooded. Let's see how cold you can be." Terras chuckled and fell to his knees. A quake rippled out from where he landed.

The ground under the students' feet lurched. Kayle screamed as he lost his balance and slipped down towards the churning canal. Rilt snagged Kayle's wrist in the nick of time, but his ribs shrieked in agony and his legs gave out. Rilt's blistered palm burst with renewed pain.

"Rilt!" Kayle's blue eyes were wide and terrified. "Rilt, don't let go, please don't let go!"

"I won't," Rilt promised, gritting his teeth. He could not inhale properly. Every breath hurt. Stretching down his other hand, he gripped Kayle with all the strength he had left and then some. Below them, the canal was a roiling channel of muddy water. The low rumble of thunder in the distance promised even more rain.

Naelen and Gareth rushed to either side of Rilt. Naelen reached down immediately with his good arm, but Kayle's grip slipped alarmingly when he tried reaching for Naelen. They tried to pull on Rilt so he could drag Kayle up to the bank. Gareth was trying to wrench the other guardrail free, but the fight earlier had clearly sapped him. The prince yelled helplessly at the metal, commanding it to yield, but to no avail. Behind them, they could hear Terras' mocking laughter about Gareth still being too soft-hearted to be an Alcaronan.

They all heard the voices calling for them. Rilt could make out Cedaran's shouts and, for a heartbeat, wanted to shout at him to stay away. With one hand securely tangled in Rilt's tunic, Naelen yelled for them to come. Gareth disappeared, presumably to get to the reinforcements.

Rain drenched Rilt's clothes and water flowed down his neck, his shoulders, his arms, and his hands. To his horror, Kayle's grip was slipping.

"Someone save Kayle!" Rilt screamed. His ribs burned. "For Creation's sake, somebody get him now!"

Kayle was digging his fingers into Rilt's hand. He gulped and smiled shakily up at his lover. "I'll be alright, Rilt. I will be."

"You will be," Rilt vowed. His throat and lungs felt raw from pain.

Gareth appeared beside him. "Hold on! Dagger's got some rope! You'll be safe!"

Kayle nodded.

There was a brilliant burst of lightning. Rilt winced from the deafening clap of thunder that followed. Impossibly, the downpour grew heavier. Rilt clung to Kayle with the desperate hope of an imminent rescue. Soon they would be safe, and he could tell Kayle how much it didn't matter who Kayle used to be. That all that mattered was how much he loved him, and that nothing could part them, not even Halden.

Abruptly, Kayle's hand slid through Rilt's grasp. The Halim scholar didn't even have time to scream before he was swept down the churning canal.

Instinctively, Rilt strained for Kayle, his mind locking on a frenzied chord that had to be the water of the canal. He couldn't breathe, trying to steady the torrents of water that pounded and boiled and rolled beneath him. Kayle was still there, he had to be, the Creators would not be so cruel to give him hope and rip it from him like this…

The humming in his ears grew so shrill that he could hear nothing else. When someone lifted him off the ground, he shook them off and staggered back towards the canal, convinced that if he could lock onto the correct note of resonance, he could bring Kayle back. His vision flickered around the edges and suddenly went dark, but still he stretched out all his senses, every nerve crying to do what he needed to do. His ribs were on fire, and his muscles were on fire, and none of it mattered except he needed to get Kayle back and safe-

And then, oblivion.

AFTER

Naelen and Wolvam were waiting by his bed when Rilt woke up.

"Kayle?" Rilt asked. His throat hurt. His lips felt parched and cracked. His burnt hand was wrapped in thin bandages.

Naelen averted his eyes. In a suspiciously thick voice, he said, "I'll inform the nurses and the duchess that you're awake."

"Kayle?" Rilt insisted, gazing at Wolvam. "Kayle?"

Wolvam brushed his dirty blond hair from his brow as he glanced out the window. It was very bright outside. His tone was unusually gentle when he spoke. "He was found this morning. Under the Glass Bridge."

"He's alright?"

Wolvam shut his eyes. "No, Rilt. He drowned."

It would have been kinder for Wolvam to stab Rilt in the heart.

"I cleaned up Room Six and I found this tucked under a pillow." The adept handed Rilt his red journal. "I read some of it. I'm sorry, I wasn't thinking when I opened it … I'm sorry."

If Rilt was not in shock, he would have been outraged. As it was, he took the journal numbly and ran his thumb over the edges.

"I'll need to ask you what you learned about fire-resonant kaedine when you're better," said Wolvam.

Rilt stared at the embossed house crest until it blurred into the cover itself. He could not feel his extremities, but he could hear his breathing. In and out. In and out. It sounded too harsh, too raw.

"I saw what you wrote about Jodius."

The young lord's attention flickered to awareness. "You know now."

"There is nothing to know," said Wolvam. He patted Rilt's knee awkwardly. "Rest, Rilt. Everything else can wait."

* * *

When Selvina saw Rilt, she immediately ran to embrace him. "You brave, reckless boy," she whispered, tears running down her beautiful face. "You saved Prince Kirzan! Why didn't you tell us you were friends with him?"

Cedaran and Galena stood side by side at the foot of the bed. Galena's eyes were red-rimmed. Once Selvina released him, Rilt held out a hand to Galena and tugged her close for a hug.

"I'm so sorry," whispered Galena, her sweet voice hoarse and low. "I'm so, so sorry. We heard the news this morning."

"How long have I been unconscious?" Rilt let go of Galena. More than anything else, he wanted to cry, but he felt lost and weightless, as though he was still asleep. There was something deeply wrong and he could not give voice to it, could not form words around it.

"Four days," Cedaran replied. He cleaned his glasses and stared at his hands. "The healer said you … you nearly burned out." He went on talking about the attack that had unfolded in the banquet hall. Apparently, Halden had stabbed two Verashki with a shard of glass before he was thrown across the room by Terras' attack.

Galena squeezed Cedaran's fingers when the young man faltered. She said, "King Eram… King Eram fought Terras. He defended Master Midusel from the other Verashki and Terras called up rock spikes and … I saw. I was behind the curtains at the musicians' dais and I saw, and I froze."

"You were frightened. Anyone would be." Cedaran went on to explain how he went searching for the others.

Uninterested, Rilt barely listened to his brother's recount. He leaned back on his pillow and stared at the high wooden ceiling, studied the chipped paint and the red-tinted shadows. There were birds singing outside—one was a blackfen, a common Enthinian pest in the fields, warbling loudly. It must be near dusk now.

Galena squeezed his fingers and sniffed. "Naelen said he'll, um. He said he'll take care of … of things. That you just need to focus on, um. Focus on recovering."

That sensation of being adrift was stronger than ever. He closed his eyes. "Mother, Ced, could I speak to Galena in private for a moment?"

"Of course, dear, and once you're well enough to travel, we're taking you home." Selvina stood up in a rustle of silks. Her dark skin was dusted over in bronze by the dusk outside. Rilt wondered why he ever trusted her judgment.

Cedaran cleared his throat and gazed at Galena. "If you want, I can wait for you outside."

"That'll be good, Ced, thank you," said the young woman.

Once he was sure his family had gone, Rilt opened his eyes and took Galena's slender, strong hands. "I will keep my promise to you, Galena."

"That's hardly important now," Galena protested.

"I will keep my promise." He breathed in with some difficulty; his ribs were bound securely. "Get me Naelen and Gareth. Or Kirzan, whatever he's calling himself now. I need their help."

* * *

"This is madness," Gareth said. "You're not well enough, Rilt. Can you even stand?"

"Not by myself, which is why I asked for you both." Rilt had managed to sit up, but even doing that put pressure on his ribs. His right ankle was bandaged, as was his left knee. He was more injured than he had first thought. "I must know."

Gareth's voice was rough and angry. "He was my best friend. Do you think I couldn't recognize him?"

For a long while, Rilt did not answer. He focused on his toes, the pulsing soreness of his ankles and knees, the pattern of the stone tiles of the healer hall. Finally, he said, "It's not about that. It's about closure. I need to be there."

Naelen studied Rilt and then quietly exited the room. He came back swiftly, pushing a chair mounted on wheels. "We'll go."

"Nael, you're not helping," Gareth said irritably.

"You'd want to if it were you."

Gareth had no rejoinder for that. He sullenly helped Rilt to the chair, and then escorted him and Naelen out to the main hall. Along the way, two wardens joined them.

Rilt paid them no attention. He paid no attention to his surrounds other than the signs showing where they were headed. His shoulders hurt and he found himself clenching his fists until his knuckles cracked.

* * *

"Your Royal Highness," a healer in green robes and gloves hurried up to them when they came to the locked wing, "You cannot be here. This is the morgue!"

"Precisely where we intend to go," said Gareth. "Only the three of us. The wardens will remain here. Go on, open it."

"But Prince Kirzan, this is against Healer Hall practice. The morgue is not a place for any patient to enter, nor any person without formal permission from Master Raman. Not even the king of Aleis and the future duke of Enthin."

"Either you let us in to view the body found this morning," Gareth said slowly, advancing on the hapless healer, "or I personally see to it that you end up in that room on a slab. Open the door."

The healer swallowed nervously.

"If it helps," said Rilt, "you can place the blame solely on me. I'm the one insisting on this. You know who I am. The twin rams on my house crest should tell you about an Arald's temperament."

Though intimidated, the healer left to seek permission from Master Raman before he grudgingly unlocked the morgue. It was bitterly cold inside, helped by the huge blocks of ice stacked along the walls. Shrouded figures lay on top of stone slabs and metal trolleys like so many loaves of bread. Each trolley had a number attached to it.

The healer wheeled out a body and then stepped aside, head bowed respectfully.

Naelen put a hand on Rilt's shoulder. "Are you sure you want to do this?"

"Yes." Rilt took a measured breath. The room smelled of frozen memories and slowly blooming rot. He unclenched his hands and nodded.

The healer folded the covering down to the body's chest. He explained quietly that a dead person who was found submerged in water for hours would look vastly different once the body was exposed to air, and that part of the skin had sloughed off due to abrasions from the rough surfaces under the bridge where the body had been found.

"Shipsuckers have very sharp edges," said the healer. "The cuts are not-"

"Shut up." Rilt pushed himself to his feet. His head swam as he scrutinized the discolored face of the dead man on the trolley.

Dark hair, skin that would have been fair if not for the green tinge and mottled bruising, lips that Rilt had known intimately but was nauseated by at this moment. He studied the corpse, willing his mind to work, to make sense of this. Or to wake up and feel relieved that this was just another nightmare.

"Turn him over."

"Lord Rilt…"

"Turn him over. I need to see his left shoulder."

The healer did as requested. The revealed skin was partly abraded, but there it was: a tattoo of a cliff rose.

Abruptly, Rilt's legs gave out. He could not stop the trembling, and when Naelen tried to help him up, he threw up all over the chilly floor. Since he hadn't eaten yet, all that came up was sour bile.

"Let's get you back to your bed," said Naelen. He heaved Rilt back into the wheeled chair, apologized to the healer, and hurried him out of the morgue. The passage back to Rilt's bed was a blur. His ears rang with a silence so thick that he could choke on it. Vaguely he registered that Gareth and Naelen were arguing with each other, but he had no fortitude left to deal with them. Instead, he covered his face with the thin pillow on the bed and waited until they left.

Then he screamed into it until he ran out of breath. He wished he could run out of tears, too.

* * *

Duke Halden did not look up from his book when Rilt limped into the study at their Izdahli mansion with Pellit's assistance. The duke's arm had recovered already. "Have you prepared for tomorrow's ceremony at the Lords' Convene? The king himself will honor you. The Black Crescent, just one step below my grandfather's Iron Thorn of Valor."

"There is nothing I want that Kirzan can give me." Rilt stood, leaning on the plain boxwood cane. The last thing he wanted was to be honored for going to Gareth's—Kirzan's—rescue, when the one he wanted most to save was lost.

"King Kirzan, even in your thoughts. You should feel proud. You've brought honor to the house of Arald." Halden set aside his book and scrutinized his son. "After your ... dalliance with Ledon Pol, I had despaired of you ever respecting your station. And then you chose to involve yourself with that ... prostitute. But you've done well, son. The king owes you a great debt. I also see that you've become friendly with Liria Alwyth. I shall withdraw my support for Evvas, on the condition that you cultivate that friendship."

Rilt held his father's gaze for a long moment. He wanted to rebuke his father for insulting Kayle, but thought better of it. Halden would never change his opinion on Kayle. Why bother? "Liria is ten times more suitable than Evvas ever was."

"If she were not secondborn and a woman, I would have supported her from the start."

"Secondborn is not second best, Father." Rilt inclined his head. "I should rest. I'm not fully recovered yet."

* * *

Pellit looked worried. "Sir, won't you reconsider?"

"You have always been more than a servant to me, Pellit, and I trust your judgment, but this time my mind is set." Rilt took a deep breath. "This is what's best for Enthin."

The page looked distressed. Rilt smiled and pressed his hand to Pellit's cheek affectionately. "You won't be out of a job, I promise. Cedaran will look after you. Now, my luggage."

Once Pellit left, Rilt sank back into the soft down pillows and closed his eyes. The silk sheets were cool to the touch and he smoothed his palms over them; he had forgotten how good they felt on his skin. He had forgotten a lot of things about living as an Arald. Already, the routine of his days in Kaedin Hall felt like a passing dream.

HONOUR

For the first time, the Lords' Convene was held in the throne room in the north wing of the palace. Through the massive floor-to-ceiling windows, everyone could see well beyond the city gates. Rilt suspected that he'd be able to see the ocean from that room on a clear day. The throne faced the windows, while rows of chairs had been placed in a semicircle around the throne, with an aisle dividing the attendees. There was a rostrum at the foot of the stairs for the officiant to manage the proceedings.

Lady Liria's confirmation to the title went without a hitch. No one wanted to back Evvas after Duke Halden withdrew his support. In addition, she and her guards had protected many of the lords at the King's Ball. No one wanted to appear ungrateful.

Lady Liria, soon to be Duchess Liria, had been at the receiving end of flirtation from nearly all the eligible bachelors of the lesser nobility in Izdahl. They would not get the duchy, of course, but should they succeed in wooing her, their children would inherit the title and the lands. Their fawning attitudes sickened Rilt. Liria, for her part, had coyly encouraged the attention. She shone like a black pearl in the sun. Her cloud of dark hair and elaborate gold jewelry drew the eye of everyone in attendance. When she winked salaciously at Rilt, the latter rolled his eyes at her outrageous performance.

Rilt listened to the proceedings with only half his mind present. The Lords' Convene was an excuse for the nobles to meet and form alliances, not to resolve issues. Earlier, during the recess, he and Galena had exchanged pleasantries with Duke Ingros of Dunte. Galena was to be rewarded for her part in foiling the plotters' attack.

Sitting beside Rilt, Cedaran was listening attentively to something about taxation, and judging by the scowl on his younger brother's face, it was something he disagreed with. It was easy to forget how young Cedaran really was, Rilt thought, watching his half-brother take notes and muttering comments under his breath.

He let his mind wander, the voices washing over him, until it was time for his father to speak.

"I have merry tidings," Duke Halden said. He was actually smiling. "In the near future, my son will wed Lady Galena Aedinal of Dunte. If any present here object to the union, please voice your concerns."

Rilt expected no resistance to the engagement. The Aedinals were lesser nobility, so the offspring of a union between the houses Arald and Aedinal would not cause a rift in succession in either Dunte or Enthin. He kept very still in his seat and wondered how much Cedaran really understood from their conversation. Duke Ingros agreed to bear witness for the engagement, and Rilt wondered how much the Aedinals would rise in status back in Dunte.

There was a murmur of congratulations from various lords and then it was time for the king to address the Lords' Convene.

Gareth—King Kirzan—held up his left hand, his other holding on to his plain iron kae staff. He looked as comfortable as a child playing dress-up. Rilt tried to pay attention.

"Four days ago, a treasonous party tried to assassinate us. My friends risked their lives to keep my father and I safe. Some of them died in doing so."

A courtier hurried forward with a tray laden with medals. The new king swept his gaze around the circle of lords. "I was sent away from Izdahl for my safety and education. I have traveled nearly the length and breadth of Aleis with little incident, and yet, if not for the brave actions of my friends, I would not have made the short distance from Kaedin Hall to the palace. Today I wish to honor my friends for all they have done for my father, and for all they have done for me."

"To my friends who stood against the treasonous Verashki at great cost to life and limb, the White Peak of Alcaronan." Oledan led the class in receiving the honor. Rilt watched dully. Ladmos kept prodding the little triangular medal of pure white steel until a stern nudge from Derone stopped him.

The four-pointed Red Star of Aleis, with the greater ice hawk of the Alcaronan crest at its heart, glittered white and crimson when the king picked one up. "For those who defended my father in his hour of need, the Red Star of Aleis."

Naelen, Felas, and Halden all received the medal. Halden, who was used to such honors, bore his with grace and dignity. Naelen and Felas both seemed slightly overwhelmed by all the attention.

"To those who led the defense of Kaedin Hall and saw to the protection of the students as well as the lords and ladies, the Black Crescent."

It was the second-highest honor the king could bestow on his subjects. It should have felt momentous. Rilt felt as though he was watching it all from a great distance as first Liria received hers, then Wolvam and the two junior adepts Wader and Minas, and himself. Perhaps there was polite applause. He was no longer listening.

The king pinned the medal to Rilt's tunic. The young man bowed, and then returned to his seat. He kept his eyes on his hands when Gareth—King Kirzan—spoke again. To Rilt, the words sounded like they were coming from a long way away, waves washing onto sand.

"There is one man I have to honor above all others. My best friend, Kayle Radieri, took on my identitiy and gave his life to save mine," he began, and all Rilt could think was: *No, no he didn't.*

It was an accident, he was terrified as he fell, you didn't feel his hand slipping through yours. You liar, you call yourself his best friend, but you let him die. He didn't die to save you. He died for a secret. I lost him because I couldn't accept the truth.

He should not have died just because you couldn't tell the truth.

No one should have died just because we couldn't take the truth.

Gareth went on about bravery and loyalty and other empty platitudes. Rilt had to grit his teeth and swallow a lump of infuriated sorrow closing up his throat. He blinked away tears. This was not Gareth speaking. This was King Kirzan. A proper king on the throne had to speak of proper things, not of shared laughter over meals and arguments and commiserating over too many essays and readings.

Eventually Kirzan finished. Everyone stood and clapped politely. Rilt remained standing when the audience sat down.

"Lord Rilt?" The king looked concerned. "Is there something you wish to say about Kayle?"

Rilt made his decision. With a deep breath, he said, "Your Majesty, I ask for permission to speak."

"You have my permission. Speak freely, my friend."

My friend. The term of endearment sounded more like a warning. He almost wished the old insult of "lordling" had been used instead. Rilt walked to the rostrum slowly, his bootheels echoing. As he turned and saw the assembled highborn, he almost faltered. For a brief moment, he considered not doing what he planned to, but Master Baelmin's voice whispered in his ear: Be kind, be courageous, and be yourself, always.

"As my father, Duke Halden, had announced earlier, Lady Galena will become duchess of Enthin. I seek your blessings for the union between Lady Galena," he beckoned to her, and she came to him, nervous and unsure, "and the future duke of Enthin, Lord Cedaran of the Arald house."

There was an explosion of silence. Rilt led the perplexed and stunned Galena down to where Cedaran sat, gaping, and put her hand atop his brother's. "Take care of each other."

"What is the meaning of this?" Duke Halden demanded. He rushed out of his place and swung Rilt about by the shoulders. "You cannot just cede your birthright and title as you wish!"

"Why not? There are enough witnesses here."

"Why are you doing this, Rilt?" King Kirzan asked.

Disengaging from his father's hold, Rilt removed the medal from his tunic and returned it to the king solemnly with both hands. "I do not deserve this, Your Majesty. A Black Crescent is bestowed on those of good character, but I am not one of these people."

Angrily, the king hissed, "What are you up to, lordling?"

"Your Majesty. I am morally unsuitable for the station."

Halden said sternly, "You are making a mockery of this convene, Rilt. Sit down."

"On the contrary, Father, I wish to make it very clear to all the esteemed lords assembled here that Cedaran is the better candidate, for two simple reasons."

"Rilt, stop speaking," Kirzan commanded, every inch the king. There was true anger seething beneath his composure, but Rilt detected a hint of alarm. Kirzan knew what was coming.

For Kayle. Rilt looked directly at the other young man. His heart pounded painfully against his ribs. "Your Majesty, as you were well aware, Kayle and I were lovers. And because I loved him, I killed Master Jodius. You know why I did that, and what we did afterwards to hide my crime. I do not believe that I should be judged for whom I loved, but I am a murderer. Hence, it is just that I forfeit the Black Crescent, along with all claim to title and land. I place my life in your hands, to be dealt with as Your Majesty pleases."

He sank to his knees, head bowed. Peace washed over him at last.

A BEGINNING

Dear Ced,

How are you? At the moment, I'm still under watch in the palace. Gareth—I mean, King Kirzan—is deciding what to do with me. He doesn't intend to kill me, but they can't keep me in here forever. Well, they could, but what would be the point? I promise that I will write you as often as I am permitted. Whatever else, you are my brother.

I never did get to tell you how sorry I am to leave the burden of the dukedom to you. We both know it is no sinecure to be duke, and I know you've only ever wanted the role of my most trusted advisor. I guess we'll have to trade places, brother mine, assuming I will be allowed out of Izdahl. This much I know: Gareth (I really can't get used to calling him King Kirzan, he's been Gareth too long) is concerned about the Verashki who got away. It's likely that someone will be sent to investigate.

They will reinstate Master Baelmin's name in the School of History, so that is one small victory, at least. He found the secret which has now revealed itself. I hope that, wherever he is now, he's satisfied.

If you're angry with me because of what I have left to you, please understand that I am deeply sorry. I beg your forgiveness, for now you have to bear also the burden of having a murderer as a brother. I hope you harbor no resentment against Kayle Radieri, and that you don't blame him for my actions.

Kayle was important to me; I loved him with a fierce, blinding passion that overtook the good sense Master Baelmin tried to smack into my head. I failed to let judgment rule my temper. What happened was entirely my fault. You would have fared better than I in this; you have always been the smarter one.

Take care of yourself, Ced. You are very dear to me. Never doubt that I love you, and that I will do all in my power (however little I have) to support you when you are Duke of Enthin.

Remember: be kind, be courageous, and be yourself.

Your loving brother,
Rilt.

* * *

Rilt glanced up from the letter when the door opened with a creak. There were other letters on the narrow table, addressed to Selvina, Galena, and Pellit, as well as Pellit's mother.

"I knocked," said Naelen. "No one answered."

"I didn't hear it," Rilt told him. He slipped the letter into an envelope and slid it across the table with the others. "Thank you for doing this."

The other Enthinian offered a thin-lipped smile and cleared his throat. "You're welcome. We've, uh, we've seen Kayle off. The cremation was … They held the cremation in the center of the lake. Gare- I mean, Kirzan, the king was there. He put the Iron Thorn in the urn. The entire university watched and, um, Gareth and I walked the urn around the lake. Liria will accompany his ashes back to Port when she leaves, with an honor guard."

Rilt felt his airway constricting. His eyes stung with emotion. When he found his voice, he said thickly, "Thank you."

"He went home with great honor," said Naelen. The pause grew heavy and poignant, both of them wishing that Rilt could have been there at the end. Sniffing once, the blond swent on briskly, "Kirzan wants me to tell you that you're going to be sent on a mission."

Tension snaked over Rilt's shoulders. "There is more you haven't said."

Naelen sighed and scratched the back of his neck. "Obviously, you won't be going alone."

"Don't tell me…" Rilt groaned, letting his head flop forward until his forehead thunked softly on the table.

"I had to tell him about the things you found out about the fire kaedine. King Kirzan was adamant on this. You'll be questioned further."

"Can't they question Terras?"

"They burned him out." At that reveal, Rilt raised his head. Naelen looked almost sad as he said, "The Kaedine Council burned him out, and he's refused to say anything other than 'there will be a reckoning'. The noble houses are calling for his public execution, and I'm fairly sure King Kirzan will do it."

Rilt wished he felt no regret for Terras' fate. He remembered how it had been the adept who sent Kayle sliding down the bank of the canal, how his followers had tried to kill his friends. He also recalled the time Terras drank with them in Oledan's room, and the way he had offered comfort to a shaken Wolvam. The kindness he showed to the students, helping them with assignments. With a deep breath, he put aside his thoughts and feelings about the adept. There was nothing he could do, would do for Terras.

They heard the clicking of boot heels in the corridor. Naelen glanced at the door and said, in a low voice, "Kirzan trusts him. I have to go; they won't allow more than one person in here." He took the letters and tucked them into his tunic pocket.

Rilt stood and grasped Naelen's arm. "Thank you. For … for telling me about—about Kayle."

"I'll miss him too." The blond patted Rilt's hand and rapped on the door. A guard opened it and Naelen swept out, nodding to the man waiting outside.

Once Naelen had left, Wolvam strode in. He was dressed in traveling robes, but with a shiny new master's badge holding a faded blue hooded cloak to his shoulder. His dirty blond hair still hung in his eyes though. "Naelen has informed you, I suppose," he said without preamble. "You're coming with me on my journeying."

"Why?"

"The fire-resonant kaedine. Those that came to Kaedin Hall can't be the only ones. The king wants me to find them; you're helping me in my enquiries."

Rilt hesitated. "But you … You know I killed Jodius. And you still want me?"

Wolvam's lips thinned briefly. His gaze pierced Rilt with its fierce honesty. "Kirzan has told me why you did it. Knowing what I know now, I might have done the same."

"I don't understand."

Wolvam sat down on the stiff bed, his face ashen. "Kayle was not the first student Jodius manipulated into providing sexual favors. I had—I came into some evidence, but the student wouldn't testify before the judges or before the other masters. I confronted Jodius before. He promised me he'd changed. I believed him."

Clenching his fists, Rilt had to make himself count to ten in his head. It was not Wolvam's fault; it was Rilt's.

"I shouldn't have killed him," said Rilt quietly. "He should have faced the judges. Been tried by the law. I'm sorry."

"Shoulds and shouldn'ts. They're of no use now, Rilt. Now, I have a mission, and I need you. Terras did not work in isolation. We need to find where the other Verashki have gone." He sat on the uncomfortable bed. "I'll need you to tell me everything you know about them."

Rilt considered his options. The reappearance of fire-resonant kaedine would undoubtedly shake up the balance of the kingdom. It had already changed his life, and taken away Kayle's. What was going to change next?

He decided.

"My late tutor, Master Baelmin, left me a letter in his will," he began.

EPILOGUE

It was dark and cold. He had lost count of the hours, but he supposed his days were numbered just the same, whether he took note of them or not. The sound of marching feet oozed through the thick ceiling, the barest hints of life beyond his cell. That was all that he was allowed of the world now. The dark, the chill, and whispers of existence.

When the heavy iron door clanged open, it was the loudest sound he had heard since he had been locked in here. Sitting up on his narrow cot, awkwardly shifting his bound hands and feet, Terras wondered if this was the day he was to witness open sky for the very last time, or if they would deny him even that.

Firelight—from a torch, perhaps—bounced off the damp stone walls. The light came from someone before the bend in the stairway. Terras had to squint against the unexpected glare, but he kept his eyes open, fearful and furious that even a pittance of light felt like a feast for his senses. A man descended the steps cautiously, silhouetted against the glow. Terras did not need the light to identify him.

"Wolvam," said Terras, and was startled by the harsh croak of his own voice. "So they have sent you to be kind to me."

"There is no kindness for you, Terras," said Wolvam. "You killed King Eram."

It took Terras a few heartbeats before he absorbed the contents of Wolvam's words. So hungry had he been for another person's company, he did not quite comprehend the other man's tone. Once he registered the hint of bitter disappointment underlying Wolvam's words, he barked a laugh.

"I killed Eram, but Gareth—Kirzan, I should say—lives. The king is dead, long live the king," sneered Terras. "I suppose he wants me quartered and paraded through all the cities."

Wolvam remained still, his assessing gaze taking in Terras' state while showing no emotion. "I persuaded him otherwise."

"Still trying to save me, Wolf?"

"Don't call me that," snapped the adept. It was the first real crack in his facade. Wolvam turned away from Terras and took a few deep breaths before facing him again. "Give us the names of your co-conspirators, and they will give you a draught. You'll die painlessly. That is … that is the best I can do."

The prisoner regarded Wolvam until the silence grew as heavy as the iron encasing his hands and feet. "We are Verashki. I cannot give you names."

"Then you'll be executed and your body thrown into the sea, and you'll never go home."

Wolvam had taken only three steps when Terras called out, "You misunderstand me."

The adept paused. For a second he looked as though he was going to proceed up and out into the light, leaving Terras behind in darkness again. Then he jogged down the stairs and walked straight to the prisoner, grabbing him by the shoulders.

"This is not a game, Terras," Wolvam hissed. "People are dead. People we care for and people we have taught are dead. I am not in a gaming mood!"

"I am not playing," said Terras. "People died because they did not know the truth. Because the kaedine hid it from the populace."

"What are the kaedine hiding then, Terras? What so-called truth gave you the right to kill the king and attack all the nobles? What gave you the right to kill our students?"

"That anyone can be kaedine!" Terras retorted. He slumped back against the wall. "Anyone. Verashki. Firash-kae. Breath of flame and fire, my friend. We—are—Verashki. I cannot give you names, because anyone, at any time, could become as dangerous as I was, as my fellow Verashki were. Are. The ruling houses, from Aleis to Alcaronan, have killed hundreds or thousands of us who discovered this truth. Yet we survive. I discovered this. I learned. I grew. All those fires. You suspected foul play. You just never thought that it'd be our own."

Even in the dim light, Terras could see that Wolvam's lips had gone thin and angry. "You lie."

"Is it a lie that I resonate with stone and yet wield fire? Believe me,

Wolf, I care not for the manner of my death, for the truth will live on. All of us who attacked that night were ready to die for the truth. But that was not all the Verashki. We are many." Terras smiled, broad and friendly despite the grime clinging to him. Only now did Wolvam see the glint of madness in those familiar eyes. "The kaedine will fail, Wolvam, and soon, there will be a reckoning. There will be no king on the throne. Kirzan should have remained Gareth Krell."

Wolvam backed away from his former friend. His hands were shaking, though whether with suppressed rage or fear, Terras could not tell. Finally, the adept squared his shoulders and headed up the stairs. Just as he reached the bend, Wolvam paused and said, without looking down, "Tell the Terras I knew that I was his friend, and that I will grieve for him."

"That Terras thanks you, Wolvam." The prisoner leaned back, eyes wide to devour the final vestiges of firelight. "For his part, he was your friend too."

The door clanged shut. Darkness embraced him again. The men outside marched away, sucking sound out from the cell, leaving him with the steady beating of his pulse and the hoarse rush of his breathing.

Read on for an excerpt from *The Kaedin Forge*, the next book in The Kaedin Trilogy.

The Kaedin Forge

"The King is dead, long live the King!"

The proclamation was made at noon in all the cities across the kingdom of Aleis. The capital city of Izdahl knew of the passing of King Eram already; this was a mere formality. The entire city lined the streets, dressed in ash-gray as was custom, and waited for the late king's iron bier to make its solemn trek to the Kingsmound in the heart of the third circle, where previous monarchs had been cremated.

Everyone who was present around the mound watched the young King Kirzan light the stack of dry hay set within a low wall of stones. They would say later that the young king had not shed tears for his father; they would say that he stood as close as was possible to the flames; they would say that he stayed until the ashes had cooled, and then he had used the Scepter of Coleri to fashion the bier into an urn for his father. They would all remember how King Kirzan personally carried the urn and walked all the way back to the palace, flanked by guards and Kingsriders all older than he, while the royal carriage veiled in gray trundled behind.

That was the last time many Izdahlis would look upon their king.

* * *

None of this spread to Fenfoss village. It was a small village sited near a claypit, with a population of perhaps two hundred adults. Nearly everyone worked either in the clay or with it. What happened in the capital city was as good as a fireside story. Only Par Odem, Par Daol and Mam Daol had ever gone as far as Dunwall, the largest city in Dunte. The furthest the rest of the villagers had gone was to Big Lake Town, which was half a day's ride on a yokebeest cart. News trickled slowly to Fenfoss, and by the time they arrive, they were olds.

Hence, when a towncrier had come to Fenfoss village and called out for them to gather, it caused quite a stir. Fresh news, straight from Big Lake!

"Are we all here?" the towncrier asked the village head.

Par Odem nodded. "Aye."

"Alright. Now, good people of Fenfoss, hear ye: King Eram has passed away and King Kirzan now bears the Scepter of Coleri. The kingdom grieves for the manner of King Eram's death, for it was not peaceful, but it was honorable, for he fell in battle defending his people against traitors. Traitors who called themselves the Verash-ki attacked the king. King Kirzan wishes these traitors to be made known to all Aleisans, that they may be forever shamed and their names never carried on by any child from this day forth." The town-crier read the proclamation from Izdahl aloud in his most dignified manner, puffed with pride that he was given this important task by the town mayor. "Terras Pollastri, from Little Pond of Dunte. Kelon Hang, from Viniel of Dunte. Rodas Damieri, from Lake Poll of Enthin…" He recited the entire list of twenty-seven names. By the end of it, he was parched. When he lowered the official scroll, he saw the solemn, plain faces of the villagers staring up at him on his pony.

"That's all," he said, impatience coloring his tone. He had seven other villages to inform. These Fenfoss villagers with their muddy hands and clay-covered feet were unsettling him.

The village chief jerked his chin at the towncrier. "We've heard all we need to, aye? There be no more news?"

"Yes, that's all."

Satisfied, Par Odem turned around and gestured curtly to one of the men. "G'wan then, git. We have three hunnerd bricks promised to Par Flekin by next fulmoon."

As a group the men returned to the mine or the kiln, leaving the women still standing in the square, looking at one another in vague concern. The towncrier huffed in irritation and urged his pony into a turn. They could have at least given him a sip of tea or something.

Once the self-important man was gone, Mam Garuna shook her old head and sniffed. "Ol' Eram, young Kirzan. None of what mat-ters to us, aye? Them lords and ladies be concerned with them big matters; we be bothered by our own little matters."

* * *

"Well, *that* certainly caught us unawares," Liria said breezily as she strolled into the meeting chamber. The king had called for his first meeting with the Privy Council. Liria was keen to find out what Kirzan was like; Naelen's description of him had not been too complimentary at first, but over time, her best friend had amended his opinion of his roommate to something near acceptance.

Duke Ingros hummed noncommittally. "It changes little. The house of Arald will stand strong, even if Rilt has disavowed his birthright."

"It was taken from him," Halden snarled as he stalked past and crashed into his seat. His glower could have darkened a summer day.

Ingros took her seat next to Halden. "Cedaran is an intelligent young man, Halden. I'm sure he'll be an honor to your house."

"He is secondborn. He cannot ever understand the burden he now bears," Halden huffed.

Liria debated if she should comment, and decided to hold her tongue for now. When she had attended the previous Lords' Convene and Privy Council in her father's stead, she had kept her mouth shut and her eyes and ears open. The only new element this time round would be King Kirzan.

The masters of the university filed in, still dressed in their somber robes with their different colored belts. Master Midusel, his beard looking more straggly than before, sank into his seat next to the newly-confirmed Duchess Liria with a sigh.

Leaning over the arm of her chair, Liria asked, "How are things at Kaedin Hall, Master Midusel?"

"We're coping," said Midusel. "Of course, there have been some losses. Five very promising adepts, eight students … it's hurt us all. I taught most of those boys myself." He shook his head, cracking his bony knuckles as he clenched his fist. "And for King Eram to die defending me… That's a blood debt, as they say."

"I wish I could have been more help," said Liria.

"You protected many innocent lives, your grace. We're already in your debt." Master Midusel smiled at her. "Time for us to do our part."

Masterhealer Ranida overheard and tilted her head. "What does that mean, Midusel? I know the Kaedin Council met up last evening."

"The king was there. He wasn't decided last night, so there's no point sharing anything until we know what he wants.".

Across the table, the dean of the Hall of the Arts tapped irritably on the table. "What's taking so long? The king should have arrived by now," complained Master Galei, his melodious voice almost petulant in tone. "I have to oversee the repairs to the hall."

"As do we all." Master Historian Veldonan traced the lines of the inlay of the table just before him. He inclined his graying head at Liria. "How fares your father, your grace?"

Liria's lips curved in a rueful smile. "Master Ranida has been to see him not too long ago. He's doing as well as can be expected, but to be honest, it will be a comfort for him to be free of his pain. It grows every day."

"Would it help for me to send my healer over to you, Liria?" Ingros inquired. "Master Jussep and Adept Pol have become quite skilled at easing pain with the distilled potions they've been crafting from Duntean vine beans. I'll run Jussep a message today, if Master Ranida will kindly supply me with a replacement."

The duchess nodded and thanked him for the offer. Master Ranida shrugged, her plain white headscarf shifting with the motion. "I'm sure any one of my master healers will be happy to go to Dunte for its warmth," she said. Liria was always surprised by the master healer's husky voice.

The heavy door swung open and a steward entered, head bowed slightly. "Your graces, my lords and ladies, please rise for the k-"

"Sit down, skip the formalities," King Kirzan snapped. "Is it necessary to announce my presence for every room I enter?"

"It is protocol, sire."

"Protocol can scorch itself. Now leave. We have matters to discuss." The young king waited until the door was shut again before he stalked to his chair at the head of the circular table. He had shucked the furred cloak and the crown, but he held on to Coleri's scepter like his life depended on it. The heavy iron staff made Kirzan look young and lost; Liria had no doubt that Kirzan felt that way and was trying to hide it. His gray eyes, so like his late father's, swept the room, taking in the different faces now observing him. Everyone was older than he, and Kirzan was very aware of that.

Halden was the first to speak. "Your majesty, I beg clemency for my son. He's still recovering from the attack and isn't in his right mind-"

"That issue will be dealt with."

"Sire-"

"Duke Halden, do not discuss his sentence! He is not of concern right now." Kirzan's thin, sallow face flushed. "I've shown as much mercy as law and custom allow. We have more pressing matters than your precious son."

Halden made as though to stand, but Ingros tapped the back of Halden's elbow. With a sidelong glance at Ingros, the duke of Enthin settled back into his chair. "I apologize. I am … distressed over Rilt."

"I understand," said Kirzan. "He is my friend."

Liria was privately amused. So Kirzan was going to be that kind of king. She leaned back in her seat and clasped her hands in her lap. She wished she could watch Duke Halden and Duke Ingros, who were both on her left, but unless she craned her neck, she'd have to satisfy herself with observing those seated in front of her. Already she could see the resentment in the set of Master Galei's jaw. The dean of law, Master Drennel, seemed similarly unimpressed.

"I don't know you personally, but since you were chosen by my father to be part of the Privy Council, I suppose I have to trust you," Kirzan went on. "I called for a meeting today because we have a few matters to discuss. First of all, what to do about the traitors."

Liria covered her lips with her fingers. Either Kirzan didn't realize what he had just done, or he didn't care, but most of the masters caught the barely veiled insult. Out of the corner of her eye, Liria saw Masters Veldonan and Ranida exchange a grim look. This was going to be very interesting.

Drennel raised a hand slightly. "Your majesty, what has become of those who were captured?"

"They are in the dungeons and will be silenced before they're interrogated," said Midusel. "The kaedine masters are overseeing this task."

"But they have conspirators and there are more of such monsters out there in the kingdom," Kirzan said. "I want them rooted from Aleis forever."

"All of them?" Duke Ingros' tone was sharp. "Your majesty, that won't sit well with the citizens. They could be anyone—their neighbors, their friends, their kin. You won't find it easy to get rid of them."

"I will have them erased from the kingdom!" Kirzan slammed an open palm on the table. "They are not Aleisans—they are Verashki. They burned down half the university, they killed my friends, they tried to kill me, they killed my father! They are not people, they are monsters, and I will end the Verashki if it's the last thing I do!"

The room fell silent. Liria lowered her lashes as she counted quietly.

On the count of three, Master Galei spoke up. "And how does the king plan to do that?"

Kirzan raised his chin slightly. "There is a test. All Aleisans will take it."

"A test?" Galei glanced around the table. "What kind of test?"

Kirzan looked at Master Midusel, who inclined his head and rose to his feet. "It is a variation of an assessment given to potential kaedine, to check if their resonance is strong enough to enrol in Kaedin Hall."

"And what will you do with those who are Verashki?" Halden crossed his beefy arms on the table.

"They will be brought here for questioning first. Should they submit to silencing, I will forgive them their trespasses against my father and this house." Kirzan's assessing gaze swept around the table. Liria was strongly reminded of birds of prey, and her lips curved slightly as she recalled the animal on the Alcaronan house crest: the greater ice eagle of the Northwyn mountain ranges. "I want the full support of the Privy Council. We will begin testing tomorrow-"

"I don't think we can do that, your majesty," Liria interrupted. She bowed her head in mute apology before she rose gracefully to her feet, the better to address the entire table and to command their attention. "There is far too much planning to be done before this test can be carried out, simply in Izdahl alone. For one, we'll have to corral people from their various towns and villages to testing stations where master kaedine can administer it. And I doubt we can do that without enlisting the assistance of armed soldiers, but as per the Treaty of Dellwash, the dukes and I do not have standing armies large enough to guarantee compliance. The rangers are stretched thin, and their attention is—rightly—on the borders and on enforcing Aleisan law, not to be wasted on herding peasants." She sat down again, careful not to look smug.

Kirzan narrowed his eyes. "If you think I will allow those murderous bastards to walk free within my kingdom-"

"I think that it will be more prudent of your majesty to let us examine your plan and add to it," said Liria with a sweet smile. "Sire, you've informed us of your desires. Let us fret over the nitty-gritty. That's what your Privy Council is for, after all."

The young king frowned. He seemed to weigh Liria's words over in his mind, before he finally nodded. "One week. I want a plan in a week."

Duke Ingros cleared his throat. "Sire, I'd advise that you allow us a month-"

"Two weeks. No more." Kirzan stood up and so did everyone else. "I'll see you then."

"Sire, what about your coronation?" asked Master Drennel before the king could exit.

Kirzan tilted his head and stared at Drennel. "I am already king. What is then the purpose of a coronation?"

"The ... the people will expect one."

"They can keep expecting. I will not have a boring, prolonged ceremony that tells the kingdom what they already know." With that, King Kirzan left, as abruptly as he had come in.

Once the door was shut, everyone started talking. Ingros shook his head and murmured, "Still very much a child. He needs someone to guide him along."

"He had someone," said Master Foram, the portly master of mathematics across the table. He had not spoken at all earlier, preferring to stare at his hands. Liria knew from her sources that Master Foram found politics bewildering and, as far as possible, kept to his work. However, most of the nobles of Izdahl respected his opinion far more than they did Master Midusel's or Master Veldonan's. She would have to win him over to her cause if she wanted to nip Kirzan's idea in the bud.

Master Midusel had gotten to his feet and was whispering something to Master Veldonan, and a frown appeared on the latter's brow. Liria darted around the table to take the master kaedin's arm before the man could slip away.

"You seemed bothered by the test, Master Midusel." Liria put on her most charming smile. "Is there something wrong with it?"

"Yes, I'm curious too," said Master Ranida. She strode over, her starched robes rustling with her movements. "What are you hiding, Midusel?"

While Midusel might have fobbed Liria away with some excuse about craft secrets, there was no escaping the calm assertiveness of the master healer. The other councilors noticed the tension in the small group and fell silent. The master kaedin sighed.

"The test helps to identify the resonance that a potential may possess," he said. "So if he has resonance for water, he may manifest a drop of water. Small kae-attunement phenomena, basically. It doesn't gauge how strong his resonance is, just whether it exists."

"So a Verashki man will manifest a small flame?" Ranida asked.

Liria caught on fast. "But a small flame doesn't stay small."

"Yes, unfortunately." Master Midusel exhaled heavily, his mousy moustache waving with his breath. "Regrettable ... accidents have occurred before."

"What sort of regrettable accidents are we talking about, Midusel?" asked Master Galei. His shrewd mouth thinned. "Did people get hurt or killed?"

The masters were all watching Midusel now. Duke Halden was still in his seat, Liria noticed. She wasn't certain if the man was even listening. At least Duke Ingros was paying attention, though his somber face was as inscrutable as always.

Midusel hemmed and hawed for a few seconds, before nodding his head. "Accidents. We tried to stop them but the fires ... they spread, fast, and when a kaedin—or kaedin potential—panics, they accelerate and magnify whatever they're doing."

Ingros sighed. "Was that what happened in Little Pond, eight years ago? The whole village burned to nothing."

"I can't say."

"Yes, you can." Halden stood up, a bear of a man. He was not looking at the cluster of councilors but he was clearly addressing them. "We are at war, Master Midusel, or on the brink of one. Tell us everything you know about these fire-breathers. They cost me a son and they cost Aleis a good king. This is not the time for secrets."

He finally looked at the master kaedin. "The more we know about those monsters, the better we can defend ourselves against them."

With Halden now commanding the council, Liria stepped back and let Midusel become the focus of the group. He began recounting what he knew of the Verashki from historical records, and the steps the kaedine of ages past had taken to quietly quell that threat.

She had strong misgivings about the entire affair. The king was lashing out because of grief, and there was no reasoning with a grieving man; he had lost his father and his best friend, by all accounts, and he wanted vengeance. But once the king's forces were sent out to capture the Verashki, what was going to happen? The Verashki would not go peacefully, and she was sure not all of those who were "fire-breathers" were opposed to the kingdom.

Not until the kingdom was opposed to them.

Liria had managed to buy Aleis two weeks of peace. She wondered if she could possibly stop a war.

Get updates on *The Kaedin Forge*, the next book in the
Kaedin Series at:

www.akleewrites.com

Or say hello to A.K. Lee on Twitter:

@aklee_writes